sweet DISTRACTION

K. BROMBERG

PRAISE FOR K. BROMBERG

"K. Bromberg always delivers intelligently written, emotionally intense, sensual romance . . ."

—*USA Today*

"K. Bromberg makes you believe in the power of true love."
—#1 *New York Times* bestselling author Audrey Carlan

"Always an absolute must-read."
—*New York Times* bestselling author Helena Hunting

"An irresistibly hot romance that stays with you long after you finish the book."
—#1 *New York Times* bestselling author Jennifer L. Armentrout

"Bromberg is a master at turning up the heat!"
—*New York Times* bestselling author Katy Evans

"Supercharged heat and full of heart. Bromberg aces it from the first page to the last."
—*New York Times* bestselling author Kylie Scott

ALSO WRITTEN BY K. BROMBERG

Driven Series
Driven
Fueled
Crashed
Raced
Aced

Driven Novels
Slow Burn
Sweet Ache
Hard Beat
Down Shift

The Player Duet
The Player
The Catch

The Malone Brothers
Worth the Fight
Worth the Risk
Worth the Fall
Control (Novella)

Wicked Ways
Resist
Reveal

Standalone
Faking It
Then You Happened
Flirting with 40
UnRaveled (Novella)
Sweet Cheeks
Sweet Rivalry (Novella)

The Play Hard Series
Hard to Handle
Hard to Hold
Hard to Score
Hard to Lose
Hard to Love

The S.I.N. Series
Last Resort
On One Condition
Final Proposal

The Redemption Series
Until You

The Full Throttle Series
Off The Grid
On The Edge
Over The Limit
Out of Control

Tangled Hearts Series
Twisted Knight
Threaded Lies

Backstage Pass Series
Sweet Ache
Sweet Regret
Sweet Surrender

Holiday Novellas
The Package
The Detour
Forever More

This one's for the readers who believe in slow burns and stolen glances. For the ones who stay up way too late waiting for the moment that burn catches fire . . .

sweet DISTRACTION

CHAPTER

one

Rocket

EIGHTY THOUSAND SCREAMING VOICES SING BACK AT US.
The sound they create surges into the dark of the arena, through the blinding lights of the rigging above, and then slams into us like a wave that crashes onto the stage.

My fingers fly over the keys of my keyboard, feeding off their energy. I'm drenched in sweat, and my pulse thunders with a never-ending rush of adrenaline.

Lights flash.

The sound riots.

Hawkin's voice roars into the mic.

Vince's guitar squeals through a lick.

Gizmo slams into his drum kit like he's trying to crack open the sky.

This is it. *The high.* The place where nothing matters—where the crowd worships us like the gods we aren't, and we live on their attention like it's the oxygen we need to breathe.

We are untouchable. Indestructible. Met as teens with dreams and now are men who get to live them out. Fucking legends in leather.

I hold the last chord longer than needed—eyes closed, chin tilted to the rafters—the moment fucking surreal.

Then Gizmo hits his drum finale, and the stage explodes in lights and fire as confetti rains down all around us.

The high is stratospheric—this dream we're living is fucking awesome.

I see it in the faces of the people in the front row. The cell phone lights swaying in the far depths of the arena. In the chants of BENT over and over as we wave goodbye one last time and jog offstage.

Backstage is chaos. Absolute fucking chaos. Security, crew, hangers-on— they all line the hallways as Hawkin, Vince, Gizmo and I take one final walk through the wide corridor toward the greenroom. I pull my sweat-soaked shirt off and chuck it onto the floor where it lands on top of Hawke's.

The adrenaline crash is coming. It doesn't matter how many times we've done this, it still hits. The shakes, the racing heart, the flash of heat that feels like it's consuming your body. The need for silence but to not be alone.

It's the weirdest fucking clash of reactions so I do the only thing I've learned to combat it—well, other than sex that is—and I grab the bottle of Jameson one of the techs hands me. No glass, no hesitation, I drink it straight from the neck.

"Jesus Christ, you're an animal." Vince laughs, pushing past me and grabbing the bottle out of my hand just long enough to take a pull himself.

I grab it back. "We just played our asses off. I earned this."

"Damn right, brother," Hawkin says, already two shots in and soaking up the post-show glow like a cigarette after a damn good bout of sex. But by the way his wife is looking at him as she sits with her legs laying across his lap, that might be happening sooner rather than later too.

A sexy blonde drapes herself around my shoulders, her tongue brushing the shell of my ear. "You were unreal out there," she murmurs.

Anne? Abby? Her name escapes me, but the suction of her lips from earlier before the show sure as shit doesn't.

I grin and decide to hell with remembering her name. Security knows to have her out of here soon. "We usually are."

Gizmo stumbles in behind us, shirt off, hair a mess, drumsticks still in his back pocket, and a newly placed wedding ring glinting off the overhead lights. "You call this an afterparty?" he shouts to no one in particular.

The greenroom smells like sweat, whiskey, and ego. Perfectly fucking BENT.

Our publicist shouts into a phone in the corner as she deals with some invisible crisis. Our manager's ordering people around and no doubt jonesing to get the fuck out of here and go home to his wife he never sees. The road crew and the women they've invited back here with them are laughing and hoping to get fucking lucky tonight.

Hawkin has Quinlan and those long legs of hers. Vince has Bristol sitting on his lap, his chin on her shoulder as they take it all in. And Gizmo is dancing drunkenly with his wife.

And then there's me . . . sizing up everyone else and contemplating if I really want to take Abby-Anne-whatever her name is to my dressing room before heading back to my house and my bed and the peace I crave.

We're in Los Angeles. The home we've longed for after what's felt like endless months on the road. That's why we made it our final stop before taking a two-month long break. We've done this long enough to know there needs to be a hiatus from the wear and tear on our bodies, our relationships . . . and *our livers*.

And thank God that break is finally here.

The music is blaring, and the lights were just dimmed, so if I want to lose myself in their shadows to have a little privacy, no one will care what I'm doing.

This is the fucking life.

It's messy, wild, loud as hell. *Ours*.

I'm Rocket fucking Caldwell. I've got platinum records on my walls and groupies waiting to unzip my jeans.

This is who I am.

This is all I've ever wanted.

I raise the bottle, take another drink, and let the burn slide down my throat like a reward. Two months off. No shows. No press.

Just excess and freedom and silence.

I tip my head back and let the buzz settle in. Savor the chaos. Own every single fucking moment of it.

But had I known this was the last night of true freedom, I would have savored the predictability more. Because up until this moment, my life felt complete. *Mine*.

CHAPTER
two

Rocket

Mʏ ᴍᴏᴜᴛʜ. Iᴛ's ᴅʀʏ ᴀs sᴀɴᴅᴘᴀᴘᴇʀ ᴀɴᴅ ᴛᴀsᴛᴇs ʟɪᴋᴇ ᴀ ʀᴇɢʀᴇᴛꜰᴜʟ combination of whiskey, remorse, and cotton.

But it has nothing on the pounding in my head. It feels like my brain is trying to claw its way out of my skull.

Fuck me.

I roll onto my stomach, bury my face into my pillow, and mutter a curse. My body is still buzzing from last night's show and the hours of chaos that followed. A blur of bodies, booze, possibly a few bad decisions, but definitely some entertaining memories.

No doubt I'll remember a few of them once this fog clears. *I hope.*

The plus side? I'm not in a hotel room, not on a bus going to the next stop . . . I'm in my own bed. In my own silence.

And thank fuck I was smart enough in my celebratory stupor last night not to have brought anyone home with me. While it might have been fun at the time, kicking them out in the morning is always a bit fucked up. Callous but needed.

I welcome the quiet. The stillness. After months on the road, days on end of bus wheels rumbling beneath me, and footsteps clomping up and down hotel hallways, it's just silence and the comfort of my own fucking bed.

Heaven.

Or at least the heaven I'll revel in for a few weeks before I get antsy to get back out there under the heat of the lights and in front of the roar of the crowd. The new town every night might suck, but the adrenaline and attention that come with this job are two highs I thrive on.

I let out a groan and stretch, arm flopping over the edge of the bed—

Bang. Bang. Bang.

I jolt from the sound and immediately bring my hands to my head as if that's going to help protect it from the sound.

Bang. Bang. Bang.

"Jesus," I mutter, dragging myself up and out of my bed. The room spins and my stomach pitches right along with it.

Who the hell is at my house this early?

I stumble down the hall toward the door. I'm in boxers but don't give a fuck because the sunlight pouring in through the windows is enough to cripple a man.

Bang. Bang. Ba—

I throw open the door. *"What?"*

The person standing on the other side is not a fan. Not paparazzi. Not a woman looking for round two. And yet I know exactly how she got past the guard at the gate because she's on my visitor's list.

I just never actually thought she'd visit unless I was in trouble or about to be arrested.

Um . . . I look both ways to see if there are police somewhere and then let my shoulders fall when I see that there's no one waiting to ambush me.

Why the hell is my lawyer standing at my door at this ungodly hour?

"Sandra?" I groan in protest.

"It's eleven, Gavin," she says using my real name. "You should already be up." Her expression is calm, professional, and totally unimpressed by the half-naked rock star glaring at her through bloodshot eyes.

Isn't that the reason I hired her as my lawyer? Dogged, unfazed, and efficient. I've never had her be that way with me, and I'm not exactly in the mood for it.

I rub a hand down my face. "Technically true. Still rude."

"Thank you for inviting me in. I'd love to take a seat." She snorts and the way she pushes past me and into my house has dread trickling through me. I shut the door and follow her determined walk and slicked-back bun.

"Is something wrong?" I ask, the mental fog clearing much faster than I would've preferred.

She spins on her heel once she reaches my kitchen, her sharp gray suit somehow making my house feel underdressed. "Depends on how you look at it."

"Is that a yes?" I ask. Her eyes track over my living space as if she's ready to judge. Thank God I only just got home so it's clean—and for some reason, I think I need that on my side in this bizarre moment. "Because I'm beginning to think you're not here to talk about contracts or rights or—"

"The name Olivia Whitmore ring a bell to you?" Her eyes narrow with the words.

"Should it? I meet a lot of people every day. Why would that name stand out?"

"Let me rephrase, and maybe the context will help. Do you remember sleeping with a woman named Olivia Whitmore?"

"Olivia?" I fumble through my scattered thoughts and try to place the face that belongs to the name. The haze clears just enough for it to register and erase any trace of alcohol that might have been left in my system.

Olivia.

A smirk toys at the corners of my lips. Her raspy voice and throaty laugh are vague but there. Long hair. Brown eyes. Incredible body. And a helluva lot of fun in the sack.

"*Olivia. Olivia Whitmore,*" she says, her smile suggestive and her eyes addictive.

"*I don't do last names, sweetheart. Never remember them.*"

"*I'll guarantee when I'm done doing the things I want to do to you that you'll remember it just fine.*"

"*Is that a dare?*"

"*It is.*"

"*Then by all means . . . dare accepted.*"

The woman *did know* how to make a lasting impression—for a while anyway. The years that have passed—and the women since then—definitely made sure of that.

"You do remember her," Sandra says, but her resigned sigh unnerves me.

I shift uncomfortably. "Vaguely, but yes. If it's who I'm thinking of, we hooked up a few years ago." I try to place the when and the where. Sometimes in this life of mine, it all runs together. "It was after we played that charity event at Hollywood Bowl. Maybe twice? Loved tequila. Red heels. Something about her laugh caught my ear. Why?"

But the minute I ask the question, I realize there can't be anything good about a woman I slept with years ago being brought up now. By my lawyer, no less.

It can only be one of two things: she's accusing me of shit I didn't do or she had a kid and is trying to say it's mine.

Both are so far-fetched it's ridiculous. Both something each of us in the band—and so many in this industry—have been accused of in the past for attention or hopes for monetary compensation.

And so far, when it's come to my bandmates, every accusation arisen over the years has been discredited.

"Whatever she's saying is bullshit. You know that. I know that." I scrub a hand through my hair. "We've been there and done that with the wannabe groupies desperate for their fifteen minutes of fame. This is the last thing I need right now."

"Ms. Whitmore died last week in a car accident."

"Oh." Her comment startles me. "I mean, I'm sorry for her family, but I don't understand what that has to do with me."

"Her will named you." Her smile is tight. Unforgiving.

"Named me for?" I ask, voice breaking and concern now front and center because the last thing I'd assume is I'm about to be left a small fortune.

Sandra doesn't respond. Instead, she opens the file in her hand and pulls out a short letter. She holds it out for me, but I don't take it. I'm scared to.

"Why would I be in her will, Sandra?" I ask. Each second that ticks by seemingly makes this situation and unwelcome house call that much worse.

"Olivia had a daughter. Poppy Grace Whitmore is her name. She's three years old."

"Nope. No way." I laugh, disbelief dripping off its edges. "There is no fucking way she's pinning a kid on me." I move about the room as if the movement can physically reject whatever it is that Sandra has come here to sell.

"I'm not pinning anything, Rocket. But Olivia left a letter stating you were the father as well as a copy of Poppy's birth certificate naming you the same."

I shake my head, and a dry laugh escapes my throat. "Right. Great. I'm the father on the birth certificate. It's stated in a letter she wrote. But the little girl has Whitmore as a last name. Help me make that make sense because . . . it fucking doesn't."

"I get you're upset. I understand why you're bucking this," she says evenly. "That's why we take a paternity test, get the results in a few days, and be done with this."

She says it so matter-of-factly—like it's a run-of-the-mill test—but inside . . . inside I'm freaking the fuck out. "She's not mine," I whisper as fear creeps into my voice. "Can't be. I always used protection."

Sandra lifts a brow. "Always?"

"Shit." I drag a hand through my hair. How many times do I jacket up after having a few too many? Did I do it right? Did I fuck up? Did . . . "Yes. No. Fuck this, Sandra."

"Like I said, a paternity test will clear this all up."

My heart pounds in my ears and drowns out reasonable thought. "Doesn't Olivia have parents or siblings? Wouldn't Penelope—"

"Poppy."

"Right. *Poppy*. Wouldn't *Poppy* be better off with someone she already knows instead of some random man she's never met before? And then what? Me, a certifiably unqualified bastard, is supposed to raise her without any warning or history of parenting at all?"

"While I can't disagree with you, Olivia explicitly stated in her letter that she didn't want her parents to have custody. Reading between the lines, it seems like they had some kind of falling out and so she wanted her to be with you. Not them."

I scrub a hand over my face and groan. The bottle of gin on the far end of the kitchen counter calls to me, begs me, to drink this all away and pretend like it's not real.

But Sandra standing in front of me with papers in her hand, ones I'm choosing to ignore, tell me otherwise. That this is very fucking real.

"Rocket. Gavin," she says quietly, her expression softening just enough to chisel away some of the shock. "We need the paternity test. I've brought a cheek swab kit to do that and get the ball rolling. Until that's confirmed or refuted, no one is doing anything. The results will give us our next steps."

"Next steps." I blow out an exaggerated breath and lace my fingers behind my head. Normally, I'd laugh this shit off and not worry, but something isn't sitting well with me. Something . . . has dread weighing heavily. "You said car accident?"

"I did. On I-405 a few nights back. Drunk driver hit her and Poppy."

"The kid was in the car?" *Jesus fucking Christ.* I blink hard and look away while my gut twists simply for the fragility of life.

"Yes. *Poppy* was there."

Right. Poppy. Fuck.

"Where is she now? Are Olivia's parents watching her in the meantime?"

"No. Child Protective Services has temporary custody of her. They've moved fast since her window of stability is small. They're looking to find someone to help ease the transition to whatever is next for her. Someone who can build trust. I was told they're looking to place her temporarily with a nanny who is familiar with trauma and might provide support while everything is figured out."

"A nanny?"

"Yes. Perhaps if this goes that way, it's someone who can stay on and help you with the transition as well, seeing as she'll already be vetted."

"Don't." I hold up my hands. The last thing I want to talk about is nannies and toddlers and— "Let's not get ahead of ourselves, okay?"

I blink hard and look around my place. Around the trophies of my life—Grammys and platinum records and pictures of a life lived alone— and wonder what the fuck is going on?

My bandmates are married. My bandmates have kids. I've watched each of them succumb to it over the years . . . but it's not something I ever had on my future radar.

Sandra sets the letter down in front of me. "The letter is short. You should read it."

I stare at the papers like they're a live grenade, but not reading them doesn't change the situation. My fingers tremble as I take it.

Rocket,

If you're reading this, then something's happened to me. I know this isn't fair to spring on you, but I didn't know how else to do it. Poppy is yours. She always has been. One look at her and you'll see it.

Our night of fun created this incredible little girl. You never asked for any of this and so I chose to keep her. I chose to love her. And even though I know those choices made her my responsibility, that doesn't mean that I didn't want to tell you a hundred times, but I was scared you wouldn't want her. I was scared you'd reject her like my parents wanted me to do. But if you are only finding out about her now, I should have told you. I hope, more than anything, that you'll want to know her. And that since you're reading this, that you'll try to give her what I no longer can.

-Olivia

I stare at the handwriting until the letters blur. I shuffle to the one beneath it—a birth certificate with my name clear as fucking day under the section for "father." If the letter didn't give me a jolt, then the birth certificate sure as shit did.

Father: Gavin Aaron Caldwell.
Mother: Olivia Francis Whitmore.
Child: Poppy Grace Whitmore.

Everything inside me goes still.

"She could be lying," I say hoarsely.

"She could," Sandra agrees.

"Why name me on this if she wasn't going to tell me?" I ask, trying to reason with logic in a situation that's completely illogical.

"There are legal ramifications that come from your name stated as the father. It allows the mother to ask for support at any given time. Things like that," Sandra says. "But she didn't. In past cases, I've seen mothers do this—name the father—maybe planning on telling Poppy the truth later in life, but . . . that's a guess."

A three-year-old little girl.

"This has to be a mistake. A total mistake." My heart hammers, and my hands shake in a way they never have before.

"Again, that's why we test. But if the results come back that she's yours . . . you need to be prepared for that. This little girl has just lost everything she's ever known and will need you."

My head drops, fingers clenched around the letter. I should feel anger. Panic. Fear.

But all I can manage is focusing on the insanity of this. The randomness on a Friday morning. The ability this might have to fuck up my pretty fucking terrific life.

"She's just a kid," I murmur. "And if she's mine . . ." I trail off, the weight of that *if* pressing harder than I expect.

Sandra doesn't answer. She doesn't need to.

Because I already know—my life might have just changed irrevocably.

And fuck if I want it to.

CHAPTER
three

THE SQUEAK OF THE SWINGS IS A CONSTANT AS I STUDY THE LITTLE girl sitting on the edge of the sandbox. *Poppy Whitmore.* She's wearing a frilly yellow top, white shorts, and clutching to her chest a pink stuffed bunny that's seen better days. Her hair is a tangle of copper curls. She absently brushes them out of her eyes as she sits and cautiously watches the other kids play.

She's in the mix of them all, yet she doesn't interact in that carefree way like the other kids do.

If I didn't know what she's been through, I'd assume she's just shy. But I do, and that makes watching her sit there silently even more heartbreaking.

"She still hasn't talked since the accident?" I ask, more to myself than to anyone.

Alan, my cousin and her CPS officer, stands beside me with his arms crossed over his chest, concern etched in the lines of his expression, and nods before looking toward Jackie who's standing on the other side of him.

Jackie was Olivia's best friend and the only connection we have to know what Poppy's life was like before the accident. Her favorite foods. Her routines. Her personality. *Her norm.*

"She hasn't in the time that I've spent with her," she says. "God only knows what she saw in that car. What she heard. What her mind has made up to fill in the gaps. I feel so helpless."

"We all do," Alan says and reaches out to squeeze her forearm in comfort. "The doctor said the mutism is not an unusual trauma response and that her speech will return in time. The main goal now though, is to give her the support she needs while we figure out the next steps for her."

"You know I'd take her in a heartbeat," Jackie says, her hand moving up to rest over her chest. Her despair and helplessness is palpable.

"I know, but legally my hands are tied here," Alan says. "The note you found in Olivia's paperwork, in addition to Poppy's birth certificate, indicates for all intents and purposes who her father is and where she should be placed. The paternity test is being administered today, and once the results come in, then we'll go from there."

"There's no question he's the father. She looks exactly like him," Jackie says.

Alan shushes her and glances my way like I just heard something I shouldn't have. "I understand," he says, "but at this time, nothing has been proven, and what you read needs to remain confidential."

"I know it does. I just . . . if it's him, like . . . how is he going to be a father when he lives the life he leads?"

"Jackie. Please. Willow is on a need-to-know basis here," Alan says, which has my interest piqued even more now.

Need to know?

What am I walking into here with this request?

"I'm sorry. I know. It's all just been a lot and—" Jackie huffs out a breath. "I'm worried about Pops. There's so much change for her already. So much instability. And now a new, random man who might be her father."

"I know. I agree. That's why I've brought in Willow," he says, referring to me like I'm an associate and not his cousin.

"But what if Rock—if he's not her dad? What then? Does she go to foster care? Do Olivia's parents get her? Just more trauma to a little girl who deserves the world." Her voice breaks on the last few words.

"We're taking it hour by hour right now. The main thing is that during all of this transition, Poppy has someone who stays by her side. Someone she becomes comfortable with so that no matter where she ends up, that person can help bridge that gap between all this new 'strangeness' and her old world." He points to me. "That's why I was able to get the special authorization from my superiors to bring in Willow. She has experience in childcare, a degree in early childhood development, and is currently between jobs."

Between jobs. I tense at the description but smile at Jackie regardless. It's too much to get into, too much to explain, and Poppy's the priority here.

"I told Alan that I'd be more than willing to help. I'm from Los Angeles, and not only am I familiar with the resources available to her as far as her care, but I'm willing to stay on and help with her transition to a new family," I say, hoping to ease her fears.

If I were in her shoes, meeting me for the first time, my fears would be far from erased. Am I a special needs teacher who used to nanny to work her way through college? Yes. Am I in any way equipped to handle a traumatized toddler? I hope I am. I have love. I have arms to hold her. I have experience with my nonverbal students.

"She's an incredible little girl who didn't deserve this," Jackie says quietly as she wipes away a tear with the back of her hand.

"Poppy," Alan calls out gently. "Come here, sweetheart."

She turns her head as she stands and moves slowly toward us. She doesn't smile nor does she frown, but rather just looks at Jackie, then Alan, before shifting to study me—the stranger in the group. Her eyes hold a weight and wariness a three-year-old shouldn't have nor can I fathom. It's almost as if that stare of hers questions if I'm as safe as the other two people I'm standing with.

"Hey there," I say softly as I crouch down so that we're eye level. She's currently grabbing hold of Jackie's leg like it's her only lifeline. "I'm Willow."

Nothing. No change in expression. No blinking. No response whatsoever.

"That's okay," I add quickly making sure I remain at eye level with her so that I'm not towering over and intimidating her. "It's a really weird name. I'd look at me with a name like that too."

For a brief second, she gives a flicker of a smile and relaxes her features slightly before they harden again.

It's something, and I'll take it.

"You know that you don't have to speak, right?" I say, assuming that everyone's asking her to talk. "Sometimes I don't feel like talking either."

She pulls her bunny tighter against her and twists her lips.

"I like the quiet. I get overwhelmed when there's too much going on, and then it makes me not want to talk at all. So I don't because it's easier. Is that what you're doing?" I ask, making her feel like she's making the choices for herself.

She might be three, but when your world is out of control, having some kind of say matters.

She nods ever so slightly. Her lips part but no words come out.

"When I feel that way, sometimes I use hand signals to tell other people what I want or how I feel." I lean in closer and whisper, "That way I get what I want but don't have to talk. You can try it if you want to."

She shifts on her feet, and a curl falls out of her pigtail into her eyes. She brushes it away but keeps her eyes on her bunny.

I try again. "Like, if you want juice or a snack or . . . just to go play on the playground."

At that, her eyes lift again to meet mine. She points to the playground and nods.

I smile. "You want to go play with the other kids?"

She nods a bit more enthusiastically this time.

"Awesome. Look at you learning how to talk with your hands. I knew you were super smart. High five?" I ask and hold my hand up. She studies it as the smallest twitch curls up the corners of her lips before softly tapping it. "Woo-hoo! Now go play, and we'll be right here when you're done. We're not going anywhere, okay?"

She takes a step toward it. Stops. Alan and Jackie both encourage her to go play, and with one more glance for reassurance, she's then off with her bunny bouncing against her hip as she walks timidly toward the slide. It's as if she knows she's supposed to want to play, but inside she's still trying to process how this world still exists without her mom in it.

"She went from vibrant and full of life to *this*," Jackie says, compassion owning her voice.

"Nothing will replace her mother or erase what she went through. Taking it day by day is the only way to handle it," I say as Poppy drops her bunny before quickly picking it up and having what appears to be a silent conversation with it as she picks pieces of grass off it.

Can I do this? Am I able to provide the stability and soft place she needs to cope with this tragic void in her life? Even more so, do I want to do this?

"Do you mind if I go play with her?" Jackie asks, already taking a few steps Poppy's way. "She just seems so lonely, so unsure of herself."

"Of course," Alan says and then recrosses his arms over his chest as we both watch Jackie scoop Poppy up in her arms and spin her around. It's not long before I feel the weight of Alan's stare on me.

"Just ask what you're going to ask, Alan," I say, eyebrows raised and decision made the moment I saw Poppy.

But he knew that. He knew I wouldn't be able to say no.

"So? Do you want to help? Do you think you can do this?" he asks.

I blow out a long, measured breath to try and bite back the emotion that has owned me since I pulled that pink slip out of the envelope. My sense of purpose was gone. My faith in the system that we're here to help kids was stripped. "I don't need a handout," I say, although figuring out how to pay the bills in the coming months had crossed my mind more than a few times.

"No one's giving you one. You lost your job. I have a job to offer. You are the most compassionate, intuitive person I know who just so happens to love kids and knows how to deal with them. And I happen to be in need of a person who is all of those things."

"You're being too kind."

He snorts. "Perhaps, but I'm also in desperate need of help. And everything I just said was true. Plus, the job is transitional."

"No one hires at this point in the school year."

"Exactly. So you can help Poppy. You can transition her to her new family. And you can either look for a new job to start in the fall when school starts or maybe finish that master's degree you've been putting off." He raises his hands in mock defense and peeks around his hands as if he were expecting me to hit him.

The thought crosses my mind—finishing my master's has been something I've been talking about for some time—but I roll my eyes instead of hitting him.

"Finishing my master's is the last thing I need to do when I'm not taking in a paycheck."

"But this *will* give you a paycheck."

Why is he making this sound so easy when I know it's not? That it wouldn't be.

"About the transitional part," I say.

"Like I told you when I called you, there's no guarantee that you'll be picked up as a long-term caregiver for Poppy, but it's a paycheck for now . . . and if the man who's being tested is confirmed as the father, I have a feeling you might just be kept on."

"You can't know that."

"I know what his lawyer has insinuated, but we'll get into that when and if the time comes."

My eyes find Poppy again where she sits on the bench next to Jackie. Her feet swing, but she doesn't play.

It's been a hot minute since I was the twenty-four-seven caregiver of a child. Those long hours I worked in college are imprinted on my brain, but so is the love and satisfaction I got from the job. No bureaucracy and red tape restricting me.

For some reason, Poppy glances up and meets my gaze. Almost as if she knows I need this to finalize my decision.

Something in my chest clicks into place. Something I can't shrug off.

"Fine. I'll do it."

"Like you were going to say no," he says and snorts.

"But only while we wait on the paternity test . . . only in the interim. I need to get my life back on track with a lasting position and paycheck."

"Noted." He pats my shoulder, aware that lack of routine is hard for me and this no job thing has created just that type of chaos. "Jackie has provided everything important for Poppy. The foods she likes. Her schedule. Her comfort items. Her routines."

"I'll have to thank her," I say, still questioning myself even though I know I'm doing the right thing.

"Okay, so we'll work out the handoff. I've already gotten your background check back and you, personally, signed off on by the powers that be. For now, I suggest you go home and pack some things. We'll put you two up in an extended stay hotel for now while we wait for the results to come in. And then go from there."

"Okay." I stand there like he just didn't tell me I'm supposed to go and pack.

I look back at the little girl with copper pigtails, and for the first time in weeks, maybe longer, something feels right.

Like maybe this distraction isn't a detour after all.

Like maybe life is trying to hand me something else.

CHAPTER
four

Rocket

THIS SILENCE I'VE BEEN DROWNING MYSELF IN IS LOUDER THAN ANY amp I've ever blown.

It echoes through my house and feels like every bad decision I've ever made is screaming back at me.

I haven't turned on music. Haven't touched an instrument. Haven't called the guys. Haven't done a damn thing but sit and wallow in a bottle or two of whiskey.

I usually love the silence and solitude after a long stretch on the road. I welcome the emptiness of my house and lack of schedule.

Not this time.

Not now.

This fucking waiting for Sandra's call is going to be my undoing.

The clock ticks. Seconds pass. Minutes drag . . . hours feel like fucking days. There's an awareness of the time. The kind you can't drown out—I've tried—even when I'm trying to convince myself I already know what the results say.

It's not mine.

She's not mine.

She can't be mine.

I rub a hand over my face, then press the heels of my palms into my eyes and try to stop the loop from running through my head. The one that's taken me days to scrape together. The highlight reel is brief and uneventful, save for a few great orgasms.

Olivia. Red heels. Dark hair. Whiskey on her breath and a laugh that carried through crowded rooms.

The last time I saw her, she kissed me like there was no tomorrow, but like she didn't want there to be one with me either. I think I said something stupid—something about us being fun while it lasted. No promises. No tomorrows. Just fun times and great orgasms.

Her words? *"Good thing I'm not a clingy bitch, or I'd have a hard time letting you walk away, Rocket Caldwell."*

Then she pulled me in for another dick-hardening kiss before winking and walking away with a smirk and a sway to her hips.

I didn't ask questions. What fucking guy would? We parted on good terms, and I never expected to see her again.

And now this . . .

She can't be mine. Poppy can't be—

Fuck.

I pick up my phone out of habit, but there are no missed calls. No messages. No new texts.

The results are supposed to be in today.

They told Sandra it would be today.

I grab a bottle of water from the fridge, crack it open, and take a swig like it's going to settle the chaos in my chest. It doesn't. No wonder, given I've been living on amber liquid out of glass bottles.

My phone buzzes in my hand.

Hawkin.

I hesitate, then swipe to answer because I can't fucking hide forever.

"What's up, man?" I try to sound like my life isn't in a fucking upheaval.

"You good, man?" he asks, curiosity tingeing the edges of his tone.

"Yeah. Why wouldn't I be?" Has the media already found out? Did someone get a large payday on this rumor?

"You've been quiet as hell. You've usually blown up the group text at least twice by now and it's been silence. You didn't even respond to Giz's last comment. It was the perfect opportunity for a classic Rocket cutdown, and you didn't take it."

"Shit, man," I say and run a hand through my hair. "I must've missed it. I've kind of been on do not disturb. Guess I needed a little recharge. Post-tour coma and all that."

"Right . . ." His tone is suspicious. "You're not dying, are you?"

"Not that I know of. Should I be touched that you care?" I joke.

"Eat shit. You know I care." He pauses. "You're acting weird and when you act weird, something's usually up."

I pinch the bridge of my nose. "I'm fine, brother. Just tired. Just catching up on sleep and choosing to ignore the world for a bit."

"You sure? You're worrying us."

Us. I bark out a laugh. "Ah, so you're the poor fucker who was picked to check in on me."

A pause. A chuckle proving I'm right. A surge of love for this family of mine I never expected to have and couldn't do without. "Something like that," he says. "I'll let you get back to your solitude or what-the-fuck-ever you're doing. Just know we're here if you need anything. Want to meet up for drinks on Thursday?"

"Maybe."

"Maybe?" He snorts. "Now I'm definitely worried."

"I—I'm just—" *Possibly having a kid by then?* Like what the actual fuck do I say? "I'll get back with you on it. For some reason I think I have something," I lie.

"Fine. Sure. You know where to find me."

Hawkin ends the call, and now I feel like shit because I just lied to one of my best friends rather than confide in him. But what good is confiding if this turns out to be nothing?

I don't even have time to put the phone down before it rings again. *Sandra.*

My stomach drops at the sight of her name on my screen. I stare at the screen for a long second before answering.

She doesn't waste any time. "The results came in."

My fingers flex against my thighs, and my heart thuds violently against my ribs. My throat hurts when I swallow. "Yeah?"

"Gavin . . . *she's yours.*"

Those two words explode like a bomb in my head.

I thought I'd braced for the reality of it. Convinced myself that I already knew—that I didn't need a lab report or a blood test or legal documentation to confirm what I'd felt in my gut.

But this?

This is different.

This is real. Indisputable.

Jesus fucking Christ.

The weight of it compresses my ribs like a vise. My breath burns in my chest. My tongue feels swollen behind my teeth.

I don't move. *Can't.*

Don't breathe. *Don't think I could if I tried.*

She says something else, but I don't hear it.

Mine.

Fuck me.

She's mine.

"Sandra." Her name is barely audible.

"You okay?" she asks solemnly.

"You're sure?" I croak. A little girl. A three-year-old whose mom just died and no doubt whose world is more fucking upside down than mine is right now.

"I'm sure." She gives me a moment to absorb this, if that's even possible.

And I don't. Can't. I do what I've always done before and focus on what's next. On shoving how I feel—lost, helpless, forced, unprepared—down and moving one foot in front of the other while I let the fog of confusion consume me. I need logistics and tangibles. Something other than the thudding of my heart.

"What does that mean?" My throat feels like acid poured over sandpaper. I'm sure it doesn't sound much better either.

"Your introduction and her placement with you will be tomorrow."

"Tomorrow?" I screech.

"It's being arranged as we speak." Her voice is so steadfast there's no wiggle room, and yet I ask my question like there is.

"What do you mean tomorrow?" I shove up out of my seat and let my long legs eat up the length of the room.

"You're her dad. You're where she belongs."

There has never been a more ludicrous statement spoken before. Not when it comes to me, anyway.

"I'm the furthest thing from a dad. I didn't even have one to know how to be one. How am I supposed to—" Full-on panic sets in. I'm split between wanting to jump in my pool and sink to its bottom, or getting in my car and driving as far the fuck away from here and her as possible.

Both make me chickenshit. Both make this real.

I love my life. I have a damn good one. Like . . .

"No one expects you to walk into this with a degree in parenting. You'll take it one day at a time. I have faith in you that you'll figure it out."

While I appreciate her encouragement, it falls on deaf ears.

"So . . . what? I have no say in the matter? Just 'surprise, you have a kid,' and it—she's dropped on my doorstep?"

"She's not a piece of luggage, so no, she won't be just dropped per se, and no, Rocket, you don't have any say in the matter because the test proved she is yours."

"She can't come tomorrow. I can't . . . I'm . . ." *On tour.* But I'm not so I can't use my go-to excuse for this. "I've got a schedule and appearances and a fucking life. I can't just become a dad and—"

"Look," she says sternly, pulling me from the spiral I'm going down. "I know this is a lot."

"A lot? Sandra . . . I'm not dad material." How can I be when my own never set anything close to an example? When my own didn't even want me?

"If you think you're lost, think of *her*. Poppy. She's a little girl who just lost her mother and is being taken away from everything she's ever known to come live with a father she's never met. If you think you're confused, think how she feels."

Fuck. This isn't happening.

"Gavin? You there?"

That silence I had drowned in all week slowly suffocates me until my chest burns and my body shakes.

"I need you to listen to me, yes?"

"I'm here."

"She currently has a caretaker . . . a nanny, so to speak, who's been looking after her this week. Apparently, Poppy's taken to her well. The nanny's name is Willow Adams. From what the CPS officer has expressed, Willow has the experience and skills that are needed—someone Poppy trusts. The state has paid for Willow's services during this transition, but it would probably be for the best to keep her on until you find someone who suits you—"

"Vet her. Hire her. Keep her on."

"Rocket, you haven't even met her."

"But that's what you were suggesting, right? Keep on the one person with any experience in this situation? Fine. Done. As we've established, I don't have the first fucking clue about having a kid. None. Nor do I know what would be needed in a nanny. If she's as good as you tell me she is, if Poppy has taken to her, then keep her on." One less fucking thing I have to do and one way to keep everything at arm's length for a while. "Pay her the fucking world to keep her on. Give her whatever she asks for—"

"I don't think—"

"Do you actually think I'm in my right mind right now to make any of these decisions? Poppy likes her. Fine. Done."

"You're not just an everyday Joe, Rocket. You have privacy concerns and—"

"Then do your job and make sure she signs an NDA and does whatever the fuck needs to be done. You've done it with everyone else who works for me, right? Then do it for her."

There's a slight pause. A sigh of measured frustration.

"I just figured you might want to meet the woman who'd be living with you before you had her sign a binding contract."

Oof.

Living with me. Jesus fucking Christ. I scrub a hand through my hair and wonder why that statement just got through to me when nothing else has. I sit down. I stand back up. I move to look out at the backyard. Then wander aimlessly through the kitchen.

The perpetual bachelor. The man who likes his space and his privacy. Now two people will be moving in.

"I think it's best if we do a contract with a probationary period of say, a few weeks to a month. If she passes and you like her, then we can sign an extension."

"You're the lawyer," I mutter.

"And you're my client so I take direction from you. Are you good with this plan?"

"Yes. Fine." I scrub a hand over my face.

"Great. I'll get going on this—"

"There's no way out of this," I state, knowing the answer and feeling like an absolute chickenshit for even suggesting it. "What about—how can—can't I be considered unfit to parent? I'm always traveling. I live a chaotic life. I mean, is there something I can do to have the courts think that?" My pulse pounds in my ears. It's the only sound louder than the silence stretching and judgment being leveled between us.

"You're better than that, Gavin. You're not *an* asshole who would do something horrible to make that happen. First, because you're a good guy and second, because you don't want to give the press the field day they'd have with it when they found out you abandoned your child, sent her to the foster system—and they *would* find out."

Yes, I'm as horrible as that comment just made me out to be.

I emit a strangled groan as I grab my neck and stop pacing. She's right. I know she's right, and yet it sounds so fucking tempting.

"Tough love time," she says. "It's going to be rocky and tough for a while. You're used to thinking about no one, and now you have to think about Poppy first. Use the nanny while you sort through your shit—be that a day or a month—but don't use her to shirk on your duties as a father. As the man I know you can be."

"You don't know shit about me," I spit out.

She makes a non-committal sound. It's a warning her words reinforce. "I'm going to give you a pass on talking to me like this due to the shock of this situation. It's a one-time thing. Please remember that."

I hang my head and grunt in response as I will away the tears that burn and my chest that aches and wonder what the fuck to do next. I know she's right and yet it sounds so fucking tempting. What the hell did Olivia's parents do that she'd rather I have her than them?

"Maybe it'll help if you talk to the guys."

"And say what?" I mutter.

"Hawkin has two little girls," she continues like I never spoke. "Vince has a son he didn't know about until he was six or seven, right? Gizmo has one on the way . . . I bet they'd be able to calm your fears."

"I'm not afraid of anything," I say and then laugh self-deprecatingly. "Who the fuck am I kidding? I'm afraid of everything."

"Do you want to see a picture of her?" Sandra asks. I don't think it's possible to steal anymore breath from my lungs, but she just did.

No.

It's my first reaction. My only reaction because seeing is believing and I don't want to believe this.

"Yes." The syllable is barely audible.

"Okay. I'll let you go so you can see the text I'm sending and process. I'll be in touch with information on when you'll meet her tomorrow."

"Mm-hmm," is my only response as I end the call a split second before my phone alerts a text.

My hands tremble, and every part of me screams not to look. I don't know how long I stare at the damn attachment like it might bite me if I click it, but eventually, my thumb moves.

The image loads slowly. Too slow. My chest tightens with each spinning second.

Fucking hell.

There she is.

A little girl with curls that have a mind of their own and a tiny gap between her front teeth. She's sitting cross-legged, clutching something pink against her chest. Her smile isn't big. It's shy and tentative, like someone told her to smile and she tried, but didn't quite trust it.

Her eyes? They punch the air from my lungs.

Big. Round. Haunted. Familiar in a way that messes with my head.

I've seen those eyes before. In a mirror. In pictures of myself when I was that age. On my fucking driver's license for Christ's sake.

Motherfucker.

I don't want to look anymore, but I can't tear my eyes away, so I zoom in, not even realizing I'm doing it until I'm studying every detail of her tiny face.

I thought I'd feel doubt. Anger. Confusion.

And I do feel all three, but I also feel overwhelmed, desperate, and inadequate.

I'm still stuck somewhere between disbelief and detonation.

I don't know what I expected to feel. But *fuck* . . . this isn't it.

This is grief, tangled in awe and wrapped in fear.

It's loss and gain in the same breath.

It's a freefall with no parachute.

And even none of those describe how fucked up I feel right now.

I don't want this. I never wanted this.

And despite those truths, all I feel is a low, aching pull. Like my heart just shifted when it needs to stay squarely where it's been for the past twenty-seven years.

She's mine.

The test proved it when all I needed was a picture of her to know.

And fuck if that doesn't scare the hell out of me.

CHAPTER
five

The non-disclosure agreement I was required to sign comes with ridiculous repercussions for breaking it.

Jackie's comments in the park about Poppy's father.

The way Alan was so secretive about all references to the paternity test.

It all clicks into place the second the front door opens, and I come face to face with Poppy's father.

A name spoken aloud or read on a piece of paper is one thing. But when that door opens and Rocket Caldwell stands before me, shoulders filling the doorway, the enormity of what I'd agreed to and who I was now working for hits me.

"Is now the time to tell you who you'll be working for?" Alan asks as I buckle Poppy into her booster seat.

"Gavin Caldwell. That's the name that was on the NDA, was it not?" I ask, clearly missing something by the smirk on his face.

"That's the name on his birth certificate, yes."

I tap Poppy on the nose and make a sound. She smiles softly. It's been a long few days spent inside the small world I created for us in a hotel room. One of snuggles and puppet shows with toilet paper rolls. Of forts made of sheets and reading books.

She didn't take to me right away—I definitely had to work at it, and she still hasn't spoken—but it's my hand she clutches tightly to. It's my eyes she veers to when asked a question so that I can speak for her. Her trust in me is growing. I hope that with time, I can begin to help her emotionally sort through whatever trauma she may have seen in that car.

I close the door on the back seat and climb in the front seat beside my cousin. His eyebrows are lifted, and the smirk still toys at the corner of his lips. "What am I missing?" I ask.

"You're a music lover," he states.

"What does that have to do with . . . wait. Who is Gavin Caldwell?" I ask, realizing not every celebrity or musician uses their real name.

"Ever heard of the band BENT?"

"Of course. Who hasn't? They're on my evergreen playlist—Rocket." His name comes out in a shocked whisper as I recall from some article I read somewhere that Rocket's last name is Caldwell.

"Bingo," Alan says as he enters the freeway and heads toward the Brentwood area of Los Angeles. "Now do you see why I've had to keep this close to the vest?"

Jesus Christ.

Rocket Caldwell.

The same feeling remains as I come face to face with someone who's come into my life on my social media and playlists for years. Who is part of the band that has sung anthems that I correlate with various parts of my adult life.

Thirty whole seconds.

On the drive over here, that's the amount of time I decided that I'd give myself to stare and ogle and be starstruck by my new and *most likely* temporary employer.

What I didn't expect was for that thirty seconds to start the second the front door to the massive house swings open. No lawyer opening it. No personal assistant holding court. No girlfriend clinging to his side. Just Rocket Caldwell, one of the biggest rock stars on the planet, standing before us. His hair is tousled. His tattoos climb up one of his arms like sin incarnate. And he leans against the frame in nothing but low-slung worn jeans, a dark V-neck shirt, and a look on his face of confused displeasure.

But he's here, on his own, facing down the fact he has a toddler he never knew he had. That means he's either the measure of a man or is hiding this new fact about his life from everyone in his.

The latter has me reserving judgment.

My thirty seconds are up.

Jesus. He packs a punch. A punch even I can feel from my position where I'm partially hidden behind Alan's shoulder.

I ogle a second longer but then Poppy stirs in my arms, and the guilt crashes down upon me.

"Mr. Caldwell," Alan says as he steps aside so that the two of us come into Rocket's full view.

Rocket's eyes—deep, reckless, familiar in an unexpected way that unsettles me—flicker down to the little girl snuggled in my arms. Poppy's sound asleep, her cheek pressed to my collarbone, thick lashes resting on rosy, round cheeks, and curls tickling her shoulders.

"While I know you're expecting us, I'm sure that this is all rather shocking to you," Alan says gently. "But I'd like you to meet your daughter, Poppy. She'll wake any second no doubt—"

"No. Leave her." Panic laces his voice as he stares at Poppy like he's trying to memorize something he didn't know existed until recently.

Like she might disappear if he blinks, but he's not sure if he actually wants her to.

But then I can see it—the shift. The second he shoves down being mesmerized and becomes . . . *indifferent?* Almost as if he's not sure he'll accept this new reality.

I wasn't sure what I expected when Alan divulged who Poppy's father was, and the whole ride over here I've been playing out this first meeting in my head. I figured it would be emotionally charged but wasn't certain what that charged emotion would be.

Or how awkward and intrusive it would feel to be a part of this moment.

Would I want a witness to me rejecting my own daughter? Because that's what his physical recoil says when he takes a step back and just stares.

"Mr. Caldwell?" Alan prompts.

The muscle in his jaw clenches as we all wait in the suspended silence. His voice is gravel when he finally speaks. "This can't be real. She can't be—"

"Like I said," Alan says, "I understand this is all quite a shock to you and will take some time to process, but the sooner we get Poppy with you and integrated into your life, the better it is for her emotionally and mentally. She's been through more than most adults can handle in a very short amount of time."

"May we come in?" I ask.

Rocket's eyes flicker to mine for the first time and then immediately back to Poppy. "Sure. Yes. Come in."

His movements are jerky. Mechanical. And if I weren't standing here, seeing the whites of his eyes, I'd question if the man was strung out.

But he's not.

He's panicked. Terrified. Unsettled in the worst way possible and not sure what to do.

The smallest part of me feels for him. I do. But an even bigger part of me feels for the little girl in my arms who'll need him to step up to the plate for her.

I just hope that he does.

Rocket ushers us inside. The interior of his home is nothing like I expected. I thought I'd find sleek modern furniture in monochromatic tones that felt cold and unlived in. Instead, I find warm tones and sprawling couches that look like you could sit down on them only to realize later you've slept for hours.

Where I thought I'd find empty booze bottles littering the coffee table and maybe a stray bra missed or stashed in a corner, from my vantage point, everything seems to be tidy and in its place.

The man leading us down the wide hallway may smell from what I assume was a late night of drinking, but he did, in fact, pick up his house. *Or he has people for that.*

But if he does, they are nowhere to be found to greet the newest addition to the household.

The hallway leads into a massive room that opens up with high, vaulted ceilings. The space has a chef's kitchen on the far side, a sitting area around a large television on the other and the whole western-facing wall has windows that overlook an extensive backyard—patio cover, fireplace, pool on one side, large grass area on the other.

And while there's a bag of trash tied up and sitting against a door, everything else is clean. No dirty dishes stacked in the sink. No random person crashed out on the couch. No bongs displayed like art on the shelves.

Yes, I've seen it all in my time working with families, but my first impression here—other than the man beside me—is that he wanted to make a good one. That he was in fact trying.

Either that or he's freakishly clean.

I'll assume he's typically somewhere in the middle on a normal day, so at least there's a sense here that he cares.

It's not a huge sign, but it's better than none at all.

He clears his throat and narrows his brows as he seems to notice anyone other than Poppy is here for the first time. "Do—uh—you want to sit down? She, uh, looks heavy."

"Yes. She's getting to be." I shift her in my arms. "Thank you."

I move toward one of those massive couches I was admiring in the other room and sit down, grateful to have some support. Carrying a sleeping toddler is like carrying dead weight.

"Forgive me. Where are my manners?" Alan says. "Mr. Caldwell, this is Willow Adams. I know Sandra has coordinated her staying on for a probationary period while—"

"Hey." Rocket's gaze finally shifts to me, and he nods in greeting.

"You ready to do this?" I ask and then cringe at the stupidest comment in the world. Of course he isn't. By the look on his face, he'd rather have every tooth pulled without Novocain than be here, but when I get nervous, I say the most awkward things.

Like that.

"No. Actually, I'm not," he deadpans, his vibrant green eyes assessing and judging and criticizing all in one fell swoop. "That's why you're here."

Oh. That's how this is going to be. Disbelief laced with anger. Rejection edged with irrefutable proof.

I stare at him, eyes narrowed, but knowing my place. I'm not exactly getting the best first impression of Rocket Caldwell.

But I'll reserve judgment. *At least, I'll try to.*

Alan clears his throat as Rocket's eyes veer back to Poppy. "All of the legalities have already been taken care of by your attorney. Paperwork, medical records, any and everything else that was found in her mother's place."

"Fine." He glances around his own home like he'd rather be anywhere else than here.

"Then it's probably time that I get going," Alan says and glances to me with a reassuring look. "A social worker will be checking in to check on how things are going in the coming days and weeks, but if you have any questions, I'll leave my card on the counter here. Willow also knows how to get ahold of me."

He runs a hand through his hair and then hangs it on the back of his neck, despair owning every ounce of his posture. "If I said no, you can't go, it wouldn't matter, would it?" he asks with a half-assed chuckle.

"No. I'm sorry. It wouldn't," Alan says.

"Our bags," I say, realizing they're still in the car.

"I'll get them," Rocket says and moves toward the door without waiting for a response.

Alan glances at me again. "You okay?"

I nod and whisper, "Yeah. It'll be fine. This is a lot for anyone." And I mean it. But that doesn't mean I'm not wary about what the coming days will bring.

"Okay. Call me for anything."

"Will do," I say as he rushes out of the house and after Rocket to get our bags out of the car.

Within seconds of the front door shutting, there's a *thunk* from our bags hitting the floor, followed by a very long, drawn-out sigh, and then a pause before the footsteps carry back my way.

I know he's there, just behind the couch, and we both sit in that uncomfortable silence as we play a game of chicken over who's going to speak first.

I decide I should.

"Thank you for bringing the bags in."

"I haven't even figured out . . . *anything*," he says.

"It's okay. She's little. She'll fit anywhere," I joke as he passes me, moves to the other side of the room, and then finally turns to face me.

"I appreciate the jokes, but this situation is far from funny."

"You're right. It's not." I tuck an errant curl off Poppy's cheek to behind her ear and when I look back up, he's studying her again.

It must be weird to look at someone, at the spitting image of you, and know they were in the world and you didn't have a clue.

"Do you prefer Rocket or Gavin?" I ask.

"I don't respond to Gavin." He snorts. "*Ever.*"

"Noted." I nod and then begin to say the spiel I've replayed over and over in my head the past few days, knowing the situation I had agreed to walk into might be difficult. And if I practice what I need to say, then at least about 30 percent of it will sound right before the rest goes off the rails. "So I know this is a weird situation for both of us. I'm here to help you. To make sure there's some stability for Poppy after everything she's gone through and to make sure that she's cared for. No doubt you've been through an emotional roller coaster too that you've yet to have time to process."

"Your point?"

"Don't kill the messenger—figuratively, of course." I lift my eyebrows and shift. "I'm here to make your life easier."

"Fine. Great. Thanks," he says. "You guys can stay on that end of the house. One room is ready. I'll have to move some stuff out of the other one for you."

"No need." I smile and shake my head. "I said I'd stay on for the first week or two while you two adjust, and then I'll work a more regular schedule."

"No. That wasn't the deal." Panic once again laces his voice. He's scared of being alone with her. "Sandra told me you were a *live-in* nanny."

"I . . . that wasn't—"

"Do I look capable of doing this alone?" he asks. "The deal is live here or the job is done."

I bark out a disbelieving laugh as Poppy stirs to life. He's so full of shit he stinks, but I'll play along. "Okay. That's fine. I'll go. I'm sure there are plenty of other qualified nannies who—"

"Name your price."

I try not to startle at his words. At his demand. The desperation in his voice speaks volumes. "It's not a matter of price. I have an apartment. A life—"

"I'll pay your rent while you're here. I'll double your salary. We'll work out a schedule that suits you." He holds his hands out, frustrated and probably used to getting exactly what he wants simply because of who he is. "Live here. Help me. Name your fucking price, just don't leave."

I close my eyes and draw in a long, deep breath. More money. Rent paid. That sound of desperation he just spoke with now embedded in my head as much as the way Poppy's fingers tighten on the piece of my shirt she has gripped in her little hands. Two people desperate and scared.

"Fine, but there are conditions."

"You already signed the contract," he says, like my statement is as preposterous as it really is.

But clearly, I hold the leverage right now.

"I did."

"You're savvy, Willow. I like that." It's the first time I see his smile. The one that I'm sure has charmed the pants off more women than I care to count. And it takes me a second to remember where I am and what I'm supposed to do and that—

But then Poppy stirs. The playful moment is gone and the levity of the situation is suddenly back and weighing down the room.

"I mean it. I'll stay. I'll be a live-in, but I will not be her sole caretaker, and you will not shirk your duties with lame excuses like I've never done this before or I never asked for this."

"The nanny has demands."

"Yes. She does," I state, and this time when he holds my eyes across the room, there's more than fear and panic in his eyes. For the first time there's a vulnerability there along with something I can't quite place. I have a feeling I'm going to have to remember I once saw it though, because as soon as it's there, it's buttoned back up and gone.

"You'll find I'm far from fucking perfect," he states.

"Aren't we all?"

"This isn't . . . Just because this is being forced on me doesn't mean I'm going to have to like it."

There is a callousness to his tone. An edge that says he's used to getting and doing whatever he wants, and *this* isn't it.

He'll come around. He has to.

As if he's suddenly uncomfortable with this conversation, he glances to the bags he dropped to the side of the couch. "This is all she has?"

"The little one is hers. It's what her mom's friend thought she might need most. Yes."

"Whatever else she needs, you can buy for her." He moves absently around his family room. He picks up a bottle of water and then sets it back down without drinking it. He pushes a magazine a few inches to the right.

He takes a step one way before retreating and then taking a seat opposite me. He's doing anything and everything but look the one place it seems his eyes are drawn to. *Poppy.*

He's nervous. Uncertain.

For a man comfortable in front of tens of thousands of people, he's definitely out of his comfort zone right now, and I keep reminding myself that as I initiate this first interaction.

"You can look at her, you know," I say softly.

His Adam's apple bobs as he closes his eyes for a beat. "I don't want—"

"You're not going to disturb her. She's three and three-year-olds sleep like a rock."

"I just," he says, but his eyes flutter up and then over to Poppy.

I loosen my hold on her now that I can use the back of the couch for support. Her body turns more, and her hair falls back and off her cheek.

Rocket's breath hitches when he sees Poppy's face for the first time. "She's still asleep," he whispers, his voice rougher now. Hesitant.

"She is," I say. "She's had a rough and very confusing few days. Nightmares. Tantrums. Missing her mom. Sleep is good for her."

He grunts but his eyes never stop running over the little girl on my lap. It's a stretch of time. Of questions in Rocket's expression that he doesn't voice aloud. It's in the bob of his Adam's apple and the shaking back and forth of his head like he still doesn't believe she's real.

If this moment feels like forever to me, I can't imagine how it feels to him.

"Do you have any questions?" I ask.

A muscle tics in his jaw before he chuckles self-deprecatingly. "Oh, I have a shit ton of them, but not a single one pertains to you."

I nod. "Understandable. Just remember that whatever those shit ton of questions are, Poppy here is caught in their crossfire and can't give you a single answer. She's innocent in all of this."

His expression shifts—offense, confusion, something wounded just beneath the surface. "Glad you assume I'd blame her."

"I don't assume anything. I'm simply stating—"

Unknowingly, Poppy steals the moment when she releases my shirt for the first time to rub her eyes. She emits the cutest little yawn before those thick lashes of hers flutter open.

Her body stiffens as awareness hits her that she's in yet another new, foreign place. Her emerald-green eyes flicker around before landing back on me. It's then and only then that a slow, sleep-drugged smile crawls over her lips.

"Hi, sleepyhead," I say to her. My smile is as automatic as the shrug of her shoulders and the refastening of her hand to my shirt. But it's the quick intake of breath that Rocket emits on the opposite side of the coffee table that owns the room.

Poppy follows my glance to where Rocket sits, face pale, almost as if he's trying not to fall apart.

Something shifts behind his eyes. And momentarily, I see a man who's terrified. Of her. Of this. Of what it might mean to love someone when you have no clue how. *Or am I projecting?*

"Rocket?" I murmur.

"I—I need a minute," he says, voice low, raw.

CHAPTER
six

Rocket

WALK OUT OF THE ROOM LIKE I'M HEADING FOR A WALL TO SLAM INTO. Or maybe I've already hit it and am still staggered from the blow.

I can't get away fast enough and the minute the door to my office shuts behind me, I press my hands to my knees and struggle to drag in a breath.

Christ.

She looks just like me.

Not in the vague, might-be-yours, could-be-a-coincidence way. No. More like in the way that punches the breath straight from your lungs.

Same green eyes—wary and watchful and way too fucking serious for someone her age.

Same messed up eyebrow that I have where the end feathers up some like my dad's did too.

And she's so small.

My breath's shaky as I scrub a hand through my hair before pulling down on the back of my neck.

Then my feet start moving—anything to abate the . . . who the fuck knows what it's called that's coursing through me. I pace across the space like action will keep me from losing it.

She's three.

Fucking three.

Which means I missed all of it. Her first steps. First words. First everything.

So the fuck what, Rock? You don't want a kid, right? What does it matter if you missed things people say should be unforgettable?

"Oh my God," I mutter and bang my forehead gently against the wall knowing it's going to do nothing to fix the situation.

This is all a bad fucking nightmare I can't wake up from, and yet she's sitting on my couch with her pink, chubby cheeks and unruly curls, like I used to have as a kid, telling me different.

She's mine.

And now she's here.

With her tiny sneakers and her tangled curls, and a damn suitcase the size of a backpack—as if that's all she needs. As if that's all she has.

And isn't that part of the problem that guts me the most?

Because it's not just her resemblance or the timing or the way her fingers curled into Willow's top like she already knows the world isn't a safe place, but rather it's the fact that her entire life fits into a zippered piece of carry-on luggage. Like she's something someone packed up and passed off.

Passed *on* so that now she's here.

My breath is as shaky as my hands when I draw it in.

This isn't a joke.

This isn't a publicity stunt like Gizmo's marriage originally was or some bullshit paternity rumor planted to salvage my reputation. There's a lot of shit like that that goes on in the industry. This? *This is real.*

The problem is—I don't know what the hell to do with her now.

I'm not a father. Far fucking from it. I'm a goddamn mess with a crazy tour schedule, a bad temper, a selfish streak a mile long, and a proven tendency to fuck things up.

I've ruined relationships, wrecked hotel rooms, and walked off stages mid-set. Christ, I couldn't even get my own parents to love me enough to care.

I've broken a lot of things.

But this?

This little girl with my eyes and nothing but a suitcase and a stranger to keep her steady?

I can't break *her*. And yet, it feels like *that* and music are all I'm good at doing.

I slide down the wall until I'm crouched on the cold tile, elbows on my knees, head between my hands.

I don't even think about Willow.

Not at first.

Not until I hear a soft, muffled giggle drift down the hall. It's not loud, but it's enough to cut through the fog clouding my thoughts.

"There's nowhere you can run, Caldwell," I say to the empty room. Nothing to save me. Nothing to fix this.

I'd beg for the chance to.

I rise to my feet slowly. Each step back down the hallway feels like curiosity mixed with trepidation. Like intrigue laced with uncertainty. But they do keep moving, one step in front of the other, until I'm standing at the edge of the hallway, watching Willow with Poppy from afar.

Willow's sitting cross-legged on the floor, her long braid of dark hair is resting over one shoulder, her expression soft but focused. Her smile is warm and sincere. Poppy is standing in front of her with a stuffed bunny tucked under her arm, while her other hand reaches out and taps Willow on the nose.

With each tap, Willow flails her arms dramatically, which causes Poppy to erupt into a fit of laughter. I watch this game play on for several minutes and fight the tilt that comes automatically to the corners of my lips.

But something is off and it takes me a second to catch it. Willow is talking. Willow is making funny sounds. Poppy's face is lighting up with expressions and reactions . . . *but she's absolutely silent.*

Is something wrong with her? The way the immediate thought hits me square in the solar plexus is unexpected and unwanted and claws at something I'm choosing to ignore. Knowingly.

Willow grins, points to her nose and then her eyes.

Poppy giggles softly, but her whole body responds—shoulders shaking, cheeks flushing, eyes lighting up.

And that crushing pressure behind my ribs? That ache in the hollow of my chest? It twists hard and sharp and deep.

Because I'm watching them . . . and for the first time, I'm not front and center on the stage. Nah, I'm the guy standing in the wings, wondering if I even belong here. Knowing this is something that scares the shit out of me.

And knowing in the past when my hand was forced at something, I bucked even harder the other way.

Right now, my hand is being forced.

I cross my arms, jaw clenched, and heart hammering.

And as grateful as I am for Willow being here, knowing how to deal with Poppy, it only serves to make me feel like I'm already failing at something.

"Why don't you come in so I can introduce you to her?" Willow asks without looking my way.

I rub my hands down my jeans-clad thighs and move into the room, jumpy like a junkie looking for his next fix.

I don't know what to do or how to act. Sure, I've been around kids. I'm not good with them, but . . . it's never really mattered. *They've never been mine.*

"I don't know what to say."

"Poppy," Willow says calmly and puts both of her tiny hands in hers. "I want you to meet my friend. This is Rocket. He's your . . ."

It's like she has no clue how hard my heart's pounding or how much that open-ended question she left dangling for me to answer just rendered me speechless.

I open my mouth and then close it. What the fuck am I? *"Friend?"* The word feels like molasses on my tongue. Overpowering, hard to swallow over, and in reality, a complete lie.

"Yes." Willow nods and offers a compassionate smile my way. *"Your friend."* She may have said something else, but all sound is drowned out as Poppy turns my way and meets my eyes for the first time. Eyes that start and stop my heart simultaneously.

"Hi," I say and smile, and then feel like an idiot when I add a wave to it after the fact.

She tilts her head to the side, her curls bouncing with the motion. Her eyes stop on the tattoos on my arms and then narrow as her lips twist in thought.

I feel judged in a way I've never felt before, in a way that matters more than any other time in my life, even though I'd swear up and down to anyone who asks me that I don't care.

But I do.

"She's not talking," I say quietly, glancing at Willow for her to stop that niggling in the back of my head that something's wrong.

Willow's nod doesn't ease that feeling at all. "Yes. The doctors say it's a trauma response to . . ."—her eyes flicker to Poppy and then back to me—"everything she saw last week. A coping mechanism that can last for however long she wants it to last."

Everything she saw last week.

"Jesus Christ," I mutter more to myself than anyone as I process those words. Yes, I knew she was in the car, but now that Poppy's here, now that I see how fucking small she is, how innocent she is, the knowledge hits differently. It wears on me differently.

"Mm-hm," Willow says as she presses a kiss to Poppy's tiny hands and then taps her on the nose as her voice softens. "But it's okay to not want to talk, isn't it, Poppy?"

Poppy nods and then looks my way, her eyes stalling on my ink again.

I hold my arms out and take a step closer. "Do you want to look at them?" I ask, causing her to startle and move behind Willow's shoulder for what I can only assume is protection. "Maybe another time, then."

I'm unable to tear my eyes away from her now that I'm this close. Now that I can see the freckles dusting the bridge of her nose or how her fingernails are painted a light pink. Now that I can see how tightly she clutches the stuffed rabbit beneath her arm or how she instinctively reached out upon seeing me to keep her hand on Willow's shoulder.

Think, Caldwell. Say something. Do something.

So I take a step back, lift my hand, and wave.

Eyes the same color as mine hold me captive as seconds stretch before she offers me a shy, hesitant smile . . . and then waves back.

CHAPTER
seven

Willow

Rocket watches Poppy's every movement. Her every expression. His arms are crossed and his body's still, almost as if he's afraid to move. Like if he breathes too loud, she'll vanish. And by the way she jumped behind my back when he took a step forward, she just might.

"She looks like me," he murmurs.

Poppy has taken a seat on the other side of the room. She wandered there herself with her stuffed animals and is setting up what I am making out to be is some sort of house on the floor with throw pillows used as a crude wall around them. She has methodically arranged her stuffed animals in a neat little line. Bunny. Fox. Elephant. All worn in the way toys get when they're loved hard and carried everywhere.

"She does. Yes," I say, knowing she's just out of earshot. Clearly, he's her *"friend"* at this point and so that'll be a whole other topic to figure out—when to tell her he's her dad.

"And the not talking thing?" His Adam's apple bobs with a fleeting glance my way.

"In simple terms, it's her way of coping."

"But she's okay, right? Nothing happened in the accident to her physically that . . ." He speaks like he should be presenting in a boardroom. Unemotional. And yet, while it can be read as not caring, the fact that he's asking when he seems so conflicted with the entire situation tells me that in fact, he does.

"Physically, yes. Emotionally . . . time will tell."

He makes a noncommittal sound as he shifts on his feet, his gaze never leaving Poppy for more than a second. Moments ago, he was looking anywhere but at her and now it seems he can't look away.

I take the moment to study the man I'll now be living with. His hair is a dark brown, a little shaggy, but only in the way it curls at his neck and over his ears. His eyes are the same vibrant green as Poppy's, but whereas hers are full of wonder, there's wariness in his. He's tall, I'd say a few inches over six foot, and while he's not bulked with muscles, it's obvious he's fit. And then there's his array of tattoos that Poppy seems completely fascinated with. They twist down one arm and over a very defined forearm stopping just before his wrist.

And on that wrist is the only flashy thing on him, what looks like a very expensive watch. It seems completely out of place with his faded jeans, navy blue V-neck shirt, and combat boots.

"This is—" He steps forward, then stops short like there's an invisible line he doesn't know how to cross. "Her mom. Olivia. I barely remember her."

I nod in response.

"Not because she wasn't anything but . . . I mean, it was just a quick thing." He groans. "I know how that sounds, how that makes me look. It's just—"

"I'm not here to judge." But I am judging and I'm wondering how common this kind of thing is for him. If the rock star stereotype is true.

I'm far from a prude, but I can't say that random hookups are my thing. Sure, I've had a few in my adult life, but my mind veers to the logistical element of this. Is this a norm for *him*? If so, does he bring women here? How am I supposed to sit with Poppy watching shows while he's having some wild, loud sex in his bedroom—wherever in the house that may be? And while I'm at it, does he throw crazy parties here? Do I need to be worried about cleanliness and the things Poppy will inevitably put in her mouth?

"But you are judging," he says, his eyebrows raised and his eyes firmly on mine now. I'm aware how willingly he shifts to topics he can argue with me on rather than interact with Poppy. It's like he starts to peek his head up from behind his guarded wall and then ducks down the minute he realizes he's doing it. "You're judging and wondering and questioning about my sex life and my reputation and everything in between."

I hold my hands up. "I'm here for Poppy."

He grunts and holds my gaze, but he doesn't defend himself or how many women he's slept with, which is where I thought this conversation I *never* wanted was going.

His eyes drift back to Poppy and her mindless playing with her stuffed animals.

"This is insane," he says to no one in particular.

"I'm going to have to agree with you on that one," I say.

He runs a hand down his face, scrubbing over his jaw, and then looks back at me. Again, it's not arrogance or deflection I see in them—it's absolute disbelief.

And buried beneath that, something I can't exactly name. Hope? Disbelief? Possibility? Disgust?

"Do you want some coffee?" he asks. Again, another way to deflect instead of sitting down with his daughter.

"Only if it's stronger than whatever it is you were drinking last night," I say, trying to ease the tension in the room.

His smirk is back. Lazy. Dangerous.

Oh. Don't do that, Rocket.

"Coffee it is," he says, already heading to the kitchen. "Last night's drink of choice was warranted for many reasons, all of which I'm sure you can understand."

"Uh-huh." I stand and run a hand down Poppy's back as I watch him move behind the kitchen island.

"You'll learn I'm an excellent host on a normal day." He pulls down two mugs. "Today is nowhere close to being normal."

"Can't disagree with you there."

I shouldn't feel this amused by his discomfort and his awkward comments to avoid facing what he's not exactly facing.

I shouldn't feel anything.

But when I glance at Poppy still playing with her animals and then over at Rocket, who looks shell-shocked . . . I know.

I know this is exactly where I'm supposed to be.

Rocket lingers in the kitchen like it's safer over there, behind the counter, behind the noise of pouring coffee and clinking mugs. Making coffee is something he can control.

How he reacts to a rosy-cheeked little girl, on the other hand, is something he can't control. In his eyes, he seems to think it's safer for him in the kitchen.

A few minutes later, he returns with a mug in one hand, the other shoved into the front pocket of his jeans.

"Coffee," he says with a shrug, holding it up like a white flag. "Fresh. Strong." He clears his throat. "Like I promised."

Poppy looks up from her spot beside me and watches him. She's not afraid but more curious and wide-eyed. There are questions in her eyes, in the furrow of her brow, and I swear she knows this new man standing near her is more than just a friend.

She studies him for a long time, far too aware for someone that young. She glances at his tattoos again, then at his hair, then at the faint scar near his eyebrow. The way her fingers twitch, it's almost as if she wants to touch him.

He sits on the edge of the coffee table, careful not to get too close but close enough that he's part of the space now.

"Do you . . . do you want something?" he asks, speaking softly and lifting his own coffee mug.

"Juice or snacks?" I add. She nods. "I have both in her bag." I start to move, but Rocket's already on his feet.

"I'll get it."

He moves to her bag and stares at it for a second too long before he lifts it gently and unzips the top.

I know what's inside—a few changes of clothes, three board books, a T-shirt of her mother's, a blanket, and pictures of her and her mom in frames wrapped protectively and stowed in the very bottom. But on top is a lunchbox that has juice and a half-open pack of fruit snacks.

He pulls the lunchbox out, his hand trembling slightly before he makes his way back and hands it to me.

Poppy tugs on my sleeve, her eyes sad despite the newfound snacks and points toward the door.

"What is it?" I ask.

Her bottom lip begins to quiver as she taps a hand over her heart—the gesture we've been using to say she wants her mommy.

A sullen reminder of why we're here and the enormous tragedy this little girl has endured.

"What does that mean?" Rocket asks.

I look up and hold his gaze. "She wants her mom," I whisper.

The air in the room shifts.

Rocket flinches like my words slapped him.

He doesn't look at her. Doesn't look at me. Just stares down at the floor, jaw flexing, and words escaping him.

"I—" He clears his throat. "I have an appointment. One I . . . couldn't reschedule."

My stomach twists.

"Of course," I say, keeping my voice steady.

"We're writing new music. Usually, they're all-night sessions. I probably won't be back until late. Later. Maybe even the morning. It just—we just go until we can't."

"Right." I nod. I also hate that I'm disappointed. Hate that I spent so much time making sure Poppy's hair was perfect and that her bows were bright. That she smelled like baby lotion, and that her outfit was adorable.

I know none of that should have mattered, but I thought first impressions were huge, and I wanted hers to be incredible. I wanted him to fall in love with her at first sight, just like I did.

Guess none of that superficial preparation mattered.

His smile is tight, and his eyes dart to anywhere but me.

"There're rooms down that hall there for you two. Big beds. Bathroom with each room." He points off to the left of the kitchen. "Third and fourth doors on the right."

"Okay. Thanks."

"Food is here in the kitchen. Plates. Drinks. Cups. Pantry." He points absently to each as he talks. *He can't get out of here fast enough.* "Make yourself at home. To get settled, I mean."

"We'll be fine," I say as graciously as I can, but I won't deny there's a chill to my tone.

His gaze flicks to Poppy once before he grabs his phone, wallet, and keys off the counter. "She, uh . . . she should eat something more than that," he says like I haven't already created a routine for her, like I haven't already built my life around taking care of kids and their needs. "You'll have to make me a list of food she—you—like, and I'll get it taken care of. Drinks. Snacks. Juice. Milk. That kind of thing."

"Uh-huh."

"I have a person—she shops for me. Cooks when I want her to—I really am sorry that I have to get out of here. We're on a schedule. A deadline and . . . *this* was unscheduled."

"How inconvenient for you," I say.

Clearly my sarcasm wasn't missed by the way he stops in his tracks and meets my eyes. There's an apology there, the ever-present dose of fear, and a little bit of anger, no doubt directed my way.

But he doesn't say anything in response. He doesn't argue with me. He just stands there leveling me with an indiscernible look while his daughter he's given a whole few minutes of his time to is sniffling beside me. *Focus on her, Willow. She's sad.*

I can see the muscle pulse in his jaw even from this distance, and with nothing more than a subtle shake of his head, he dumps the coffee he barely touched in the sink, raps his knuckles on the counter, and walks out of the kitchen.

The door clicks shut behind him.

And Poppy's eyes stay locked on the direction I'm looking . . . maybe because I am. Or worse, maybe because, despite her age, she senses rejection.

What's he going to do when he can't run away or hide behind making coffee anymore? What's going to happen when he has to face the reality that Poppy is his daughter?

I guess that's when we'll see the true man that Rocket Caldwell really is.

CHAPTER
eight

Rocket

I DON'T REMEMBER DRIVING HERE.

I needed to escape. Needed fresh air and distance from this new reality that I haven't been given any time to accept. *She* was just thrown squarely in my face. Somewhere between slamming the front door and getting behind the wheel, my brain just . . . blanked. Went quiet. Like maybe it's protecting me from myself.

Or maybe it knows I need backup.

So I called the only people who have ever showed up when everything else in my life went to shit.

The band. My brothers from other mothers. What feels at times like the only family I have.

And now I'm in Hawkin's backyard, sitting around the fire pit with a beer in my hand and a heart that won't stop hammering against my ribs like it's begging for someone else to carry the weight.

Vince is here, his legs stretched out and his bottle of beer resting on his thigh. He's got that same unreadable expression on his face he always wears before he says something that'll either destroy you or save you.

At this point, I'm not sure which I'd prefer.

Gizmo's sprawled in a lounger, hands tapping idly on the armrest to a beat he hears in his head. His time here is limited because of plans he'd previously made with his wife.

And then there's Hawkin himself, the resident but loyal-as-hell shit-stirrer—well, at least when I'm out of commission like I seem to be now—leaning back in an Adirondack chair and looking at me through the flames like he owns the night.

They're the only family I've ever trusted. As much as I hate to admit it, I need them more now than ever before.

That's why I came here, isn't it?

"So," Giz says, his fingers still tapping as he speaks. "What's with the urgent group text? You sounded like someone important died, and yet all you fuckers are here so clearly that isn't the case."

I chuckle, but it's not a good sound. It's hollow and sharp and so very similar to the sound of Gizmo's about this time last year when his life was turning to shit.

And everything turned out okay for him.

Remember that, Rock. It all turned out okay.

I glance at each of them, then drag a hand over my face. "I have a kid."

Silence. Then—

"Funny, Rock. You're the last fucking guy here who needs a kid," Gizmo says and then takes a sip of his beer.

And on a normal day, I'd laugh with him and agree. But it's not any fucking day. It's today, and my closest friends are laughing because they think I'd be a joke of a father stings. *It shouldn't.*

"Jesus. I thought you were serious for a second," Hawkin says and barks out a laugh.

Vince studies me over the neck of his beer, his eyes quiet but assessing. "He *is* being serious."

One of them snorts and another chokes on the sip he just took, but I'm too busy holding Vince's stare.

"Rock?" Gizmo asks as he sits forward until I have the courage to look over at him.

I nod. That's all I give them, but I sure as fuck have their attention now. For the first time in days, I feel like I can finally breathe.

"Like . . . a real one?" Hawkin asks, brow lifted. "Not the 'I might have knocked someone up' kind?"

"She's three." Fuck, those two words sound as shredded as I feel. "And she's at my house. Right now."

Gizmo spits out the sip he's taking. "Three? *Dude*. What the fuck?"

"You left a three-year-old alone at your house?" Hawkin says, eyes widening but tone playful. "Pretty sure that will get you a call from CPS."

"It's crossed my mind," I say.

"That's one way out of this for sure," Gizmo says. "But seriously, let me repeat myself. What the actual fuck, dude?"

"I found out last week. Was waiting for the paternity test to disprove what it proved."

"And now your silence makes sense," Hawkin says, meeting my eyes and nodding. "You could've told us."

"I know. I just . . . I'm here now," I say, realizing I probably hurt their feelings by not saying shit. That wasn't my intention. "Found out last night she's mine. She showed up on my doorstep today. Well, CPS, her nanny, and her."

"Fuck," one of them sighs out.

"That about sums it up." I chuckle.

"Wait. Showed up at your house? Where is her mom?" Vince asks.

"Passed away in a car accident. That's why Poppy's here." Acid churns in my stomach, and I feel like a dick for saying it so nonchalantly.

"Poppy?" Hawkin asks. He's sitting forward now with his knees on his elbows.

"Yes," I say.

"Okay." Gizmo holds his hands up. "We need details because you know the minute we get home the wives are going to say we neglected to ask the right shit. But first, before you say all that"—he pats a hand on my leg—"you okay? How are you doing?"

"Fucked in the head. Not believing it when there's proof. Trying to figure out how the fuck to go from here when it feels like I'm staring down shit I never wanted to stare at."

"Understandable," Hawkin says.

And then I give them the details. How Sandra called me out of the fucking blue a week ago. The shock. The denial. The waiting game for the paternity test, and now Poppy sitting in my house somewhere right now while I sit here like a chickenshit.

"Should we remember Olivia?" Vince murmurs as if he's trying to place her.

"I hate to sound like a callous prick, but not more than any of the others. I mean—"

"We get it," Gizmo says. "We've been doing this a long time. Hard to remember every face we meet and every woman who's occupied our beds—"

"Or dressing room," Hawkin says.

"Or tour bus," Vince adds.

"Or basically *any-fucking-where*." I shrug and chuckle, grateful for the levity. For them knowing what I need. "It is me, after all."

"Especially in those early years," Hawkin says, and we all laugh as he lifts his beer to his lips. For a moment, it seems as if each one of us see reruns of those freshman years in our heads. "Fuck, man. *A kid?*"

"Yeah," I say quietly as everyone stares at the fire lost in their thoughts over the news. As they accept that I'm a dad. Me. *Rowdy, nonstop, life of the fucking party, Rocket.*

And maybe that's what I needed. To be among the people who I know would accept me—mistakes and all.

Vince clears his throat and is the first to speak. "What do you need?"

I blink. "What?"

"You didn't call us because you wanted to relive your greatest hits with Olivia. You called us because you're spiraling. We know you." His eyes lock on to mine. "So, we're here. What do you need from us?"

I exhale and hate that tears of frustration are burning the backs of my eyes. And then the fact that they're threatening makes me even angrier. "To turn back time to four years ago and tell me not to sleep with Olivia Whitmore." The words are out and even though they are true, it bugs me that I said them.

Huge green eyes and bouncing curls flash through my mind.

A little mini-me.

"What-the-ever-loving-fuck am I going to do?" I ask.

"It's rubber meets the road time," Vince says, voice level.

Gizmo coughs out a laugh. "Clearly Rocket doesn't know much about rubbers."

"Fuck off." I flip him the bird. "I always use one."

"Clearly not well enough," Hawkin jokes.

I laugh, but it dies a quick death.

"If there's one thing I know from my own experience," Vince says, referring to finding out he had a son with his high school sweetheart he didn't know about, "is that you can't run from this. Jagger was the last thing I ever wanted but fuck, Rock, now I can't imagine what my life would be like without him."

He has a point, but Jagger's mom—now Vince's wife—has always been *the one* for him. He's loved her since high school. This whole thing with Oliva is nowhere near the same scenario. "This isn't the same."

"So, what?" Gizmo asks with a judgmental lift of his brows.

My stomach twists. "She's got my damn eyes," I whisper. That sucks the air out of the backyard.

"Let's hope she doesn't have your stubborn streak, or you're fucking screwed, dude," Gizmo says.

"Look," Hawkin, our problem solver, says matter-of-factly. "It's simple. You adapt and adjust. The upside is you have a nanny already to help."

"Willow." All three heads turn my way. "The nanny."

"Oh. Right. *Willow*," Hawkin continues and shrugs like how were they supposed to know that. "You have her to help you so that's a start because you're being thrown directly into the fire. And then you take this break between legs of the tour to figure shit out."

"It's not that easy," I say.

"No one will ever say parenting is easy," Vince says through a self-deprecating laugh. "But it's more of a plan than you have. Three, you said?"

I nod.

"Tough fucking age, but like Vince said, you have the nanny who she knows and who will do everything you need her to do to help out," Hawkin says.

"She's not talking," I blurt out. "Because of the trauma of seeing her mom, you know . . . I don't know why I felt the need to say that."

Gizmo nods. "Because you already care about her."

I start to protest but Vince holds up his hand. "Don't," he warns me. "She okay otherwise?"

I startle at the question. One I should know the answer to but don't. Willow would have told me otherwise, wouldn't she? "Yeah. I think so."

"Okay. So you go from there," Hawkin says. "One step at a time. One minute at a time. One hour at a time. That's all you can do."

"I have no idea how to be a dad," I blurt out. It's the one thing that keeps circling in my head. "I never had one. I don't have a clue how to be or what to do or how to not fuck her up."

"It's a valid fear," Vince says.

"But you're not going to fuck her up," Gizmo says. "We wouldn't let you."

"Use us," Hawkin says instantly.

"Yep. Use us." Vince taps the neck of his beer against mine. "We're basically the gold fucking standard when it comes to fatherhood."

"You mean chaos and bribery?" Giz teases.

"Hey, my kids are still alive and moderately polite," Hawkin says.

"Never mind. *Don't* use us as examples"—Vince shrugs and laughs—"we were barely functioning humans five years ago—"

"Speak for yourselves." Giz raises his hand. "I've been emotionally stable since . . . well, at least since last Tuesday. Just ask Hendrix," he says, referring to his wife.

I grin despite myself, and the knot in my chest eases slightly. This is what I needed. My brothers. Their banter. Their levity. Their understanding. *Their unconditional support.*

It's not going to make what's ahead in the days to come any easier, but that suffocating, isolating feeling I felt yesterday has lessened.

"You don't have to do it alone," Vince says. "Seriously, bro. We've got you."

"Thanks. I . . . just thanks," I say.

"And Willow?" Hawkin asks, eyebrows lifted and smirk widening. "You didn't mention much about the nanny."

I know these guys better than I know myself and can already guess where this conversation is headed.

I roll my eyes and take a long pull from my beer. "What about her?"

"She hot?" Hawke continues.

No. *Yes.* Christ if I can even really remember, because I was so goddamn focused on Poppy.

That's a lie.

A flat-out, bald-faced lie.

Willow is pretty in the girl-next-door way. Natural. Unassuming. Completely not my type at all.

"He's not answering," Gizmo says. "That means she's definitely hot."

"Road trip to Rock's house to check her out," Vince says, no doubt because he knows it'll get under my skin.

I hold my hand up before the other two agree. "I was a bit preoccupied meeting *my kid* for the first time. I didn't notice," I lie, to which a roar of protests go up.

"You're so full of shit, Rock, you stink," Vince says. "Tell me what other time you've been in a room with a woman and haven't noticed her?" He levels me with a look. "I distinctly remember that time you had to get stitches in your ass. You were drunk as hell and could tell me what every single nurse in that emergency department looked like. So, uh, try again."

I roll my eyes and set my empty bottle down with a thud and downplay. "She's . . . okay, I guess. Just not my type."

"You mean her tits weren't up to her neck, and she didn't immediately run up and grind herself against you, begging for your time?" Hawkin says to a round of laughter.

"Fuck off." *These assholes.* "No. More like she has zero interest in me. Wasn't fazed by who I was in the least."

"So, she's perfect for you, then?" Giz asks around a mouthful of pretzels.

"Exactly your type," Vince adds, grinning. "Not being fazed means she'd humble you and that giant-ass ego of yours real quick."

"Don't you guys have anything better to do?" I ask.

"You're the one who got on the *bat phone* and called this emergency meeting, so nope, apparently we don't have anything better to do than bust your balls over how you're going to fall head over heels for the hot nanny," Hawkin says.

"Jesus, wait until the wives figure this one out. You won't be able to get them and their matchmaking out of your house." Vince chuckles.

And he's right. I know my texts will be lighting up within minutes of them finding this out.

"I appreciate you guys trying to make me laugh, but you're *batshit* crazy. Besides the fact that she's taking care of a toddler for me I never even knew existed. Pretty sure she has a less than stellar opinion of me."

"That's how you know it could be real love." Hawkin pats his chest and sighs. "Already pissing her off before she's even met you. Talk about starting with a good foundation. Something you can build true feelings off." I flip him off, and everyone laughs. "I mean, if she were just here for your abs and your complete dysfunction, then we all know it would never last. But hatred? Now that's something you can rally around."

"Bite me," I say, but I'm laughing now. For real this time.

Willow will be Poppy's nanny for as long as I need it. There will never be anything more than that. Of that I have no doubt.

CHAPTER
nine

Poppy's out cold.

Her face is planted into the pillow with one arm thrown over her bunny's neck. Her tiny mouth is slack as she breathes evenly and her fingers keep twitching. Hopefully, she's lost in a dream of imaginary fun.

She looks how I want to be—dead to the world and oblivious to the chaos we just stepped into—but sleep eludes me.

It must be this big, empty house that calls for me. Of course I'd love to explore it, to fall more in love with it than I already have, but truth be told, I need to do some toddler proofing.

I lived with several families in my college years when I nannied and when I first arrived, it would always feel like I was intruding on their space. They'd tell me to make myself at home. They'd encourage me to feel like what's theirs is mine, but it always takes some time to sink into that feeling. To not feel like a stranger sneaking around and invading other people's privacy.

And then, when you add to that whose house I'm currently in, it makes things even more . . . *weird*.

Poppy pulls me from my thoughts. She makes a small mewling sound and then murmurs, "*Mommy*."

It's the first and only time I've heard her adorable voice, and it's a heartbreaking one at that.

Undoubtedly this was going to be hard—uprooting a three-year-old from all she's known and who's just lost her mom—but I also wondered if she'd be so wrapped up in all these changes that she'd slowly adjust without realizing what she's lost.

I can help ease her sadness when she's awake, but there's not much I can do to chase the nightmares away when she sleeps.

So far she's been such a trooper. My smile is bittersweet as I tuck the blanket up over her side, gently brush a curl from her cheek, and back out of the room, leaving it cracked open so that I can hear her if she needs me.

I'm exhausted. The emotional toll of the day, of worrying about her and meeting Rocket for the first time, has hit me hard now that I'm alone. I'm hungry and welcome the solitude and silence of the house.

What I learned a long time ago with this live-in nanny gig is coming back to me now—when your charge is sleeping, savor the time for yourself.

To have a glass of wine. To catch up with friends. To read a book. To simply step outside of my world of sticky hands and cherubic cheeks and be a twenty-six-year-old woman.

It's not always an easy feat to achieve, but right now is the perfect time. I have a sleeping toddler and a silent house.

And I'm freaking starving.

I grab my phone with the baby monitor connected to it and head toward the kitchen with the intention of getting a better lay of the land beyond where the dishes and pantry are.

As I move down the hall, I take stock of what borders the rooms we're in. Yes, their doors are closed, but it's my job to make sure Poppy is safe and secure. Therefore, I need to know if she were to open one of the doors and go in, what she'd find. Some gym equipment she could hurt herself climbing on? A collector's room where everything is glass or breakable? Or who knows what else?

I am in a rock star's house, and they have reputations for a reason, right?

Let's hope I don't find anything embarrassing this time around. Not on the first day when my initial impression of Rocket is still forming and amendable.

The first bedroom beside Poppy's is mine, so I pass it and open the next door to find an office. I stand in the doorway in awe of the platinum records lining two of the four walls. One after another with a few gold ones mixed in there.

And then it hits me squarely in the gut that I'm at *the* Rocket Caldwell's house.

Like . . . *holy shit.*

Those are real, and there are dozens of them. I itch to walk in there and look closer at each and every one, but I'll wait to do that until Rocket invites me to do so. While he may be a public figure, this is his private space.

But before I can let the picture of what all those accolades paint sink in, my phone rings in my hand. I jump to turn the ringer off, afraid of waking up Poppy, and answer the call immediately.

My best friend's face fills the FaceTime screen.

"Tell me everything," Lily says as I hold the phone up.

"About?"

"Um, about your hush-hush new boss—wait. What are those on the wall behind you? Records? Like shiny ones on the wall."

"No. Don't be ridiculous." I shut the door and rush down the hall toward the kitchen. Awesome. Perfect. Breaching the NDA on the first day of the job wasn't on my bingo card today.

"You're such a fucking liar. Your new boss is a singer, isn't he?"

"Lily," I warn as I prop the phone on the kitchen island and take a seat at one of the barstools facing it. "I can't—"

"Hold on," she says and the phone goes dark as she does something I can't see. "55687 Fairgate Road."

"What?" I screech.

"We shared our locations on Find My iPhone for safety. Remember that? And now you went to live with some strange man you'd never met before. You bet your ass I just checked the address so I know where you are in case you go missing or something."

"You listen to too many true crime podcasts."

"Don't hate your girl for being prepared," she teases. "But if I were to look up the address of that house and—*holy shit.*" Lily's eyes grow wide, and her jaw drops open.

"Christ," I mutter under my breath.

"Willow Adams, please tell me that you are not at the house the sleuths on Reddit are telling me that address belongs to."

"I'm not. Don't know what you're talking about." *Kill me now.*

"Ha. You *so* are, hence why all the stupid secrecy and—why are you there? He doesn't have a kid, so who are you—"

"Lily, I signed an NDA. I can't talk about anything."

"Okay. Fine. I wouldn't want you to get *bent* out of shape or anything." She grins and winks at her double entendre. I do the only thing I can—I shake my head and sigh.

"I still can't say anything."

"You didn't. You haven't. You took a new job as a nanny for an orphaned little girl and her newly found father. At an address I double-checked to make sure an axe murderer hadn't accosted you only to find it's owned by an incredibly famous rock star . . . and here we are." Her grin is contagious.

I glance around the open space before looking back to her. "You have to promise not to—"

"You know my word is good. All I did was FaceTime you. I didn't even mention any name so we could be talking about anyone." She rolls her eyes.

"I know. You're right. I just . . ."

My guilt rides high. I do *not* want to be responsible for how the media finds out that Rocket Caldwell has a daughter. I know I can trust Lily with my life. She's not exactly the social butterfly, nor would she have any reason to blab, and yet, the non-disclosure agreement I signed said no one is to know.

Call me a rule follower.

"Relax." She sighs. "You are such a rule follower, it's ridiculous," she says having no clue that she's just voiced my thoughts. "But oh my God. You know what this means, right? Your face is going to be splashed over every damn tabloid."

"No, it's not." I shake my head to reject the thought and the fear it evokes. "Rocket has security in his neighborhood. A guard shack and privacy clauses. My pay is through an LLC, so there is nothing connecting me to him."

She snorts. "Except the fact that you're living in his house. You've clearly never seen how rabid superfans are."

"Let's hope not," I murmur but wonder how long Poppy and I will remain under the public radar.

She then claps her hands together. "Now, tell me everything."

I hesitate for a second and then welcome the chance to talk to someone about this very odd situation I'm in.

"Not much to tell, really. He was only here for like an hour max."

"And that's one hour more than I'll ever have or will. One hour more than I have to make the qualified decision of his certifiable hotness. Like, is he simply just hot-HOT or is he more the totally and completely fuckably hot-HOT."

"Jesus." I know he's not home, but I glance around the great room as her voice carries through the empty space.

Leave it to Lily to lay that question out there.

And to force me to think about something I probably haven't wanted to admit to myself.

"He's . . ." *Sexy. Even better in person. Attractive.* "Yeah. He's hot."

"Willow. I need more," she whines playfully.

"What do you want me to say? That he's totally and completely fuckably hot-HOT?" I whisper and play along. "Like dangerously hot. Leather pants, tattoos, lean-muscle, man-who's-lived-some-shit hot?"

Lily's eyes go wide. "Well, hell. Now I'm gonna need to get my vibrator out and picture him all the while. Wait." She narrows her eyes. "Your text said you thought your new boss was emotionally constipated though."

"Oh, he is. Fully. Emotionally unavailable, defensive, occasionally charming in a *what happened in your childhood* kind of way—"

"So then he's perfectly your type? Too fucked up to get attached but hot enough to have some good, dirty fun with."

I snort and rest my elbows on the counter so that I can stare straight into the phone. "Nope. Nope. And oh, *nope.* He's my boss, Lil. Even having this conversation makes me feel like I'm breaking all kinds of ethical boundaries."

"God forbid you break a rule now and again."

"I'm here for Poppy—first and foremost—not for—"

"And still, it's crossed your mind at least once since you got there."

"Changing subjects," I say.

Lily gasps and points at the screen. "You're so full of shit. You only say that when you want to avoid reality. You *so* want to climb that man like a tree."

"Lily. Stop. That's en—"

A floorboard creaks.

I jump, heart hammering in my chest, and whip my head toward the opposite side of the kitchen.

To right where Rocket is standing. Shirtless. In the dark. Looking like the fuckably-HOT rock god he actually is with a glass in his hand and a bemused expression that says he heard everything.

Oh. My. God.

I reach for my phone and fumble it in a desperate attempt to hang up on Lily.

"Willow? You still there—"

I successfully end the call and shut her up.

But now I'm faced with something way more embarrassing. Way more . . . real.

Did he hear me say that? *Fuckably-HOT?*

Dying now would be a much better option than meeting his eyes.

I give myself a few seconds, but when I finally look up again, Rocket's watching me with an unreadable expression. His mouth twitches like he's fighting a smile. *At least there's that.*

If there were a hole to crawl into right now, I'd be the first one to dive headfirst into it.

"Hi. Um. *Hi*," I say. My voice just screeched like nails on a chalkboard.

"Didn't mean to scare you," he murmurs. "Didn't mean to *interrupt.*" He moves past me toward the fridge. My eyes try not to track the way his sweatpants hang low on his hips. Or the trail of ink running down his ribs. Or the fact that he smells like clean soap and exhaustion and something stupidly masculine.

This is not helping.

"Didn't catch much," he says absently.

I nod too fast. "Cool. Yep. That's great." *I want to die.*

Don't look at him, Willow. Don't . . . for the love of God that's much easier to think than do because the man is . . . there. Right before me.

Looking like that.

Smelling like that.

He just oozes sex appeal even when he's not trying to.

"Everything good?" he asks as he empties the last sip of his drink and sets the glass down on the counter.

"I thought you said you'd be gone until the morning." Why is my voice shaky?

"That was the plan." He opens the fridge. Shuts it. Moves to the pantry. "Plans change."

"Was this some kind of test?" I blurt out.

He stops and glances over his shoulder. "Test?"

"To see if I was going to rip you off? To see if I'm trustworthy?" I shrug. *To see if I'm going to admit to my bestie how fuckable you are.*

"Nah. Everything I have here is replaceable." His eyes hold mine. The silence stretches. He studies me, eyes wandering down to my tank and shorts.

Shit. I didn't put a bra on because I didn't expect to see him.

And yes, of course, right as rain, I can feel my nipples hardening and no doubt pressing against the thin fabric of my tank top.

Just awesome.

Maybe he won't notice. Maybe . . . who the fuck am I kidding? He notices, all right. I see the bob of his Adam's apple. The tightening of his jaw. The twitching of his fingers.

"You'll know if I'm testing you, Willow."

The way he says my name. It's the first time I actually think he has, and it has chills running over my skin.

This is wrong.

All kinds of wrong.

I have never, ever thought one of the dads I've worked for in the past have been hot. I never, ever even remotely considered the thoughts I am thinking in the odd instances I found myself completely alone with the father before.

But I'm thinking them now.

"Did you need something?" he asks, eyebrows narrowing. The food it seems we both came in here for completely forgotten for the moment.

My eyes dart down to his abs. To the low-slung waistband of his sweats.

Big mistake. *Huge.*

"I was out here to look at—we need to talk about . . . toddler-proofing."

He chuckles, turns to rest his ass on the counter, and crosses his arms over his chest. Of course his biceps flex with the motion and make his tattoos dance.

"Toddler-proofing?" He lifts an eyebrow. "That's what you want to choose to talk about right now?"

I swallow forcibly and hope to God he can't hear it like I just did. "Yes. Proofing." It's better than letting my eyes wander and my thoughts drift.

He angles his head to the side, and I can't tell if this whole situation is an act. If he's so used to toying with fans and groupies that he knows how to use his looks to make someone else uncomfortable. Or win them over.

And I'm falling right into that trap.

"Aren't you ever off the clock?" he asks.

"Does that mean you'd like to step in and take over with her?" I ask. I challenge. A simple comment to knock me back into Willow-the-Nanny-ville and out of Rocket-is-a-rock-god-ville.

And the clenching of his jaw gives me the answer.

No. He's not ready.

No. The time spent writing music—if that's even where he went—didn't suddenly make him realize that he has a daughter and he needs to figure his shit out.

Emotionally constipated. Yes, that still fits.

"Ever heard of the word no?" he asks, not answering the question.

"Meaning?" I'm confused.

"Instead of toddler-proofing. The word *no* should work."

That comment gives me all I need to know about his experience with kids.

"Of course." My smile is taunting. "Works perfectly. Just say it, and a three-year-old falls right in line."

"Sure. Fine. Whatever. Do what you need to do," he says with an indifferent flicker of his fingers.

"Thank you. I was . . . if I was looking around, I just didn't want you to think I was snooping or anything."

"How would I know that if I weren't here?" he asks, turns back to the open pantry, and starts picking items up and then putting them back down.

"Cameras. Security measures that people like you probably have."

"People like me?"

"Famous. Someone people stalk. I don't know."

He wobbles his head back and forth like he's contemplating my description of him. Clearly he's okay with it because he continues on arguing. "There are only cameras on the outside," he says. "Never had a need for them inside before." He moves toward me, stopping right in front of me. I have to angle my head up to meet his eyes. I pray the sudden thumping of my pulse isn't noticeable in my neck because I feel like it's visible from a mile away. "Do I need to worry about you, Willow?"

His voice. The timbre. Those words. The seductive quality to them is undeniable. I want to step away from him, to gain some space, and yet he's right in front of me—so close that I can see the flecks of gold on the center of his irises.

"No. Of course not."

"Why do I make you nervous?" he asks as he reaches out and puts his hand on the counter beside me.

"You—uh—don't. Just new places, new faces. They make me jumpy."

The subtle nod says he's not buying the lie I'm selling. "I'll keep that in mind," he murmurs and leans in even closer.

"Thanks." The syllable is breathless. Embarrassing. But he's so close, and all I can smell is him as he fills my entire line of sight.

"Willow?"

"Hmm?"

He leans a little closer and whispers. "I need to get in the drawer."

"Oh. Yes." I jump out of the way and in the course of doing so, run smack dab into the front of him so we're pressed together chest to knees.

I jolt back the other way so that my ass hits against the drawer he just opened and slams it shut again.

It's a series of mortifying moments of my awkward ineptitude, and while my cheeks are burning red, Rocket chuckles mercilessly.

Almost as if this is the comedic relief he didn't know he needed after the day's events.

"I'm sorry," he says as he continues to laugh, moves to the fridge, and opens the freezer door. "But that was funny as fuck."

"Hilarious." I roll my eyes. "For the record, it's not going to work with me and this situation."

He looks over his shoulder, and his brows furrow. "What isn't?"

"What you've fallen back on your whole life."

"You've lost me." He pulls out two pints of ice cream from the freezer and sets them down on the counter between us.

"Your good looks and sweet-talking mouth."

He chuckles and the sound is pure danger. "Can't say I've even been accused of it being sweet. Dirty for sure, but definitely not sweet."

I stare at him, my body reacting to his words and the innuendo. And falling right into what I just accused him of doing. "See? Right there? You're doing it."

His grin is lightning-quick. Of course he knows he's doing it. Why does it feel like I've just laid down a challenge he'll gladly accept?

"Relax. People misconstrue me being nice with flirting. They're two completely different things."

Every part of me wants to walk through that door he just opened and ask what the difference is in his eyes. The other part of me needs to save my sanity because, no doubt, his answer will replay in my head over and over as I stare at the ceiling and try to fall asleep tonight.

But his comment repeats in my head as he slides the two spoons from the drawer and places them beside the pints of ice cream.

"Ice cream always makes everything better, doesn't it?" He lifts his chin toward the pints.

"Who said I needed to make anything better?"

He levels me with a gaze and a smirk. "Your silence did." He taps the tops of both pints—Rocky Road and salted caramel—and lifts his brows at me. "How often do you do this?"

"Which part of it?"

"Pick up your life at a moment's notice to go take care of someone else's kid?"

"I haven't. Not since I was in college."

"Why not?"

"I'm a teacher. I teach." Good one, Willow. "I was laid off due to budgetary cuts and knew a CPS employee who had an immediate need for someone with experience. I needed a job. They needed help with Poppy. So here I am."

"So you're an experienced nanny who's out of experience."

"Are you questioning my qualifications?" I ask.

"Far from it. Just curious."

"I'm more than qualified."

He raises his hands. "Never questioned if you were, Wills."

It takes me a second to hear the nickname. To process that he's calling me it. To realize I like it when I don't want to like it. "It's Willow."

He chews his bottom lip and nods. "So which flavor, Wills?"

I eye him dubiously, but the sound of my stomach growling breaks through the silence and has a grin crawling over his lips. He pushes the two flavors toward me.

"C'mon. Don't be shy. Break ice cream with me," he jokes. The man goes from seductive to intimidating to welcoming so fast that it's hard to keep up.

"Fine. Thanks." I select Rocky Road, offer a smile as I make sure to keep my distance from him as I do, and then take a seat on the opposite side of the island to him.

"Rocky Road. That choice says a lot about a person."

"What's that?"

"It says you like a little chaos with your sweetness. Nuts and marshmallows mean you're definitely not afraid to make things complicated. You went straight for the flavor that doesn't play it safe."

I bark out a laugh. "All that from an ice cream flavor?"

He nods. "Everything says something if you're listening loud enough."

"And what does salted caramel say about you?" I ask.

He purses his lips and nods. "It says I like depth. A little edge. I'm not out there chasing sprinkles and whipped cream because I want my satisfaction to come from the ice cream itself."

"Please tell me you just made that up because . . ." I can't stop laughing.

"That lame, huh?"

"More than."

"You put me on the spot." He reaches out his spoon and taps it against mine sitting on the counter. "Cheers."

I stare at him as he opens the lid of his and takes his first bite in silence. I do the same, afraid of being caught staring for too long. Afraid of being charmed by a man who just toasted our spoons like it wasn't a big deal at all. I welcome the reprieve to process my thoughts and try to figure out who exactly this irreverent woman is because she is nothing like me.

I'm straightforward. I'm black and white. I've . . . never sat in a dimly lit kitchen eating ice cream with my employer.

And I've never sat and wondered what his kiss tastes and feels like.

But I just did, and now my cheeks are flush and my body is keenly aware of him.

I shake my head to clear it. It's just because of who he is when you're used to stuffy accountants and strait-laced lawyers.

"I lied to you," he says, breaking the silence.

My breath hitches, but I think I succeed in keeping the same expression. "About?"

"I didn't have plans tonight. I needed . . . a breather, a moment to process . . . I don't fucking know, but I just needed to get some space." He runs a hand through his hair. "From my own house. How fucked up is that?"

There's a rawness to him. To his voice. An honesty I haven't seen yet.

He's not the performer right now. Not the cocky guy on stage soaking up all the fans screaming his name.

Just Gavin Caldwell—unfiltered and fraying a little at the edges.

And he's making an admission that most people wouldn't to a woman they barely know.

I nod slowly and meet his eyes. "You had something major sprung on you."

"I'm not a bad guy," he says. "I just . . . never wanted to have kids. Never thought I'd be this. And it's overwhelming to have someone make that choice for you and then be thrown into it three years later without warning."

"That's valid," I say.

"Every part of me wants to buck against the idea that she's mine, but she's my goddamn reflection."

I don't say anything. I don't need to. He sees what anyone would see from the outside, but that doesn't mean he's going to accept it without a fight.

"Fuck." The word is a long, drawn-out sigh that emotes exactly how he's feeling. I've seen families where the children are the afterthought. Not necessarily *loathed* but not exactly wanted. The career-driven parents who believed that having kids was just part of life's goals—*checking off the list.* They're the parents who reluctantly bond with their mini-mes, but it takes time. Sometimes more than others.

"It's not always something that's automatic," I say. "The connection. The loving your child. Sometimes it takes work and time, but it happens eventually."

"I'm well the fuck aware of that. I've lived it. I know that. But you're wrong. It doesn't always happen," he says, and by the aversion of his gaze back down to his bowl, I can tell he fears that he's said too much.

But it's enough for me to know he has scars from his past resulting in the emotional tumult he feels right now.

That I can at least work with.

"This is one of those moments," I say finally. "Where you either jump . . . or you don't. You can sit on the ledge for a while, but at some point, you have to decide who you are and what you're going to be to her."

He studies me. Really studies me like he's trying to decide whether he hates that I see him or if he's grateful for it.

"You know, you're the second person who's said something like that to me tonight. I appreciate the sentiment, but I'm not quite there to appreciate it just yet."

"Noted and I appreciate the honesty."

He scoots his stool out, grabs his ice cream and spoon, and looks at me. "I'll leave you be. I'm sure the last thing you wanted when you came out here was some surly asshole like me."

Before I can respond, he turns to go. I think I'm slightly relieved that he does so that I can overthink this entire interaction. But before I can even start, when he's halfway down the darkened hall, he pauses and then tosses over his shoulder. "Good thing your boss is fuckably hot because I heard he's emotionally constipated."

I blink.

My mouth falls open.

And then he disappears into the dark, chuckling.

Shit.

CHAPTER
Ten

Rocket

IT'S BEEN THREE DAYS.

Three days of tiptoeing around my own house like it belongs to some-one else. Three days of waking up late and staying up later. Of pretending I'm answering emails I haven't even opened so that I have a reason to stay behind my office's closed door. Then there's my blasting music to avoid the sound of muted giggles and hearing enthusiastic praise.

Because yes, I need to come to terms with the inevitable but fuck, man, Rome wasn't built in a day, and I'm far less emotionally evolved.

I bang on the keyboards to feel. I wail into a mic to get that shit off my chest. I run errands that I don't need to run to escape my own fucking house.

Three days of *her*.

Willow.

The nanny.

The nanny who shocked me with her thin tank top and assessing eyes.

And yes, it was a dick move to flirt with her the other night. But doesn't it prove I'm unfit to be a father if I'm struggling to get *her* out of my mind?

Yes. That makes me a fucking douchebag. It says I'm still thinking with my cock and not enough with my brain. *Which seems to be what got me into this mess in the first place.*

My brothers have checked in, but I haven't told them I'm ignoring the bigger picture—*I have a daughter*—and considering my pleasure over the little girl's needs.

My phone alerts a text. I hang my head and chuckle in exasperation. No doubt it's the guys checking in. *Again.* And razzing the fuck out of me. *Again.*

> Vince: How's the hot nanny?

> Me: For the tenth time. She's not my type. Not even close.

> Gizmo: Doth protest too much.

> Me: Since when the fuck do you quote Shakespeare?

> Gizmo: Always full of surprises over here.

> Hawkin: We need a pic of her. Or a last name so we can look her up on social media. (This is Quinlan. You're holding out on us!)

I chuckle. Of course, Hawkin's wife would accost his phone since I'm not giving her shit.

> Hawkin: And it's okay to like the nanny. You have to blow off some steam somehow, right?

> Gizmo: Blow being the operative word there.

> Vince: Ah. That's why he didn't answer my call. He was otherwise occupied.

> Me: Was on a run. Too hard to talk and run.

> Hawkin: Already giving excuses in case he answers and is out of breath.

> Me: You guys are assholes.

> Gizmo: Yes. Yes, we are.

I shake my head. All this shit and the irony is that Willow isn't even my type. Not even close. She's independent and grounded and far too sharp for a guy like me. I like chaos. Attitude. A little edge. Not much push-back.

She walks around here in cutoffs and messy braids and makes juice boxes look like tactical gear. She's sunshine and sass and soft curves wrapped in no-nonsense.

And other than in the kitchen that first night, she's a goddamn defensive armor when it comes to Poppy. Almost like she's protecting her from me like any intelligent, assuming person in their right mind would do.

Or maybe she's giving me time to adjust.

Vince: You're not answering. That means you're pissed.

Me: Not pissed.

Hawkin: You good, man?

Me: That's debatable? I don't fucking know? All of the above?

All I know is I'm distracted with music, with working out, with thoughts of her. Wondering what her hair looks like when it's out of that braid or what her voice would sound like moaning my name.

Juvenile shit. Bait and switch shit so I can escape reality. But valid thoughts none the fuck less.

Vince: When can we meet Poppy?

Gizmo: And the hot nanny?

Me: Thinking one big scary man is enough for her to deal with right now.

Hawkin: Fair.

Gizmo: So we'll stay away for now. We'll hold off the wives as long as we can.

Vince: Might need reinforcements for that.

Hawkin: We're here if you need us.

The boys went quiet after Hawkin's comment so I spent an hour in the home gym, working out to escape the strangers in my house but thinking about them the whole goddamn time.

I drop the barbell to the mat and stretch out my arms after a brutal set. Sweat drips down my chest as music pounds through the built-in speakers, but I welcome the burn, the pain, and everything in between.

Movement outside the window catches my eye.

The far corner of the front yard grass. A slip and slide with water spraying up from its pontoon-like sides, casting rainbows across the lawn.

I step to the window and crane my neck.

And that's what I get for looking at my own front lawn. For spying on the nanny. For caring what the fuck is going on.

Willow's out there. Obviously, but it's the black two-piece she's wearing—modest but still giving me enough to look at—that's caught my attention, and the laugh I can see her emitting but can't hear.

Then there's Poppy in a sunshine-yellow bathing suit with pigtails high and a smile like I've yet to see from her.

Something twinges in me at the sight of it but I shake it away.

And then without thinking, I feel compelled to move toward a window with a better view.

They're running through the sprinklers barefoot. Poppy squeals in delight, flapping her hands and spinning in circles before flopping on the slip and slide. She only goes a few feet, but by her ecstatic reaction, she doesn't care.

Willow runs over to her, drops to her ass, and slides a few feet until she bumps into Poppy.

There's another round of giggles as Poppy tries to get up and then slips and falls again. It looks like they sign something back and forth to each other before Willow gets up, takes Poppy by the ankles, and then pulls her down the slide before sling-shotting her down the rest of the plastic.

When Poppy reaches the end and rolls with dramatic flair onto the grass, Willow throws her hands up in the air and jumps up and down, clearly her biggest cheerleader.

My eyes are drawn back to Willow now. How can they not be? Her hair is still in that damn braid, but it's loosened so strands have fallen out and are stuck to her shoulders. Her body is compact, like a gymnast's, but with subtle curves. But it's her face that owns me. Her animated expressions and the way they emote everything she's feeling.

Then there are her eyes—dark brown, framed with thick lashes. They always seem full of life, like she's never looked at the world through a jaded lens. Why is that so intriguing to me?

"It's because you're fucked up, Rock."

"Thanks, Vince. Appreciate the love," I joke.

"What can I say? Truth and love often go hand in hand." He shrugs through the FaceTime connection. "You're thinking about the nanny because you're not used to women who seemingly have it all together from the get-go."

"Who said I was thinking about the nanny?"

"Well, you and I are trying to figure out the lyrics but you keep looking out the window of your office, and it's not the gardener you're checking out. I know that for a fucking fact."

"Maybe it's at Poppy."

He snorts and then barks out a laugh. "Not with that look on your face it's not. Look, it's okay to be curious about her."

"Why are we talking about her again?" I ask and glance over to where they are playing to make sure they can't hear me. *"You guys are more obsessed with her . . ."* than I am.

"Because you're used to chicks with daddy issues—case in point, Poppy's mom. Women who use sexuality as a way to gain or trap something. Females who don't care if they're used simply so they can gain clout for sleeping with you. But Willow seems like none of that."

I scrub a hand through my hair and sigh. *"She wouldn't be my daughter's nanny if she were."*

"That's the first time you've said that."

"Said what?"

His smile is quiet, but his eyes are knowing as he gives me a nod and lets me digest that tidbit. *"My daughter."*

My conversation with Vince yesterday comes back to me as my attention veers over to Poppy. Back to her playful spinning that has her starting to wobble and weave as she stops, but the world keeps rotating around her. She staggers as she holds her hands out for imaginary walls to hold her up as the dizziness subsides.

She is all smiles and laughter and innocence. She's lit up, completely unrecognizable from the quiet, cautious girl who arrived three days ago.

What was her life like before . . . everything? Did she have a yard to play in? Grass under her feet and sunshine on her skin?

The Olivia I knew briefly was a decent person who I'd assume took her daughter for walks in the park and cuddled her every night . . . but that's the thing, it's supposition. I just don't know.

The gut punch that thought evokes is real and one I don't think will ever truly be answered.

Willow picks Poppy up from her dizzy stagger and pulls her in for a hug. They are unsteady and fall back onto the grass holding each other tightly, all while Willow lavishes her with affection.

And I'm . . . I'm jealous.

Of a three-year-old.

Of her laughter.

Of Willow being the one who gets to see it and bring it out in her.

I scrub a hand down my face. *Don't go out there, Rock. Leave them be.*

But my feet move before my brain agrees.

By the time I push open the front door and step outside, the music from the portable speaker they brought outside shifts into a pop summer track with a catchy beat. Noticeably not rock, which strangely has a smile tugging on my lips.

Willow is at the hose spigot, turning the water off and the arches of water spraying on the plastic slide are slowly growing smaller and smaller. Poppy is crouched near a bed of flowers, squatting and sticking her nose in them and sniffing them audibly.

Willow turns just as I reach the edge of the patio.

Her eyes widen slightly when she sees me. I'm shirtless from my workout. She's nearly dripping. We both freeze like we've caught each other naked when our state of undress is so very normal.

But nothing about this feels normal.

Her eyes skim down my chest—quick, involuntary—and then snap back to my face with a faint blush creeping into her cheeks.

I clear my throat. "Didn't know you were throwing a rave out here."

"We were hydrating the grass," she says.

"Oh. Is that what we're calling it now?"

Willow grins, quick and crooked, and then looks away like it costs her something to keep it playful. *At least there's that.*

"Poppy wanted to cool off, and I thought it was a good opportunity to get her outside in the sun for a bit and get some of her energy out."

"She's smiling," I murmur.

Willow nods as she angles her head and studies me. "Yes. She is. More and more. It takes time to build trust, even with a three-year-old."

I'm not sure if that's a dig or a suggestion, but I just nod and hold those brown eyes. "Suggestion noted."

"That's not what I meant. That it was a suggestion." Her cheeks flush with color. She's flustered. "That you're doing something wrong."

"Wills, I'm doing everything wrong. I know it." I glance over to Poppy where she's studying the flowers. "It's hard to break cycles you've lived in your whole life."

I don't know why my candor surprises her. I've never really been one to beat around the bush, but by the slight shock open of her lips, I can tell it does.

"We're also practicing our words."

"She's talking?" My head whips to Poppy and then back to Willow.

"No. Sorry. Only in her sleep. I didn't—I meant I'm pointing out things in the yard and trying to use the limited amount of ASL—American Sign

Language—that I know to try and give her words while she's choosing not to talk."

"Why do you say it like that? That she's *choosing* not to talk?"

"She's not really. Her brain has shut down that ability for her—or held it closer, depending on how you look at it—to protect her in some way. But none of what happened is under her control. When I tell her she's making the choice not to talk, I'm trying to give her some control back. It's a play on words that a toddler wouldn't catch but that an adult would."

I nod. *Show me how to do it. Teach me the right words to say.* But the words don't come out, so I deflect. "You do know there's a pool in the backyard, right? You could have taken her there instead."

"I'm well aware."

"Why not use it?"

"Your house is big and beautiful and a marvel of wonders to this little girl who grew up in a studio apartment. If I show her the pool, if I take her to it, then it becomes a thing she wants to do all the time. It becomes a threat to her safety."

"What?"

"Right now, she's scared of it. If I take her in and show her it, if she loves it, then I have to worry more about her slipping out the door to go to it." She looks at me like I'm an idiot. "There's no pool fence, Rocket. Sure, you have a perimeter fence or whatever was needed to pass inspection when it was installed, but there's nothing that prevents her from walking out that back door and falling in it and dropping to the bottom. No sensors on the doors telling me a back door has been opened and a toddler has escaped to the backyard. So we're focusing on the front yard, on places that are safer for now until I can introduce her properly elsewhere."

I nod, I understand, but a fucking pool fence that will block the view I paid a shit ton for? Like . . .

"I can turn the door chimes on. It's part of my alarm system. That's easy." And the damn sound going off will drive me crazy, but whatever.

"Thank you. It'll help in all aspects when knowing if she opens a door or not, but the pool still worries me."

"Fuck," I mutter and scrub a hand through my hair.

"She was getting cooped up. I thought this would be okay. I hope you don't—"

"No. It's totally fine. It was . . . is cute."

I follow Willow's glance over to where Poppy is now picking blades of grass, and then throwing them up in the air and giggling as they fall down like confetti. Her curls are still damp—ringlets in pigtails—and her cheeks are flushed pink.

She's adorable. Beautiful with her green eyes and olive complexion.

I stare at her, trying to process how that little perfect being somehow came partly from me, and then wonder how the fuck to talk to her. And wanting to, thinking about it, means that I've accepted this whole . . . situation, but I'm just not there yet. Immature? *Perhaps*. Real? *Very*.

"She seems so happy," I murmur absently.

Willow's gaze softens. "Right now, she is. The nightmares come when she sleeps. Almost every night, really. That's why I'm trying to tire her out so maybe she might be so tired they don't come."

Jesus. What do I say to that? If I felt helpless before, I feel even more helpless now. "Is there anything that can be done to help her?"

"I have an appointment scheduled with a play therapist. Sandra had your assistant put Poppy on your medical insurance so I called around and found an opening next week. It won't fix things overnight, but it's a start. That and time and trust." She smiles at Poppy. "Kids are way more resilient than they're given credit for."

"It's like you're her world right now."

Willow looks at me—right at me—and for once, doesn't blink. "It's because I'm all she has."

Those words hit me just as hard as the jealousy. The truth to them. The honesty that I'm not being what Poppy needs to be right now.

I shift, trying to shake off the weight that suddenly feels like it's pressing on my chest. Poppy turns our way and smiles.

"Poppy," Willow says. "Come show your favorite flower to Daddy." Willow sucks in a breath the minute she realizes what she's said.

The same damn second that I hear it.

I freeze. The uncertainty of that term and the negative connotation it's held for me my whole life, startling me. The one I don't want to own yet.

"I'm sorry," Willow murmurs to me, regret woven into it. "I didn't mean to—it was a slip of the—"

Poppy bounds up to us, breaking the tension. She holds three different colored flowers in her hands as she steps up to me, head angled as she studies me like a grown-up would. Her brow is furrowed and expression confused.

Willow's head shakes back and forth emphatically. "No. I meant friend," she says, sounding anxious.

I could tell her it's okay. I could say it's no big deal, but for some reason, I don't. Maybe she's right. Maybe I am emotionally constipated, but a part of me wants to see how this plays out.

Will Poppy hear the term, *the label,* and simply believe it? Does she even know what it means since she's never had one? Or if she does know what it means, will she reject the thought that this man kneeling in front of her, covered in weird markings and who is clearly scared of her, as being her dad?

Does it matter?

Yes. It does. And I hate that it does.

All I know is that by prolonging this reveal the harder it's going to be for Poppy. Again, *selfish asshole.*

Poppy points to me, and between the expression on her face and the shrug of her shoulders, I know she's asking Willow, "Then who is he?" in reference to me.

Willow moves abruptly, heads toward the planter, and picks up a decorative garden stone I have in one of my flower beds. It's about three inches wide and light gray in color with black swirls of sediment in it. She moves back to us, drops to her knees beside Poppy, and holds the stone out to her.

Poppy furrows her brows but takes the rock and then giggles when her hand dips under its weight. She hums a sound, almost as if to say how heavy it is.

"I know," Willow says. She points to the stone in Poppy's hands and then points to me and says. "Rock."

"I'm her rock?" I say out of reflex but unknowingly play into the game Willow is setting up.

"More like her rock"—Willow points to the stone and then to me—"*et!*" The way she says the last part has Poppy erupting into a fit of laughter before scrambling to get closer to me.

I suck in a breath as she steps into my personal space, closer than she's ever been before to me. Her eyes grow big as she holds the rock up next to my face . . . and then bursts out laughing again. This time, it's a deep belly giggle that has chills chasing over my skin and something cracking over that hardened shell of my heart.

And fuck . . . I don't like how it feels.

She waits until the laughter subsides and tries it again. This time when she sticks the rock next to my face, I say, "Rock," and then I throw my arms up in the air and say, "Et!"

She falls into another fit of belly giggles so her pigtails bounce and her hands tighten on the rock in her hand.

"Don't look now, Rocket, but someone thinks you're funny."

I nod because my tongue feels thick in my mouth. I don't know why I just did that, but it feels good to have made her laugh.

The breeze kicks up. Willow's hair dances across her shoulders, and Poppy keeps laughing.

Suddenly, I don't want to leave and finish my workout or hop on another Zoom with Gizmo.

I want to stay right here, standing on the patio, watching my daught—*Poppy*—laugh and trying to figure out how to be someone she can count on.

I want to ask Willow how she knows so much. I want to know what makes her think I have what it takes to do this when I don't even know.

Too much.

Too quick.

Just too fucking much.

But instead, I step back and clear my throat, retreating toward the door.

"Rocket?" Willow calls after me.

"I've gotta finish what I was doing," I mumble, embarrassed that I can't keep my emotions in check. Uncertain when it seems like that's where I've lived the past two weeks. "I have to—yeah—you know . . ."

And like a goddamn coward, I retreat into my house.

Why? Why has a garden rock, a giggle, and bouncing curls brought me to my knees? Why, after all these years of success with BENT, am I only able to focus on the thought that I'm a failure? That this—being good at being a dad—is something I'll never be able to do?

Why can't I accept this? Accept her? "Why the fuck not?" I grit out as I shut the door behind me.

Sure I've failed in the past. But that failure only ever affected me.

If I fail this time around? The consequences would be so much greater. Would affect more than just me.

Fuck.

CHAPTER
eleven

Willow

Poppy's quiet time stretches longer than usual. And I'm afraid to jinx it, but it's peaceful for the first time since I've come into her life. The sunshine and our outdoor adventure worked.

She's curled up in her blankets, bunny tucked under one arm, hair damp from the sprinklers earlier, and cheeks flushed from the sun. I press a kiss to her temple, ease the door mostly closed, and walk barefoot into the kitchen.

The house is quiet. Still. Rocket must have left again. If that fear in his eyes earlier is any indication, he'll probably be gone the rest of the night like he's been wont to do. I've noticed his pattern over the past few days. Watch from afar, *try* to engage, engage, and then get spooked when he realizes he's curious and wants to know more.

But today she laughed with him. Today Poppy bypassed looking at all the colorful ink she seems so fascinated with and stepped up to him to play with the damn rock.

Baby steps.

I can only hope this is the first of many interactions. Of Poppy starting to look at Rocket as more than just the guy in the background and as Rocket starting to trust himself and who he is. What he can be for her.

And if he doesn't? Fuck. That would be brutal. Poppy would have no one, and I know CPS would have no other choice than to put her in the system. She'd fall only deeper into her own mind and that little bit of sunshine I've gotten to see in her would be erased completely.

No. It's not going to happen. I won't let it. I have to do everything in my power to help facilitate Rocket to see that he can do this. That this little cherubic girl is the best thing that's ever happened to him.

I meander through the great room, taking it in. Everything looks placed professionally. Sure there are photos of Rocket with people, but I doubt he's the one who put them there. And the few personal touches that are about, seem to all be with his bandmates or revolving around them.

There are no pictures of people who look like family. No older woman or man to whom I can see a resemblance in.

For a man in the public eye, there's so little about his early life online. A single mother. A youth spent pushing the limits of trouble. A chance meeting at a party with Vince and Hawkin that changed the direction of his life.

I find my way outside to the back patio and curl into the corner of the outside patio furniture. The couch is just outside of the sliding doors so I can hear Poppy if she needs me, but so I can enjoy a different aspect of this incredible house in my downtime.

Plus, the idea of getting my master's degree has stayed front and center in my mind since Alan suggested it. That and with the extra cash coming in from Rocket unexpectedly paying me double what I'd agreed to, to begin with, the idea is becoming more of a reality. So maybe I'll look into getting into a program.

But for now, I soak in the welcome silence and the moments without being needed. I keep thinking about the pictures inside and how lonely that might be.

Without thinking, I pick up my phone, scroll to the name I'm looking for, and hit call.

She answers almost immediately. "Willow?"

"Hi, Mom."

"Oh, baby. You sound tired."

"I'm good. Just . . . busy."

"Busy because your new boss is running you ragged and an asshole, or busy because you love your new charge and aren't giving yourself any time because you're so worried about her?"

"Neither." I sigh. "More like I'm just plain ol' tired. Teaching is one type of exhaustion. I think I forgot the whole other type of exhaustion that comes with being a nanny at a kid's beck and call every second of every day."

She chuckles, and I picture her settling into her chair in her reading nook and smiling. "Okay. Fine. I'll give you that." She pauses. "So things are good?

"Yes. My charge, Poppy, she's adorable with all these curls and these big green eyes. We're slowly figuring each other out, but yes, I'm already head over heels in love with her."

"Like I expected anything less."

"There was that little boy—Brad. I was not a fan of his. Remember?"

She laughs. "The stories you used to tell. I do remember. And the family you're working for? They're treating you well?"

"Just a single dad."

She makes a noncommittal sound that borders on disapproval and concern. "Don't let him take advantage of you," she murmurs.

I open my mouth and then close it as images of Rocket earlier come to mind. Him standing on the porch in low-slung workout shorts and rivulets of sweat running down his chest. His hair in disarray, and those eyes of his guard every emotion his bobbing Adam's apple and shifting feet hinted at.

"I know, Mom. He's nice. He's fine. He's . . . it's fine."

"And you? You're *fine* too?"

And there it is. The question I should've expected, but have been so wrapped up in making sure Poppy was thriving that I kind of lost track of time.

That's a lie. I didn't. But maybe this year it'll hurt a little less.

"Yes. I know. It's coming up," I say, beating her to the punch.

A quiet stretch passes between us. No static. Just that comfortable silence that exists when the other person knows exactly what you mean without needing the words.

"Five years," she murmurs.

"Forever and yesterday all at the same time," I say.

"He'd be happy for you. I think of that often. James would be so happy for you and where you are in life. He was always your biggest cheerleader."

She's right. I know she is, but it doesn't make it sting any less. He was my best friend, the man I had pictured sharing tomorrows with, and then he was just . . . gone. You can't prepare for that sort of loss. You can only grieve, one day at a time, until the hole his loss created lessens. *Dulls.*

"I called his mom last week just to check in on her. They're doing fine. Obsessed with their new grandchild. His sister named him James after her brother. Thank God for that for them."

"Hmm," I say.

"Didn't mean to bring the conversation down. I was just . . . wanted to make sure you were okay."

I let her words sink in. "It's been three years, Mom. I loved him, but I don't think about him every day like I used to, and for the longest time the guilt of that would weigh me down. But I can't help that he went to bed in his dorm that night and didn't wake up the next morning." The emotions I felt that morning come back on the drop of a dime. Aren't they supposed to fade with time? "Just like I can't feel guilty for still being alive and wanting to make the most of it."

"Oh, honey. I never meant to make you feel that way." Her voice wobbles with regret.

"You didn't." I sigh and lean my head back on the chair and close my eyes for a beat. The scars James's death left run deep. My ever-running and unfounded guilt that I should've seen something or known. How I've not dated or allowed myself to get attached to someone since. How it feels like our close friend—basically family—dynamic has changed.

"That was nice of you to call his parents. I'm sure they were happy to hear from you."

"It was good to catch up. Now . . . tell me about what you've been up to otherwise, or else Dad will pepper me with questions when he gets home from the driving range, and I won't have any info to give him."

"Like I said, I'm just getting settled here. I'm thinking about starting back at getting my master's again. I'll have time on my hands for an online course or two—"

"Says the woman who just said she's exhausted."

"I know, but you know how important education is to me. How I set goals and need to accomplish them, and because of cost and time, this fell to the wayside. Now it seems I have a bit more of both than I'm used to, so I figured maybe I'll look into it."

"Honey, you know we wish we could help more."

"You're still paying off loans from my undergrad. You are *not* helping me with this."

"It's still hard as a parent to not be able to give you more."

I smile. "You've given me more than I could've ever asked for. I'm fine. I just need to do this for myself."

"I understand." She tsks like she tends to do when she's going to change subjects. "So the Napa trip with Lily is off, I take it?"

"More postponed than off. We'll get there. It's on my list of places to see."

"Sometimes I marvel at how you came from me." She laughs. "So driven and self-sufficient. So focused on making things better for everyone else. I'm forever proud of you, Willow."

Her words warm me.

We talk about nothing for a few minutes. My dad's retirement project—refinishing the shed. My sister's new boyfriend who apparently thinks quinoa is a type of pasta. And then her voice softens again.

"I'm glad you called," she says.

"Me too."

"I was worried after the layoffs. I know how much you loved your job and your kids and their families."

"I still do. I miss them. I feel like I let them down, but in the same token, I'm needed here."

"You sound . . . different. Content."

Maybe because I'm right where I'm supposed to be. Making a difference for someone who needs it most. For now, at least.

"I am. Things are good for me."

"No mother will ever complain about hearing that." I can hear her smile in her voice. "I'll call you later this week, okay?"

"Sounds good."

I end the call, set the phone on the cushion beside me, and let the silence wrap around me. My thoughts dizzy about the past and swirl regarding the future, but I keep coming back to the simple fact of how damn lucky I am. Poppy will never get to have that type of phone call with her mom. She'll never hear the pride and the praise in her voice—or rather, see it on her face being directed at her.

But I can and have and do so regularly. And I'll never take that for granted.

"Enjoying the sun?"

I jump at the sound of Rocket's voice. When I turn, he's standing on the far side of the couch. Barefoot. Hair tousled. A sexy smile tilting up one corner of his mouth.

"We have to stop meeting like this. My heart isn't going to handle living here," I tease.

His grin widens as he steps forward. "The door was open. I figured you didn't mind the company."

"It's your house. You don't need to apologize for anything." I shift to collect my laptop and phone and—

"No. You're fine." He digs his hands in the pockets of his jeans and rocks on his heels. "I looked out the window and . . . you looked happy is all."

"I am, I guess."

"You guess?" He chuckles.

"Yeah, I mean. I just talked to my mom, and she always makes me feel good about everything."

He raises a brow and slowly lowers himself onto the couch opposite me, stretching out his legs with a groan.

"You close with her?"

"Yeah. With both of my parents."

He grunts like he doesn't know what that feels like. I study him for a moment, the flicker of emotion behind those eyes that always seem too guarded for their own good.

"I take it by that response that you're not with yours?" I lead and wonder if he'll shed some light on the few things he's said over the past week I've been here.

He sighs. "There's a reason I loved music. It allowed me to drown everything out when it got too loud at home."

"I'm sorry."

"Don't be." He shrugs. "I could say I turned out just fine, but from where you stand, I'm sure you think that's debatable."

"That's a setup if I've ever heard one."

"Not a setup when it's the truth."

"I'm still not taking the bait," I say playfully.

"No smart-mouthed comment? No underhanded slight?"

I slide a glance his way and meet him smile for smile. "I'm working on taming them."

"No. Never. And especially not on my account." He crosses an ankle onto his other knee. "No one ever had fun walking the straight and narrow."

"I'll keep that in mind, although I do have a feeling my knack for both of those things might be why I got laid off from my teaching job."

"Teaching job?" He sounds surprised.

"Yes. Before this." I explain about being a nanny in college. About my teaching position being eliminated due to budgetary cuts. About the opportunity to help Poppy coming along at the perfect time.

"I'm sorry for you, but their loss is my gain."

"Thank you," I say quietly and force myself to look out over the valley than where I want to—at him.

"So, Miss Willow Adams, tell me about you."

I start to laugh, thinking that he's joking. Why would a man of his stature—one who's met kings and presidents—be interested in anything about me? But when I give into the pull, into his silence, and look his way, he's staring intently at me and waiting patiently.

I'm not used to this side of him, and for some reason I hesitate. Maybe I know that letting him in could be a huge mistake for me.

"Clearly, you come from a good home, have a career path that you love, but what makes you, you? What is it that you desire?"

I quirk my eyebrows. "Desire is a loaded word."

"So was that bathing suit you had on earlier," he says without missing a beat, "but I managed to cope just fine, now didn't I?"

My eyes flash over to his and hold.

Oh.

He *noticed.*

And now that I know he did, I can't help but wonder if that's why I picked it this morning. Why I reached past two perfectly respectable one-pieces and chose the one that tied behind my neck and dipped low in the back. The one that made me feel a little more . . . seen.

He doesn't look away. Neither do I.

"You're trouble," I finally murmur, folding my arms.

"Perhaps." He grins. "*Definitely.* It makes life more interesting."

I laugh, despite myself. The sound floats between us as he puts his elbow on the back of the couch and rests his head on his hand. "You didn't answer me," he says. "What makes you, you?"

I shift, playing with the hem of my shirt. "I guess I'm still figuring that out."

"No rehearsed speech about how you've always wanted to work with kids and make the world a better place?"

"Oh, I definitely want to make the world better. But not in a 'Miss America, here's my platform' way. I just want to leave people better than I found them. Especially the small ones."

"That's a damn good answer." And just when I think he's going to leave it there, he asks, "What interested you about teaching? And why the special needs field?"

"My mom was a teacher. It's in the blood." I toggle my head from side to side. "And I had a cousin who was special needs. I always hated how outside of our family, when we were at school, she needed a little more of everything than everybody else, and her mom had to fight so damn hard to get it. Not everyone is comfortable around kids who need more—I am. So I figured why not specialize in that field."

"Impressive."

"Not really. More just being a good human." I smile. "God, that sounds cheesy—"

"But I like it. It feels right when you say it."

"So why the laptop? Should I worry you're searching for teaching openings now because you're sick of your current boss? Don't have me panicking, Wills."

"No. God. I just . . . I started my master's a while back." Ran . . . out of money. Time. Bandwidth. "And now I'm thinking of starting back up during this lull, so to speak."

"You're telling me I'm a lull?" He barks out a laugh. "Can't say that word has ever been used to describe me before."

"No. I didn't mean it like that. I meant—"

He waves a hand to stop me from explaining. "Master's in what?"

"Special education."

"Quit being so impressive," he groans. "You're making me look bad."

"How many platinum records do you have on the wall in your office? Please." I snort. "What about you?"

He blinks. "What about me?"

"Who are you? Not Rocket—the rock star—but more the guy underneath all of that. The guy the world doesn't always see. What makes you tick?"

He goes still. Not defensive. Just caught off guard.

And for the first time since I met him, I think I might have asked a question he doesn't already have a practiced answer for.

"You can read about me anywhere on any site on the internet. I can't promise it's all accurate but it's true enough."

"You're right. I can look you up and I have." I have no shame in admitting it, and by the lift of his eyebrows, I think he is surprised by the admission.

"But you want more."

"I want more. I want the non-media trained answers."

"I assure you media training doesn't work on me. What you see is what you get."

"Noted, but appease me."

He sighs. "Willow."

"Call me a greedy bitch."

He chortles out a laugh. "That's the last thing I'd call you, but we'll go with it."

"Good. Tell me about Gavin."

"I'd rather talk about Rocket," he deflects.

"Noted. But Gavin is the person here without the media or the world watching his every move. Gavin is the man trying to figure out why he's curious about Poppy but keeps her at arm's length. Gavin is the man I see glimpses of." I shrug.

"Gavin is a man I don't know anymore."

"Don't tell me you had a secret life as a choir boy."

His mouth twitches. "Worse. I wanted to be an astronaut."

"No way." I definitely wasn't expecting that answer.

"I had this cheap, plastic helmet I wouldn't take off for months. A Halloween costume discard I saw in a thrift store window when we were walking by. I had to beg my mom for it. Her boyfriend at the time ended up buying it for me to shut me up and occupy me. Man, I loved that thing. I ate cereal in it. Slept in it. Called myself Rocket Man."

"Is that where the name came from?"

"Yup. Stuck in fifth grade after I made a presentation about space exploration. One of my drawings I did—I used to draw all the time—was mixed in the papers I brought to school. It was an image of my helmet with Rocket Man written in block letters. Some great work, if I say so myself." His chuckle is bittersweet. "Anyway, the class prick—some asshole who needed a lot of fucking love in life—picked up the drawing and played keep away from me with it. Held it up for the class and called me Rocket to get a laugh. It stuck."

"I bet that brat straightens his shoulders every time he sees you all the million places people see you, and brags to others that he's the one who made your name for you."

"Probably." He runs a hand through his hair and eases back in his seat, more comfortable now. Maybe because he doesn't think I'm going to grill him on where his head's at with Poppy.

"So, what happened to being an astronaut?"

"First time I went on a roller coaster, one of those upside down ones . . . I learned I'm not a big fan of being upside down. Ended that dream real quick."

"Valid point," I say. "So you became a rock star instead. Fair trade."

He barks out a laugh. "Can't complain at how life worked out for me."

"Neither would I. It must have been a wild ride."

"Is. Was. Continues to be." He scrubs a hand over his face and a mischievous smile stays in his wake. "The wildest of all rides."

"Even better than going upside down?"

"Way better." He looks out toward the pool and his expression changes like he's reliving some of the greatest hits of his career. "If you would've asked little Gavin Caldwell if he could've ever dreamed this would be his house and his life, he would've told you that you were crazy."

He appreciates it.

I'm not sure why that notion strikes me so poignantly in the moment, but it does. Here is a superstar who I thought was so spoiled and selfish, who has done this for so long that he took it all for granted, and yet here is *Gavin*, telling me otherwise.

But just like I'm having a hard time reconciling Rocket with Gavin, I'm also struggling to see this man before me and not understand his reluctance to acknowledge Poppy.

Hell, might as well bring that up while we're at it . . .

"You haven't been around much," I say quietly.

He tenses. "Meaning?"

"Nothing. Just . . ."

"I have a feeling there is nothing you say without intention."

I chuckle because he's right. I raise my hand to make light of it. "Guilty as charged."

He nods. "You'll find I'm normally straight to the point."

"Who's also my boss."

"Semantics." He shrugs and smirks. "Speak your mind, Willow."

"Well, the first night I was here, you escaped to get drunk. Just about everything about Poppy was a shock to your system—her being alive, her being here, you name it. Understandably. It's been almost a week and now you're just escaping to go to the store and random places for no reason at all."

"Because learning one has a child should be a seamless transition, right?"

"No. That's not what I meant. It's just . . ." *She's a good little girl. I see in your eyes you know that, you believe that, and yet you keep your distance. I don't understand how you can even resist her.*

He watches me for a beat, then says, "I'm still here." And those three words could mean so many things.

You're questioning me, and I'm still here.

I found out I have a daughter, and I'm still here.

I scrunch my nose up because as frustrated as I am at him and what appears to be a lack of progress, those three words say more than I thought they did moments ago.

I'm still here.

"I stand corrected," I say, barely audible.

"I don't want you to stand corrected," he says, voice flat but irritated. "I want you to understand where I am. Who I am. A guy who deals in facts. Who needs concretes. Who . . . just had his world rocked and is trying to process it all."

I meet his eyes—calm, certain—and challenge him when I have no business challenging him. "Her being here? Her reaction when she looks at you, and you feel that punch in your gut, or have the oxygen sucked out of your lungs—you know? The times you decide you need to bolt? That's your proof, Rocket. That's enough for you to know you need her as much as she needs you. You might not know it yet. You might not acknowledge it yet. But it's there, and you fucking know it."

He sighs and gets up, moving toward the edge of the patio. The sun peeking through the slats of the patio cover outlines his frame—broad shoulders, long legs, hands planted on his hips as he stares out at the view beyond.

He paints a striking picture. Broken. Beautiful. Unmoored.

"You pay me to be her advocate," I say. "To give her the best. To look out for her. You being a part of her life is looking out for her."

He hangs his head and rolls his shoulders. "Look," he says without turning to look my way. "I didn't grow up with a dad. I had a mom who worked double shifts and who had a rotating door of boyfriends, all of which taught me exactly who I never wanted to be."

I don't say anything.

"I don't know how to do this," he says. "I don't know how to be what she needs. I hope I can get my shit together and figure it out. But frankly, in the meantime, in between time, if I stop moving, I might start thinking. And if I start thinking, I'll realize how badly I could fuck this up."

"Said every parent *ever* in one way or another," I murmur and draw a look my way.

His eyes hold such a depth of emotion, but his expression is unreadable. "I have everything I've ever wanted. Money. Fame. Notoriety. I never have to worry about anything again. And then all of a sudden, the one thing I never wanted, the one thing my childhood fucked me up and told me I never wanted, shows up on my doorstep. I had no fucking choice in the matter."

And this time, when he looks back to the view beyond, I don't press any further.

I gather my things and leave him be.

I've pushed enough.

I was hoping he'd push back more. I was hoping he'd ask me *how*. Because it's only in fighting that you can sometimes see your true self and face your worst fears.

And it seems that Poppy is that to Rocket.

CHAPTER
twelve

Rocket

Poppy's sitting on the kitchen counter, legs crossed, and a mixing bowl in front of her. She has a wooden spoon that's way too big for her little hands, and yet her face is twisted in concentration as she stirs the ingredients.

"Awesome job," Willow says, her face animated with pride, as she steps up beside her and holds out two eggs. "Are you sure you can do it?"

Poppy nods emphatically so that her pigtails bob. The wooden spoon is forgotten where it rests against the bowl in her quest for the eggs. Her face lights up when Willow places one in her cupped hands.

Such a simple thing—cracking the eggs—but clearly it makes her feel like a big kid. That's not something I ever would have thought of letting her do.

Willow stands beside Poppy and gently guides her little hands as she cracks an egg into the bowl. She hits it a little too hard. The broken shell crumbles, and the yolk dribbles down the edge of the bowl, but the pride on her face and the belly giggle she emits? Adorable.

I stand rooted in place and just stare.

Not at the chaos. Not at the cookie mess or the noise or the fact that a toddler is barefoot and sitting on my damn marble countertops.

But at them.

Willow, with her easy warmth and steady hands. Poppy, with her wide eyes and giggles and impossibly perfect smile.

Then the realization hits me, and I'm gutted all over again. I'll never be able to do that. *Be like Willow.* I'll never be that soft. That safe. That steady.

Poppy'll never laugh like that with me.

I'm the guy with shadows where memories should be. With wounds that have scarred over but never truly healed beneath. The man who used to dream of rockets and stars and escape routes because the world inside his own house was too transient to live in with new boyfriends always coming and going.

"You need to get lost tonight."

"Mom." I look toward the window where it's already dark. "I can't. It's—freezing out there."

"You don't have to sit out in the backyard. The back seat of the car though." I look up from the sketch I'm making. Her eyeliner is dark and smudged. Her lips are bright pink and her lipstick stretches beyond the outline of her lips. Her dress is tight and shows more of her than any son ever wants to see of their mother.

Here we go again.

"Again? Can't we have some time without a new guy coming around?" It's like an ever-revolving fucking door. One leaves. A new one gets brought in, is treated like a fucking king only until he isn't, and then he's out the door for the new man in the wings.

"Without a new guy?" she screeches. It's as if I just told her she's going to have to cut off an arm—or God forbid, spend any amount of alone time with her son. "Who do you think helps to pay for all these nice things we have?" The slur of her words says she's been drinking. Clearly she doesn't think too highly of him herself if she has to drink before the first date.

Nice things? I take a look around our place and almost laugh at that comment. But I know better than to speak up. I know the consequences of pissing off my mom, who will then tell the new boyfriend I'm an ungrateful prick. And that means either an ass whooping or less food or being forced to sleep outside while they moan and groan and do gross things out in here.

"Yep. Sure." I huff the words out as I gather some things to occupy me in the car while I sit there tonight.

"Grab a blanket. I don't want you to get cold," she says. "That back window still isn't rolling all the way up."

"Got it."

"I'll wake you for school in the morning."

No, you won't. "Okay."

"And I promise I'll tell this one I have a kid sooner than the last one. They just never seem to want to stay around when they know I have you."

"Uh-huh." *That's what you said with the last guy.*

My childhood wasn't a home. *It was survival.*

The parade of men that passed through taught me exactly what I never wanted to be. Loneliness that dug its claws in deep and never let go. Affection wasn't shown, and it sure as fuck wasn't taught . . . and yet I'm just supposed to know how to give it? To show it? To . . . I don't know what with it?

To have sex with a woman—then time after sex—it's one thing. It's a thank-you. A reaction. A means to an end. But to a little girl who asks nothing of you—from you—and who you're terrified of ruining? That's a whole different level of comprehension.

My phone buzzes in my hand and pulls me from my never-ending thoughts.

Vince: Sorry, we held them off as long as we could

I blink.

"The hell does that—"

Ding-dong.

Fuck. It's such a rare sound, one that means whoever's here is already on my approval list at the guard shack. Between the text and that knowledge, I already know who it is.

Poppy whips her head up like a rabbit about to bolt.

Willow shoots me a look. "Do you know who that is?"

"No," I lie.

But I do.

I open the door, and there they are. A feminine wall of energy. Perfume. Designer handbags. Matching grins.

Quinlan. Bristol. Hendrix.

I'm fucked.

"Get out of the way, Caldwell," Quinlan says as she puts a hand on my chest and pushes past me. "You've been holding out too long so we took matters into our own hands."

Bristol presses a kiss to my cheek as she brushes past. "This was all her idea."

Hendrix pulls me in for a quick, sympathetic hug. "It was all our idea."

And with a sigh, I follow behind my bandmates' wives and their quest to finally meet Poppy.

The gasps come first. Then the squeals of delight and clapping of hands. I trail close enough behind to see Poppy's face as she takes in these three new faces. She sits a little taller with a glance from Willow to me and then back to them.

"Look at her curls," Bristol says, practically vibrating as she steps into the kitchen.

"And those Caldwell eyes," Quinlan says.

Hendrix? She doesn't even speak—she just makes a squeaky noise in her throat and beelines for the counter.

Poppy shrinks a little as Willow steps closer to her, and she tries to figure out what the hell is going on.

"Hey, whoa—maybe ease in—" But the wave of my hands over my head is futile. They're already descending.

Willow smiles at Poppy and leans in. "It's okay, sweetie. They're Dadd—Rocket's friends and are just excited to meet you."

Poppy peeks over her shoulder at the women standing there staring at her expectantly.

Then she nods, just once, as her shoulders square and her smile lights up her face. And just like that . . . she lets them in.

Literally and figuratively.

"Oooh, she's a brave one," Quinlan coos, crouching to eye level. "That's good. We like brave girls."

"She's gorgeous," Bristol says. "Look at her eyes. She's totally a mini you, Rocket."

I choke. "What?"

"I said she looks like you," Bristol says, glancing back at me with a wink. "It's unmistakable."

Quinlan grins and sits on a barstool in front of Poppy, lowering her voice like she's trading secrets. "Are you making these cookies all by yourself? Wow. You really are smart."

Poppy's lips curl. The tiniest smile.

I blink again.

What the hell is happening? It's like estrogen central in here. Between the pitch of their voices and them all talking at once, overwhelmed is an understatement.

"Guys. Hello," I try again. I clap my hands to get their attention. "Everyone. This is Willow. Willow, this is Quinlan. Hendrix. Bristol." Each one lifts their hand as I call their name. "Everyone."

There's a rushed cacophony of sound as greetings and hugs are exchanged so fast my head spins.

"Willow is one of us now. Accepted and liked," Bristol says making Willow's eyes widen and head startle. I think she's just as shell-shocked by this whirlwind as Poppy.

"You can go now," Hendrix says to me with a dismissive wave of her hand. "We can take it from here."

She doesn't wait for me to say a word. Instead, she reaches out and runs a fingertip over Poppy's red painted toenails. "So pretty. That's my favorite color."

Poppy practically preens under her compliment.

I take a step back, more like a stumble back, to sink into a chair by the window, and watch the chaos take shape.

And Willow steps into it seamlessly. I'm not sure why I expected otherwise, but she does calmly. Effortlessly. Steadily with a hand on Poppy's back as they finish making the cookie dough while praise flies like confetti.

They love both of them.

Of course they do.

My phone buzzes again. I expect it to be another apology from the guys. Instead it's Quinlan.

Quinlan: No wonder you're hiding her from the guys. They'd razz the shit out of you if they knew how perfect she was for you.

I glance across the room, meet her eyes, and deliberately scratch my cheek with my middle finger. She lifts her brows and barks out a laugh that has everyone glancing her way. She just shakes it in a never-mind gesture.

And they just go on and on.

Bristol is now showing Poppy a sparkly bracelet and promising to bring a matching one next time. Hendrix has somehow built a pillow fort out of my throw cushions for after the cookies are done, and Poppy is trying to decide whether she even wants to finish them or if the fort is more inviting.

And I just sit there.

Watching it unfold. Watching my old world integrate with this new one I don't quite understand yet. Watching three women accept *my* daughter. One who doesn't talk but who they all completely understand.

This is what normal looks like.

What *real* looks like.

They know how to be. How to talk to kids. How to read moods. How to offer snacks and build trust without even thinking about it.

And then there's me.

Sitting here like a fucking tourist in a life I think I want but can't quite recognize.

Like I missed the memo that came with fatherhood and domesticity and knowing what to do when a kid cries or clings or stares up at you like you're supposed to have answers.

I stand up too fast. My throat burns and chest hurts and head spins. I bump into the table behind the couch. Willow notices the sound and looks my way.

"Everything okay?" Willow mouths, her head tilting toward me as she brushes a curl from Poppy's cheek.

"Yeah. I just . . . I'll be back."

I step out of the room, into the hallway, and away from all of it. I lean against the wall and drag a hand down my face.

It's all perfect.

Too perfect.

And I don't know how to exist inside perfect without breaking something.

I need air. To get out of here. To . . . get some space. I head toward the garage, slam the door behind me, and do the only thing I can—I drive.

Through the Hollywood Hills, past the winding streets that know me too well. I roll the windows down and blast music loud enough to drown out the voice in my head in an attempt to make my own rhythm in its place.

My fingers tap against the steering wheel—a chord, a beat, a melody I don't understand that's inside of me, fighting its way out.

I drive until the traffic fades and the chaos dies down. Until the ache in my chest eases and doesn't feel like it's going to suffocate me.

I hit the Pacific Coast Highway and head for Santa Monica where the sun's dipping now and will soon cast its colors over the horizon. The beach has always held peace for me so I'm grateful that I find an empty spot to pull into amid the grifters, the diehard surfers, and the tourists.

The beach is a place where everybody belongs, regardless of how fucked up their life is, and right now I feel that more than anything.

But my life isn't fucked up. That's the catch, isn't it? It's just . . . changed at the drop of a dime. How do you adjust and adapt to something you never saw coming? How do you look at something you unknowingly created and try to love it when you've always felt that part of you was broken?

Fuck, man.

I take in everything around me. The waves crashing in the distance. The tourists strolling along the boardwalk and taking pictures of the sunset. And I just sit in my car and breathe.

But my heartbeat doesn't go back to normal.

I don't think it ever will.

My phone buzzes against the console. I expect it to be Willow. It's Vince. I'm not sure if that's better or worse.

Vince can read me like a book. There's no hiding anything from him, and no doubt he'll most likely hand me my ass. Motherfucker.

I sigh and answer.

"Hey. You good, man?" he asks.

"Why wouldn't I be?"

"Because you missed our call with the label."

"Fuck." *Shit.* I could blame it on the wives coming over, but I don't even try. I tell him the truth. "It slipped my mind. I have a lot going on. I didn't—"

"Fine. Whatever. We covered for you, but . . . you don't miss shit like that." He pauses and lets the concern loaded in his voice wash over me. "You okay?"

I open my mouth to speak, but words don't come out—just a strangled sound instead.

"You're spiraling. Nothing else needs to be said. Where are you?" he asks.

"The piano bar."

He chuckles at our inside joke that this is where I write my best music. "I should've assumed. The waves big?"

"Can't say I'm paying attention," I say, eyes fixed on the stretch of Pacific outside my windshield.

"Valid." He pauses. "You working your shit out? You writing music? Did our wives drive you to walk into the ocean and never come back?"

I chuckle at that.

"Seriously though, do I need to come get you because you're gonna cause trouble?"

"No," I say through an exhale. "I'm good. Well, not really. I just need . . ."

"To breathe?" he finishes for me.

"Something like that." Poppy on the counter with her little bare feet crossed and her pigtails bouncing flash through my mind.

"You drinking?"

If I have any more visuals like that, I'm going to be.

"Not yet," I murmur. "Most likely not far off though."

Another pause. Just long enough to mean something. "Don't do anything stupid, Rock."

My chuckle sounds bitter. "Never."

"That wasn't too convincing."

"Wasn't trying to be."

He cusses softly, and it sounds like he scrubs a hand over his face. "When you're in a better headspace, remind me to tell you about the time I found out about Jagger," he says, referring to his son. "How Hawkin had to bail me out of jail at two in the morning because I punched a guy and then sat in the bed of a truck—probably not too far from where you might be right now—for a long time while Hawke straightened my ass out."

A real laugh escapes me this time. "At least I haven't punched anyone out."

"*Yet.*"

"Yes. *Yet.*" I twist my lips as the horizon swallows the last bit of the sun. "I'm an asshole, right? Like she just lost her mom, and I'm here feeling sorry for myself that I have to grow the fuck up when I don't want to."

"Or maybe you're worried you have to actually be the man you thought you could never be."

And there he goes with the zinger.

"Christ," I mutter.

"Feel the emotions, brother. Own them. It'll be easier to come to terms with them than it will be to keep outrunning them."

I stare out at the crashing waves. At the last remnants of color fading to dark on the horizon.

"I don't know how," I admit.

"You don't have to know. Just don't run from it. Especially not now."

"That's all I know how to do."

His silence tells me he understands, but doesn't want to hijack my feelings or my confusion, by telling me about his experience in a similar situation. He knows that'll make me feel pathetic, and I'm grateful that he stays silent.

"Here's what you need to do. You need to go find a bar and then park your car. Go in. Get shitfaced if you'd like. Don't if you don't. Leave your keys with the bartender, and I'll get your car picked up and brought home for you. Do what you need to do. Drink. Fuck. Cry. Rage. Whatever it is that helps, but when you walk through the door of your house, you need to not bring that back with you."

I grunt.

"It's going to be okay. I promise. Just . . . remember we love you, okay? Even if you don't believe in that shit."

I grunt, throat too tight to do much more.

Then I end the call.

Because if I say anything else, the pieces I've held together for the past week are going to crack open completely.

And if they do, I'm afraid I won't be able to put them back.

Vince is right. I start the engine. I drive back over the roads I took hours ago and end up parked in the lot of a dark, seedy-as-fuck bar. Perfection.

I sit there for a few minutes before I go in, alone with my silence and the weight of two words I never thought I'd hear.

She's yours.

And I wonder what it's going to take to finally believe it.

And if I will ever be able to father a little girl who has no one else.

CHAPTER
thirteen

T HE HOUSE IS DARK. UNNERVINGLY STILL.

I know Rocket came home—saw the headlights in the driveway, heard the front door click sometime after midnight, felt the subtle shift in the air—but I didn't hear his footsteps after that. I've gotten used to his late hours. The clatter in the kitchen or the low hum of the television on, but tonight, there was none of that.

Nor was there an answer to the text I sent him an hour ago. **Are you okay?**

I should leave it alone and respect the boundary he's obviously put in place. Something triggered him earlier. It was almost as if seeing all the women in his life together, doting on his daughter, flustered him.

Or made this more real than it already has been.

I stand in the kitchen, uncertain why I'm not going to bed. Call me weird and reaching, but something about the silence feels wrong, especially after Rocket tore out of here earlier without an explanation.

The travertine tiles are cool beneath my feet as I move through the hall, past the living room and the kitchen. With a quick glance at Poppy sleeping quietly on the baby monitor in hand, I move down the corridor that leads to the studio and game room. Somewhere near the end of it, I hear it—a low, repetitive clack . . . clack . . . clack.

A pool table? *Clack.* Has to be a pool table.

I hesitate at the cracked doorway, unsure if I'm about to walk into something I don't want to see. A drunkfest? Drugs? A woman? A broken man?

My concern outweighs my fear.

I push the door open.

The room glows with a single low-hung pendant light over the green felt. The light is dim and hints at pinball machines on the far side, arcade-style gaming units, and various other man cave items at the edge of the shadows.

But it's Rocket who holds my attention.

He's standing with his back to me, pool cue in one hand, shoulders tight, and bare feet planted as he bends over the table. He moves with quick precision, and within seconds the sound of balls smashing together violently echoes in the quiet.

As if on autopilot—or deep in thought—he moves to the far end of the table and collects the balls to rack the shot again. His face is etched in concentration and his lips move as if he's talking to himself but no sound is coming out.

He lines up the break again. Hits the ball. Hard. And *clack* fills the room once again.

"Rocket . . ."

He doesn't turn. Doesn't even startle. It's almost as if he already knew I was here and was just biding his time. Either that or the empty bottle of whatever it is on the table against the wall and the glass beside it are enough of an indicator that he's numb.

"You probably don't want to be around me right now," he finally says, voice gravel smoothed by sandpaper, as he moves back around the table to hit another ball.

"Why?" I ask, drawn into the room and him in a way I've never been with someone before.

"Because I've drank more than is reasonable. Because I'm pissed. And because when both of those things happen, I typically like to fuck them out of my system and, Wills . . ."—he tsks and turns toward me for the first time, eyes flashing with a glint of something that borders on danger and desire—"... you're within reach."

My breath catches.

His stare pins me in place. I'm standing in the doorway, but I feel anchored, cornered, like I'm on fire from the inside out.

And I hate the way my body responds. The heat that pulses low in my belly. The goosebumps that skim over my arms. The part of me that freezes and wants him to reach for me.

"What are you upset about?" I finally ask, trying to keep my voice steady.

But I already know. I saw it earlier before he left—the defeat and the hope. And I sure as shit see it now—the fear and the predetermined failure.

"Just am." His tone's flat, indifferent. The exact opposite of what the look he gave me says he is.

"You're full of shit."

He takes a step toward me, slow and deliberate. "And you're not?"

I lift my chin. "I'm not the one brooding in the dark with an empty bottle and taking whatever you've got going there out on a ball and a stick."

"No," he says, circling the table, "but you're the one who pretends she's immune to fucking everything."

"Immune?" I bark out a laugh and challenge. "Define *everything*."

He stops at the corner of the table, arms braced, gaze smoldering. "Me."

My heart stutters.

Immune to him? Fucking hell. I've been standing in the lion's den each and every day since I've been here—never more so than right now—and he thinks I'm unaffected by him?

"You say you're here to look out for everyone else," he continues. "So tell me, Willow. Who's looking out for you? Who's going to protect you?"

"I don't need protecting."

"From me?" His chuckle is dark. Suggestive. Wrecked. "Sure, you don't."

I swallow hard, throat dry. Rocket's making me feel things I shouldn't feel. He's making me want things I have no business wanting. Not now. Not because he's my boss. Not because he's clearly been drinking.

"Because I'm drunk. Because I'm pissed. And because when both of those things happen, I typically like to fuck them out of my system and, Wills, you're within reach."

Am I attracted to Rocket? Who wouldn't be? Have I thought about acting on that? No. I simply can't. *It's not what I'm here for.*

But those words, adding to the wickedly sexual vibes in the room right now?

My body wholeheartedly disagrees.

I do the only thing I can to bring us back to where we need to be. To throw cold water on this conversation. "So who'd you go to so you could fuck it out of your system tonight?"

He doesn't stutter. "That question has no place in this moment, but I'll answer because you asked." He leans forward, eyes trained on mine. "No one."

"And what is *this moment?*" I ask, chills chasing over my skin. "Because I'm not used to men who warn me away, stare at me like they want me, but then talk in circles."

"What are you used to then? The boy next door? A man with smooth hands, lack of conviction, and emotional maturity?"

James flashes in my mind. A gentle giant. My first love.

And nothing like the edgy, mercurial, and incredibly sexy man in front of me.

"Grow up, Rocket." Isn't that what this is all about? Poppy's presence is forcing him to grow up? And yet everything I've seen about him screams grown-ass man. "You don't get to have an opinion on what I'm used to. You don't know anything about me."

His smile is a slow, wicked crawl over his lips. "I know your hands are trembling, and the pulse in your neck is pounding so hard I can see it." He closes the space between us in two long strides, his voice low when he next speaks. "This moment is when I should walk away. When I should go to my bedroom, grab another bottle to drown out the noise, and close the door. When I should pretend I didn't think about that bikini you wore or the way your laugh got under my skin."

I take a step back. He follows.

"But instead," he murmurs, "I'm wondering what you taste like. If your mouth is just as clever, just as smart, when it's consumed with mine. When it's wrapped around me. If you'd still talk back when you're gasping for—"

His hands land on either side of me, braced against the wall behind my shoulders, seconds before he kisses me.

It's not soft.

It's not sweet.

It's desperate. Punishing.

It's suffering, like holding a grenade with the pin already pulled.

I gasp into it, but I don't pull back. Not right away. Because he's fire and fury and grief, and his mouth on mine cracks something wide open in me that I'm too scared to admit to. Too scared to acknowledge.

His hand grazes my waist. *The chills chase.* My fingers fist in his shirt. *The ache burns.* We break apart for a breath—my hands against his chest and his knee between my thighs—and that's all it takes.

Reality slams into us.

He jerks back.

I stagger forward and away from him.

For a long beat, neither of us says a word. Our breathing is ragged. My lips tingle. My chest heaves like I've just sprinted a mile.

But his eyes hold mine. Those pools of green are pure torment that don't look away.

I bolt.

Embarrassed. Ashamed. Turned on. Desperate for more when *more* is a mistake.

I run to my room, shut the door behind me, and slide down the smooth wood until my ass is on the floor. My chest heaves, and I press my hand over my mouth like I'm not sure if I want to remember his taste or scratch it out.

Who am I kidding? I don't think I'll ever forget his taste again. Whiskey mixed with hunger. Desire mixed with desperation. Need edged with a violent want. Wrong mixed with—

I hear Poppy stir on the monitor and look at my phone to see her sigh softly before rolling on to her side.

I push myself up.

What the hell did I just do? What did I just risk for her?

I just kissed her dad. My boss. I just crossed a line I can't take back.

I scrub a hand over my face knowing, if given the chance again, I'd probably do the same.

How can one man—one moment—make me feel more alive than I've felt since James died?

Maybe even more than when James was alive?

What fire did Rocket just stoke with that kiss?

And why—fucking hell, *why*—do I fear that I don't want it put out?

CHAPTER
fourteen

Avoiding Rocket turns out to be easier than I expected.

At least at first.

I wake up early. I'm dead tired—sleep was hard to come by for obvious reasons—but I figure if I get up early and am occupied with Poppy by the time he gets to us, that will make both our lives easier.

And a lot harder for him to talk to me. Alone.

Then again, will he? Or will he just pass it off as no big deal since he's probably used to women willing to do anything for his attention?

Luckily for me, Poppy's in a great mood. The sounds she makes to communicate—muted grunts, quiet sighs, emphatic assent—are more frequent now. Louder. Insistent. The therapist thinks she'll be talking sooner rather than later but emphasized there is no "expected" timeframe.

But it feels like she is. Like she wants to. Sure the nightmares still come, but there's more space between them than there was before.

And last night there were none.

So Poppy hums to herself as she eats breakfast. I hold a one-way conversation with her that's responded to with more giggles than grunts. We take our routine morning walk through the neighborhood where I point out colors and flowers and insects we see on the way. When we get back, we practice our alphabet and sight words. We stack magnetic tiles until they collapse like tiny neon skyscrapers. All while I make every effort to avoid the hallway to his studio and keep clear of every corner of the house he might be in.

If I hear his footsteps, I go the other way. Every time I catch a glimpse of his silhouette down the hall, I duck into a room and stay there. But avoiding him doesn't stop my stomach from fluttering or from my pulse racing like it's being chased.

I need to get out more. If there's one thing the infatuation with the kiss has taught me is that I'm narrowing my world too much. I *need* to step away from the house so that Poppy doesn't consume my entire world . . . nor thoughts of Rocket and his kissable lips.

So I make a plan. A schedule for me. A new routine for Poppy with built-in quiet time, more time at the park, library days, music therapy appointments—space.

And a note.

I leave it on the counter in the kitchen like I'm dropping off an invoice.

Rocket,

Now that Poppy has more of a routine down, I'd like to adjust my hours and take off two evenings each week.

I've written out Poppy's modified routine and mealtimes. She'll be asleep most nights by seven. I'm giving you notice in case you need to arrange for someone else to come in and care for her, either a babysitter or one of the guys' wives, if you're unable to watch her.

Thank you,

Willow

Clinical. Professional. Safe. And options for him if he chooses not to watch her himself.

But all this—a new schedule and a posted letter—doesn't save me from what I've been avoiding all day.

Knock. Knock.

Dread drops in my stomach at the sound because there's only one person it could be.

I glance over to where Poppy is curled up in her favorite chair by the window. She has a dozen or so picture books on her lap and around her as she goes through one after another and "reads" to them.

"Willow?" Rocket's voice sounds rough. Tired. Frayed around the edges like a guitar string about to snap. "I know it's late, but do you have a minute?"

I stare at the knob. At the place my hand wants to reach but doesn't. Can't.

"If this is about the schedule I left on the counter," I say, trying to keep my voice even, "we can talk about it in the morning."

"Schedule? Not sure what you're talking about, so no, it's not."

Shit.

I rest my forehead against the door and draw in a fortifying breath. It's amazing how I've managed to keep myself so busy all day—crafts, playing, music, mindless chores—but just the sound of his voice on the other side of this door brings the feelings from last night crashing back.

"It's about last night," he says.

Oof.

"There's nothing to talk about."

"There is," he says. "Come on. Open up."

Can he hear my heart pounding like I can?

"Don't worry about it," I say as casually as I can, aware that Poppy is within earshot. "You were drunk. Overwhelmed. I just happened to be there. Like you said, you like to *F* whatever it is out of your system, and I was . . . within reach."

There's a rustle. A muffled curse. What sounds like a long, ragged breath through clenched teeth.

"I shouldn't have said that."

"But you did." I pause and state what has bugged me all day. "And you weren't lying, were you?"

Silence for a beat. "It'd had been a long night. I was blowing off steam in the privacy of my own home. You were in the wrong place at the wrong time, Wills. That's all."

"Otherwise, you wouldn't give me a second thought."

"Exactly."

The admission hits way harder than I had anticipated.

Not because I didn't expect something indifferent—he's a rock star, after all, no doubt a master of detachment if his night with Olivia is any indication—but because part of me hoped the kiss wasn't simply because I was a body in the blast radius. And ego wise, those words are a pretty brutal blow to my self-esteem.

But I didn't walk away knowing all of that before I even stepped foot in that room and that's on me.

"This conversation would be so much easier if I could see you," he says.

I hesitate for a beat and then open the door.

He's standing there in joggers, a black tee, and barefoot again. His hair is messy and face is unshaven. He looks like he's been wrestling with things he doesn't know how to say.

That makes me feel a little better. At least I'm not the only one grappling with how to speak about what happened.

And at least he's addressing it when I chose to avoid him all day, so there's that.

But for fuck's sake, the moment our eyes meet, I relive it all over again. The treacherous heat. The bone-melting kiss. The undeniable tension.

The *oh fuck* that followed right after.

"Hi," he says, eyebrows lifting and then a sheepish, lopsided smile.

Jesus. Why does he have to be so attractive?

I glance over to where Poppy is still "reading" to make sure she's okay and then back to him.

"It's open. You see me. What more needs to be said?" I ask stoically.

"Look. I screwed up. I shouldn't have kissed you. I've been messed up since you got here, and I took advantage of the situation simply because you know that. I apologize, and I'm sure I'll apologize again. I don't want this to affect things," he says gruffly.

"Because you screwed up or because you're afraid I'll leave, and you'll have to figure out Poppy all on your own?"

"Truth?"

"Preferably."

"*Both.*"

I exhale and nod. "What if I tell you that leaving is still on the table?"

"What?" His voice cracks in disbelief.

I shrug. "You heard me. When are we going to talk about the hard stuff? When does Poppy become the priority rather than every other thing in your orbit?"

He blanches at the comment and shakes his head. His breath stutters— barely there, but enough to catch. His eyes narrow, not in anger, but hesitation.

Then he shakes his head. "We're not talking about Poppy. We're talking about this, here, us. The kiss that never should have happened."

"Noted," I say and try not to feel the knife twisting. No girl wants to be seen as an opportunity to be used. "But, Rocket, just like you can't kiss me one minute and have an excuse for why it can't happen next, you can't have a daughter living under your roof and keep her at arm's length because your fears are greater than your hopes. And the fact that the kiss is what you're addressing and not what you need from me to help you bridge that gap with *your daughter* speaks louder than anything else."

"That's a low blow."

"It's the truth, though, right? Later when you're replaying this conversation in your head, that's the part that will be repeated the most."

"Fuck." He takes a few steps away and runs a hand through his hair, but he doesn't refute me. Doesn't even try. At least there's that. "I meant what I said, okay? I don't want this getting in the way of you staying. You're good for her. And she needs stability. She needs more than me." He looks at me again, and this time the flicker of pain in his eyes is real.

That's it, isn't it?

"You're more than enough for her," I say, needing him to hear that. Needing to chase away that vulnerability that's wavering in his voice.

"Like I said, thank you for staying." Blasé. Matter of fact.

I fold my arms over my chest and lift my chin with defiance. "I'm not staying for you."

A twitch at the corner of his mouth, not a smirk, not a smile, but more of an understanding. "Noted."

We stand there, locked in a moment where I feel like he wants to say more.

Then a soft sound breaks it.

We both glance over toward the chair where Poppy lies curled in a ball, fast asleep. The noise was from the books piled on her lap that slowly slid off and fell to the floor with one soft thump after another. She has one arm flung over her bunny, and her mouth is slightly open but curled up in a soft smile, much like the one Rocket just gave me.

I watch him watch her. His eyes soften, and so many muscles in his face flicker but don't fully commit to the expression. It's like he wants to but isn't allowing himself to.

"Do you want to move her to her bed?" I ask quietly.

He watches her for a long time. His expression softens, but his mouth is pulled tight as he struggles internally with his flood of emotions. "No. That's okay." He takes a step back. "She knows you better. I'd startle her."

My heart falls. It's a valid comment, and yet, I'm disappointed. "You can still try. It's not like you're a stranger."

"I—uh . . ." His Adam's apple bobs. *How* he looks at her contrasts his words and I'm holding tight to that. "I don't want her to be scared of me."

It's an admission at best and an excuse at worst. "Rocket," I murmur.

"You can't undo fear. I know that for a fact, okay? Call me callous. Call me distant. Tell me I'm struggling and need to do a better job . . . but don't make me do something that's going to make her afraid of me."

His words hit me hard. The conviction behind them even more so. I struck a nerve—clearly—but that nerve also allowed me a glimpse of what drives Rocket's distance. What stops him from closing the distance. What drives him to that realm of indifference where he has one foot stepping closer and the other pointed out the door.

This, I can deal with. Honesty. Truth. Fear. *That,* I can build from.

"I hear you and appreciate your honesty." I nod.

"Have a good night," he says. Our eyes meet as he nods and then closes the door he so desperately wanted open a few minutes ago.

Click.

And I'm alone again. Just as I should be. In the silence of a room accented by Poppy's soft snores.

That sound, along with the ones of his footsteps going down the hall, is the only reminder I need that this isn't about me. *Poppy comes first.*

I sit on the edge of the bed and stare at her. I'm here to do a job. I can ignore that lingering sense of attraction and chemistry. I don't need to add that to this already tricky and sensitive situation.

He kissed me. He pushed me away. One shouldn't have happened. The other should be the reason why it shouldn't happen again.

In any other world but here, would I be disappointed by that? Of course. Without a doubt. The man kissed me, and I felt more alive than I have in years. Not since grief hollowed me out and left me waiting for someone to spark something in me again.

But this is not what I'm here for.

And I need to be okay with that.

CHAPTER
fifteen

Willow

T HE MINUTE POPPY'S DOWN FOR HER NAP AND THE HOUSE FALLS quiet, I step out onto the back patio with my phone at my ear and an iced coffee I made purely for the ritual of it.

I need five minutes. Just five to feel like myself again.

And the person who I know will pick up on the third ring will do just that. And as if on cue, she answers with her usual dramatic flair.

"Please tell me the hot rock god has a private chef who cooks you gourmet pancakes in the shape of his abs," Lily says in one long breath.

I laugh before I even sit down. "Sorry. No pancakes. No abs. And he barely speaks in the mornings unless it's to grumble at the coffee maker."

She gasps. "Oh my God, is he one of those 'don't talk to me before caffeine' men? Because honestly, same."

I settle into a lounge chair, stretching my legs. "He's more of a 'don't talk to me ever' kind of man."

Lily snorts. "When you look that good, you don't need to talk."

"Let's not tell him that."

She chuckles. "So he's still grumpy and mysterious. That tracks."

"If that's what you want to call it." There are so many things I want to say to her, tell her, but I can't. Not just because of my NDA but because I don't know how I even feel about them myself.

"What aren't you telling me?"

"Who said I was hiding anything?"

"You. Your silence." Lily sighs. "You're an open book. That's what makes you *you*. But right now you're not saying shit."

"You really do have an active imagination. How have I never noticed it before?" I chuckle.

"You did. You know I'm over here filling your lack of communication with thoughts about how the man is kissing you senseless in between snack time and *Goodnight Moon*."

I go quiet and then snort in a half-hearted attempt to play off her words.

"Wait." Her tone sharpens. "*No way*."

"I didn't say anything."

"Exactly," she says, triumphant. "Oh my God. He kissed you?"

I press the heel of my palm to my forehead and scrunch my nose up. "No. Not officially. There was a moment. A brief second, but then we jumped back because it was a mistake."

"Forget the fact that I'm freaking out that Rocket fucking Caldwell kissed you—like OH MY GOD, WILLOW—and listen to me when I tell you the *we shouldn't have kissed* is ten times worse than the full-blown, all-in, fully committed kiss. You play it on a loop like a messed-up song you hate-love."

"It never should have happened," I murmur.

"When your boss is as hot as he is, all is forgiven."

"It's complicated."

"No shit. Well, I demand a full debrief in person. Soon," she says, switching back to lighthearted. "We need margaritas and judgment and at least one dance floor."

A smile tugs at my mouth. "Soon. I promise."

"Good. Because I miss you in that irrational, clingy best friend kind of way."

We both laugh, and for a second, I forget about the tension in this house, the letter, the girl with the quiet eyes, and the man who's a contradiction in more ways than one.

"Soon," I say again.

"Soon."

We hang up.

And even though nothing's changed, I feel a little more like myself again.

CHAPTER
sixteen

Rocket

O THERWISE, YOU WOULDN'T GIVE ME A SECOND THOUGHT.

Willow's words from the other night loop in my head like a hook stuck on repeat. One I keep jotting down but can't seem to write the chorus for. They replay over and fucking over, and I hate how loud they scream.

Because it's a total fucking lie. Not give her a second thought? Does she realize that goddam kiss nearly ruined me? That I've thought about it more times than is probably healthy?

I groan, dragging both hands through my hair and tipping my head back toward the ceiling of the studio. Because isn't that exactly what I've done? Thought about her? Wanted her? Fought against taking her?

She's just a distraction, Rock.

That's all she is.

So I don't have to focus on the terrifying part. The part that's three years old and sleeps with a bunny and has eyes that look exactly like mine. The part that I'm struggling with. I know I need to get over my own fears, I know I need to figure my shit out . . . and I know my failure to do so is one hundred percent on me.

No one else.

And it's a fucking miserable place to be.

"Hello?" Hawkin's voice cuts through my thoughts. "Earth to Rocket. You in there, fucker?"

I blink and look up.

We're in the studio—guitars slung, mics hot, drumsticks at the ready— and by the jump of colored bars on the computer screens on the opposite side of the glass, the track is still rolling in the background. Apparently, I've spaced the hell out mid-verse.

"Yeah. Sorry. I—uh—"

"You just stopped playing," Vince says from the corner and lifts a brow. "Mid-chorus you just stopped playing. Do we need to be worried? Call an ambulance?"

"Call an escort," Gizmo mutters, and the guys snicker.

"I'm fine," I say.

"Oh, so you already got the escort, and that's why you're so tired?" Hawkin chimes in.

"When have any of us ever had to pay for pussy?" I flip them off, but by the nods, I've made my point.

I yawn, only fueling their speculation that I had a hard night. Too bad it's not for what they think it was.

"Can we just—can you guys shut up and play?" I ask.

"Wow," Gizmo says, twirling a drumstick between his fingers. "Touchy-touchy."

"We can, but if you're going to drift off to space—"

"*Rocket* off to space," Gizmo adds in a lame attempt at a joke that earns him snorts.

"And forget where you are again? It's better if we just call it a day," Vince says dryly.

"Lead us in, Giz," I say through gritted teeth. I came here today to get lost in the music to find a bit more of myself. It's what I've always needed. Today is no different.

I position my hands at the keyboard on the ready as Gizmo counts us in.

And for a few glorious minutes, I disappear. Into Gizmo's steady beat. With Vince's guitar riffs. And with Hawkin's gritty voice as he plays with the lyrics we've been testing on this new song. My fingers move on the keys as my foot taps out the count.

Giz adjusts his tempo and the rest of us quicken the pace.

"Nah, I don't like that," Vince shouts over the music as he keeps playing but then directs the pace half a beat slower.

We adjust to him.

This is what ten years together does. It allows us to know each other, to anticipate each other, and for now, to work like a well-oiled machine.

Because there are definitely times when we've been at each other's throats.

I close my eyes and just play. This is what I've needed. It's one thing to sit in my studio at home and play. It's another to be with my brothers and let the music we create grab hold of something feral in me. The ache. The anger. The want. The confusion. And it burns through my veins like gasoline.

The chords are dirty. The drums hit hard. The lyrics blur into noise.

But . . . I feel like I can breathe.

We finish the chorus, sweat on our brows, chests heaving, and the reverb still humming in the floorboards.

"Damn," Hawkin says, pulling his shirt over his head, wiping his face with it. "Should we test that out next leg?"

"Feels like something," Vince agrees.

There's a collective nod between the four of us as Vince pulls the guitar strap over his head and Giz sets his drumsticks down before guzzling a bottle of water.

"Hey, Rock?" Giz says.

"Hmm?"

"Are we going to talk about your . . . situationship?" he asks and has Vince and Hawke looking my way for a reaction.

"There is no *situationship*, whatever the hell that is."

"Situation and relationship combined," Gizmo says. "Duh."

Hawkin barks out a laugh. "Hendrix has you watching way too many episodes of *Real Housewives* or whatever if you're using terms like that."

"No clue what the fuck you're talking about," Gizmo continues. And I'm fine with that. So long as the focus is on him, it's off me. "I heard it in the bakery the other day. I stopped to pick Hendrix up and overheard some girls in the front using it."

"No doubt those girls were teenagers speaking, so let's save our dignity, Giz, and not bring them here," Vince says with a chuckle, but his arms are crossed over his chest, and he's leaning back. He's thinking. And then he turns and looks at me. "The man does have a point."

"And what is that?" I ask, feigning like I already forgot.

"What are you going to do about the tour? The nanny coming?" he asks. "Or is she staying home so you can go back to fucking your way through each city like the good ol' days?"

I laugh—but it's hollow. "Sounds tempting."

Except it's not. In fact, it's the last fucking thing on my mind.

"*Sounds tempting* because you're already fucking her and over her, or *sounds tempting* because it'll keep you occupied so you don't fuck her?" Hawkin asks. There's sarcasm in his tone, but there's also something else. Curiosity? Speculation? "Which one is it?"

"How about it sounds tempting because it's none of your fucking business?" I say and flash a smile I'm sure doesn't reach my eyes.

"They were right," Vince murmurs.

"Who was right?" Irritation peppers my tone.

"When they brought pizza over the other day for their little party with Poppy, Bristol said the two of you were avoiding each other," Vince says, referring to when their wives came over two days ago.

"Glad to know they have a pulse on things in my house."

"Dude, why the fuck are you so uptight?" Gizmo says.

"Because he needs to get laid," Hawkin whispers.

"She's not like your usual type," Vince says out of the blue.

"What the hell does that mean? You've never even met her."

"You're right. We haven't because we've been giving you space because we're good like that. We're waiting for you to invite us over," Hawkin says.

"And have you harass her like this? No fucking way," I mutter.

"Well according to Hendrix, Willow's hot but definitely not your type," Gizmo says.

"What does that even fucking mean?" I shout. I'm so fed up.

"It means," Hawkin jumps in, "that she's not down for a quick fuck and posting a social media picture to brag about who she spent the night with."

"You guys have never met her so your opinions are moot."

"*Moot?*" Giz asks, lifting his eyebrows. "Rock always goes for the thesaurus when he gets defensive. The question is, what are you defensive about?"

"Unless of course, you like her," Hawkin says. "And it doesn't take a thesaurus-wielding rocket scientist to know a woman who spends her days taking care of other people's kids and living in their house isn't exactly a fuck-her-and-chuck-her woman."

"Jesus," I mutter.

"And to emphasize Hawke's point, it's not like you can just sleep with her and wash your hands of her like you typically do," Vince says.

"Like we all used to do," I say. "Just because you're all married fuckers now doesn't mean I don't remember."

"Look, asshole," Gizmo says. "They have a point. You sleep with Willow, you ruin that whole situationship. If Willow leaves, then Poppy gets the short end of the stick. *Again.*"

I rub the back of my neck. "Can we just play? Please?"

"Dude, you have a fucking kid," Hawkin says and shakes his head. "I mean fucking the nanny is all good and well, but why are we focusing on that instead of Poppy?"

"Because it's way fucking easier," I shout. Silence weighs down the studio as they all stare at me. Shocked.

"Talk to us," Vince says.

"And say what? I'm a horrible father?" My voice cracks, the admission eating me alive inside.

"I refuse to believe that," Hawkin says. "We all had fucked-up families. Isn't that partly why we commiserated so well in the beginning? We understood each other and where we were coming from. We all get it. The fear of failing our kids. Of being our parents. Of fucking our kids up more than our parents did us."

The lump in my throat grows bigger with each passing second.

"But here's the thing, Rock," Vince says, "if you don't show up, then you're letting that fucker who walked out on you when you were one year old win. You're letting your selfish, revolving-door-of-a-mother win. You're better than both of them. All of us can vouch for it."

"The best thing about kids is they forgive and forget and are willing to love you for simply nothing. That's why our parents' actions hurt so bad," Gizmo says.

"We know it's hard, but you've gotta show up. You have to try. Be there for Poppy even if it's just to watch the same stupid show over and over and over until your ears bleed," Hawkin says, and Vince chuckles.

Fuck. Tears well, one falls over, and I wipe it away as fast as I can as I turn my back from them and take a few steps to compose myself.

My chest burns with shame. But there's also . . . hope and a desire to do what they're saying I should. From knowing they understand me when no one else possibly could. From knowing they believe in me.

I sniffle and am just about to turn back around when Gizmo says, "You're right. Talking about fucking the nanny is way easier than this."

Laughter rings out. *God, I love these guys.*

"So for clarification, have you or have you not fucked the nanny yet?" Hawkin asks.

My middle fingers go up, and I feel the ground steady beneath me a bit more. I welcome it.

"Must be a world record for him," Gizmo says. "Three whole weeks. No pussy. Write it down, boys."

"Oh shit, someone call Guinness," Vince adds, tapping the snare. "Get this man a trophy."

"Or a condom."

"Or a cold shower."

"No, no," Hawkin says with mock seriousness. "I feel a song coming on."

Gizmo kicks in a quick beat on his drums. Without prompting, Vince grabs his acoustic and throws in some chaotic chord progressions. Hawkin starts singing in an exaggerated and horrible falsetto.

She walked in with juice boxes, hair in a bun,

Thought she was here for the kid, not the fun.

Vince starts in, and you can barely hear the lyrics through his laughter.

She's a sweet distraction, pure satisfaction,

Got the nanny cam catching all the action.

They both point to Gizmo and wait for him to add on. He's on it in a second.

She's in the kitchen making grilled cheese,

He's behind her like, drop to your knees.

Hawkin holds his hand up to indicate he's going next.

Finger-paint on the fridge, bra on the floor,

Who needs a tour bus when she locks the door?

They're laughing so hard Hawkin nearly drops his water. Giz is bent over his drum set holding his stomach, shoulders shaking, and Vince just shakes his head like he's already finishing writing the chorus in his brain.

And as if on cue, all three look my way, and I do the only thing I can do—I laugh with them. "You guys are regular fucking comedians."

"We can keep going," Gizmo says and lifts his sticks.

"No. Please." I hold my hands up. "That's the last thing I need repeating in my head when I go home and come face to face with Willow."

"One more," Hawkin says and jumps right into the lyrics.

So don't ask where he's been or what he's doing tonight . . .

He's busy with the nanny.

And she's doing him right.

"Please tell me we were recording that," Vince says as he wipes tears of laughter from his eyes.

"That's our next Grammy winner right there. Sweet Distraction," Gizmo says and hits the cymbal to accentuate his words.

"Fucking hilarious," I say with a heavy dose of sarcasm in between bouts of laughter.

"You're laughing. That means we did our job," Hawkin says.

CHAPTER
seventeen

Willow

I'm halfway through the financial aid form I'm filling out online when I hear the door creak open.

I lift my gaze from the glow of my laptop to see him standing there. Rocket.

Hair mussed like he's been dragging his hands through it. Tattoos disappearing beneath the sleeves of a worn tee. His expression somewhere between exhaustion and something rawer. Like the kind of tired that has nothing to do with sleep.

He doesn't speak right away. Just stands in the entryway to the kitchen like he's not sure if he should come in.

"Hey." I close the laptop gently. "How was the writing session?"

"Meh." He shrugs but gets the most playful tilt to the corner of his lips despite the somberness in his expression. "Funny. What I needed."

"That's good then, isn't it?"

"Yeah." Another muted response.

I angle my head to the side and study him. "What is it?"

He shifts his weight from one foot to the other, fingers flexing like they want to grab something.

"I, uh—" He drags in a breath. "I wanted to say I'm sorry."

That gets my full attention. I swivel on the barstool and face him head-on. "For what?"

"For not trying hard enough." His voice is low but certain. "With Poppy. With this whole thing."

My heart stutters.

"I'm not good at this," he says, stepping forward. "None of it. I've been trying to act like I'm unaffected, but the truth is . . . I don't have a damn clue what I'm doing. She's a kid. And I'm just—me."

I swallow the lump building in my throat. "Rocket—"

"I keep waiting for someone to come in and tell me I don't qualify. That this was a mistake. That someone better is on the way. Someone who knows what bedtime songs are supposed to sound like or what to do when she wakes up crying in the middle of the night asking for her mom." His voice cracks a little, just enough for the edge to fray.

"No one knows those things off the bat. That's something you learn with time. With trial and error," I say, desperate to ask him what brought this epiphany on. Was it his bandmates? Was it their wives who reported back after our pizza party a few nights ago when I didn't have answers for their endless questions about how much Rocket participated?

Was it a combination of both?

"Don't get me wrong, I love that you're asking all these questions. That you feel comfortable doing so when I know it's probably super hard for you to do so, but where's all this coming from?"

His nod is slow and knowing, and it does nothing to erase the wariness in his posture. "She looks at me like I matter, Wills. *And that's terrifying.* Because what if I screw this up?"

"You won't," I say softly.

"You don't know that."

"No. But I know what she needs."

He looks up at me then, eyes dark and open in a way I haven't seen before.

"And that's you." His shoulders hitch at my words, and so I keep going. "All she wants is your time. That's it. Time and love and laughter. She's a kid.

She doesn't care about being perfect. She just wants to know she's wanted. That someone's going to show up."

He nods, jaw tight.

"She doesn't need a rock star," I add. "She needs you. However messy and uncertain that is."

"I'm definitely both of those," he says and pulls on the back of his neck.

"Does any of this have to do with your own childhood?"

He freezes.

There's a flicker of something in his eyes—pain maybe. Regret. A thousand unspoken things.

"Sorry. I didn't mean to pry. I'm simply trying to understand you more so that I can better help you."

"I didn't exactly have stellar role models," he says quietly. "My dad wasn't around, and my mom needed a man—any man, she wasn't particular—to feed her self-worth at the expense of a validating relationship with her only son. *Me.*"

A sad smile tugs at the corner of my lips. "Well, lucky for you, Poppy just wants you to be *next* to her. *Want* her. She doesn't care if you know what you're doing. Color perfectly inside the lines in her coloring books. Let her put glitter stickers on your arm. It doesn't matter. Being with her gives her confidence to brave her new world."

He huffs a small laugh. "Is that what you had on your arm the other day?"

"The other day?" I laugh. "Try every day. I swear she's trying to give me tattoos like yours, so there's that."

That gets a real smile from him. A smile that makes you feel like maybe the man underneath the guarded sarcasm and tattoos is someone still learning how to be whole. "Probably not the best thing for a three-year-old to be fascinated with."

"We'll take little wins where we can," I say as he walks to the freezer, grabs a pint of ice cream, and wordlessly takes a spoon from the drawer. No bowl. No apology. Just peels back the lid and starts eating straight from the container.

I stay quiet, just watching him. What does tonight's flavor choice say about him? "Moose tracks, huh?"

His grin is devilishly quick and lights up his face. "It says I'm basically the dessert version of trust issues. You think you're getting plain vanilla with a few chocolate swirls, but there's so much more within its depths. I like the surprise I get in every bite."

"Again, that made no sense." I laugh.

"Just like me," he says. He takes another bite as we sit in silence for a beat before he looks back up. "I'm ready to do better, Wills."

I nod. *And I'm here to help you, Gavin Caldwell.*

CHAPTER
eighteen

Rocket

"Is this a bad time?" Sandra's voice booms through the car speaker as I merge onto I-605.

"I'm driving. It's fine. What's up?"

"You alone?"

"Yes." I draw the word out because those two words she just asked already have me sitting taller.

"And everything's good?"

"Uh-huh. As good as can be," I say. "What is it?"

"I got a call earlier today." There's an edge to her voice, a sudden chill to her tone. "Olivia's parents have entered the picture."

"I don't know what that means. I thought they were estranged. I thought—"

"Well, they were finally found and claimed Olivia from the ME's office."

"So they're going to give her a proper burial. I . . . I didn't know that hadn't happened." And now I feel like an asshole for it. "I would have done it. I . . . what are you telling me, Sandra? What does it mean *they've entered the picture?*"

"Her parents have hired counsel and plan on filing for custody of Poppy."

My stomach drops. "What?"

"Let me back up. As of now, they're filing for visitation, but the lawyer has hinted at your chaotic life and lack of stability, which causes me to think they're going to file for full custody."

My world that was slowly righting itself, tilts again. "Okay." The word is barely audible as I try to process Sandra's hypothesis. "They can do that?"

"They can, yes. It's not easy to prove, but there are ample pictures and documentation that it wouldn't be too hard to paint an unfavorable picture."

Her silence eats up the line, giving me time to think.

Three weeks ago, I'd say this was a good thing. That Poppy would gain a more traditional family with better stability and perhaps even blood ties to a larger family.

But now the thought has my pulse racing.

"Sandra, I . . . *fuck.*" Maybe they're still the better option. Maybe they have a better foundation to do this seeing as they've already raised a child.

"You have options," she says. "You can fight any petitions they file or you can agree to them, offer support to stem any future filings for monetary support, and wash your hands of the whole situation."

I shake my head and scrub a hand over my face. "This is crazy. They want their granddaughter but didn't fight hard enough to want their daughter when she was alive?"

"I know. I understand what you're saying."

"Why were they estranged? Can they answer that for you because I've yet to get an explanation on that one?"

"You know how families are. One little thing snowballs into something bigger and both sides are too stubborn to take the first step."

I scrub a hand through my hair. "What happened between them What was their one little thing?"

"From what I can tell they didn't want Olivia to chase her Hollywood dreams. Told her if she left for Los Angeles they weren't going to support her. She left. They fought. The only time she'd call home was for more money—over and over again—until they cut her off and said no more. She was angry at them. They were angry she got pregnant out of wedlock and thought she'd had an abortion. The tiny rift became bigger, both sides refusing to give an inch."

I can see how that can happen. I know other families that have fallen apart for far less . . . and yet, now they want to step up? Now they care? Poppy is three years old. "Sandra, I don't even know what to say. I'm still just getting the hang of this—"

"This is what you wanted originally, right? To be deemed unfit and unable to parent Poppy? Were those not your words?"

That's not fair. But I don't say *that* because she's right. That is what I said. It is what I asked. Things are different now, though.

But are they? What have you done to step up to the plate, Caldwell?

"Is that what you want?" she pushes, putting me on the spot.

My silence is my answer. It's also the only way I can run away from the situation.

My exhale is long and slow. "She doesn't even know them," I whisper.

"She didn't know you, either," Sandra says softly.

"Fucking hell."

Because isn't that the truth. An even bigger truth is how she's been in my house for three weeks, and we're still fucking strangers.

She didn't know you, either.

Her words wreck me because she's not wrong.

What is *best for Poppy?*

"Well, lucky for you, Poppy just wants you to be next to her. Want her. She doesn't care if you know what you're doing. Being with her gives her confidence to brave her new world."

Like the boys were for me, would it be enough if I was simply in her corner, helping her be brave?

CHAPTER
nineteen

Rocket

> Hawkin: Thought of some more lyrics.
>
> Me: This isn't helping our next album get written.
>
> Hawkin: No, but it's making you laugh. Here's a verse:

It started with snack time, ended in sin,
One minute she's reading, the next she's all in.
She's got bedtime vibes and after-dark plans,
Who knew the nanny came with such great hands?

I sit in my driveway and shake my head. The smile's there, but the stress of Sandra's phone call lingers like a hangover after a long bender.

"Thanks, brother," I say to no one as I rest my head against the headrest and stare at my house. The lights are on in the family room and kitchen. All I want to do is go inside, but how the hell can I when this fucking storm cloud is hovering over my head?

How do I fight for something I only just started believing was worth fighting for?

Having the money and means to take care of someone doesn't always mean you're the right person for the job. It doesn't make you qualified.

Maybe it won't end up how Sandra thinks. Maybe Olivia's parents are just desperate to have a piece of their daughter in their life and want visitation rights. Nothing more. Nothing less.

And maybe I've never sold out stadiums night after night before.

Fuck, man.

This is what you wanted, Rock. Your freedom back. Your ability to choose if you want to be responsible, depending on the situation. A house void of sippy cups and stuffed animals stuck between couch cushions. Not having to think of anyone other than yourself and what's best for your bandmates.

The thoughts swirl and nag. This invisible war that started before I even knew I had skin in the game, and now I'm just . . . I don't know what the fuck I am.

All I know is that the old me would have taken the easy way out. Hands up. Hands off. Walked away.

But the new me?

New me? What the fuck, it's been a month, dude. There's no way you've changed that much.

But when I unlock and open my front door, the house is quiet. The kind of quiet that used to be comforting but now just feels hollow and unsettling.

How the hell did that happen?

I don't know why I stand there instead of heading to my room or game room like usual. Maybe I *don't* want to be alone tonight. Maybe I'm curious what Poppy and Willow are doing. Maybe I don't desperately crave the solitude like I used to because I have skin in the game and a riot of thoughts in my head.

The silence tells me to move on. To go to bed. And just as I decide to do that, I hear something. It's not music or the hum of a television. It's something softer.

Singing? Is that Willow?

I don't hesitate. My feet move toward the sound like I don't even have a say in the matter.

Her voice grows louder as I approach. At first, I think it's a lullaby, but then stop when I hear the chorus. It's one of our ballads.

I don't know why that moves me. People all over the world sing our songs, and yet I stop at the open doorway of Poppy's bedroom and listen.

Willow's sitting against the headboard. Her feet are bare and crossed at the ankles. Her hair is loose and in waves over her shoulder. And then there's Poppy, curled against Willow's chest like a heartbeat outside her own body.

She continues singing softly, her voice not half-bad, while she strokes Poppy's back in slow, even motions. Her face is soft and calm in a way I've never figured out how to be.

My gaze moves to Poppy. *To my daughter.*

For the first time, that word doesn't get stuck in my throat. It doesn't unsettle me or feel like a punch to the gut. *It just is.*

She simply is.

She's asleep. Her tiny hand clutches Willow's shirt, and one foot is kicked out from under the blanket. Her curls are sticking up all over the place, and her pajamas are pink. She looks a mess in that way that little kids do when they get hot and sweaty while they sleep. *And she looks safe.*

Fucking hell. The way that thought hits me . . .

I suddenly want to be that for her too despite the fear.

I can be that. I can do that. I can make myself enough for her, right?

Maybe knowing—*experiencing*—what not to do could make me know what to do?

I have to try. I have to . . .

She makes the softest of sounds and snuggles deeper into Willow. Something in my chest tightens—it's fear *gripped in hope.*

But not over her being here.

What's it going to take from me to be exactly who she needs me to be? I don't know the answer, but . . . I have to try.

Poppy's a walking mirror of everything I never thought I'd deserve. And now her grandparents want her? Strangers, but family. People with actual histories and photos and maybe a swing set in the backyard. People who probably know how to bake cookies without a tutorial and don't need a nanny to show them how to raise a kid because they've already done it before.

Would she be better off with them?

No. The answer is definitive in my head, but logic questions that.

My chest aches with the weight of it, and I step into the room before I can talk myself out of it.

"Hey," I say quietly.

Willow lifts her head, and when her eyes find mine, they light up. "Hi." She scrunches her nose. It's rather adorable. "How embarrassing to get caught butchering one of your songs."

"Not at all. I liked it."

"It's ridiculous. I don't know." She's flustered, and it's cute. "I thought it might be nice for her to get used to your music. Kind of like it would help her get to know you or something. Whatever."

"Don't apologize." I look around the room. Willow has done her best to make the space softer, more welcoming for a toddler. Stuffed animal chairs. A mini table with plastic chairs and an organizer of some sort on the top. A stack of books in the corner. How stupid was I not to think of it before? "Is there anything else you need for her? Not that I'm not late to the party or anything," I joke.

She smooths a hand over Poppy's curls and smiles softly. "Thank you. It's been fine so far. She's comfortable in her space, and that's important for when I eventually leave."

Leave. The word is like a knife to my chest. I'd like to the think it's merely because of the panic factor of doing this all on my own, but I know better than that.

My house feels different. My life's been altered. And it's not because I have a new roommate.

It's because of her.

"Rocket? You okay?" she asks.

"Yeah. Fine." I offer a smile. "We're not talking about you leaving unless you want me having a heart attack. Anything else you need though?"

"Maybe just more of you." Her voice is soft, knowing, and more than anything, searching. Am I still going to try harder like I said I was the other night? Am I still willing to be what's expected of me?

Our eyes hold, and I nod. "I'm here right now."

"You are." She tilts her head and studies me. "You can come in, you know."

I take a step forward. Then another.

Poppy stirs when I get close. Her eyes flutter open, sleepy and sluggish, and land on me. For a second, I think she might cry. Instead, she lifts one tiny hand, fingers reaching out toward me, fingers flickering in a wave as the slightest smile ghosts her lips.

It's a barely-there smile, but it punches a hole through my ribs and makes my heart feel so different.

Then she lays her head back on Willow's chest and sighs, already drifting again.

My tongue feels heavy in my mouth, and thoughts I've never had before seem to own my mind.

"She asked for Olivia again," Willow says, interrupting my thoughts. I welcome the change in topic but not the heaviness of the new one.

"Was she okay?"

"Hmm. I don't know that she'll ever be *okay*—her mom was her world—but we can do our best to support her."

"I know you said the therapist said she was making progress, helping her cope better. Is it still working?"

"Two days a week isn't going to take away the pain, but it'll help. Her therapist said to expect the nightmares to lessen but that they'll pop up every now and again. She said to try and keep her mom alive for Poppy as much as possible . . ."

"Which is hard since neither of us really knew her."

"True, but I've pieced together the life I think she had from pictures I found on social media. From talking to her mom's best friend, Jackie, who I'd love to let Poppy see. I show the pictures to Poppy, and when she's in them, I ask her if she remembers that day. I try and talk about her so that Poppy isn't afraid to when she finally speaks."

"You're amazing," I whisper. All this for my daughter, someone she's not even related to, while I sat and debated and stood idly by.

"Not amazing." Her smile is soft and flips my stomach. "Just trying to help your tiny human."

"Thank you," I murmur, feeling overwhelmed. "For that. For this. For . . . just thank you."

She nods and jokes, "That's what you pay me for."

"Funny thing is, Wills, I think even if I didn't pay you, you'd still try and do it because that's just who you are."

"You might be right." Her cheeks flush and eyes blink. She pats the bed beside her. "Come. Sit."

I hesitate.

She raises an eyebrow like she knows I'll do it anyway.

She's right. I do.

Poppy's foot brushes my thigh as I settle in beside the two of them on

Poppy's bed. Willow's shoulder grazes mine, and the silence between us is comfortable. *It feels earned.*

"She doesn't roll off this in the middle of the night?" I ask.

"There are sides that I raise up once she's asleep."

"There are?" I look down at the net-rail contraption thing and chuckle. "Guess you have it covered."

"I do indeed. What's on your mind, Rocket?" she asks.

"The usual."

She angles her head to the side and meets my eyes. She searches for something I'm not certain of. "It's more than the usual. What's wrong?"

I almost say it.

Almost tell her about the call. About the grandparents. About how this irrational fear I suddenly have that they might be able to provide Poppy with more than I can—emotionally, developmentally, and more. That I might lose the first thing I've ever wanted that didn't come in the form of applause or adrenaline or escape.

But I stop myself.

Because what if she thinks less of me?

What if saying it out loud makes it real?

Instead, I shake my head. I hesitate. My sigh could be misinterpreted a million different ways, but I'm past caring. "Help me understand," I finally say. "How can I be better?"

Her body stiffens beside mine. "Be you. That's all she needs."

I snort, but when she places her hand on mine and squeezes, the sarcastic comment on my tongue dies.

"Sing your songs to her. Hum them. Dance to them. Make your voice familiar to her. Not just talking to me but to her. Pick one of your favorites, twist the words around, and make it about her. *Make it hers.*"

Her words hit home. Take root. Grow into seeds of hope.

"Okay. I'll try."

"Trying is all she wants."

I reach out and run my thumb over her tiny fingers. "She makes me feel helpless," I say as Willow rubs her thumb back and forth over the top of my hand. "She doesn't talk, and so I don't know what she wants or needs and as a man, that's not easy."

Willow nods, but I'm left wondering what kind of voodoo magic this woman has. I don't talk about my feelings, and I sure as shit don't admit I'm helpless. Yet here in a span of a few weeks, I've cracked open like a book and am saying shit I'd never thought I'd say.

"Did your mom ever look at you, and you just knew she loved you? That she was proud of you?" Willow asks.

The question slams into me. There's no need to search for a memory that I know doesn't exist. I've tried. I refuse to try again and come up empty-handed. "Next example," I say drolly.

Willow nods, not pushing. "Okay, then what about with the guys?" she says. "You're onstage, and you can't talk to each other above the music, right? And yet you know what they're saying. It's the look they give you. Your bandmates' cues. Their energy. You *just* know. That's how it is with Poppy. She just knows you care about her through looks and actions."

I glance at her. "Yeah?"

"Yeah," she says. "There's so much more to communication for her than words. There's hand gestures and expressions and touch. She uses all of those things to communicate with you."

She wiggles her fingers in her sleep that are still in my hand. Her skin is so soft. So warm.

"You make it look easy," I murmur.

Willow smiles. "No. It's never easy. I just have more practice."

Poppy stirs so that her beloved bunny falls into my lap. I pick it up and toy with the ears. The damn thing has seen better days.

The same could be said for me.

When I look up, Willow's watching me. Her expression is guarded, but her eyes hold nothing but warmth. There's no judgment in them. No mockery. "Thank you for being patient with me. For helping teach me. I just hope I can be the man and father she deserves. I just hope I can make her love me."

Her eyes fill with tears—quick and quiet—and I don't know why that hits me hardest. Why her softness undoes me more than any song ever has.

"You will be. You already are. It's just hiding," she says. "She'll love you because you're her dad. She'll trust you because you won't let her down. She'll want you to be the one to hold her because you're where she'll feel safest."

"That's a tall order."

"So was becoming a world famous rock star and you kicked ass at that, right?"

CHAPTER
twenty

I CAN'T SLEEP.

Not because I'm uncomfortable or because Poppy is restless. She's tucked in tight in her bed next door to mine, snoring softly, with her favorite rabbit under one arm and one finger twirled in a curl of her hair.

No, I can't sleep because of his comment. *I just hope I can make her love me.* It plays on a loop in my head, along with the image of Rocket sitting beside me with his broad shoulders tense and his brow furrowed. It was as if letting me see that side of him took everything he had.

And that wrecked me a little.

So after tossing and turning, I give up on sleep, tug on a sweatshirt, and pad quietly down the hallway and into the kitchen.

The house is dimly lit by a soft glow spilling from the family room.

I turn the corner and find him there. Rocket's sitting on the couch with one arm sprawled over its back and a glass in his other hand. Whiskey, probably. The drink you sip when you're chasing silence.

Or regretting your choices.

He paints a striking picture. A lonely one. He's staring out the windows at the Los Angeles valley beyond. It's a glittering stretch of chaos that eventually falls dark when it hits the Pacific.

He has to know I'm here. It's not like I tiptoed into the room, but he doesn't turn or look my way. He just lifts his glass to his lips and then lowers it back down after he takes a sip.

I'm drawn to him in a way I've never been to a man before. Is it because I think I can fix him? Is it because he's so different from the people in my small circle, and there's a thrill to that?

"You're up late," I say.

He doesn't look over. "You too." He shrugs. "I'm a night owl. It's way too early for me to sleep."

I hover for a second, figuring he probably wants to be alone.

"Come sit," he murmurs.

I know before I take a step that this is the point of no return for me. It's not his looks or personality or fame that attracts me, though . . . it's his vulnerability. His willingness to try. That's what is blurring lines for me that were so well defined before.

I cross the room and sink into the opposite end of the couch, pulling my knees up under me. I look out toward the same view that's captured his attention. "Thanks for letting me join you."

He nods. "Do you want a drink?"

"No. I'm okay. Thank you, though."

"Can't sleep?"

"Lots on my mind," I say.

"Those forms you've been filling out for college?"

You.

"Something like that," I say.

We sit there like that for a minute, saying nothing and just watching the world outside move by.

He breaks the silence first. "Tour starts again in a few weeks."

I glance over. "You excited to get back to doing what you love?"

He makes a face I can't decipher. "I don't know. Usually, yeah. But now . . ."

"Now there's a three-year-old in the picture."

"And her nanny," he adds, a crooked grin crawling over his lips. "Ever been on tour before?"

I snort. "You heard my singing earlier. Of course I have. With talent like that, I've sold out stadiums."

Everything about him relaxes. "Damn, you must have been the one who broke our record."

"I was. I hate to break it to you." I smile at him and contemplate that I should have taken that drink he offered.

"Don't worry. We'll win that title back."

"I have no doubt."

"So are you excited to go on tour with us then?"

My head startles. "I—uh—figured I'd be staying back with Poppy. That way you can have a bit of your old life back, and I can . . . get her used to her new one."

He narrows his eyebrows, but his only response is, "Right."

The word feels hostile. Irritated. And here I thought I was giving him what he wants. "Poppy's barely settled. It's a big ask, throwing her into another unknown. Constant changes. New places. Loud crowds." I rest my chin on my knee and cave to the need to explain. "I think Poppy's doing okay because she has structure right now. The idea of upending that . . ."

He nods slowly. "And if I'm not around, how am I supposed to connect with her?"

The question is quiet. Honest. I look at him, really look at him.

For the first time, I believe he gets it. That he's not just going through the motions or waiting for the storm to pass. That he's actually trying.

"I don't know. When it comes down to it, it's your call what you want to do. She's your daughter."

"You mean I'm her *rock . . . et,*" he says and pretends to hold a rock next to his ear that makes us both chuckle.

"Yes. You are her rock . . . *et.*"

"God, that made me laugh. Her expression and giggle and . . . she's funny," he muses over the lip of his glass.

"Probably a bad choice on my end to pick up a rock for comparison, but I was startled."

"I like it. Don't apologize." He takes another sip and darts his tongue out to lick his lips. "At some point soon, I need to tell her I'm her dad. Does she even know what that is?"

"It's a good idea to . . . and if I'm honest, I don't know how much she knows. She overheard us talking. She's overheard the wives talking about the two of you looking like each other. She's a very intelligent little girl. She might already know."

He scrubs a hand over his face, and the scraping sound of his stubble fills the room.

I rest my head on the side of the couch, sink farther into the plush couch, and meet his gaze. "Why music, Rocket? Where did that start?"

He lifts his brows and chuckles at some memory only he knows. "Because it was the only thing that made sense when nothing else did." He shrugs. "Because when I couldn't say how I felt, I could play it, even when I didn't understand it myself."

"I get that." Maybe I need to get Poppy an instrument. Maybe that will help her feel connected to Rocket.

"I never knew my dad. My mom had a revolving door of boyfriends. She was so busy trying to keep them around—for their money, for the way she thought they gave her value, for an escape from having to be a mom, I guess. I was pretty much left to raise myself so she could entertain them. I spent a lot of nights shut in my bedroom or on the back porch or falling asleep in the back seat of the car as to not disturb her and whatever she had going on so I used music to keep me company."

A lump forms in my throat. There's nothing I can say or do to change the damage of his past, but it does give me some explanation as to why he fears fatherhood. I had a hunch, but he just confirmed it.

"How did you settle on the keyboard?" That should move us to safer territory.

His grin is lightning quick and mischievous as fuck. "Diana Finkleman."

"Who?" I laugh because the way he says her name with mesmerized awe is like a grade-school kid who has a crush.

"She was a friend's sister. Taught piano down at the local church. She was so hot. So . . . *developed* for a sophomore."

"Oh, Jesus."

"I was a freshman, and at that age all it takes is a stiff breeze to make you hard. Can you blame me?"

"No," I say through a laugh, wondering what a teenage Rocket was like.

"Dude, everybody wanted her. I mean, I didn't come from a church-faring family or anything," he says. "But that church had some damn good cookies."

"And they had Diana teaching piano lessons."

"Exactly." He gives a shake of his head. "The church was quiet. There wasn't any yelling. And when Diana sat beside me, her chest would brush my arm every time she leaned in to show me finger positions and scales and . . ."

"And so you asked her to show you again and again."

"I did."

"And you fell in love with the piano."

"More like I fell in love with her and the attention she gave me because I had a knack for it."

"You were good."

"I was good. I could listen to a song or series of notes and play it back without needing sheet music or practice."

"That's incredible."

"I was fortunate to have that knack. The more people I meet in the industry, the more I realized it's rare. But yeah, learning piano wasn't sexy at the time, but it earned me my first kiss with Diana," he admits and grins. "And it came in handy."

"Clearly."

"Gizmo and I met Vince and Hawkin at a house party years later. They were talking about putting a band together. I convinced them they needed someone who could play the keyboard."

"And the rest is history?"

"Something like that." He shrugs. "Four guys from fucked-up homes figuring their own shit out. We gravitated toward each other. Became friends. Now are brothers."

"That's a cool story." I grab the pillow and hug it to my chest. "Thank you for sharing."

He reaches out and tugs on one of my bare feet. "Why don't you have a boyfriend?"

The question catches me off guard. "I mean, if you wanted to change the subject, you should be a little less subtle. There's no way I would've gotten the hint."

"Why beat around the bush?" But his hand is still on the top of my foot, and his thumb is still brushing absently back and forth. "So . . ."

"I had one. Once."

"Once?" He nudges me with his shoulder. "You have to give me more than that."

I pick at the hem of my sleeve. "His name was James. We grew up together. Family friends we'd vacation with. Barbecue with. We went from making mud pies in my mom's garden as kids to first kisses at high school dances. He was a good guy."

"I'd expect nothing less if you liked him."

My smile is bittersweet. All those memories I still hold dear and paint such a great light on my youth. Almost every memory of family vacations has him in it. Every birthday party or holiday growing up includes him.

"First love turned into college sweethearts. We made the long-distance thing work even though it was just across town. Never really discussed the future but knew we'd end up together. And then one day in our junior year of college, I got the call from his mom that he was gone."

I can still feel the memory so clearly. Can hear the emotion in his mom's voice. Can remember feeling like my heart had been ripped out and shattered.

"Gone, gone?" Rocket asks, his expression flooded with compassion.

"Gone, gone." I sigh. "It was a fluke thing. An undiagnosed congenital heart defect. He went to bed then just never woke up."

"I'm so sorry, Willow."

"It's okay. It was years ago."

"Years don't erase the hurt. They just dull the edges."

"Spoken like a songwriter," I tease.

His smile is cheerless. "And I imagine you swore off relationships after that for good reason."

"More like I swore off possible hurt from losing someone again."

"Valid." He toggles his head from side to side. "You threw yourself into school, then work. I bet it's way easier to get lost in that than put yourself out there again."

I raise a hand. "Guilty as charged."

"If you don't get attached, then you can't get hurt, right?" Truer words have never been spoken. "We're the same but different," he says.

"How so?"

"You don't date because you know how bad the heartbreak is. I feared getting to know Poppy because I know how bad the heartbreak is when a parent lets you down." He takes another sip. "The same, but different."

"The same but different," I repeat. "Is that your excuse why you don't have someone? Or I guess I should say many someones?"

He chuckles. "My life is chaotic. What you're seeing now—me being at home, the quiet, the calm—it's the exception, not the rule. The rest of the time, it's press and performances and hotels and flights and no sleep and running on caffeine."

"And whiskey and women galore," I say with an infused cheer.

He looks at me while I berate myself for making a second comment about the abundant women in his life although, I've yet to see that side of him. I sound like a jealous lover when I have no right to feel that way.

"That comes with the territory," he says slowly. "*If I want it to.*"

I clear my throat. His hand on my foot feels like a brand now. Hot. Noticeable. Something I should pull away from yet I sit and welcome the burn.

"Does it bug you?" he asks.

"What?"

"My lifestyle. The stereotypes. *Your* suppositions."

I swallow. "Why should it?"

He shrugs, eyes on mine. "Because you seem pretty strait-laced."

"There's a difference between being strait-laced and thinking there needs to be something behind sleeping with someone simply because they're there."

"I'm thinking that's a dig, but I accept it." He looks down where his hand is on my foot before he slowly scrapes its way up my body. I never believed someone could fuck you with their eyes before, but I'm feeling well and thoroughly fucked right now. "Don't you ever do something just because it feels good, Willow?"

It's a loaded question and one that I feel right down to the apex of my thighs.

"I like to do a lot of things because they feel good." I straighten my back and try not to be offended.

"You're not selling that too well." He chuckles.

"No. I'm serious. Sometimes it's the holding out that makes it better in the long run. It's the wait. The anticipation. The going to piano lessons just so Diana Finklebottom or whatever her name is can brush her boob against you that makes it *that much more.*"

"So you're saying a guy like me doesn't appreciate anticipation?"

"I don't know. You tell me? *Do you?*"

"*Humph.*" He twists his lips, and his fingers trail beneath the hem of my joggers and up the back of my calf.

"I don't see someone like you ever accepting or wanting a guy like me."

Accepting him? Wanting him? My stomach twists.

But I don't say what I'm thinking—that I do want him, despite everything. Despite his past. Despite mine.

"We all pretend to be someone we're not," I murmur, not completely sure what I mean by the comment. "I mean, until we meet the right person."

The silence that follows is heavy, not uncomfortable, but thick with all the things I'm not certain either of us know to say.

"And who, Willow Adams, is it that you're pretending to be?" His voice is low and seductive. A challenge and an invitation.

He moves first with just a shift of his knee. Followed by a tilt of his head and a look that lingers.

"No one," I whisper once I'm able to find my voice.

His hand slides up to cup my face, his thumb rubbing back and forth over the line of my jaw. For a second, I forget to breathe. For a moment, I realize the burn his hand on my foot caused has nothing on the way my entire body feels right now. Ablaze.

Then he leans in. There's no hesitation on his part and just a stuttered breath on mine before he brushes his lips lightly against mine.

Once.

Twice.

Then the kiss delves deeper, coaxing something out of me I didn't know was still alive. It's not rushed. Not demanding. It's reverent. Intentional. Like he's waiting to see if I'll pull away.

I don't.

And I don't want to think about the dozen reasons I should.

The hunger is still there, stronger than the last time and stoked from the anticipation of this possibly happening again, but it's subtler. It's more controlled.

And I'm not sure if that intimidates or excites me.

My fingers reach for the hem of his shirt, fisting the soft cotton like I need something to hold on to. Like I need to feel his skin beneath to know this is real. That he's real.

But instead of letting me touch him, instead of allowing me to initiate the next steps of whatever this is, he pulls me closer, his hand finding mine and gently pressing it to his chest. Over his heart.

He pulls back just enough to whisper, "No. Just this."

I blink, startled. Breathless.

He sees it—the hurt—the flicker of doubt behind my eyes.

Like I'm not enough.

Like I'm not what he wants.

But then he smiles. Slow. Soft.

"Don't read into it," he murmurs as he tugs on my bottom lip. "Let's not pretend to be something we're not."

His thumb brushes over my knuckles.

"Just enjoy the moment," he says before slipping his tongue between my lips and deepening the kiss. "The anticipation."

And it makes me wonder. Is Rocket trying *not* to sleep with me? To keep this light?

Not necessarily because he doesn't want me . . . but so he doesn't need me?

Right now, I'm not sure which is more dangerous.

CHAPTER
twenty-one

Willow

Tap. Tap. Tap.

I groan and snuggle into the warmth of the bed beneath me. My sheets smell like Rocket. Somewhere in my fogged brain, I both recognize his scent and realize it's because his cologne rubbed off on me when we kissed last night.

I'm definitely not complaining about that.

Just as I doze back off, it happens again. *Tap. Tap. Tap.* Persistent. Soft but determined.

"Poppy . . ." I whisper, all but begging for a few more minutes of sleep. *Tap. Tap. Tap.*

Then I hear it. A giggle that's high-pitched and amused.

My brain struggles to wake, but thoughts start to connect, one after another. They start to make sense.

The bed is warm beneath me. Really warm. Too warm.

Wait. It's not the bed. It's the couch.

Rocket's couch.

And there's a heartbeat under my cheek.

My eyes blink open, and I come face to face with a black T-shirt and the faint scent of cedar and citrus and sin.

Sin?

I lift my head. Oh. *Oh.* Oooh!

I'm not just curled up on the couch. I'm curled up on Rocket.

Like, on top of him.

Like, my entire body is sprawled across his chest like he's a mattress made of rock star.

I'm definitely awake now. Like blood-pumping, body-heating, every-nerve-ending aware type of awake. It's not just the feel of him beneath me, but it's the tensing of his hand on my lower back pulling me into him when I go to move and his slight groan of protest.

I blink away the sunlight and startle when I see a pair of very curious green eyes about a foot from me. Poppy stands at the side of us, head tilted and if her expression is any indication, absolutely delighted.

"Oh shit," I whisper.

And then I move. Fast. Perhaps too fast because when I bolt upright, I forget about the concept of gravity and the coordination needed to *dismount* properly. My hand flies out to brace myself, only to land directly on Rocket's crotch.

Specifically . . . on the morning part of it. The very erect, very hard morning part of it.

I freeze. In his sleepy state, he grunts and adjusts his hips to grind his erection into my hand.

With a noncommittal sound, I launch myself off him like I've touched an open flame. Of course, that causes me to narrowly miss a giggling Poppy and end up colliding full-force with the coffee table. My shin slams into its edge, which causes me to hop on one foot and then fall in glorious fashion to the floor with a thump—ass up, face flat on the ground.

Before I can even hope to salvage any of my dignity, I feel Rocket's hands on my hips from behind and hear Poppy giggling so hard she snorts.

But even through the pain in my shin and my dignity in shambles, my body immediately heats as the feel of his thighs against my ass and his hands helping to move me to a seated position.

"Good morning." He chuckles a sleep-drugged rumble when our eyes meet for the first time. *Jesus.* The sight of him and that low, even voice of his that scrapes over my skin does things to my insides. "You all right?"

But I don't respond—can't—because his hand is sliding up my pant leg to check my shin.

"Willow?" he asks, causing me to look up from where I'm focused on his hand running over my skin and meet his eyes. Every neuron I have short-circuits, because God help me, all I can think about is last night.

The way he kissed me—slow and sinful and devastating. The way he held my hand to his chest and whispered, "Just this." The way that when the kissing ended, we just sat where we were with my head on his shoulder and talked about trivial things because it felt like neither of us wanted to leave the moment.

There was no rush to an end game—just time and well-focused attention that surprised me.

And right now, kneeling there between my knees, his palm brushing over my leg in that careful way that's anything but careful—he's giving me the exact same look he gave me last night.

Like he remembers.

Like he feels it too.

"Sorry. I'm fine. I'm good. I just went to get up and . . ." *And I all but wrapped my hand around your cock.*

Kill me now. Please. Because by the way he glances lazily down toward his lap, he knows exactly where my thoughts are. "Didn't think *it* would scare you that much."

"It's not *it*. I wasn't—I didn't mean to—" My cheeks heat. I try not to look at the very obvious issue below his sweatpants. Thankfully, the one shielded from Poppy, who's standing there with her hands over her mouth stifling her giggles.

"It's okay if you are," he says, that sheepish, sleep-drugged smile tilting up one corner of his mouth.

The bastard's glowing. Disheveled hair. Creased shirt. That scruff that's begging for my fingers to run over it. He looks like a man who could wreck you and then cook you breakfast.

And apparently, make you fall asleep on his chest like some idiot who forgot she has boundaries.

I press a hand to my face. "I'm fine. I'll be fine. You're"—I wave my hand in his direction as my cheeks burn even brighter—"clearly more than fine. I can't believe I fell asleep here. There. On you."

Rocket flashes a grin. "Can't blame you. I'm pretty comfortable."

Poppy giggles again and breaks the trance he has over me.

And then the guilt hits. Here I am thinking of Rocket and his dick and my hormones and neglecting the reason I'm here in the first place.

"Poppy," I say as she giggles again and points at Rocket's hair and how it's standing all over the place.

She points to "rock" and then says "*et*," before laughing. The kind of belly giggle that you can't help but smile at.

"Yeah, yeah," he says and then messes his hair up further. Poppy erupts in another fit. "You try sleeping with a human blanket on your chest." He glances at me and winks. "Not that I'm complaining one damn bit."

Oh God. I bury my face in my hands. "Please stop talking."

"Nope. I'm enjoying this too much."

"What about it exactly are you enjoying?" I ask as I pull Poppy into my lap out of reflex for a good morning hug.

She hugs me back and then bends over to look at my shin, giving me a clear line of sight to Rocket and his half-cocked grin. "Seeing you a little mussed up. The hair is down. I now know you're a good snuggler on top of being a great kisser. Guess there's something to be said for that anticipation, huh?"

"Rocket. You can't say that. Poppy can—"

"Hear me. I know. What's the big deal? We both like you. Why hide it?"

I stare at him and his casualness, my jaw lax and mind stuttering over how easy this seems for him.

What happened to the emotionally constipated man from a month ago?

And then something happens before I can respond to him. He stands abruptly and reaches for Poppy's hand. There are no words, no coaxing, no anything.

She takes it.

Just like that. No hesitation. No second-guessing. No wide-eyed uncertainty. Her small fingers wrap around his pointer finger.

"You hungry?" Rocket asks her. Her eyes grow wide, and she giggles before looking back at me to make sure it's okay she goes with him.

I nod and then freeze in place, shin still smarting but heart swelling.

Because this? This is the first time he's taken to her all on his own. To say it wrecks me is an understatement. To say it's *everything* is an even bigger one.

I stay where I am and watch the two of them.

He's barefoot, shirt wrinkled, and hair's a mess. She's wild curls, pink frills, and a wide grin. Poppy is still giggling as she twirls under their joined hands like it's a game only she understands.

And then Rocket looks down at her with a soft, crooked smile.

His guard is down. His walls are gone. And I let myself stare. Let myself take it in. Because I've never seen anything so beautiful in my life.

He glances back at me.

"I don't mind you looking," he says, voice amused. "I don't mind you touching, either."

I choke on air and start coughing.

He winks. "Just next time, maybe give a guy some warning so I can ensure I'm at tip-top form."

My face might never recover from this shade of red.

He makes a show of lifting Poppy up onto the counter before looking my way and saying a little quieter and a bit more seriously, "I like you, Willow Adams."

I blink, and my breath burns in my chest as I lift my eyebrows in response. "That's kind of a new thing for me."

The world tilts because he's not joking. Not deflecting. Not putting on a show. I've gotten to know him well enough to know that he means it.

He turns to Poppy. "How about pancakes, Popstar? I have no fuc—freaking clue how to make them. They'll probably taste like crap, but we'll try." He moves toward the cupboards and then turns back to look at her while I smile at the new nickname he's given her. "Oh, and I know I'm not supposed to cuss. It's a vice. I'll work on not cussing if you work on talking to me, okay?" He holds out a hand to shake hers.

She looks at it, then takes it and shakes it with a definitive nod.

"Okay," he says. "Now let's get those pancakes burning."

He does a little dance that has her clapping her hands together, and all I can do is sit where I am and stare, reeling as I think of last night. The kiss. The way he held my hand to his chest. *Just this.*

And now this morning—with his daughter. With me.

And I know.

I'm fucked.

Well and truly, absolutely fucked.

CHAPTER
twenty-two

Rocket

THE SUN IS SETTING, THE CREW IS WORKING AT A SNAIL'S FUCKING PACE, and the guy running the auger keeps glancing at me like I'm going to sign his ass to a record label. Normally I don't supervise shit like this, but since we're off tour, the bands' personal assistants were given the first month off, and this is on me.

Plus? This is something I want to do myself, like a dad who has his shit together.

Newsflash. I don't.

At least that was my thought until these guys started dragging ass and taking twice as long as I was promised.

How hard is it to core some holes in the concrete and slip those tiny posts for the child fence into them?

My cell is tucked between my shoulder and ear while I move one of their rusted drill bits off the cushion of my patio furniture. Sandra drones on in her clipped tone about power of attorney and rights and who the fuck knows what else because as usual, I stopped listening ten minutes ago.

"You've stopped listening, haven't you?" she asks.

"Of course not. I never tune out."

Her laugh is rich and throaty and sounds like she's upped her occasional cigarette to several packs a day. "You forget how long you've been my client."

"Yeah. Yeah." I roll my eyes and move to pick up a piece of plastic trash that has fallen out of one of the boxes the workers have opened.

"So, how's it going? How's dad life?" Her tone is cautious. Searching.

"It's good. Better. Poppy's adjusting well and getting more comfortable with . . . all the changes. Willow's keeping everything under control."

"That's good. Great. And how are you feeling about it all?"

Memories of the past four weeks flash through my head. It feels like forever and just a minute—but the moments flicker like a slideshow through my head. Poppy giggling on the kitchen counter the other morning and painting with pancake batter on the kitchen counter. Her on a tricycle on the back grass, crashing into the cones I set up for a racecourse. Stacking blocks up as high as we could before I used my head to ram them and knock them down—just so I could hear that belly giggle over and over. The memories are starting to stack up, and the fact that there are some amazing ones causes my chest to ache in the best way. I smile. "I'm slowly adjusting. It's a big life change that I'm figuring out." I wave to the contractors as they say goodnight and head home. "You got any idea what Olivia's parents are thinking? You don't just call without a reason. Are they going push this?"

There's a pause on the line. I'm not going to like what comes next.

"I'm not certain yet, but my gut tells me that we need to start preparing for it. Testimonials from family and friends, people who know how you are with kids."

My stomach tightens, and I bark out a dry laugh. "That might be tough because I've never exactly been around kids before. Not until"—I glance toward the back door—"now."

"You have your bandmates and their kids. You've spent time with them, and no doubt they'll vouch for you."

"Exactly. That means it won't hold any weight because they're expected to vouch for me."

"What about the nanny?"

"Nanny?" I repeat the word like it's foreign because I realize I'm staring right at Willow, and every goddamn coherent thought I had seconds ago, vanishes.

Fuck me.

She's standing in the doorway, and she's not in the same athleisure outfits she's usually in with her trademark braid.

Not in the least.

The black dress she has on? It clings to every dip and curve and thought I shouldn't be having.

Her legs? They look a mile long in those heels, and I'm not ashamed to say I have immediate thoughts about what they'd look like digging into my ass as I fuck her.

Her lips? They're painted a sinful shade of red, and the way she looks at me says she doesn't have a shred of regret in her choices.

"Rocket? You still there?" Sandra asks.

"Uh, yeah . . . I have to go though. Something just came up." *Like my cock.* I hang up before she can ask why.

My dick aches. My fingers itch to touch. My lips beg to taste.

So much for anticipation.

This is full-blown torture. Like skintight, lipstick-wearing, legs-bared torture.

My swallow gets stuck over the desire lodged in my throat. "Going somewhere?"

Her slow crawl of a smile is a temptation in and of itself. "Yep. Tonight's my night off. Remember. We talked about it last week. I suggested you call over Quinlan or Hendrix if you couldn't handle it alone. It's on the schedule I gave you."

"Schedule?" *There was a schedule?*

"Yes. We talked—"

"We did." I shake my head. "I'm having a hard time thinking anything at the moment with you standing there looking like that."

"Oh."

The way those lips shock in a puckered O have even more thoughts springing up.

"I thought you said you were going out for coffee . . . or something." Like knitting. Or dog sitting. Or anything that doesn't involve that dress.

"Plans changed."

No shit. Plans can unchange real fucking quickly.

"So a book club meeting?" I ask.

She grins. "Not tonight. Tonight we're going out."

"Looking like that?"

I'm doing everything in my power to keep my eyes on hers, but they keep dragging lower.

That dress . . . *Jesus.*

She glances down, then runs her hands slowly down the front of her dress—right where my hands want to be.

"Why? Is something wrong with it? Did I get deodorant—"

"No. God, no." My voice breaks and gives a hint at what my insides feel like.

What's it feel like to want, Rock?

We stare at each other.

Everything I've been trying not to think about overwhelms my thoughts—the curve of her hips, the way her mouth tastes when she bites her lip, the way she said my name that night I almost—

No.

Stop.

"Wait." Her head startles, and she looks at the backyard while my eyes stay trained on hers. "You put in a pool fence?" she asks, her voice a mixture of surprise and gratitude.

"Yes. That's what the guys were doing back there. For Poppy." I grunt because fuck the pool fence. Especially when Willow's going out tonight looking like that.

Other guys are going to see her tonight. Guys who'll look at her and think the same sinful things I'm thinking right now. And they'll be allowed to do something about it while I'm over here trying to fucking prove anticipation is all that. I never want to hear the word again.

"Rocket." Her voice is soft, and tears well in her eyes. She either has no clue what I'm thinking, or she's a damn good actress. She motions to the pool fence. "That's the sweetest thing ever."

I shrug and swallow. "Poppy can come out here now. Play back here without you having to worry."

"Thank you."

I swear to God if she steps up and gives me a kiss on the cheek to thank me, that dress will be on the floor in seconds.

Walk toward me, Willow. Pretty. Please.

"Poppy is 'reading' books on the couch," she says. "Already fed and bathed. You know what to do next."

"Yep. Get the wiggles out with music. Brush teeth then whatever it is she wants to do before bedtime. I've got it covered, Wills."

I'd rather have you covered, though.

How can she seem so unfazed? So nonchalant? But the thought lasts for a split second as her own eyes drag down the length of me and no doubt see my cock straining against the seam of my jeans.

A smirk plays at the corner of her lips. She fucking knows she's turning me inside out, and she's amused.

"Who are you going with?" I ask it like it's casual, like I'm not dying inside.

"My friend."

"Friend?" If she says Bob or Steve, she's not leaving.

"Yes. Lily."

I breathe a little easier. "Where are you going?"

Willow chuckles. "What is this? Twenty questions?"

No, but it's about to be. Because if I think about her out there in that dress for one more second, I'm going to handcuff her to the goddamn kitchen table.

"Where to?"

Willow shrugs. "Lily makes the plans. I just go along with them."

Of course, Lily does. Of course, this is the one time she decides to be spontaneous and hot as fuck at the same time.

My palms sweat. My chest tightens. I want to be chill. I want to nod and let her go and act like this is no big deal, but instead, "Give me your phone."

"Why?" She laughs the word out.

I hold my hand out. "Just . . . give it."

She narrows her eyes but hands it over.

It only takes me a few seconds to do what I need to do. To make a clear but subtle statement about where my head—and where my cock hopes—to be at.

I hold it back out to her just as a car horn honks out front.

"Perfect timing," she says.

"You have fun," I lie.

"Bye, Pops," she calls over my shoulder into the family room. "I'll be back in a while like we talked about, but you'll be asleep. I'll give you more kisses when I get home."

Poppy's curls bounce as she nods, but she doesn't get up. She keeps turning the pages of her board book. In the moment, I'm not realizing it, but I know later it'll sink in that her lack of a reaction means she's comfortable with me.

"Maybe I should—"

"Go," I say. "We'll be fine.

"You sure?" She smiles, and the sight of it tugs on something inside me that I don't understand.

"I'm sure." Seconds ago, I was needing her to stay and now I'm begging her to go. *Get a grip, Caldwell.*

But before I can say anything more, the door closes behind her.

I stare after her like I've just been punched in the gut.

What the actual fuck is she doing to me?

I'm jealous—of the nanny. *The fucking nanny.*

I could snap my fingers and have a pool filled with naked women and get lost in any number of them. Women who wouldn't hesitate. Women who wouldn't ask me questions or talk about anticipation or wear goddamn dresses that make my whole body hurt.

But I don't want any of them.

I want her.

And that? That's the most dangerous part of all.

CHAPTER
twenty-three

Willow

I CLOSE THE DOOR BEHIND ME AND IMMEDIATELY REGRET EVERYTHING.

Because my skin's still tingling. My dress suddenly feels tighter. And Rocket? He looked at me like I was the problem and the solution all in one.

Holy hell.

That look. It wasn't just attraction. It was possession. Like he'd already played out every conceivable way to undress me in his head and was now choosing which one to act on.

And it did something to me. To my insides. Something violent and stupid and reckless.

God, I want to go back inside.

But I force myself toward the curb where Lily's waiting, engine idling, lip gloss shimmering, looking like she's about five seconds from screaming something wildly inappropriate out the window like she's sixteen again.

"Get your ass in the car, girl," she shouts out the open window, proving my hunch and our long-standing friendship true. "I was about to come knock on the door, hoping that fine-as-fuck man would open it and give me more fuel for my fiddle box."

"Fiddle box?" I slide into the passenger seat with a laugh, tugging down the hem of my dress and trying to reassemble my dignity.

"Yes. Fiddle box. Men have spank banks. I, the demure and modest woman that I am"—she rolls her eyes—"have a fiddle box."

"Jesus, Lil." I bark out a cough. "You're incorrigible."

Lily flashes me an unapologetic grin and slaps my thigh. "Don't act like you didn't look that good on purpose. You knew what you were doing."

"And what was I doing?" I play along, acting way more innocent than I am.

"No doubt he's in there having a heart attack right now over that dress. Or he might be in an ice-cold shower using you as his own spank bank."

I shake my head but then think about what Rocket was overseeing today.

The pool fence.

He put in a pool fence.

Not because someone made him. Not because it was convenient. *But because of Poppy.*

Because he thought of her.

Because he wants her safe.

Because he gets it.

And that's real. *That is sexy.* Well, not any sexier than the way he looked at me. The way the scrape of his eyes over my skin made me feel. The way his Adam's apple kept bobbing as if I'd personally offended him by looking this hot on my night off.

My grin's relentless at the thought. The anticipation war I waged?

I just won. Hands down. No question.

"Hello? Earth to Willow?"

"Sorry. I . . . I was distracted."

"No shit? Everything good with Poppy? She's not upset—"

"No. She's good. We've done practice runs with me going to the store a few times and talked about it repeatedly. She was completely fine with me leaving." More than I expected.

"So it's not Poppy. But your cheeks are flushed, and you're grinning like someone just licked your neck and if he did and you're holding out on me, so help me God, Willow—"

"No." I snort. "Nothing of the sort has happened." *Yet.* I squeeze my thighs together to abate the ache his looks just gave me and hope she doesn't notice.

She typically notices everything.

With one last look at the front door in hopes of a peek at Rocket, she puts the car in gear, and I breathe a sigh of relief that she's so preoccupied she didn't notice. "Do you have any idea how many gates and security booths I had to go through to get in here? Thank God you cleared me with security. This neighborhood is like Fort freaking Knox. I half expected a retinal scan back there."

I laugh and roll my eyes . . . and that's when I see it. The little green Venmo notification on my phone screen:

Payment Received: $300 from Rocket Caldwell.

Three hundred dollars? *What the hell?*

I can't open the app fast enough to see why or what or . . . again, *what the hell?*

Within seconds, it's open, and I startle when I see the note that went with the payment:

Memo: Because I'm the only one who'll be buying you drinks tonight.

I freeze and love that something deep down in me burns brightly. "Oh my God," I say, not really thinking.

Lily slams on the brakes. "What? What's wrong?"

"Look." I hold my phone out for her to see.

"Holy. Shit." Lily's eyes widen.

"Right?" I cough the word out in equal parts disbelief and excitement.

"Are you serious right now?"

"I don't even know what to say." I shake my head and reread the note for what feels like the tenth time already.

"Say nothing," she says and starts driving again. "You're not going back like you already want to do. And don't give me that look. It's written all over your face. Believe me. I get it. I'd be running back, stripping off my clothes, if I got that text. But we—"

"We?"

"Yes, we are going out. We are going to dance. We are going to flirt with hot guys. And the whole time, you'll know that Rocket freaking Caldwell is at home pining for you."

"That's ridiculous. He is not going to be pining for me. And who the hell says *pining* anymore anyway?"

"The woman who just read her best friend's phone and saw a man sent her money so no other man gets close to her tonight." She purses her lips and shakes her head. "Girl, that man wants you, and he wants you *bad*."

I look out the window at the quiet street, at the night stretching in front of us, and all I can think about is that Lily's right.

I already want to head back home and reap the rewards of what I've sown.

"Don't even think about it," she murmurs, reading my mind, and guns the engine out of the gate to the community.

What's Rocket doing right now? Pacing? Staring at his phone? Still hard from just looking at me?

God help me, I hope so.

And I really hope I survive this night without escaping out a club side door and sneaking my way back home.

CHAPTER
twenty-four

Rocket

I'M NOT GONNA LIE, I WAS COCKY AS FUCK THINKING I COULD DO THIS. Once I got over the image of Willow in that dress and remembered this was her night off, my first thought? How hard can this be? I've watched her for store runs. I've played with her while Willow went out for a run. This is just that, times a few hours.

Turns out I was wrong. This is way harder than I thought.

It's me. It's quiet. And there's a tiny person in front of me holding a raggedy stuffed bunny, blinking at me to ask where her entertainment is.

I should be used to this. I entertain for a living. But not little people and not someone who doesn't talk back.

Lord help me, I'm trying though.

"So, Popstar, what do you want to do now?" I ask. She blinks, tilts her head and chews on the ear of her bunny. "I mean, I know we're supposed to get the wiggles out, but how about I show you something that I love? Something that you've looked at but never gotten to touch?"

Her shoulders straighten. I have her attention now.

I hold out my hand for her, and when she takes it, we move to the front room where the piano is. I sit on the bench and pat my thigh. "C'mon." Her eyes widen to epic proportions. She's not supposed to touch this. "I'll show you."

She hesitates only a second before stepping forward, carefully climbing onto my lap like she's unsure whether I'm testing her and she'll be in trouble for taking the invite.

I move with slow, deliberate motions and settle her on my lap. Her body's small and warm and solid. Her curls tickle my chin.

"You want me to play something?" I ask.

Her head bobs, and I begin a slow but upbeat lullaby. I don't remember the name but I'm sure Diana Finkleman would be proud that I still remember it all these years later.

She moves to the sounds I create. Her body sways between my arms as I work the keys. When I finish, she claps and squeaks in excitement. In pure joy.

My smile's automatic. My heart's full that I can share this with her. That I can create this for her.

"Do you want to try?" I ask, and her nod is immediate. "Okay. Tap where I point."

Her fingers hit the first key and she jolts back almost as if she can't believe she did that.

"Good job. That was all you. Let's do it again."

And so we do. Key after key. We begin playing a jilted melody that lacks in finesse what it makes up in heart. She babbles sounds with it, showing me what her voice might sound like someday.

But her frustration comes too. She miss-hits keys and tenses up. The palm of her hand presses down and makes a jarring sound that causes her to grunt in irritation.

"It's okay, Pops. Daddy's got you," I say. Then freeze.

Poppy's fingers aren't moving anymore. She turns slowly so that she can look up at me at the same time I realize what I just said.

Our eyes lock. Hold.

Her eyebrows narrow. Question.

She points at me and I nod, the words barely audible when I find them again. "Yes. I'm your daddy."

Her lips twist as she studies me. As she reaches up a hand and runs it down the side of my face—almost as if touching is believing—before pulling it back. And then she gives me the slightest of nods, acceptance without question, before pointing to the piano keys and asking me to show her again.

I'm not sure how long it takes for me to exhale the breath I'm holding, but when I do, the world is still spinning. My heart's still beating. And nothing's really changed other than Poppy knows, and she didn't scream and cry over it.

She hits a few more. Soft. Then louder.

She giggles.

It's the first sound I've heard from her all day.

And it wrecks me in the best damn way.

"You're a natural," I tell her. "Better watch out. I might lose my job."

She presses three keys at once. It sounds like chaos. Beautiful, innocent chaos.

I press a few notes of my own. A simple little melody, nothing serious. She watches my hands, then tries to copy them with hers. She gets it all wrong, and we both laugh—mine quiet, hers hidden in the crinkle of her eyes.

"Wanna make up a song?" I ask. "Just you and me?"

She nods, curls bouncing.

So we do.

It's nonsense and messy and too many sharps and flats.

But it's ours.

And right now, it's exactly what we need. It's perfect.

But that perfection doesn't hold us over until bedtime. We build blocks simply so I can hear her laughter.

Every time I get my tower to a certain height, she swings her arm and knocks it over. I react by falling back and flailing, which causes her to mimic me as she holds her belly that hurts from laughing so hard.

A smile tugs at the corners of my lips.

That sound—her laughter—is pure and wholesome, and I'll never tire of hearing it.

"You're a menace," I say as I prop myself up on my elbows and exaggerate how tired I am from building and it being knocked over.

She just laughs and throws the red block again. When it hits me on the shoulder, I flop back again and earn more giggles.

I lay on my back with my eyes closed and just soak in the sound. This might be the weirdest version of happiness I've ever known.

But it doesn't last.

Twenty minutes later, just like the piano, the block game has worn itself out. We've read the stack of books and drunk the juice she told me she wanted, which is now in her hand despite her teeth already being brushed, is no longer what she wants.

Enter the meltdown phase.

A big one—by my standards anyway.

She's on the floor, little hands balled into fists, tears streaking down her cheeks. It doesn't take long for that to lead to foot stomping followed by rocking back and forth on the ground hysterics.

Over what? I have no idea but isn't that par for the course?

I'm at a loss—for what to say. For what to do. For . . . fucking anything.

"Hey, hey. No. Poppy, it's okay."

But it's not. She's sobbing now. Loud, choked sounds fill the room. The kind that rips straight through you and makes you feel helpless.

I panic.

Do I call someone? Willow's out of the picture. She deserves her night off, and I refuse to let her know I can't handle it.

One of the bandmates' wives—Quinlan? Bristol? Hendrix?

I reach for my phone and grip it tightly as the sobbing gets louder, but I stop myself from calling someone for help.

Wait. What was that thing? The thing the nurse told Hawkin's wife when I went to visit them right after they'd had their first baby?

Skin-to-skin. Skin-on-skin? That's a thing, right?

For babies. For newborns. But I'm fucking desperate here, and I'll try it. It can't hurt. I strip my shirt over my head as Poppy wails louder.

I pick up her squirming body, then sit down on the couch and lift her into my lap.

She fights it for a second, hands hit and feet kick as I hold her close.

This isn't going to work. But just as helplessness kicks in, her little hand flattens against my chest. She lifts her head and pauses, brow furrowed and attention distracted when she sees the ink on my chest.

This is what's going to save the day for me? My tattoos? *Fucking figures.*

She begins tracing the intricate designs. Her touch is slow and curious as her sobs subside to sniffles and silent hitches of her shoulders. She stops every few seconds and looks closer at one of the designs as if she's trying to figure out the colors or where to trace next, her eyes widening and lips moving as she whispers to herself in words only she understands.

Not sure what else to do, I begin to sing and am rewarded instantly with her flattening her palm first and then her cheek against my chest as she feels the vibrations. She looks up at me and smiles—her eyes red and cheeks splotchy—but it's still a smile. I'll take it.

We sit like this for some time, me singing silly verses of BENT songs—in the best of my ability lullaby form—and her tracing my tattoos. With each minute that passes, her breathing begins to even out, and her hand begins to slow. She curls up against my chest, her tiny body fitting into mine like she's always belonged there.

"Daddy." I swear she whispers it but when I look down at her, she's sound asleep.

Did I hear that? Did I wish it into existence? I don't know, but I love the warmth that rushes through me, even at the thought of her saying it.

So I just sit here with one arm wrapped around her and the other stroking her back.

I breathe in everything about my daughter—the scent of her shampoo, the weight of her head against my chest, the soft twitching as she falls asleep.

It settles something in my chest I didn't know was out of place until now.

It makes up my mind for me like I ever had a choice.

I want to earn the right to be her dad.

Not because I have no choice.

Not because the court says I have to be.

But because she's mine.

CHAPTER
twenty-five

THE WORLD SPINS A LITTLE MORE OFF-KEY AS I SHUT LILY'S CAR DOOR behind me and make my way up the walkway.

I'm not drunk, but just warm. Floaty. In that lovely buzz that lowers your guard and makes you believe your own ridiculous thoughts.

Like the one where I remember thinking Rocket wanted me.

Yeah. Right.

I press my hand against the front door to steady myself. The short respite has every second of the past four hours replaying through my head. The time spent trying to enjoy myself but thinking about Rocket instead.

There were plenty of guys paying attention to me. Flirty glances, dirty jokes, and attempts at buying drinks, but every one of them fell flat.

And annoyingly, I know it's because none of them were *him*.

None of them looked at me like I was the only woman in the room. None of them stared at my mouth like they were starving.

None of them were Rocket fucking Caldwell.

"A good night's sleep will fix it," I mutter to myself as I unlock the front door.

That or a toe-curling, mind-bending orgasm.

I shut the door as quietly as possible and slip off my shoes so they don't click on the floor and make too much noise. I don't make it five steps into the great room before I stop.

Because I see them.

Rocket on the couch, shirtless and hair tousled, with his head tilted back, his eyes closed, and one arm wrapped around her. And then there's Poppy, curled up on his chest with her hand splayed over his heart like it belongs there.

My heart cracks open.

He's never looked sexier and for reasons way beyond what he physically looks like. It's not lust I feel. It's a deeper sensation that I don't have a name for yet. It's terrifying and invigorating.

I struggle to find a breath and fear that if I look away, when I look back, the sight of them together will be gone. Like this is some weird dream that will disappear.

But it doesn't. Not when Rocket stirs and blinks awake slowly. He yawns quietly as his eyes find mine, and a sluggish smile plays on his lips.

"You're home early."

Early? I guess by *his* standards, midnight is early, but not for me.

"Did you have a good time?" he asks.

"Yes." It's partially true. I had a good time because I was with Lily, but my thoughts were here. On him. "No complaints." I set my heels down and take a step closer. "Looks like you two got along."

He shifts slightly, careful not to jostle her. "It wasn't all smooth sailing. We struggled to communicate for a bit, had some tantrums, played some piano, but we worked it out."

I smile. "You most definitely did."

He stands carefully with Poppy still curled against him. The sight staggers me. It's the first time I've seen him carry her. The first time I've seen her cherubic curls and chubby cheeks pressed against his inked skin. And the first time I've seen him show such tenderness with her.

It's disarming. It's sexy.

"Let me go tuck her in," he says quietly and disappears down the hallway to her bedroom.

I follow him until the dark hallway engulfs him and then lean on the kitchen island, swaying slightly, my buzz mixing with adrenaline and want.

I feel brave. Hell, I feel dangerous.

I was just surrounded by attractive, eligible men, and yet the only one I wanted to come home to is in the other room, putting his daughter to bed—shirtless, inked, and unknowingly shattering every norm I've ever held tight.

You never crush on your boss.

You never want your charge's dad.

You never cross that line.

Oblivious to my thoughts, Rocket walks back into the kitchen a minute later, rubbing the back of his neck. "How was your night?" he asks as he busies himself doing nothing of significance in the kitchen.

I don't respond until he lifts his eyes and meets mine. "You already asked. I already answered. I said it was fine."

He lifts his brows and murmurs, "Hmm."

"Hmm?" I repeat. He looks ridiculously sexy right now. Rumpled, a little tired, muscles flexed as he shoves his hands in his pockets, and tattoos shifting with every move. "What does 'hmm' mean?"

He takes a step closer, that lazy confidence radiating off him again, except this time it's edged with something darker. Hungrier.

Guess I'm not the only one who wants more.

"*Hmm* as in I think you had one of two plans tonight."

"Plans?"

"Yeah. Plans. Either you orchestrated tonight to force me to bond with Poppy . . ." He toggles his head from side to side. "Or to make me jealous."

"Why would I try to make you jealous?" The last word hitches as he steps closer.

His smile is lopsided. Cocky. "Because I want you. Because I haven't stopped wanting you."

Hello, Rocket. And hello to that sweet ache between my thighs.

"Good," I state and lift a lone brow in challenge.

He leans in, eyes locked on mine. "Good? I never figured you for a tease, Wills."

"Maybe I'm not teasing. Maybe it's mutual. Maybe I want you just as much."

And that's all it takes.

One challenging statement. One tilt of my head. One lift of my chin.

He reaches out, his hands sliding to my hips and pulling me flush against him in one sharp, fluid motion.

"Is that so?" he asks, gravel straining his voice.

I don't answer—can't—because his mouth is on mine.

His kiss is demanding—hungry, consuming, perfect—with his lips parting mine, tongue brushing deep, hands gripping me like he's starved and I'm the only thing on the menu.

My muted, broken moan is all it takes.

He picks me up without warning, one arm under my ass as my legs lock around him, and our lips meet to take more.

"Rock—"

"You planned this, didn't you?" he asks, his breath warm as his lips brush against my neck.

My chuckle turns into a moan as I lean back and meet his eyes. "If I say yes, will you shut up and kiss me again?"

He flashes a wicked grin. "You're damn right I will. That and a hell of a lot more."

And then he's carrying me down the hallway into his bedroom.

CHAPTER
twenty-six

M Y BODY IGNITES—EVERY MUSCLE, EVERY NERVE ENDING, EVERY INCH of skin aflame—as our lips burn, tongues dance, and teeth graze.

This fierce desire is new to me. Maybe it's the liquid courage, maybe it's the weeks of cat and mouse between us—the kisses with no end game, the desire that was one long slow burn—and maybe it's the knowledge that all of that is coming to a head in the most deliriously delicious way.

We shed our clothes between kisses. A whirlwind of fabric—my dress, his pants—hands roaming as we do.

I trail my hands down his broad shoulders to the ridges of his abs and slip them beneath the waistband of his boxers. He's hot and hard and pulses against my hand instantly.

His groan is all I need to hear. The only confirmation I need to know we're both all in on this. That we're both desperate for more than a kiss, for more than a touch.

My fingers twist in his hair as he stoops down so his tongue can circle and lips close over my nipple. He sucks, and the combination of the heat of his mouth and the pressure of his touch has me writhing beneath his touch. Begging for more. Needing more.

"Rock," I moan. It's a soft plea that only intensifies as he hooks his fingers in the fabric of my panties and pulls them to the side. I'm already wet, already slick for his touch. And when the pads of his fingers slide between my slit and find me ready for him, his guttural groan melds with my sharp inhale.

"Do you know how long I've waited for this moment?" he murmurs, kissing up to my neck. I can't answer—my focus is on his hair between my fingers, the warmth of his breath, and the way he guides my leg up on the bed so that he can tuck his fingers inside me.

My breath catches, and my body melts into him. Into his touch and the sensations they evoke. The way he pulls his fingers out and trails them to my clit, rubbing gentle circles there. I press my hips into him, begging for more friction and the sparks that ignite with each touch.

His lips find mine again. "You didn't answer, Wills," he growls. "Do you know?"

My mind races, consumed by how perfectly his finger hits my most sensitive spot.

"That first night in the kitchen. You in that tank top with your nipples against the fabric. Do you know how badly I wanted to lift you onto the counter and fuck you into oblivion? It was so much easier thinking about that, obsessing over that than the reason you were actually here."

He tugs my hair, tilting my head back so I meet his eyes. My mouth falls open, neck exposed.

"Then that black fucking bathing suit. Modest but fuck if it wasn't the biggest cock tease in the world." He scrapes his teeth up the line of my neck, and my body bucks from the contrasting sensations. "You were my escape from day one. Thinking about you. Hating myself for thinking about you. Wanting you and hating myself for wanting you."

I gasp as he pushes his fingers back inside me, as they prepare me for him.

"You were my obsession. My escape. A constant reminder of the changes that were here and at the same time tempting me with that damn fucking braid and smart fucking mouth."

His mouth finds mine again. His tongue mimics his fingers.

"Talk to me. Tell me you wanted this just as bad. Tell me you thought about me as much as I did you." His words zing through me like electricity. Their truth even more so.

Held by my hair, there's nowhere to hide—only the ragged rasp of my breath and the slick, rhythmic sound of his fingers in me.

I've never been this turned on in my life, and it's not just from his fingers and lips, but from his words. His confessions. Knowing how much he's desired me this whole time.

He tugs on my bottom lip with his teeth. "Now tell me what you want, Wills."

I draw a steadying breath, stare back at him, and speak for the first time. "You, Rocket. I want you—inside me, on me, fucking me, drowning in me."

His approving chuckle rumbles as he kisses me. "Nanny has a mouth on her."

There's something about the way he says it. The toying, playful way when his cock is hard against me and his fingers are filling me that make them seem so much . . . more.

Before I can think too hard over any of it, he strips off his boxers with his free hand—his erection springs free, perfect and hard—but his dark eyes hold me more.

He watches me take it in, and I dart my tongue out to lick my bottom lip. He's a sight for sore eyes. Ridged muscles colored with intricate ink. Broad shoulders narrowing down to trim hips, strong thighs, and a sizable cock in between.

My mouth waters looking at him. At anticipating what he'll feel like.

"These weeks have been endless foreplay, Wills. I should be pushing you down and fucking you into oblivion but Christ, woman, I want this to last. Need this to last."

I curl my hand around his cock and begin to stroke him. Slow, long slides of my hand over its soft, velvety skin. His shoulders tense, his head falls back, and his lips call out my name.

"I dreamed about this. About you." His voice is like sandpaper, and his words have heat creeping into my cheeks. But he cups my face, thumb stroking my jaw. "Don't blush. Not with me."

He withdraws his fingers and traces the curve of my ass before turning me around slowly and unclasping my bra. My breath hitches at his lips grazing my shoulder. "Yes?" he asks.

"Yes."

He pats my ass and steps back. "Now crawl onto that bed and think how you want to be fucked." I turn to see him reaching for a condom out of his nightstand. "Soft? Slow? Testing my restraint?" I sit on the edge of the bed as he steps into the moonlight. He rips open the foil packet and then begins to roll the condom on as I watch, legs spreading willingly as I scoot back. "Or hard, fast, so deep you feel me in your stomach?" My mouth is dry, thighs ache. He crawls on the bed between my thighs and taps his cock against me. "Christ, Wills, that pussy of yours is the prettiest color of pink." He runs one hand up my thigh. "Stunning. Sexy. Do you taste as good as you look?"

Before I can answer, he's between my legs again, hands on my thighs, mouth on me. His guttural groan vibrates inside me as his tongue and fingers delve into me, mastering every slick slide of it.

His stubble scrapes my inner thighs. His warmth envelops me, and his hands brace my legs open. His tongue plunges.

I moan as each flick of his tongue has me coiling tighter. I clutch the sheets and dig my heels in as he quickens the motions—fingers and tongue in a relentless rhythm.

"Don't stop," I moan, hands fisting in his hair, back arching off the bed.

"Come for me, Wills," he murmurs, and my hips buck against his lips.

"I want you to fuck me."

"Not yet, baby. Not until you do this for me," he says as the bed shakes, and as he finger-fucks me into my climax.

"Oh. My. God." My orgasm rips through me. It's like a jolt of lightning—searing, white-hot heat that holds me hostage and owns my every reaction—trembling, pulsing, breath-robbing.

But he kisses me through its waves as it surges again and then ebbs back down.

He watches me. Close up. Unfiltered. His eyes drag over me as my arousal glistens on his chin and mouth. "You're a drug, you know that?" He gently tugs on my bottom lip, and my eyes flash open. "Quiet and sleepy. Drag me along and toy with me with tastes of what you have to offer, and then you go out looking like this, tasting like this . . . begging me to fuck you."

"Pretty please."

He cups one of my breasts, his thumb flicking over my pebbled nipple while his mouth closes around the other one. I squirm beneath his touch, my body still hypersensitive from my orgasm. My squirming only serves to grind my thigh against the thickness of his cock.

"Atta girl. Tell me what you want again." His smile is dangerous. Appealing. Only for me.

My tongue delves into his mouth as my hands grip the back of his neck. "You. Now. Or I could always go back to the club to find someone—"

He silences me with a kiss, then slides in with a single, slow sweep. "Think you can take it all?" he challenges. "I know you can." He thrusts deeper and groans, "More?"

I'm stretched beyond full yet desperate for more. "More," I moan.

He pushes a fraction farther. "There you go, Wills. There's my girl taking me all in."

My eyes roll back, and my lips part as the delicious burn intensifies. "Yes," I gasp. "Please, yes."

He withdraws, drenched in my arousal—the sound of it filling the room—then lifts my hips to accommodate another thrust. Then another. Each one stronger than the last. Each one dragging over nerves and gloriously fulfilling needs. *Who knew I wanted that?*

Sensations overload. The crest of his cock hitting that rough patch of nerves inside. The way his thumb adds the perfect friction to my clit. The feel of his strong thighs between mine. The absolute sexiness of his expression as he watches himself bury himself to the hilt inside of me.

I drown in the feel of it all. I welcome it. I revel in the sensations.

But they're too much and not enough all at the same time. I want it to last but need it to hurry up.

"Please," I beg.

He grips my neck and pulls me into a moan-fueled kiss that only pushes him deeper. "I need more," I whisper. He obliges by fucking me harder, faster—our bodies slapping, his fingers digging into my hips, driving us both toward the edge.

The orgasm crashes through me with reckless abandon. There's no other way to describe the blissful devastation it wreaks on my every muscle and nerve. My toes curl, legs shake, and pussy pulses as I cry out.

Yet he doesn't stop, doesn't pause this time around because he's too busy chasing his own climax.

"Fuck," he cries out as his hips jerk and body bucks. As his hands grip and eyes hold mine.

As the line has undoubtedly and pleasurably been crossed.

CHAPTER
twenty-seven

Rocket

I WAKE UP SLOWLY.

Not from exhaustion. No, although my body feels used in all the best kinds of ways, but rather from replaying last night in my mind.

Willow standing before me, naked with those eyes of hers daring me to lose control.

The strangled moan she emitted as I pushed into her.

The sting of her teeth when she sank them into my shoulder as she came.

There was nothing calm about what happened between us. No careful seduction, no finesse.

It was hot and frantic and needy in a way that sex hasn't been for me in . . . maybe ever.

Sex is usually pleasure. A guaranteed win. A reprieve and a reward.

But this? With Willow? Last night was hunger. Connection. Anticipation as a definite escape, but that held more meaning than normal.

And I'm not quite sure what to make of it. But one surefire way not to is to do it again.

My chuckle is sluggish as I roll over, ready to pull her into me again. Ready to lose myself in her again . . . except when I reach out, the bed's empty.

No warm body. No long hair tangled on my pillow. Just the comforter folded back and an empty spot where she was.

Shit.

I sit up slowly, blinking against the sunlight bleeding through the curtain, and scrub a hand over my face.

I shouldn't care. This is a classic Rocket Caldwell move—be gone in the morning to avoid attachment.

And yet . . . *fuck*. Where is she?

I mean we had sex. Great sex. Memorable—even if I'm still thinking about it.

Does she regret it? Is she already chalking it up to being buzzed? The fact that she lives here and can't leave without seeing me again?

But I don't take her as a one-night stand girl.

Yet the bed is empty. Her clothes are gone.

And why the hell does that bug me?

But before I can spiral further, my bedroom door creaks open . . . and there she is.

Wearing my T-shirt, hair a mess, legs bare, carrying two mugs of coffee, and a smug-ass look on her face.

My dick instantly salutes the situation.

But when she meets my gaze, her eyes narrow, and her lips pinch. "You thought I did the walk of shame back to my bedroom."

"Why would I think that?" I play it off.

"You did, didn't you?" She looks bewildered as she holds out a coffee mug to me.

"Well, it doesn't do a man's ego a lot of good when he wakes up and the woman he wants is gone."

"Uh-huh." She sits on the edge of the bed, her knee bent, giving me a hint of what I want just beneath. "Because you've never snuck out in the middle of the night so you don't have to wake up to whoever you just spent the night with?" A smile toys at the corner of her mouth. "Please, correct me if I'm wrong."

I smirk, leaning back on my elbows as my eyes take in her nipples pressing against my shirt and then dip lower. "I don't do the walk of shame," I say playfully.

"Neither do I."

"Says the woman wearing the sex shirt she ripped off me last night."

"You weren't wearing a shirt when I got home." Her eyes scrape down my chest, and her chest hitches. "That's part of the reason we're sitting here like this right now."

"That's all it takes with you? No shirt and you're ready to go?"

"It did last night." She fights a smile. "Shirt was on the dresser. Didn't think you'd mind if I borrowed it."

"By all means—I'm definitely not complaining."

She takes a sip of her coffee like she didn't hear that, but her cheeks go pink.

It's fucking hot.

She dips her eyes down toward her coffee and studies it like it's one of her textbooks. Why do I get the feeling that I'm about to get the straight-and-narrow Willow?

"Wills?"

"Hmm?"

"Just say it."

Her eyes flicker up to me and then back to her coffee. "I get that this could be . . . awkward. You know, since we slept together—"

"We did?" I tease.

"And that I live here. That I work for you. Like . . . I understand if this is just a one-time thing and you want—"

"Did you rehearse this in your head while you were making coffee?"

"Maybe." She sighs. "Maybe even before I got up."

I chuckle. "Then clearly I didn't fuck you properly if you were up that early and not exhausted."

She nearly chokes on her coffee, coughing into the rim of the mug.

I grin like an idiot. That comment definitely got under her skin—and not in the way I did last night. But still . . .

What the fuck am I even doing, saying this shit?

I've never lived with a woman I've slept with. Never had coffee or had the morning-after banter with someone walking around my house in my shirt.

This is a whole new level of domestic chaos I wasn't prepared for.

"Hey." I reach out and rub a hand over her knee and squeeze. "How about we just go along with whatever happens, huh?"

She studies me over the top of her mug. Her expression is quiet, unreadable, and for a second, I think she's going to backpedal—gladly take the walk of shame and not look back. *To her room.*

"You paid for my drinks last night."

Interesting. Where is she going with this? I nod. "I did."

"Were you trying to get me drunk?"

I chuckle and lean toward her, brushing my fingers across the hem of her shirt—er, my shirt—grazing her thigh. Goosebumps chase over her skin.

"The thought of any man touching you was enough to drive me crazy. But your theory works too."

She laughs, and damn, that sound and the way her tits jiggle against the fabric could wreck me if I let it.

She sets her mug down on the nightstand and then takes mine and does the same before I even get to enjoy it.

She's freeing our hands.

Does that mean morning sex? *Fuck.* I'm here for it. I'm already ready for it. I'm—

"So, fine. Yes, to let's just see how it goes, but we need to lay some ground rules—"

I groan and flop back on the bed, dragging the sheets over my face. Not exactly what I had in mind. "Strait-laced, rule-loving Willow is back. I knew it. Just when I was starting to like you."

She grins and runs a fingertip up the sheet that's covering my thigh. My cock bobs beneath the thin fabric. She lifts her eyebrows and meets my eyes. "You do like me."

"Don't push it."

"But I can fuck it?" She crawls up to straddle my hips with zero hesitation and a wicked look in her eyes. Her bare thighs pin me down.

"Willow," I groan as she grinds over me and the sheet. I can feel the heat of her pussy. The wetness soaking through.

"You want to throw the rules out the window, Rock?"

"I do." She grinds. "Right now, I definitely do."

Her hands slide down my chest, fingers tickling the skin as her mouth stops just short of touching mine. "Guess you'll just have to convince me."

She presses her lips to mine as she grinds her hips again. We sink into the kiss. It's slow, deep—*hot*—scrambling all thoughts other than her. Now.

And just as I'm about to flip her over and do just that, Poppy's voice yells down the hall. It's a panicked sound—probably because she can't find one of us.

Willow freezes, and she drops her forehead to my chest. She groans but is already jumping off the bed.

"I'll go," I say.

"Not with that, you won't." She motions to my erection and scrubs a hand through her hair.

I watch her walk out the bedroom door. The sun halos around her, and her tanned legs move down the hallway until I can't see her anymore.

I stare at the ceiling and wonder how the hell my life got turned upside down by a nanny, a three-year-old, and a night like last night that was damn-fucking-fantastic.

Christ, Rocket. When did you get so soft?

CHAPTER
twenty-eight

Willow

It's almost disturbingly easy.

This morning after—well, more like the *night after*—our first time.

I thought there might be awkwardness that came with time and reflection after we both separated this morning to do our daily routines. I assumed Rocket—freewheeling, fly-by-the-seat-of-his-pants Rocket—would realize he just slept with the woman he lives with and now feels a tad trapped. And me, the overthinking, stress-case me, would mind-fuck what happened seven ways from Sunday so that all interactions would feel awkward and be laced with my unfounded panic.

What I didn't expect was this ease. This sense that nothing has changed and everything has simultaneously, but that, in and of itself, isn't a terrible thing. Or the texts that came randomly throughout the day from behind the soundproofed studio walls.

> Rocket: Poppy good today? How was your walk? Find any new bugs for her to squeal over?

Rocket: Stuck trying to figure lyrics out. Will be shut in here a while longer.

Rocket: Dinner together later?

I replay them in my head now as we move around the kitchen like we've done it a hundred times—like we've choreographed it naturally. I pull the veggies from the fridge just as Rocket slides a pan onto the stove. He steps back to grab silverware and trails a hand down the middle of my back on the way.

Not in a possessive way. Not overtly sexual.

Just . . . warm. Affectionate.

Which, honestly, throws me more than anything else could. I never took Rocket Caldwell to be an affectionate guy.

Maybe it's just because I live here. Maybe he's trying to make me feel comfortable.

And maybe you need to stop invalidating this moment, Willow, and just go the fuck along with it and see how it goes.

I glance at him as he opens the drawer for knives, humming something low under his breath—probably a melody he doesn't realize he's writing.

I shouldn't like this as much as I do. The easy rhythm. The casual glances. The comfort in the unforced silence.

It feels a little like playing house, *which sounds weird*. It sounds like I'm a crazed person who's planning a wedding and a future . . . but that's not what I'm talking about. There is this grown-up feel to it. A toddler sitting on the barstool playing with her plastic animal set that Quinlan got her. Rocket setting the table while I prep the vegetables.

It's not like we're pretending, but rather we're just enjoying the moment. The feeling.

"No. Just this. Don't read into it. Let's not pretend to be something we're not. Just enjoy the moment. The anticipation."

Those were his words, his advice, that night we kissed on the couch, and I think they're worth repeating right now.

Whatever this is, I like it . . . maybe a little too much.

"Smells good," he says, nodding toward the sizzling pan.

"Yeah, well. You'll change your mind once you taste it and realize I forgot the salt."

"I like bland food."

"You're lying."

"I am." He grins and bumps my hip with his.

Poppy's bunny is seated beside her like it's playing too. She glances up briefly as we laugh, then goes right back to her plastic figures.

She looks so . . . settled. Content.

"How'd the lyrics go?" I ask.

"Don't ask." He sighs and takes a bite of the carrot stick in his hand. The snap of it is so loud Poppy laughs. "It's a frustrating process."

"I can't imagine. I'm not creative in the least."

"No, but you're smart. Like that master's you're going to get."

"Pulled that one from thin air," I say around a chuckle.

"You talked about it in your sleep."

"What? I did?" I glance over to Poppy and then back.

Rocket nods. "Yep. You did. It was a fascinating conversation but then left me wondering if I uh . . . did my *job* properly since you were still coherent."

I stand there, hands at my sides, cheeks flushing, and stare at him like he's crazy. "I don't even know what to say."

"That and you let me know I need to eat more vegetables." He snaps the carrot again when he bites it.

I smile. "That tracks."

He passes by again and this time brushes a knuckle down the curve of my arm. It's the gentlest touch, but it echoes long after he moves past me.

"I can't believe the tour is closing in," I say, trying to keep my voice light. "I feel like we're just settling into this routine."

His eyes flick to mine, and I swear there's something in them—regret maybe. Or dismay. He doesn't answer right away.

"It's always a mix of excitement and dread before we leave. We've done it enough times over the years that we don't think twice about it. It just hits differently this time around with"—he glances toward Poppy and then back to me—"everything."

"Understandably."

Instead, he leans against the counter and studies me for a beat. I hold his stare, curious about what's going on behind those eyes of his.

"I think she said *Daddy* last night," he whispers.

My head whips toward him so fast I nearly drop the spatula. "She did?" I don't know what's more overwhelming, the fact that she spoke or the word she chose to speak. "What?" I glance Poppy's way. Her head's still down, seemingly oblivious to this conversation. "How?"

He nods slowly, his expression stoic but the corners of his mouth turning up. "We were playing on the piano together—she's wicked talented, by the way. A pop star in the making, right Popstar?"

Poppy doesn't look up, just waves him off with one hand like *please, I'm playing.*

Rocket grins, moves toward her, and kisses the top of her head. He moves back to stand beside me, resting his hips against the island so that his back is to her. He keeps his voice low when he talks. "Anyway, I absently said that "Daddy's got you." I didn't make it weird. Just said it. She didn't flinch. She just looked up to meet my eyes to make sure I said what she thought I said before nodding and going back to the song we were making."

I wish I could've seen that moment. Been a fly on the wall in the room with them, but I also kind of love that it's something that belongs only to them.

"There was an epic meltdown shortly after," he adds and chuckles, pulling the plates out of the cupboard. "She got tired, probably overstimulated from the change in routine. It took me a while to figure out what to do, but I did. Got her calmed by tracing my tattoos—hence the lack of a shirt." He flashes me a suggestive grin. "And just as she was falling asleep, I swear I heard her whisper it."

My chest tightens. "Really?"

"Or maybe I didn't hear it." He shrugs. "It was so soft, almost like she didn't mean to. But I swear it was there."

He doesn't look at me, just watches the chicken sizzle in the pan, and I wonder what that felt like for him. I don't have to wonder long because he looks back over to me, our gazes holding, and says, "It was cool."

The pride in his expression guts me. So does the surprise and the vulnerability tucked in behind it, like he's still trying to believe he deserves the title she gave him.

And as I watch him now—this man who spent years living loud and recklessly, quietly falling into the role of something steady and real—I realize something.

Maybe Poppy's not the only one healing here.

CHAPTER
twenty-nine

Willow

I KNOW SOMETHING'S UP THE SECOND Rocket WALKS INTO THE KITCHEN mid-mug of coffee and freezes when he looks at his phone screen.

He groans and then looks over at me. "I apologize in advance for whatever is about to happen."

"What—"

BANG. BANG. BANG.

It's not a polite knock but more of a kick-down-the-door, open-up-we're-the-police kind of knock.

Rocket winces seconds before the door opens.

Three men stride in like they own the place. Three men who a majority of the world would know by sight but who have caught Rocket on his heels.

"Caldwell. Brother. We're here," the one in front—Hawkin Play—yells. He's tall and lean, with dark blond hair and a smile that screams trouble. He cuffs the side of Rocket's shoulder gruffly and then clocks me immediately and grins. "Well, well, well. You must be the one he's been hiding from us."

The one behind him—dark hair, gorgeous eyes, and a grin that could light up a room—Vincent Jennings stops just inside the threshold and lets out a long whistle. "Damn, Bristol was right. You're real. He was making excuses why we couldn't meet you."

"I wasn't making excuses," Rocket says and pushes Vince's shoulder playfully. "I was protecting her from you and . . . from *this*."

"You're such a fucking liar," Gizmo says as he clears the doorway before walking up to me and holding out a hand. "Jase Gizmodo. Nice to meet you, Willow."

"Nice to meet you too," I say, feeling a little overwhelmed.

"That's Hawkin." Hawkin salutes. "And Vince." Vince steps in and presses a kiss to my cheek. "And you met Giz," Rocket says. "And whatever they say, they're full of shit."

He says the words, he sounds exasperated, but Rocket came to life the minute his best friends walked in the room, and that makes me smile.

"Full of shit? Us?" Vince mutters as he grabs a banana from the fruit bowl like he lives here. "What were the bets we had?"

"Secret girlfriend."

"Witness protection."

"A new fetish."

They call out faster than I can keep track of who's saying them.

"None of those," I say. "I'm just Willow. Just the nanny. None of the dramatics needed." I look at them all, chuckle, and say more to myself than anyone else, "And you're the infamous band."

"Infamous and underappreciated," Gizmo says, already walking around the living room like he's casing the place.

I glance over at Rocket. His expression seems to be switching between hatred and love as his two worlds crash together.

"You're here, why?" Rocket asks.

"Songwriting session," Gizmo says brightly. "Emergency inspiration. Couldn't wait."

"You just wanted to meet Willow," Rocket mutters.

"Damn right," Hawkin says. "Quinlan's already decided she's one of our girls, so it's only you who's been hiding her like she's a national treasure or ugly, and we just proved the latter wrong, so . . . there's that."

"And we wanted to meet *her*," Vince adds as Poppy peeks her head around the corner from where she was playing in her bedroom. She came out to see what all the chaos is about, and now three men, three strangers, have all turned their attention on her.

She's got her bunny clutched in one arm and an expression that says *who the hell are these people and why are they so loud?*

"Ohhh my God, is this her?" Gizmo drops into a crouch and holds out a hand. "You must be Princess Poppy. We've heard all about you."

Poppy glances to me, uncertain.

"It's okay, sweetheart," I say. "They're dad—Rocket's friends. And loud."

"Hey there," Vince says, dropping to his knees and softening his voice, holding out his hand to her. "I'm sorry we were so loud. I'm Vince, and it's very nice to meet you."

Poppy looks at the hand, then back to him before her tiny hand disappears inside of it as they shake. She looks around again before slowly walking forward. She stops in front of Hawkin and, after a long beat, holds out to him a sparkly sticker shaped like a rainbow.

He stares at it like it's made of gold. "For me?"

She nods emphatically as Gizmo groans. "Of course, that's who she goes to first. That's who everybody crushes on."

A chuckle goes through the room as four men watch a precious little girl. She walks over to the pantry and opens the door to decide on a snack, already bored with the adults.

But I'm not. I'm fascinated and in a little awe of the men standing before me.

"We've got so many questions," Vince says, hopping up to sit on the counter.

"Like how you've been here almost a month and have never met us—"

"Nor have you smothered Rocket with a pillow yet for being annoying. Impressive," Hawkin tsks.

"Some days are easier than others," I tease.

"She's a saint. A saint, I tell you," Gizmo says and hooks an arm around Rocket's neck affectionately.

"I thought you said we were writing," Rocket says and takes a few steps toward his studio. The only thing I can think is he's terrified that his bandmates are set to embarrass the hell out of him when it comes to me. Or embarrass me.

"We'll get there. We wanted to talk to Willow first," Hawkin says.

"Nope. I don't trust you assholes as far as I can throw you," Rocket says and physically puts his hands on Gizmo's shoulders to steer him down the hall.

Before Gizmo disappears around the corner, he points at me. "You're awesome, Willow. Glad we met. And Poppy? Playdate, soon?"

"Way too good for him," Vince says as he follows suit.

"Seconded," Hawkin chimes in. "Or is that thirds?"

He laughs, and then they're gone from my sight, but I can still hear their laughter echoing off the walls until the studio door shuts.

No doubt Rocket's real torment is about to begin.

I turn to Poppy, who's now sitting on the floor, sorting through her sticker collection like nothing unusual just happened.

"They're . . . a lot," I say.

She glances up, eyes wide, grin big, and nods in agreement.

CHAPTER
thinty

Rocket

I DON'T EVEN GET THE DOOR CLOSED BEFORE VINCE SAYS, "So, we like her."

I grunt and move to my office chair. They're not here to write music. They're here to harass the shit out of me. "You're not supposed to like her. You're supposed to meet her, nod politely, and leave without traumatizing the child."

"Poppy loved us," Gizmo argues, flopping into the armchair. "She gave Hawkin a rainbow sticker. That's basically saying they're best friends for life."

"You scared the shit out of her."

"She was getting snacks. I promise you, she'll be fine," Vince says. "Let's talk about the real problem."

"Nope."

"Yes," Hawkin chimes in. "You lied to us."

"About what?" I roll my eyes.

"About how fucking hot Willow is." Gizmo blows out a long, low whistle.

"Like the wives told us she was pretty, but pretty in a woman's eyes and hot in a man's eyes are two totally different definitions."

"He speaks the truth," Hawkin says.

"She's not hot," I say automatically. "She's—"

"Stunning," Gizmo finishes for me. "Cool as hell. Amazing with Poppy, or she still wouldn't be here. And she puts up with your stubborn, grumpy ass, which basically makes her a unicorn."

She is.

"She's not a unicorn," I refute.

"Oh, she's definitely magical," Vince says and crosses his arms over his chest. "That's why you've already slept with her and are hiding it from us."

I glare at him. "What are we, sixteen now?"

"He's dodging the question," Hawkin says and playfully punches Vince's arm. "He's already sealed the deal."

"I'm not encouraging any of this," I say.

Gizmo grins. "So that's a yes."

"I swear to God—"

"It's the walk," Hawkin cuts in. "The post-getting-laid walk. You've been floating for two days. You smiled at the sunrise yesterday."

"What the hell are you talking about?" I bark out through a laugh—even though he's not wrong. "You didn't even see me yesterday, and it was fucking cloudy outside so you couldn't see the sunrise."

"You still smiled at it," he says. "I may not have seen you, but I know you. *We* know you."

I prop my elbows on the mixing board and drop my head into my hands. "You guys are impossible."

"No," Vince says. "We're observant. And invested."

"In your sex life," Gizmo adds cheerfully.

"In your happiness," Vince corrects. "And from what it looks like, what it seems like, even with all this change that's happened to you lately, you seem happy."

I look up slowly.

And yeah—maybe I'm dying inside a little. Because the truth is, they're not wrong. The house doesn't feel like mine anymore. Not really.

It feels better. Lighter. There's laughter in the halls and coffee cups that aren't mine on the counter. There's hummed lullabies and belly giggles. There's walking down the hall in the morning in anticipation that I'm looking forward to seeing the two girls.

And yes, while that terrifies the shit out of me, it's also different. Good.

Will it keep? Fuck if I know.

I clear my throat. "Let's write something."

"Nah, we just came to razz the fuck out of you," Gizmo says.

I shoot him a look. "You're assholes."

"We can be even bigger ones," Hawkin says as he turns the knob on the studio door. "We can tell Willow all about our song we made about her."

"Sweet Distraction," Vince says.

"Met her in a juice box haze . . ." Gizmo sings as he shuts the door behind him.

I lift my middle fingers at the direction of their backs, but I'm smiling.

And I don't even try to hide it.

CHAPTER
thirty-one

Willow

THE SUN'S HOT, THE WATER'S PERFECTLY COOL, AND ROCKET CALDWELL is currently the most distracting man on the planet.

He's in black swim shorts and nothing else, standing thigh-deep in the shallow end of his pool like some kind of tattooed rock god.

Oh, wait. *He is.*

The way the droplets roll down his chest should be illegal. His abs flex every time he moves. And don't even get me started on his low rumble of a laugh whenever Poppy does something cute.

And she is damn cute. Poppy's wearing bright pink floaties and is perched on the pool's Baja shelf with a purple plastic narwhal in one hand and a de-termined expression on her face. She tosses it as far as she can. When it lands with a splash, she throws her arms up to cheer it on and then waits for it pa-tiently—or not so patiently—to come back.

Rocket laughs. "Popstar, you're going be dangerous with that arm," he says. This time when she throws it, it hits him, and he responds by being overdramatic, pretending he's wounded, and falling backward into the water. She erupts in a fit of giggles and then plops down in the water herself, letting her floaties keep her on its surface where she's playing beside me.

I smile as Rocket moves to my side, where I'm sitting on the submerged step with the water at my waist. Our thighs brush against each other's, and all it takes is that little touch to have memories skittering through me.

Three nights ago.

His hands.

His mouth.

The way he groaned my name like a confession.

The memory lives rent free in my head but leaves so many questions unanswered.

Like, what the hell happens when you live with someone you've slept with? Do you sneak around once Poppy goes to sleep? Do I initiate that desire that's on constant simmer or wait for him to invite me to his room at night?

I mean, he had no problem pulling me into his office, out of Poppy's view, and kissing me senseless earlier, but how much is too much since we see each other every day?

When do you cross the line from being playful to clingy to way too much?

What exactly are the rules?

"You're overthinking something," Rocket says and takes a sip from his can of beer on the edge of the pool.

I immediately sputter. "No. Not at all. Just thinking about . . . something I—uh need to add to my to-do list."

Rocket smirks. "Very important to remember in this moment." He doesn't buy it for a second.

"It is." I snort and tug on Poppy's hand so that she comes a little closer to me. "Truth? I have a million things going on. It was nothing in particular."

"Anything I can help with?" The way his eyes scrape over me says he's thinking what I'm thinking. "Need a distraction? Me to walk past you shirtless in the hall? A late-night . . . snack break?"

My cheeks flush, but at least I'm not the only one sitting here dying a slow death of arousal. "Perhaps. I mean . . ."

"All that to-do list making must make you tense. I'm sure a little release would help you out."

"Yes. That might be exactly what I need." I chuckle as he clears his throat and subtly adjusts himself as he moves his waist below the waterline so Poppy doesn't notice his erection.

He walks off the step and into the pool. I study the lines of his back and wonder what it is that's bugging him. He hasn't quite been himself the past few days—or at least the easygoing man I've grown to know.

Normally, I'd think it's that we had sex and having to see me—a conquest—every day is panic inducing to him, but his comments just calmed that overthinking frenzy. So this . . . this is something different.

"I'll ask the same," I say to him. "What are you overthinking about?"

"Not overthinking . . . I just needed to talk to you about a few things."

His words still cause dread to lurch in my stomach. "Like?"

He watches Poppy for a beat, then looks at me. "As you know, the second leg of the tour is coming up."

"Yes." The white elephant in the room has made its presence known. I've been waiting for this—the *I'll be gone, and you can hold down the fort here* talk—I just didn't think it would feel like this. Like a door opening and a cliff nearing all at the same time.

"Thoughts on if you want to come?" His eyebrows lift from behind his sunglasses. "I think it's a good idea if you do."

My heart flips from equal parts hope and panic.

"Like . . . what exactly would I do while you're on tour?" I chuckle self-deprecatingly. I've never picked up my life for anyone—well, besides coming and being his nanny now that I think about it—so the idea is a tad unsettling.

"When you nannied in college, did you ever go on vacation with the family you were working for? It's the same thing, is it not? You go on tour with us, but everything stays the same—you take care of Poppy, you can work on those online enrichment classes you were talking about to get ready for your master's—other than the downside of being in a new hotel room every couple of days, you'll have new cities and places to explore with Poppy."

"Rocket, I . . ." *But I'm also sleeping with you.* How exactly does that play in this?

But I don't want to ask, don't want to define, or assume something I just took for granted—that whatever this is between us is exclusive.

"The best part is that this leg is short. So by the time you're sick of traveling, it'll be done, and we'll be back here." Rocket catches the narwhal that Poppy tosses at him and then he tosses it back to her delight.

"Again," she shouts, and both Rocket and I suck in breaths as our heads whip so that we look at each other and then immediately back to Poppy.

"Poppy! Look at you using your words," I sing as Rocket swoops her up and spins her around, pressing a kiss to her cheek.

She giggles and snuggles her head under the curve of his neck, her face shining with pride.

Rocket murmurs something in her ear that I can't hear or read from his lips because her pink floatie blocks my view, but when he asks her, "Do you want me to throw it again?"

She nods but keeps her arms locked around his neck so he settles back down on the step beside me with Poppy on his lap and the most joyful expression on his face.

"So what do you say about the tour, Wills?" he asks as both he and Poppy stare at me with matching eyes.

Excitement bubbles up. So does trepidation. Clearly, he's never broken a toddler's routine before. But . . . at the same time, this is the chance of a lifetime, isn't it?

"You've never mentioned us going with you before. Why now?"

He presses a kiss to the top of Poppy's head and shrugs. "I wasn't sure. Things were up in the air with her and where things stood. Now they're not."

Is it stupid that the smallest, romantic part of me wanted him to say it was because he wanted me there? That he wanted to show me his life and what touring is like? That he wanted to share it with me?

But that's my crazy talking.

We've slept together one time. It's not like we've discussed monogamy or exclusivity or any of that.

Do I want to go on tour with him? Do I want to see fans and other women fawn all over him? What if I woke up early to take Poppy somewhere, and I were to see a woman sneak out of his hotel room?

Jealously streaks through me at the thought.

"Hello? Earth to Willow. What are you thinking?"

I draw in a measured breath. "That's . . . a lot."

He nods slowly. "A lot, as in too much time with me? As in, you can't nanny properly or you're afraid I'll be a different person on tour? As in . . . what, exactly?"

"As in testing the boundaries of all the things when we're just getting used to this situation altogether."

"You think I'm going to have you in one hotel room and bring someone back to another, don't you?" he asks in coded wording since we have Poppy sitting with us.

I would never have expected to hear hurt in his voice, but it's there, and it hits me just as hard as the pained look he gives me.

"I didn't say that."

"You didn't have to." He holds my stare and gives the slightest shake of his head as if he's disappointed in me.

"It was one time. It would sound unhinged if I assumed that there was more or that we were exclu—"

"I kissed you earlier." My eyes grow wide, and I glance at Poppy, prepared to protest but he waves me away. "What? Let her know. I don't care."

"Rocket, you're being—"

"Irrational? Yes. I am. Just like you're being."

"I just—"

"Then make it more than one time, Wills. Make it every night. Make it whatever you want so that when we leave this house to go on tour, you're secure enough in whatever this is here that you're not afraid I can't control my urges with other women."

I stare at him—eyes blinking, jaw lax, brain stuttering—and try to wrap my head around what he just said.

How did I go from wondering how to bring it up to him just laying it out there in a matter of minutes? How did I end up looking like the ass here?

"And if you say no, then I'm going to tell you, as your employer, you don't have a choice because it's important for Poppy to be with me and continue to grow this bond. She can see what I do, and you guys can explore new places. Plus, *I want you there.*"

My whole body warms with affection for this man who's a continuous contradiction.

"Rock . . . you really know how to sweet-talk a girl."

He shrugs and winks nonchalantly. "I've had some practice. So . . . yes?"

I bite the inside of my cheek as I study him. He's serious. And I'm insane for actually considering it. *Right? "Yes."*

Poppy points to her juice on the table and grunts, so Rocket lifts her out of the pool and onto the deck. We both watch her walk over to it and sit in the shade to drink it. My mind buzzes with the conversation we just had. With the implications. With the way his words made me feel.

"Wait . . . you said you wanted to talk about *a few things*. What are the other things?"

He sighs, his tone shifting as he glances over to make sure Poppy is still in the shade. "My lawyer called a few days ago."

Nothing good ever seems to come from those words.

"What is it?"

"Olivia's parents—Poppy's grandparents—have petitioned for custody of Poppy."

"How is that possible? On what grounds?"

"According to the petition they filed earlier today, they claim that my lifestyle is unsuitable for a toddler. They're claiming I'm unstable, always on the road, and that it'll be detrimental to Poppy. That she'll be raised by a nanny if she's living with me, whereas they'd raise her if she were with them."

His words twist my stomach. "And?"

"And what?"

"And how do we fight this? What is it we need to do to put this to rest?"

His grin is loaded with pride. "Whatever it takes."

Those three words have relief surging through me, but it's tangled in something messy. A month ago I didn't even know him, and now I'm emotionally overloaded—I'm now a part of this fight too.

"*Whatever it takes*," I whisper back.

"Dadda," Poppy yells seconds before the narwhal comes flying past our heads.

We don't even glance at the narwhal because we both look at Poppy and grin at her. She looks at us like she doesn't understand what the big deal is, and so we leave it as is despite both of us screaming inside. At her second word. At the significance.

And when the moment passes, when she giggles and picks up more of her toys to throw in the pool like she didn't just rock our world, I steal a glance at Rocket.

He's staring at her, with love and pride and awe and everything in between etched in the lines of his expression. He looks at me and nods.

"There's no way I'm losing her, Willow. No way in hell. We're just getting started."

It shouldn't feel like a promise, but it does.

Still, my voice is quieter now when I speak.

CHAPTER
thirty-two

Willow

"**W**ELL, THAT DIDN'T TAKE LONG," ROCKET SAYS, HIS VOICE LOADED with sarcasm as he holds out his phone.

I stop walking on the tarmac and level him with a dubious look. "What?"

"See for yourself."

Before I even look at the screen, I have a feeling I already know I'm not going to like what I see. It's something I've been dreading.

It's a picture of the three of us—Rocket, Poppy, and me—getting into the car an hour ago to head to our current location, the airport. I'm holding Poppy's hand, and Rocket has my backpack slung over his shoulder as he helps the two of us into the waiting car. The way our heads are ducked down, we look like something out of a scandalous celebrity exposé.

Funny, especially when I had no idea a camera was anywhere in sight.

The headline above it reads, ROCKET CALDWELL'S SECRET DAUGHTER AND THE NANNY HEAD TO NEXT LEG OF TOUR

I stare at it for a beat, appreciating that the picture is at least flattering while holding back the absolute panic from seeing my face on a celebrity gossip site.

Lily was right. It was bound to happen even with all the precautions taken.

Handing it back, of course, I pretend like I'm unfazed.

"Well, at least they got the headline right. Could be worse. They could've said I'm an escort or something who's been harboring your secret love child."

He snorts. "That's probably coming next."

"Awesome." Sarcasm drips from the word. "Good thing I breached my boss's unyielding NDA and gave my parents the heads-up."

"I heard he's a real asshole."

"Will I be punished?" I ask playfully, which causes desire to flare in his eyes.

"Later," he growls.

"Promise?"

I have no idea why I'm unfazed by the article and the chaos that's about to unfold with us going on this tour. Maybe it's because of the man beside me and the little girl he's pulling from the car and her booster seat.

Happiness gives you a healthy dose of tolerance.

Rocket presses a kiss to Poppy's temple as she tucks her bunny farther under her arm. "I apologize. Again."

"We've talked about it. We knew it was coming. I'm surprised it hasn't happened sooner," I say.

"I know, but I'm not sure how they got into my neighborhood. That place is usually sealed pretty tight. I'll have our PR team put out a press release to set the record straight. That Poppy is my daughter. That you are my nanny. It'll cause the field day we know it will, but hopefully because she's a minor, they'll be more respectful of the situation. We can hope, at least." He snorts. "I'm sure there will be a lot of supposition, someone will offer a shit ton of money for the sordid story that doesn't exist, but for now, they'll assume what they want."

The words are easy for him, smooth and practiced like it's just another Tuesday.

And for him? It probably is.

But me? I glance around the tarmac at the luxury jet gleaming in the late-morning sun and wonder if there are more photographers hidden somewhere, waiting to snap the next shot.

Not long ago, I was meeting Poppy for the first time, worried about how she'd adapt to the trauma of losing her mom and the enormous changes in her own little world. Not to mention ordinary things like nap schedule, what would keep her stimulated the most, and her likes and dislikes. *Now?* I'm on the other side of the gossip site, photographed as if I'm someone important and part of Rocket's rich and famous world.

This is so far from normal I don't even have a name for it. It's like I'm on a different planet and yet somehow, I'm here.

Rocket glances my way and must sense the spiral happening behind my eyes. He bumps his arm against mine. "Hey. Ignore the photo. It's not a big deal. It'll blow over in a few days. Whatever it takes, right?"

I smile through the unsettled feeling. "Whatever it takes."

"No doubt some starlet somewhere will do something stupid, and this will blow away sooner rather than later. I promise."

"As we go on tour in the public eye." I roll my eyes and chuckle.

"Point taken. So this is it," Rocket says as we stop in front of a gray jet. It looks sleek and ridiculously expensive. I stand in front of its stairs and don't care that I stare up at it in awe.

Rocket gestures toward the plane with his chin. "Well, no time like the present to lose your private jet virginity."

And if I wasn't freaking out before, I sure as hell am now.

Because stepping into a freaking Learjet when I've never even flown first class before is a whole new level of "how is this my life?"

We carefully climb the stairs. My first impression when I peek inside the door is that it's sleek and bright and smells like leather and expensive aftershave.

And of course, sitting in that lush leather at the far end of the cabin is the rest of BENT: Hawkin Play. Vince Jennings. And Jase "Gizmo" Gizmodo.

I falter those first few steps inside the jet when I see them there. Sure, I met them at the house, but seeing them again in their private jet about to blast off on tour adds a whole different element to my current situation. One that seems so bizarrely removed from the life I had two months ago.

Poppy has no idea she's in the presence of rock royalty and is currently too busy dragging her rolling unicorn backpack behind her to care.

"Willow!" Hawkin calls out when he looks up and sees me. He rises from his seat and steps forward to offer a kiss to my cheek in greeting. Then, as I'm in the midst of doing the same with all the rest of the guys, they're giving high fives to Poppy.

"Welcome to your first tour," Vince says with a wink and then ushers me to an open seat.

Gizmo looks at me, then back at Rocket, and then back at me. "Fuck, man. I stand by the fact that you're still way too hot to be his nanny."

I cough over my next breath of air. "Well, I'm not technically *his* nanny," I joke, which causes a bout of laughter to ring out.

"Shh. We have baby ears here," Hawkin says, and as if on cue, Poppy scrambles up in the seat beside Hawkin's.

"Another female in love with Hawkin. Exactly what we don't need," Vince mutters.

A laugh rings out, and Gizmo tugs on one of Poppy's pigtails. She giggles. "Are you going to be my new backstage troublemaker?"

"You don't need any help," Rocket says.

Our laughs combine, and just like that, we all fall into this weird normalcy that only cements itself further as we buckle in our seats and take to the sky. They're warm, funny, and clearly ready to fold Poppy into the band family like she's been here all along.

I accept the glass of wine the stewardess hands me. Hawkin holds his up across the aisle to mock toast me.

"We're glad you're coming with us," Hawkin says. "Touring's crazy, but there's nothing in the world like it. Just keep your headphones charged to protect your ears—and tune us out—and don't ever, under any circumstances, eat the chili the venue provides."

I laugh. "Noted."

"Small spaces and chili don't go together," Vince says, to which everyone makes some kind of agreement. But Rocket rolls his eyes almost as if he's embarrassed that they said that in front of me. It's adorable.

"And"—Gizmo holds up his finger to make his own point—"don't believe anything Hawke says after midnight or before coffee."

"Those are life and death timeframes," Hawkin jokes.

"Moving on to Rocket's idiosyncrasies," Gizmo says.

"Nope. Not going there," Rocket says, waving his hands. "Let's not scare Willow off just yet."

"Because you need the nanny," Vince says but gives me a look that says he knows more than he's letting on.

Did Rocket tell them we've hooked up?

My cheeks flush red, and I cringe at the thought. Then again, all three are married men, so maybe they're just living vicariously through their brother and his exploits.

Exploits? Jesus, Willow.

While I've been in my own head and coloring absently with Poppy on the table between us, the conversation has carried on. They're all joking back and forth, but it's Rocket I focus on. He taps his wine glass against mine and smiles.

"See? We're all just normal guys," he says but then shifts his gaze over to Poppy.

I watch Rocket watching her.

Earlier today, he was standoffish. He seemed tense, and his words were clipped like maybe he was nervous about this. About bringing us here. Yes, he said this is what he wanted, but saying it and seeing it happen are two totally different things.

It worried me. I thought maybe we'd bitten off more than we could chew too fast. That this might be a bad idea.

But now as I watch him, he's leaning back, relaxed and grinning.

Poppy babbles something and throws her rabbit into Vince's lap.

The guys cheer like she just won a Grammy.

I don't think I've met a more resilient three-year-old in my life. She only just lost her mom, has had her life uprooted, living with strangers, and yet here, she's simply adapting. *Thriving.* She's incredible.

And Rocket?

He finally looks like he's where he belongs.

With his bandmates. With his daughter. And heading to do what he loves.

CHAPTER
thirty-three

T HE FLOOR OF THE ARENA SHAKES BENEATH MY FEET.

The bass coming through the speakers thunders through my chest.

The lasers and lights spin crazily through the darkness.

And the crowd? They're absolutely feral.

Tens of thousands of people packed into this giant arena are screaming and singing and moving like one big wave that surges up over and over again.

And in the middle of it all, standing center stage, owning what feels like the universe, is BENT.

Hawkin may be singing, but it's Rocket my eyes are trained on. Shirt drenched with sweat. Hair wild and damp. A complicated array of keyboards and synths constructed around him that he moves fluidly from one to another as needed.

His hips move with the beat. His mouth curls into a smirk when he joins in with the other guys and growls out the chorus. God help me. The man knows exactly what he's doing up there.

It's not just music.

It's foreplay.

Or at least that's how my mind's spinning it.

"Hello, Atlanta. How we doing tonight?" Hawkin asks when the song's done. The crowd works itself into a frenzy replying.

"I don't think they're ready for us," Vince says.

"No one ever is," Gizmo joins in as he taps his drumsticks a few times.

"But we're ready for you," Rocket says. "Let's get loud tonight, yeah?"

The crowd roars.

My stomach flips.

Rocket knows precisely where the camera crew is and winks directly into the lens, so it's shown on the giant video screens that flank both sides of the stage.

A small part of me swears it's at me.

Yes, I've fallen under Rocket's charm.

I'm toast.

Beside me, Poppy bounces with her pink headphones snug over her ears. She looks absolutely adorable and strangely, as if she was meant to be here. She's clutching her little rabbit and smiling so hard her cheeks might break.

I tap her on the shoulder and give her a thumbs-up sign.

She nods fast, curls bouncing, eyes wide, and grin growing. My heart squeezes at the sight.

We dance sillily as the song plays on, and with my eyes trained on Rocket.

This whole tour life? It's absolute chaos. The different hotels and tour bus miles and different cities, but this right here, right now? It's magic.

After the last encore's played and the show's over, backstage would not exactly be considered much calmer. The band winds down in the greenroom. They have towels over their shoulders, beers in their hands, and by their animated conversations, they're still buzzing with adrenaline.

I sit on the couch, Poppy curled beside me. Her headphones are still on, the crackers she was snacking on have fallen sideways onto the seat beside her, and her eyes are closed. I can't believe she lasted this long. No doubt this whole schedule thing will have to be adjusted as the tour rolls on, but in my opinion, it's important she sees Rocket on stage. For her to see what he does and who her dad is.

The guys playfully relive moments from onstage. Screwups or miscues that no one else would've picked up on except for them. It's fun to simply observe them and their brotherhood, but just like Poppy, I'm fading from exhaustion too.

I shift in my seat, take a sip of my wine, and will myself to stay awake.

But when I look up, that problem disappears when I meet Rocket's eyes.

His look? It's not innocent. It's dark. It's heated.

It says I remember how you tasted, and I haven't stopped thinking about it since.

And I feel it. *Everywhere.*

The ridiculous relief I feel that he still wants me is chased away by something much stronger—desire.

We haven't been on tour for more than a few days, but Poppy's had a rough time adjusting to unfamiliar places and settling down at night. That means that even with adjoining rooms with Rocket, she's been sleeping in the bed beside mine, and if I move in the slightest, she wakes up panicked.

Which means other than a few stolen kisses that tell me he's still interested, there hasn't been a single act of sex.

And while that might be a blessing in disguise because it forces us to take whatever *this* is, slow. It also creates one hell of a slow burn that I'm hoping will explode into a wildfire sooner rather than later.

That also means I'm currently one flirty Rocket smirk away from combusting in public.

Hendrix slides in beside me. A week into the tour, she showed up and for the past few weeks I've come to find that Gizmo's wife is bright and bold and completely unapologetic. I love her for it. We've become closer over the last few days, in huge part because Poppy is infatuated with her, and I'm incredibly grateful she's on tour with us.

She nudges me and talks quietly. "You look like you need a stiffer drink. Or an orgasm. Or both."

I choke. "Jesus."

"Tell me I'm wrong."

I say nothing because the glance that Rocket just gave me is scorching.

She just laughs and leans over to brush a curl out of Poppy's face. "She's sound asleep."

"The headphones help with that. Much easier to fall asleep when you can't exactly hear the noise all around you."

"True." She pats my leg. "Want me to watch her for a bit? Give you a break?"

I blink. "Seriously?"

"Seriously. She likes me. Plus if she wakes up, I can ply her with snacks and screen time. I'll convince her that Hendrix is a perfect name for that new teddy bear Rocket bought her today." She knocks her knee against mine. "Go. Rehydrate. Flirt with the rock star some more. I'll text if you're needed."

For a split second, I hesitate.

And then I close my eyes and nod. "You're a goddess, Hendrix."

She winks. "I know."

With one last look at Poppy, I wander down the hallway looking for water or maybe just a second to catch my breath. At home, I can leave Poppy to play in her room or watch shows in the great room. Here, I don't have that freedom, and Poppy doesn't have that comfort to do so . . . and so it's been me, on call, twenty-four seven. Yes, that's my job, but a break every now and again is welcome.

Especially when that break means I might get some alone time with Rocket.

But before I even make it to the end of the corridor, a door opens, and I'm grabbed.

"*Hey!*"

"Shhh," he whispers as his hand closes over my mouth and he yanks me into a dressing room—his dressing room—and kicks the door closed behind us.

Seems like he was looking for the same thing I was. Thank God.

My back hits the wall, and then his mouth's on mine. Hot. Urgent. *Starved.*

His hands are on my hips, fingers digging in, his body flush against mine.

Rocket's voice is gravel. "If you keep looking at me the way you were during sound check, before we went on stage, or in the greenroom earlier, I swear to God, I'm going to want to write a song about the things I want to do to you."

"What do you want to do to me?" My words are breathless, but my body's screaming.

"Everything."

He kisses me again, teeth dragging over my lower lip, and one hand sliding under my shirt like he can't stand that there's a barrier between us.

"I want you on this couch. Want your legs wrapped around me. Want you moaning my name like you need me to stop but will die if I do . . . like you forgot you had rules."

I moan against his mouth, my hands fisting in the fabric of his shirt. "You're insatiable."

Rocket kisses his way down the line of my throat. "I've been watching you for days. Walking around like you don't know how fucking hot you are." A nip against my collarbone. "Not seeing every goddamn person in the room turn their heads when you pass by." He presses harder against me, and I feel *all* of him. "Not knowing I jack off in the shower thinking about what you felt like, what you tasted like, because I couldn't have you again." He slides a hand between my thighs and groans. It's a sound I'll come back to in my naughty dreams. "I want you. Here. Now."

I lean back and meet his eyes. I love how the green has darkened and how the roughness of his palms feel over my skin. "Then take me," I whisper.

CHAPTER
thirty-four

Rocket

L IKE I'M GOING TO RESIST THAT OFFER.

Not when it's been fucking days since I've had her.

Not after seeing her in that tight-ass top and jeans that hug her curves.

And especially not after the high of a fucking killer show. All I want to do is bury myself in her tight fucking pussy and come until my head dizzies and my balls empty.

There's nothing gentle about our coming together. Not the scrape of her fingernails down my back or the way I peel her jeans down to her mid-thigh.

And definitely not the way I feel when I see those red lace panties, which are nothing more than strings and lace fucking tucked against my fucking heaven.

"Christ, Wills."

"Red's your favorite color, right?" she teases as she yanks on the buttons of my pants.

"Right behind the pink of your pussy," I murmur as my hand dives into her hair and brings her against me.

I want to touch her everywhere. Fuck her everywhere. Lick her everywhere.

And if the trolley cart and voices outside the locked door are any indication, time is limited.

"Pink? Is that so?" she asks coyly as she makes a show of pushing against my chest to give her space.

Of wriggling her jeans farther down her legs to her knees.

And of slowly turning around and bending over so I have the perfect fucking view.

Her ass. Her pussy. The goddamn arousal glistening in the dim lights.

"Fucking hell," I groan.

She looks over her shoulder at me, eyes alive and lips curved up in a smile. "Fuck me like a rock star, Rocket."

I stroke my cock, my mind already three steps ahead of my hand jacketing it up.

"Is that what you want?" I tease as I line up my cock at her slit and rub it through her wetness.

She wiggles her ass against me. My balls tighten at the sight, scent, and anticipation.

This woman will be my undoing.

And I'm fucking here for it.

I slap a hand on the globe of her ass and her pussy tightens around the top of my cock as I push into her.

Bliss. Absolute fucking bliss. The way I fit inside her. The way she grips me. The way my balls fit against her clit. The way my hand pulls against her shoulder to force myself deeper into her.

And more than anything, the way she fucking groans my name like I'm heaven and hell. Like I'm salvation and sin. Like I'm tomorrow and forever.

Her fingertips grip the couch as I drive into her, every thrust a little harder than the last.

She meets me stroke for stroke, squeezing me tight, daring me to lose control, to come undone the way she's unraveling beneath my hands.

I move my hand from her shoulder to her hair, grabbing a fistful, just the way she likes. I pull her upright so she's flush with my chest. She arches against me—ass, back, one hand reaching back to grip my thigh in a greedy show of possession that's hot as fuck.

My mouth's at her ear, breath hot, as I pound into her. "You want it like this? Harder? Faster? Deeper?"

She gasps as I show her what I mean. Each slap of skin's an assault on our senses. Every drive in is one step closer to oblivion.

"I don't care but don't you dare fucking stop," she grates out as her hips circle against me in a reckless rhythm.

My other hand slips between her thighs, thumb pressed to her clit, circling, pressing, demanding. She flinches and moans, the sound rough and desperate, and I feel her pulse around me, a ripple that rises and falls, and then rises again.

I'm fucking gone at the sound. Absolutely gone as it shatters my restraint. I flex against her, my body burning bright as the sounds, sights, and sensations overwhelm me. Control me. Push me to the edge of no control.

She pushes back into me even harder, mouth open and head thrown back as her orgasm hits. *Yes* is a never-ending word from her lips as her body rocks and pussy spasms around my cock.

It only takes seconds for me to follow. For me to shatter to fucking pieces, coming so goddamn hard my head dizzies and vision goes black.

It's her. Every goddamn thing is different with her.

That's my last thought, my only thought, as the world goes soft around me. We collapse onto the couch together, me on the bottom and her sitting on me, my front to her back. Our breathing is hard, and our hearts are racing as I slowly slip out of her.

But I don't let her go just yet. I wrap my arms around her and rest my chin on her shoulder as I come down from the high.

"Top ten," she pants, turning so her mussed hair hits my cheek.

"Top three," I correct. "Hands down. Top three."

She laughs, short and raw, then squirms to look at me. Her eyes are sex-drugged and bright. "Did I ever tell you I like you, Rocket?" She snorts. "Especially when you can deliver on what I asked for like that."

"Fuck me like a rock star, Rocket."

"I kind of like you too."

CHAPTER
thirty-five

Rocket

Willow and Poppy are running through the grass in front of me.

For a second, I don't move. I forget the chaos in my head that the call I'm expecting is creating. The distraction allows me to just sit on the bench, elbows on my knees, and watch them like my life's on the other side of a movie screen.

Two people who weren't part of my every day . . . hell, my life, not long ago and now who . . . I don't know what.

Who I don't see living my life without.

The thought is there. It's subtle. It's terrifying.

At least, Poppy, right? Because I'm not ready to be thinking shit like that about Willow.

And yet . . .

I scrub a hand over my face. This is fucking crazy talk. Crazy talk expedited by unusual circumstances like living in the same house, the same hotel, as the woman you're sleeping with.

But Willow's laugh draws me back. She's barefoot, holding Poppy's hand as they chase bubbles blown from some tiny wand she pulled from her damn tote bag of tricks she carries around that seems to solve all problems. Poppy shrieks, her rabbit's tucked under one arm, her curls bounce with every step, and determination is written all over her face like she's on a mission to catch every single one.

They're beautiful.

And beautiful in a way that makes my chest ache and constrict simultaneously.

Willow turns and catches me watching. She grins and winks.

Yep. I'm fucked.

And not just in the way that makes my balls tighten and wants to fuck. It's as though the something that's been missing from my life seems *not* to be missing anymore.

Yeah, I'm definitely fucked.

My phone rings and yanks me from my thoughts.

"Hey, Sandra."

"Gavin."

I already hate her tone. "Why do you sound like that?"

"It doesn't exactly look good, bode well, what-the-hell-ever you want to call it, that you're fucking the nanny."

I wince as I glance back at Willow and Poppy, "Who said I was?"

"Rocket," she says and sighs. "It doesn't matter whether you are or you aren't. It matters what public perception is. Not that it's any of my business, but are you?"

I stare down at my boots, scuffed and half-buried in mulch. *Fuck.*

"Your silence says it all."

"I have a daughter. I have a nanny. Both are on tour with me."

"So your PR team has told the world, but how do you think that's going to look on the stand when Willow goes to vouch for you in the custody hearing? Do you think her word is going to hold any weight? The young nanny dazzled by the rock star?"

I clench my jaw. "Why does there even have to be a hearing? Olivia stated that I was Poppy's father. The paternity test proved it. She also listed me as legal guardian to *our* daughter. Why do her grandparents get to even file for custody?"

"Because they're claiming you're not fit to parent."

"Fuck that."

"Hence, the nanny and her word needing to hold weight."

"Are you asking me to lie? Asking her to lie?"

"So it's true," she says, and I don't respond. "And, no. I'd never ask that." She pauses and then exhales like she's gearing up for something worse. "You'll be in Des Moines soon, right?"

"Yeah. Don't ask me the day, though. They're already running together."

"I know your schedule."

"And?" I drag the word out. For some reason, I hate where this is headed.

"Olivia's parents live an hour outside the city. I think it would go a long way if you met up with them. Let them spend time with Poppy."

The words slam into me harder than I expect. "Wait. What?"

"You heard me. I think you showing cooperation by meeting them half-way here shows that you're willing to share her with them, let them see her, not shut them out . . . it might go a long way with the judge."

"As opposed to what?"

"As opposed to the hundreds and thousands of pictures on the internet of you partying hard."

"All done before I knew about Poppy. Plus, who says being a parent means you can't let loose every now and again?"

"Right now it's about optics."

"Why can't it be based on the here and now?" I'm getting irritated.

"Agreed, but I think this would be a good move on your part. They've requested an opportunity to see her, and rather than go through the courts for this like your hand is being forced, it might look better if you agree to it."

"You want me to just give her to them?"

"I want you to let them *see* her. You can stay in the same room, sit at a different table, I don't know . . . but no, I'm not saying to hand her over without supervising. They probably want to—*need* to—grieve the loss of Olivia through her. They never knew they had a granddaughter. Maybe let that love soften whatever they're holding on to. It might help the case. More than that, it might help them. It might be good for Poppy when she's older to know more of her family."

I hear what she's saying, but I don't have to like it. I get to my feet, needing to move. "They could take her."

"Rocket—"

"They could walk off with her and then what?"

Her breath is stuttered. "They won't."

"You can't promise that."

"You're right. I can't, but we have to believe the best in people. Otherwise, you spend your life not trusting people."

I grunt and stare at Willow again. She's crouched beside Poppy now, blowing a new round of bubbles, letting her fall backward into the grass with a delighted shriek.

Fuck, man.

"Just think about it. Let me know in the next day or two."

The call ends, and I barely remember sliding the phone back into my pocket because I'm jogging across the grass.

And then I dive next to the two of them in a purposely clumsy, dramatic flair. Poppy shrieks and puts her hands on both of my cheeks.

"Swings?" I half-shout, half-wheeze the word before blowing a raspberry on Poppy's cheek.

Willow raises an eyebrow, breathless and smiling at the same time Poppy shrieks and points to the swings before taking off in a toddler-speed sprint toward the playground. I'm on my feet in seconds, running after her. As I get close, I scoop her up and spin her in a circle.

She emits her addictive belly giggle as I lower her into the toddler swing and begin to push her gently.

Her curls lift and fall with the movement. Her eyes are wide and her smile is . . . it's incredible.

Willow slides into the swing beside her, and for a second, the two of them are in rhythm.

Back and forth—the sun on our faces—Poppy's giggles the music I never knew I needed.

Because if I hear it, that means I'm doing something right. That means I'm not messing up yet.

Something in me cracks open. It's the weirdest, most foreign, most gratifying feeling that I couldn't put words to if I tried.

This is what it's supposed to feel like.

This weightlessness.

This connection.

Did my mom ever feel this way about me? Did she ever swing beside me in some forgotten park and feel like she might actually be enough?

Nah. I didn't matter to her. I was a burden. A responsibility she hid.

Never.

Poppy will never feel like that. I'll never let her.

When she swings forward, she lifts her head up so that she can look at me. Our eyes meet. *Fuck me. She's absolutely adorable.*

And . . . mine.

And I'm not sure I've ever felt more whole.

CHAPTER
thirty-six

Willow

THE RECORD STORE SMELLS LIKE OLD STORIES, DUST, AND VINYL. It's the kind of nostalgia you can't bottle.

Poppy's curled up on a beanbag in the middle of the store. She's content watching the lava lamps that the old record store has on various display cases. They mesmerize her, and I welcome the quiet as she's been rather fussy today.

It was a long night to say the least. A nightmare yanked her from her sleep and produced murmurings of *"Mommy."* The only thing that calmed her was snuggling with Rocket as she traced the tattoos on his chest until she fell asleep.

Then a Zoom therapy call this morning. Not exactly the easiest when you're on the road and the therapist has a hands-on approach, but consistency is more important than anything and so we're doing the best we can with it.

Tour life is simply chaotic. Messy. Incredible and tough simultaneously.

The guys have been welcoming. The buses are a new experience. The hotels have run together so much so that they all seem the same.

But the way Rocket is with Poppy? The way he's learning how to be a dad in the in-between moments of all the chaos? How he's doing his best to communicate better with her? How when she's cranky and insufferable, he puts her head on his chest and sings so the vibrations calm her down?

All those little moments with her, the ones I try to be invisible for or watch from afar, are what's making me slowly fall for Rocket Caldwell.

Then of course, there's the sex. Um . . . *wow*. Like . . . the man knows how to make a woman feel *everything*. And since Poppy has mostly coped better with all these changes than I anticipated—she's the definition of resilient—sneaking into the adjoining room at night has been an easier feat.

And then there are times like this. Rocket surprising me on an off day with a trip to explore the city. Lunch in a rowboat so Poppy can feed the ducks. A merry-go-round ride. And now this . . . us, slow-dancing mid-aisle, between the jazz and the rock sections. It's impromptu and sweet and to-tally unexpected.

"This doesn't seem very rock star-ish of you," I murmur.

"I'm trying to sneak a kiss in the middle of a music store. Can't get more rock star than that."

"Hmm." I narrow my eyes at him and twist my lips.

"What? You can think of somewhere better?"

He spins me out and twirls me back in so I land solidly against him. My chuckle is seductive as I lean in and whisper, "I can think of a few other places that would be even sexier."

"Name the place, sweetheart."

"Rooftop? Sound booth? *Our bed at home?*"

He groans when I say the last one—we've both been saying how much we miss home—but luckily for me, he didn't catch the *our bed* part.

Would that spook him?

I don't know how it would since we're basically living together, but I'll leave it be.

"You know what, Wills? You just threw down the gauntlet. I definitely intend to pick it up," Rocket says.

"I'll be waiting."

"And I'll be wanting." His hand is on my back, warm and possessive. His other hand curls around mine so that his thumb brushes lazy circles against my palm as we sway in the middle of the empty aisle.

The song coming through the speaker ends and a new one begins. It's a seductive jazz number that's slower. Sexier. The kind that wraps around you and dares you not to feel.

Rocket leans in, voice low and rough. "I didn't expect to enjoy this as much as I am."

"The record store?" I lean back to meet his eyes.

He shakes his head, a soft laugh rumbling in his chest. "No. The tour. You two being here. Exploring with you. It's . . . so vastly different from what I'm used to."

My pulse jumps because it's not just the words, but rather the way he says them. Like he's trying to understand them too, because they're so unfamiliar.

"I'm hoping that's a good thing."

"Very. I've had a lot of things in my life. Noise. Fame. Girls. Chaos." He pauses, his thumb absently brushing over the back of my hand. "But this? It's . . . more. Not in the way I thought I wanted. But in a way I didn't know I needed."

My throat tightens, and I don't know what to say. Because this still isn't a declaration. It's not a label. It isn't a promise. *But it's honest.*

And coming from him that means something.

He gives me a slow, shy smile. "Let's just say I'm starting to like the quiet. You've made me like the quiet."

Something shifts in the moment. It's intimate and undeniable. How can that simple statement mean so very much to me?

My chest presses into his, and his hand slides up my back beneath the hem of my shirt. And when he lowers his head, lips so damn close to mine, I feel it.

I want it.

But then he freezes.

I feel the hesitation before I see it. His hand stiffens. His eyes flick sideways toward the store window. And then he pulls back so casually it hurts.

Like we didn't just share a moment.

I blink, still swaying slightly, heart thudding in my throat, and confusion front and center as he moves about the store.

"Rocket?" I ask, trying to understand the sudden shift in his demeanor.

He gives a shake of his head before walking back toward me, but keeping a display of records that fall waist high between us.

I look away, pretending to check on Poppy, and trying to weirdly not feel rejected. I can acknowledge that it's a valid emotion to feel.

"Hey. Look at me."

"You don't have to explain anything," I say.

"I do. I didn't kiss you just now because I panicked. I looked up and thought, what if someone takes a picture? What if that gets put on social media? How will that affect you when you take the stand in the custody hearing?"

"Affect me or affect you?" I ask, confused how we could spend all day together in public places, places where photos of us close together were undoubtedly taken, but now he says that?

"Both? Your credibility and selfishly my ability to keep Poppy. A picture getting out of us slow-dancing and kissing in public will decimate your credibility to vouch for me. You're my nanny, Willow. Not my girlfriend. Not 'officially' anyway. That's how they'll see it."

He's not wrong. My stomach pitches at the thought. And yet stupidly, that small rejection lingers like a bruise.

"Right. I forgot. My opinion comes with a disclaimer."

His jaw tics. He closes his eyes for a beat. "Fuck, Willow. I'm trying to protect you."

"I know. I'm sorry. I shouldn't have said that."

But that doesn't mean that it didn't seem like he's embarrassed for the world to see me with him. That he wants to keep me a secret to keep his approachability up.

I move toward the end of my aisle, and he mirrors my action in his. When I go to walk past him to hang with Poppy, he catches my wrist.

"Don't walk away. I told you how I felt. *The quiet*. That still stands all these minutes later," he teases.

I can't help my smile or the sudden embarrassment regarding my overreaction.

And before I can answer, he's tugging me around the corner, behind one of the taller shelves, half-shadowed by bins of dusty cassette tapes and forgotten band posters, but still with a direct line of sight to Poppy.

"No cameras here," he murmurs before cupping my face and kissing me.

His mouth is hot and demanding but tender and reverent. He kisses me like I'm not just a secret or a mistake or a risk.

He kisses me like I matter.

And when he finally pulls back, breath ragged, pupils dark, he rests his forehead against mine.

"In case you misunderstood what my lips just did, I'll repeat myself with words. I want to kiss you every goddamn second I'm around you, Willow. Just give me time to figure out how to do it without losing everything in the process."

CHAPTER
thirty-seven

Willow

THE HOTEL ROOM IS QUIET FOR ONCE.

Poppy's napping in the bed behind me, her little body curled around her rabbit like it's an extension of her spine. I'm in the corner by the window, phone pressed to my ear, eyes trained on the skyline of downtown Des Moines, and trying not to feel like the walls are closing in.

"Girl. You realize you're freaking everywhere, right? TikTok, Insta, random-ass gossip blogs I didn't even know existed." Lily snorts. "Did I not tell you this was going to happen?"

"Yes. You did. You were right." I groan and sink lower into the chair, dragging a hand over my face. "I'm just the nanny though." It's a lie that very few people, including her, know differently on, but it bears repeating.

The people jumping out of bushes to blind me with their flashes, who have no regard for Poppy or how scared it makes her, are my least favorite part of this trip.

Yes, it comes with the territory—or so I'm learning—but it doesn't make them any less of an asshole.

"Just the nanny? More like you're officially the hot new thing," she says.

"Which also makes me the hated new thing."

"Fuck them," she asserts in a way that only she can. Like those two words are empowering rather than angry.

"I mean . . . yeah. But it's still a mess."

"You realize how crazy this all is, right? Like . . . you're in Iowa. On tour. With a rock star. His kid. And you're literally the center of internet speculation."

"Trust me. I realize it. Every second of every day." I sigh. "It's both the coolest thing I've ever done in my life and also the most draining."

"Because all of the great sex you're getting to have?" she teases playfully.

"I was going more for the emotionally draining aspect." I can't help the quiet smile that spreads across my lips. "But that doesn't hurt either."

She snorts. "I'm living vicariously through you in that aspect and only that aspect."

"Noted."

She goes quiet for a second, then says, "Just so you know, when these articles say, 'a source says' . . . that source is not me."

"I never thought you were—"

"A few calls came in—you know, fake PR people, paparazzi, one girl who claimed to be writing a documentary on the 'domestic lives of the rich and famous'—people who have connected us as friends through social media, but—"

I groan. "God, Lil, I'm sorry."

"—and I told all of them you're just his nanny and then blocked the number."

I laugh, but it's hollow. "I appreciate the help, but no one believes that. Not anymore."

"But they'll believe Chris Hemsworth had an alien baby with a rhinoceros or whatever that shit was I saw in the *National Enquirer* the other day."

"Yes, because men get passes and women get blamed. It's fine. I've stopped trying to figure people out. The thing is, I wouldn't care about any of it, but me being with Rocket—or the public thinking I am—isn't a good thing. It'll risk my credibility at the custody hearing. The outcome. It's a total shitshow."

I glance back at the bed. Poppy shifts in her sleep, lips twitching like she's dreaming of something that makes her happy. Probably the zoo.

She loved the zoo.

Just like she loved the inflatable park and all its slides in St. Louis. The pirate ship hotel pool in Omaha. The petting zoo with the goats that tried to eat her pigtails. The band that spoils her like crazy and makes her laugh and feel loved, treating her like she's one of their own.

Then there's Rocket. She lights up the room when he walks in. Everything about her shifts and changes, and it's the most incredible sight to watch.

All of it.

And now we're both trying to navigate this insane meeting tomorrow with Olivia's parents, and I can feel the stress emanating off him even when he's smiling.

But I know his lawyer is right—seeing she has other family is good for Poppy. That might look favorable to a judge if this custody protest moves forward. It's necessary, even if it's terrifying.

"How's she doing?"

"She's a kid. She adjusts well. I mean, she misses her routine. She still ends up crawling into bed with me halfway through the night, but she's happy. She's loved. It shows."

"And how's *your* heart, Willow Adams?"

That question lodges somewhere behind my ribs. "I love her. Plain and simple. She's hard not to."

"I wasn't talking about Poppy," Lily says quietly.

Ooof. That one hits me in the gut. Having to face reality—and own your emotions will do that to a girl.

"In case you misunderstood what my lips just did, I'll repeat myself with words. I want to kiss you every goddamn second I'm around you, Willow. Just give me time to figure out how to do it without losing everything in the process."

I stare out the window at the fading sky, and then at the blur of cars below. How I appreciate Rocket's words. He's already at tonight's venue, doing all of the pre-show checks, interviews, and the typical pre-concert meet-and-greets. I'll leave it up to Poppy if she wants to attend the concert tonight. Some nights she wants to dance, other nights she wants to snuggle, watch cartoons, and eat room service.

She thinks it's the coolest thing in the world that food can be delivered to your bedroom.

"Willow?"

"I'm trying to protect it. I swear I am. But he makes it really hard." The words catch in my throat. This—these feelings that keep growing—weren't supposed to happen.

"Because he's not who you thought he'd be?" she asks.

"Exactly. I mean, he's . . . good." I pause and then say the next part more to myself than to her. "That sounds weird. He's good, but not in a perfect, polished way, but in this raw, gritty, *I'll bleed for you* kind of way. He shows up. He tries. He fights."

"Sounds like someone you could fall for."

"Truth?" I ask.

"Always."

"I think I already have."

We sit in silence for a beat, connected by the hum of the line and the weight of what I just admitted.

"I'm happy for you. You deserve to be swept off your feet and shown the world. But two things . . ."

"Oh, God, you're going to make a list."

"I am." She chuckles. "First, he's a star, but you also deserve the limelight. Second, protect your heart, but don't guard it so hard that you run from something real."

"I'm not. I'm just scared of what happens when the spotlight fades."

"Then make sure you've got something that still shines when it does."

CHAPTER
thirty-eight

Rocket

'VE PLAYED TO EIGHTY THOUSAND SCREAMING FANS WITHOUT MISSING a beat.

I've stood half-drunk on rooftops while paparazzi chased a car they thought I was in like a pack of wolves on the city streets below.

I confronted my mom when I was a teenager and told her I no longer wanted her in my life because all she brought me was hurt, even though I knew that meant I might become homeless.

But nothing, and I mean nothing, has made my hands sweat like this moment. Like right now.

I tap my fingers against the paper coffee cup, trying to abate some of the tension. It doesn't work. My palms are slick, and my knee won't stop bouncing.

Because I'm terrified of losing my daughter.

I've never met Olivia's parents before. Never even heard their names until recently—Jean and Denny Whitmore. And now I've invited them to a coffee shop two blocks from the venue like I'm not about to be their worst nightmare in real time. Or them, mine.

Grief? Anger? A slap across the face?

I can easily handle that, but what I didn't expect was the weight of silence that enters before they even say a word.

Mrs. Whitmore walks in first—spine stiff, shoulders tight, her purse clutched like it's the only thing keeping her upright. Mr. Whitmore's not far behind. His stare lands on me and doesn't leave. It's cold. Controlled.

I stand before they reach the table. "Mr. and Mrs. Whitmore—"

"You have some nerve thinking you're better for her than we are," Mr. Whitmore says. His jaw's clenched so tight I don't know how his teeth aren't cracking.

I nod and struggle with what to say. Everything I had planned in my head has disappeared. "I just wanted to talk. About Poppy."

Mrs. Whitmore looks at me with an unreadable expression. "You mean *your* daughter, now that Olivia is gone?"

"Yes, she *is* my daughter," I say quietly, hands gripping the coffee cup so hard it buckles in the middle. "But she's also your granddaughter. I'm not trying to take her away from you."

For the slightest second, Mrs. Whitmore's face softens, but Mr. Whitmore escalates the situation. "Take her away from us? We'll be taking her away from you, you piece of shit. She's all we have left of our daughter," he says contemptuously. "We've already buried our child. We're not going to stand by while the man who didn't give a damn about Olivia pretends he can raise her."

My throat locks up, and I bite back the inherent reflex to be defensive. Willow was right. She said they'd be angry due to their misplaced grief. She said they'd take it out on me and that I couldn't take the bait.

She didn't say how fucking hard that would be.

I clear my throat. "I know you're hurting. I recognize and acknowledge that," I say, voice scraping raw as I do everything I can to be the mature one in this conversation. Fuck, is it hard. "But she's still my daughter."

Mr. Whitmore's eyes flare. "You didn't care about Olivia," he repeats.

"Just because the time we spent together wasn't long . . . doesn't mean I didn't care about her. On a different level." There is no easy way to answer that question.

Mrs. Whitmore's brows lift, but I continue.

"I didn't know about Poppy. If I had—" I stop, swallow the lump forming in my throat. "I would've shown up. I would've helped in every way possible. I would have been there from day one."

"Would you have?" Mr. Whitmore asks. "Or would you have ghosted her like every other headline says you do?"

That one stings.

But I take the hit because he's probably right. I'm not the same man I was three months ago. I give him that response, knowing now what I would have missed out on had the old me found out Olivia was pregnant.

And I also take the hit without arguing because he's grieving. Because that pain doesn't always know where to go, and maybe I'm the only place it can land.

"Headlines are just that, sir. You can find one to fit whichever narrative you wish to paint. But since Poppy has come into my life, I'm more conscious now about my choices and decisions than ever."

Mrs. Whitmore places a gentle hand on her husband's arm. It seems like it's a silent request, like she can't handle living in his pain anymore.

He looks at her, hesitates, and then leans back in his chair. Clearly he's letting her take the lead now.

She turns to me, voice quieter now, but still firm.

"Thank you for agreeing to meet with us," she says as her hand tightens on her husband's arm. "May we still meet Poppy?"

My pulse races. "Yeah. Of course." I look outside the window of the coffee shop where Willow just appeared and nod for her to come in. "She should know you. You're part of her family. I'm not sure if Sandra informed you, but Poppy isn't talking much. It's a traumatic response to being with Olivia when . . . in the car during the accident." Mrs. Whitmore blinks back tears. "She's been seeing therapists to help her and has started saying words, but it's sporadic. She can hear you and understands, she just chooses not to speak right now. So in case she doesn't respond verbally, that's why."

The bell above the coffee shop door jingles as Willow walks in with Poppy on her hip. She spots me instantly and wriggles to get down.

Mrs. Whitmore sucks in an audible breath that expresses so much pain. It's a humbling sound, but one I think I understand now.

Willow lowers Poppy, and she instantly runs to where I'm sitting. She looks at me and then to the strangers sitting across from me as she wraps one hand around my arm and the other tighter on her rabbit.

"Hey, Popstar," I say as Willow steps up beside me and behind Poppy. "These are your mommy's parents. Your grandparents."

Poppy's eyebrows furrow for a split second before she shifts to face them, her head tilting to its side as she studies them.

"Remember how we talked earlier about how they really wanted to meet you? Isn't it special that you can meet and know your mommy's mommy and daddy?" She twists her fingers into the hem of my shirt as if she's deciding how she feels about this and them. "Like we talked about earlier, I know they might seem like strangers, but all they want to do is hang out here in the coffee shop, get to know you and bunny, and maybe buy you a treat or two."

"Whatever treat you want," Mrs. Whitmore says, voice shaky. "We just want to get to know you and be friends."

Poppy twists her lips and looks back to me. "Willow and I are going to sit right over there." I point to the far side of the smaller, basically empty café. "If you need us or feel scared like we might leave you, you can look and see that we haven't."

Her fingers twist a little more, and then after a long, long moment, she lets go. I can see her trying to be brave, as she cautiously moves closer to Mrs. Whitmore and points to the little purple dragon stuffed animal she's produced from her purse.

"Hi there," Mrs. Whitmore whispers in a broken voice as tears flood her eyes. "This is for you. Your mommy used to have one just like it when she was little."

Mr. Whitmore stays frozen in place, but the way he works his throat looks like he's swallowing broken glass.

Mrs. Whitmore reaches up and runs the back of her hand down Poppy's cheek, and her shoulders shudder as she fights the emotion. "This is your grandpa," she says and points to Mr. Whitmore.

Willow rocks on her heels, clearly as uncomfortable as I am. We feel weird standing here, like we're invading their privacy, but at the same time, we need to do what's best for Poppy.

I clear my throat. "Poppy, are you okay if we sit right there?" I point to the table and chairs about fifteen feet away.

She glances at the table and then back to me several times before nodding.

"Okay. We'll be right there. We're not going anywhere," I repeat.

"Thank you," Mrs. Whitmore says.

Willow moves to the table with me, her arm brushing mine. She doesn't say anything as we walk, but I feel her gaze on me.

We take a seat, and I give an unsteady but encouraging smile to Poppy who's making sure we actually sit down. Once Poppy is convinced that we're not leaving and turns her attention back to the Whitmores, Willow reaches out to hold my hand as I struggle not to look back toward them.

"You did good," Willow murmurs.

I don't answer. I don't know if I can.

Besides the guys, Poppy is the first person I've ever cared about. The first person to show me what unconditional love is.

It's an overwhelming feeling.

As is what I feel for Willow. I hated but appreciated that Vince made me talk about it last night. About the woman seated across the table.

"So? You and Willow good?" Vince asks. His tone is quiet, reflective. Way different from the teasing tone the guys typically use with me.

They know Willow and I are fucking. They know I haven't entertained any-one else in my dressing room—or elsewhere.

But his tone, the look on his face, and the bottle of beer he slides in front of me say I'm about to get a Vincent Jennings, big brother chat.

This should be interesting.

"Good? Yeah, I guess?" He raises his eyebrows at me. I roll my eyes. "You're asking because why?"

"Being on tour can be a lot. Pressure. Togetherness. Annoyance. You guys managing that all right?"

"Yeah. There's been none of that."

"Huh."

"Huh? Dude. Do you forget she lives with me at home? That she came in not thinking too highly of me, therefore, there wasn't many more ways to go than up when it came to her opinion of me."

"True. You were kind of an asshole. But I like this guy you are now. Poppy's changed you . . . for the better."

"Poppy and Willow," I murmur more to myself than to anyone.

His eyebrows shoot up. "You included her in that statement."

I nod slowly, trying to figure out what he's getting at. "I did. Why?"

"No reason."

"You wouldn't have said it if there wasn't a reason."

"It's just that when you start including a woman in the reasons you've become

a better man, then maybe it's time to look a little closer at that woman. At that relationship. And maybe, you know, figure out how to hold on a little tighter to it."

His words aren't anything I haven't been thinking in the dark of the night when I stare at the ceiling with Willow nearby. But hearing them out loud, knowing someone else has noticed it, is huge. Jarring. Fucking with my head.

"It's so different with her."

"You need to ask yourself this. If there were no Poppy, if that side of it were to go away, would you still feel the same about her?"

"Yes."

He nods. It's slow and measured as is his next sip of his beer. "Well, there's that."

Talking emotions is not my strong suit. Never has been. But this is Vince, and Vince is . . . the sounding board in our group. Plus, he's been through this in his own way.

I draw in a deep breath and just talk without fear of judgment. "I've never known anyone that I can be comfortable in silence with yet still feel . . . heard." Damn, I wish this beer were something stronger. "She likes me for me. She saw the worst before she saw the better. She doesn't expect me to be . . . perfect."

"She just wants you to show up, right?"

"Yeah."

"Don't fuck that up, Rock. I've watched her with you and you're right. She's cool. She's fucking amazing with Poppy."

I laugh because he's right.

She's fucking amazing with Poppy. Don't know how I would have gotten through the last five weeks without her.

The chime on the door pulls me from my thoughts and back to the woman before me. To the situation at hand.

Willow is watching Poppy—eyes soft, smile faint.

"If there were no Poppy, if that side of it were to go away, would you still feel the same about her?"

Yes.

And for the first time, I let myself wonder . . . what if this isn't just temporary?

What if this is the beginning of something I never believed I could have? That I *deserve* to have?

To quote Vince, *don't fuck it up.*

CHAPTER
thirty-nine

Willow

P OPPY'S CURLED UP IN THE BACK SEAT, WRAPPED IN THE SOFT BLANKET she never sleeps without, bunny tucked under her chin, one chubby arm flung above her head. She's out cold—so peaceful it makes me smile. The nightmares haven't completely gone. I feared that seeing her grandparents today might conjure up more thoughts about her mom, about what happened, but for now, she sleeps. I had questioned whether she'd be able to understand *who* the Whitmores were outside of the context of her mom. But I don't think she did.

For now, she seems at peace.

And then there's the man beside me . . .

We're parked on a quiet overlook just outside the city, headlights off, the sky overhead a wash of smoky twilight. Down below, a runway glows in the distance, blue and red lights marking the stretch of tarmac where planes roar into the air every few minutes.

One takes off now. Rocket sits watching it, tracking its ascent from one side of the runway until it's up and gone.

I huff a small laugh. "Don't you get enough of airplanes with all the travel?"

He shrugs. "It lets me think."

I haven't seen this expression all day. I wouldn't exactly describe it as calm, but more like the closest thing I've seen to that.

He's been tense ever since we pulled up to the coffee shop. Since Poppy's tiny hand twisted in his shirt, and her grandparents spent time with her. Since the weight of what he thought they'd say, what they'd take, what they might judge—all of it—landed like a brick on his shoulders.

I watched it happen.

I also watched it fade.

Not all at once. But slowly. After Poppy climbed into her grandmother's lap without fear. After her grandfather crouched down to show her an old photo of Olivia. After Rocket sat at the table a few feet away, silent and tense, holding his breath as he waited for the other shoe to drop . . . that never actually dropped.

And now, here we are. A car full of quiet space. No more tension, just leftover adrenaline and exhaustion. Maybe something else, too.

I study him for a second, the slope of his shoulders, the way his hands sit loosely on his thighs now instead of clenched like they were earlier. There's still worry around his eyes, but it's not sharp anymore. It's softer. Reflective.

I reach over and slide my hand into his and link our fingers together.

He looks down like he wasn't expecting it, but he doesn't pull away. It's his way of letting me in. It's his way of welcoming me into the quiet with him.

"Do you feel okay?" I ask softly. "About what happened?"

He nods, staring ahead at the next plane lining up to take off. "Yes. No. It went better than I thought, I guess. They didn't try to take her—new fear unlocked. Didn't try to turn her against me—which is always a bonus. It was just . . . weird, but I can't explain why."

"They love her. She's all they have left of their daughter."

"I know. But those things scare me."

I squeeze his hand. "It would scare anyone."

"I didn't want them to see me as the guy Olivia used to know. The one who partied too hard and couldn't commit to anything longer than a tour cycle."

"You're not that guy anymore," I whisper.

He doesn't answer, doesn't disagree, but he squeezes my hand back.

"It's okay to be scared. To have irrational fears about the silliest thing hurting her. That's just part of being a parent—or so I'm told."

"It's weird. I went from caring about no one but myself to feeling like more of my thoughts than not are about you and Poppy and if you're okay or have what you need or . . . it's ridiculous."

It may be, but the comment makes me smile. Makes me feel so much a part of his world and center to know he cares like that about me.

"It must be maddening," I tease.

He presses a kiss to our joined hands but doesn't look my way as he chuckles. "I kind of like it . . . *when I'm not worrying.*"

Another plane rumbles past, climbing fast, disappearing into the clouds, as I rest my head on his shoulder.

He doesn't move. Doesn't react. We just sit like this—fingers tangled and thoughts unspoken—but not alone.

And then *I* realize something.

Rocket Caldwell has made me like the quiet, too.

CHAPTER
forty

Willow

Rocket's dressing room is quiet.

Poppy's asleep on the couch in the corner. Her headphones are on to help block out the noise, and under each arm is tucked both her bunny and new dragon. The noise outside the door in the hallway is continuous. Crew members rushing back and forth, cases being wheeled where they need to be, management doing their thing.

So I welcome this bout of peace before the chaos of the concert starts. And as with every night, I'll let Poppy dictate if she wants to watch it, whether she wants to play backstage in the greenroom, or if she just wants to go back to the hotel and play there.

It's her choice. It has been the entire trip.

I sink down into the chair on the far side of the room, phone pressed to my ear, waiting for her to pick up.

"Hi Momma. How are you?"

"Willow. So good to hear your voice," she says. "How's the road treating you?"

I smile. "So far, so good. Tiring. Exhilarating. A once-in-a-lifetime experience."

"So you're having fun then? Are the crowds wild? Is Poppy doing okay?"

"Yeah. She's adjusting better than I thought she would." I tuck my knees beneath me. "She loves watching Rocket do sound check. I think she believes he's a superhero."

"Well, he does have that tall-dark-and-brooding thing going for him," Mom says with a laugh. "Though I wouldn't say that to his face."

"I'm not sure he'd disagree."

She's quiet for a beat, then asks, "Are you doing okay?"

"I'm fine," I answer quickly.

"Willow."

I sigh. "I'm good, Mom. Really."

"You're awfully quiet, honey. Are you sure you're okay?"

I close my eyes and rest my head against the wall. "Yeah," I say softly. "I am."

Another pause. Then, gentle as ever, "You've fallen for him, haven't you?"

The words hang there.

I don't speak.

I don't have to.

My mom knows me better than anybody so arguing the point would be moot. She already knows.

I can feel the truth thrum through my chest like a second heartbeat, but saying it out loud feels too big, too real, too soon. I swallow hard, eyes burning slightly. "I'm taking it day by day," I lie to the both of us. "We'll see what happens when we return to everyday life back in Los Angeles."

Yes, I am.

"I'm happy for you. Proud of your maturity," she says, no trace of judgment in her tone. Just love. "You deserve to have whatever it is that you want to happen, happen. To be happy. To let that heart of yours feel as much love as you give."

I press my fingers to my lips, emotions swelling like an unexpected tide.

"Thanks, Mom," I whisper.

"Anytime, baby. Just promise me one thing."

"What?"

"Don't run from it just because it scares you. Sometimes the biggest risks lead to the best kind of love."

I nod, even though she can't see it.

"I won't."

And for the first time since this tour started, I believe it.

CHAPTER
forty-one

Willow

T HE WATER IS CALM, LIKE POLISHED GLASS, AND THE SUN IS HIGH AND bright in the sky.

We're anchored somewhere just outside the city, far enough from the marina that the noise of the world feels like it belongs to someone else.

No paparazzi. No schedule. No distractions. No fear of being caught for being more than nanny and boss.

Just the two of us.

Rocket chartered the boat for the day and arranged for Poppy to hang out with Hendrix. He said he wanted us to have something that felt normal. That felt like we were any other couple out for a day.

Couple.

That word gave me pause. We've never labeled what we are. Never really spoken about it in more than general terms . . . and so to hear him give us one felt amazing.

Lily may have sent me several lewd texts with accompanying emojis after I texted her about it. *Of course.*

And now I'm stretched out on a padded sun lounger in a bikini, hair twisted up in a knot, and skin warm from both the sun and the champagne. Rocket's lying beside me, sunglasses on, shirt off, and one knee bent casually.

The boat's gentle sway makes me sleepy.

"I figured you needed a break from taking care of someone else."

I peek over at him with my hand shielding my eyes. "Does that include you?" I ask coyly.

"We'll get to that in a second." His grin is lightning fast. "And from being under the microscope you never knowingly agreed to be under."

"I'm a big girl, I can handle myself."

"No one said you couldn't."

"So . . . no Poppy. No new activities to figure out or where to explore. No paparazzi or prying eyes," I say and glance over to the last place I saw any crew members. They do a great job of staying hidden, but I still know they're there. It's so foreign to have people waiting on me. It makes me feel guilty.

"Nope. None of that," Rocket says as his eyes scrape over every inch of my body. "No computer to stress over that master's program you will be starting up again soon."

"Don't remind me. I'm already stressing over it."

"You have it partially done. You'll kick ass on the rest of it. I have faith in you."

"At least someone does," I laugh. "So what exactly would you like me to focus on instead?"

He shifts so that his growing erection under his swim trunks is hard to miss. "Pretty obvious answer."

I roll my eyes, but my cheeks flush anyway. "Wow. So subtle."

He grins, slow and wicked.

I sit up and move to the edge of his lounger so that my knees bracket his hips. I settle there so I can enjoy the feel of his cock pressing against the fabric of my suit and then lean down and brush my lips over his.

The kiss is lazy at first. Sun warmed and unhurried.

But then he tilts his head, deepens it, and suddenly the kiss ignites. It's all tongue and growls and the press of his hands against my back like he's trying to map my curves.

I get lost in the kiss. In the feel of him. The taste of him. My body heats and hums and rocks against his cock, wanting to rush this moment to get to the next while also wanting to savor every damn second of it.

And then reality hits me and I pull back a fraction. "There are people on this boat," I whisper.

"And?" he murmurs against my lips.

"I don't want to get caught by staff."

"Staff?" He cups the back of my neck and pulls me back in for another kiss. "Listen to yourself adjusting to this lifestyle. You sound like you were born on a yacht."

I press my forehead to his and exhale a laugh. "This is crazy, right?" The yacht. The ocean on a random Wednesday in July. The rock star I'm currently straddling. "Like batshit crazy."

"Only if we pretend it doesn't feel good," he says and grinds his hips up, hitting me right where it makes me sigh.

"Oh, please." I swat at his chest, but he catches my wrist and brings my palm to his lips to kiss it.

The action is so intimate that it takes me aback for a second.

Just long enough for one of the crew members to head over and replace our downed drinks with fresh ones.

"Thank you," we both say as I shift to sit beside him on his lounger. He's on his back, I'm on my side, and our fingers of one hand are tangled together as I listen to his heartbeat beneath my ear on his chest.

The fingertips of his other hand trail lazily up and down my back as a seagull squawks overhead. "You ever think about how insane the past months have been?"

"All the time."

"I mean, you're on the verge of surviving a national tour, the relentless media attention, a toddler on the road, three rock stars who are sarcastic as fuck, *and* me."

Each time he adds on, my grin grows wider. "It's definitely been a ride." I press a kiss to his chest. "Life would've been a whole lot easier without that last one, though."

"Funny."

"I try to be."

Those fingers of his start tickling my sides until I'm squirming and begging him to stop. He chuckles and presses a kiss to the top of my head.

I look up at him and study his face. The way the corners of his eyes crinkle. The way he seems more relaxed today than I've ever seen him, like he's no longer carrying the weight of the world.

Feelings I've never had before inundate me. I loved James—with my whole heart—but I never looked at him and felt such adoration. Devotion. Like everything ends and begins with him.

But how is that possible when we've only known each other for such a brief time? "*It's the pressure cooker of the situation. It speeds things up and makes everything that much more intense.*" Isn't that what my mom said when I spoke to her last week?

"What is it?" he asks, brow furrowed.

"Nothing."

Panic hits me. Like, I feel this way, but how does he feel? I know this is more than he's ever had with anyone else—at least according to the guys—and yet . . . what does that mean?

"Come on. Tell me."

"I don't think I could ever live this life," I blurt out, afraid he's seeing right through me and my thoughts.

His laughter fades. Not abruptly, just slow enough that I don't register what I've said until the silence stretches between us.

I glance over. His expression's impassive, but his jaw is tense.

"Rocket? What's wrong? I don't mean to sound ungrateful or anything for all that you've done for me and the experiences I've had."

He doesn't respond at first. I study his profile as I prop my head on my hand and wait for him to speak.

When he finally does, he doesn't look at me. "You really don't think you could live this life?"

There's no teasing now. No glint of mischief. Just that slow, burning intensity I'm starting to crave.

I sit up, tuck my knees under me, and meet his eyes. "I didn't mean it like that. I just . . . I'm not used to this. Chartering boats. Private security. Headlines about what I'm wearing. It's a world I've never understood and am now suddenly a part of."

"Maybe it doesn't have to be like that," he says and reaches for me, thumb brushing over my cheek like he's trying to decide something.

I feel the shift in him again. The depth scares me a little because it's real.

And then he kisses me.

Not the way he usually does—full of swagger and hunger and heat.

This one is slow. Deliberate. The kind of kiss that says *I see you*. Even if I don't know what the hell that means yet.

His hands slide down my sides, over my hips, anchoring me to him.

And I stop thinking altogether.

Because when he touches me like this, I forget every logical reason why this could never work.

CHAPTER
forty-two

Willow

It's strange being back in a house that doesn't move. No lost room keys and going to the wrong room number. No late-night crew laughing as they load our luggage so we can move on to the next city. No opening another suitcase in yet another hotel room and forgetting what city we're in. No working to make the new hotel room yet another adventure so that Poppy was comfortable and happy.

Just stillness.

And quiet.

And the soft snores of Poppy sleeping in the room next to mine.

I stand at the window in an oversized T-shirt and panties, and stare out at the darkness beyond.

It feels good to be home. Even though it isn't mine, per se, it feels good to be able to let Poppy wander freely and not worry about her getting lost or someone taking her. And I think she feels it too because she was so adamant that she play on her own this evening in her chair by the window.

It feels great to be able to take a shower and not wonder what weird things other guests have done in them. And don't even get me started on the comforter situation.

I hear footsteps, prepare to see Poppy standing there, but when I look up, it's Rocket. He's standing in the doorway, no shirt, hands shoved in a pair of well-worn jeans, and a look on his face I can't decipher.

Every part of my body has a visceral reaction to the sight of him standing there—including my heart. It feels like that sucker breaks out of my rib cage and lands squarely at his feet.

"Hey."

"Hey." He leans a shoulder on the frame. "You're in my shirt."

I look down and blush. "I am. It smells like you." I smile sheepishly. "I like that."

"And I like seeing you in it." He runs a hand through his hair. "What serious thought was I interrupting?"

"Nothing. Everything." I shake my head. "Just how I need to decide whether I'm going to jump headfirst back into this master's program or consider going on this interview I got for that position at the elementary school."

"The one on the far side of town?"

I nod. It's a position. Far from here. One that would make it too hard to be a nanny and work at the same time. One that would *change everything*.

"I vote for staying the nanny and finishing your master's. But that's because I'm a selfish bastard and can't quite imagine this house without you in it anymore."

Our eyes meet. Hold. His words take root and warm me. Who doesn't like to feel needed? Who doesn't like to hear that you are?

But his words say more than that. They say live here with me. *Stay here with me. I want to do this with you.*

Or maybe that's what I want to believe they mean.

"I've already told you I'd pay for the master's program."

"I know, and I told you I don't need you to. Your generosity has already made it easy for me to complete my master's program." *And set me up to pay off my existing student loan debt.*

"Maybe I don't want you to have any reason to want to leave." He tilts his head, eyes drifting lazily across the room before locking on mine. "You're way over here in the house . . . and I'm way over there."

"Damn architect."

"I know. I was thinking of calling him up and having the rock starrest of all rock star tantrums over it," he says playfully.

"Oh, no. *Not that.*" My smile is genuine, and my heart has never felt this . . . full.

"The tour meant you were just right here. Next to me. All the time."

My pulse skips a beat. God, the way he said that—so casual, so devastating—it's almost like he's stating a fact. Like he doesn't even realize he's cracking something open inside me.

"It is your house. You're more than welcome to try out your guest bed . . . if you want." I shift.

He approaches me slowly, eyes playful. "Never done that before."

I laugh. "You've never slept in your guest rooms?"

He sits on the edge of my bed and gives it a quick bounce, testing the springs like he's making a very serious decision.

"Nope. Never."

And then, before I can say anything else, he reaches for me, tugs me gently between his knees, and wraps his arms around my waist. His head presses against my stomach like I'm the comfort he wants.

My fingers sink into his hair instinctively. It's soft and still damp at the base of his neck. I run my nails lightly over his scalp, and his body relaxes against me like I've just flipped some hidden switch.

"That feels good," he murmurs. "Keep doing it, and I'm going to fall asleep. I feel like I haven't slept in months."

"Because I don't think we have." We did. We slept, but how good do you really sleep when every place is somewhere new? "But the tour was good. The reviews were incredible."

"They were." He nods. "And I got to show you and Poppy some of the country and some of my world."

My throat tightens. "Yes. You did."

He tilts his head up. It's too tempting, and so I give in to my need, take my time, and lean down to brush my lips against his. The kiss isn't rushed. It isn't playful.

It's slow.

It's sensual.

It's a thank-you, a don't stop, and a *you matter to me more than I can explain*, all contained in this simple touch of our lips.

There's a whimper from Poppy's room. I rest my forehead against

Rocket's to listen, and then I hear it again. I press a kiss to his head before slipping out to check on her.

I expected a rough night. Sure, she's back home and she's tired from playing with less restrictions, but I also look at it as another reminder that her mom isn't here. Just because she's three and can't effectively communicate that she misses her, doesn't mean she doesn't.

I sneak in and adjust her blanket around her and her bunny, press a kiss to her curls, and murmur, "Love you," before walking out.

When I return to my bedroom, Rocket is propped up against the pillows, one arm behind his head, eyes closed like he's finally fallen asleep.

I study him—the lines of his body, the relaxed look on his face, how he looks lying in my bed waiting for me—and my heart thunders. It's never been more apparent than right now that I'm in love with Rocket Caldwell.

Ooof.

That's a huge admission I've been dancing around with tricks like saying *I'm falling for him.* Well, I'm way past falling.

I shut the door gently and slide in beside him.

"Come here, you," he murmurs as he pulls me against him so that my head is on his chest. I trace the lines of his tattoos, much like Poppy does, as his chest rises and falls.

We lie there for a few minutes, the darkness wrapping around us, before his voice breaks the silence. "I'm terrified of the hearing."

"I know you are, but I think it'll be fine."

"I have a past. It's not horrible, but it's been public. Wild years. Exaggerated headlines. Bad decisions."

"We all deserve a little grace for the things we did when we were younger."

"I hope that's true. But what if it's not enough? What if I lose her, Willow? What if—"

I press my fingers to his lips. "Shh. We're not thinking things like that."

"But—"

I kiss him to stop the words. To stop the negative thoughts. It's a slow, tantalizing kiss, as I try to anchor him to this moment. To me. To everything he's become instead of everything he's afraid he used to be.

And he lets me own this moment. He allows me to direct us to a place where sensation and feeling rule. And when my hand trails over his chest, down his stomach, and dips beneath his waistband, he handcuffs my wrist.

"No." He growls low in his throat and flips me gently onto my back.

"You took care of me on tour . . . and now I'm going to show you how good it feels to be taken care of in return."

His mouth trails down my stomach lighting a fire in its wake and burning his touch into my memory before positioning himself between my thighs.

He looks up at me in the dim light as he leans down and kisses me through my panties. His breath is a whisper against my skin. I arch reflexively into his mouth as my nerves sing, and my body aches.

I'm aware of the ache at my core, and of the tremble in my thighs as he slides his tongue along the edge of my underwear. The tip of his tongue teases, taunts, and tempts.

Our eyes meet through the dim light, and there's a darkness in his gaze that's equal parts hunger and adoration. A look that owns me in unexpected ways.

Almost as if he's confused which one should take center stage. Almost as if he's never had to choose before.

I reach down and thread my fingers through his hair, nails scraping lightly against his scalp as he presses his mouth hard against me, lips parting, tongue insistent and slow through the fabric. I grip his shoulders, helpless, dizzy against the sheets, and desperate for more.

He pulls my panties aside and glides a finger inside, featherlight. My body answers him instantly, greedy and wanting. Hungry and insatiable. He takes his time, hot breaths, featherlight touches, and murmured praise.

When he finally puts his mouth on me, I arch. I want to call his name, but can't form the sound. For a moment, the world telescopes to just this. To just us. To his warm tongue and the searing-hot pleasure. His rhythm is careful. Patient. Methodical. Skilled.

The orgasm is a slow build. The crest of a wave that pushes me up then pulls me under with an intensity I revel in.

"Come on, Wills. There you go," he murmurs, his lips against my belly as he lets me ride out my high.

And I do, but my thought as I come down is how he deserves to feel the same. How I want to return the favor.

He protests when I push him off me. When I press his shoulders to the bed and lick my lips in anticipation.

"Turnabout is fair play, right?" I say suggestively. He sucks in a breath as I trail my finger down his chest right to where his cock bobs in his pants.

"By all means." He chuckles then groans as I waste no time taking him in my mouth.

And I don't mess around. The very first bob of my head takes him all the way to the back of my throat until it can't go any farther.

"Fucking hell, Wills," he groans out, his hand going straight to the back of my head and fisting in my hair there.

It urges me on, the way my name sounds in his gritty voice. The way it feels to know I'm bringing him as much pleasure as he did me.

My lips work a rhythm, and his hips stutter, and my own pleasure lingers in the air like a benediction for us both.

He's not gentle as he fucks my mouth. He's not rough either. More like a man on the cusp of losing control but holding tightly to that one last thread remaining. The last thing holding him back.

It's in the way his hands keep tightening and flexing in my hair. How his chest shivers beneath my palm. The way he strangles on the guttural sounds clawing up his throat.

I smile around him, my lips tightening so I can drive him wild. I love the way he loses control, how the tattoos and the tough talk and the sprawl of his body all melt into a desperate need for my touch and my touch alone.

His thighs tense beneath my palms, but I take my time, slow and then faster, listening to the way his breath hitches, the way he breathes my name like a prayer and a plea.

"Wills, Jesus." He presses his head back into the pillow, his control unraveling with each second. Each time I pull back, I look up at him, and his eyes—lids heavy, pupils wide, undone—are the best reward.

When he finally comes apart, he shudders so hard it nearly lifts him off the bed, both hands tight in my hair, as if he's afraid I'll vanish. Another moment, and he collapses, boneless and spent, and starts to laugh.

"What?"

He leans up on one elbow and cups my cheek with his free hand, thumb smearing along my jaw. "Are you trying to ruin me, Wills?" he says, shaking his head in disbelief.

I shrug coyly, proud of garnering that reaction. I look him up and down. "Good. You look better ruined."

CHAPTER
forty-three

Rocket's been pacing the house all morning like he's trying to outrun something he can't name.

He's showered. Changed. Ignored calls from the guys—who no doubt know he's stressing. Tossed on a hoodie, then ripped it off again. Tried to eat. Left his plate where it was, barely touched, to walk back and forth on the grass out back. Stayed there staring at the ground for what felt like forever before rushing into his studio. Tried to play a few things in there but then cursed loudly and stalked back out.

Now he's leaning against the window frame in the living room, staring out at the street like it might hold the answers to the custody hearing he's dreading. He's too afraid to admit that, of course.

Because that's what this is all about. Nerves. Fear. The unknown.

I don't need to hear him confess a thing to know he's spiraling. I can hear his deep breaths from the other side of the room. He doesn't look at me when I speak. He checks on Poppy every fifteen minutes like he's already missing her.

"Hey, Caldwell."

"Hmm." He keeps staring at the street.

"I'm restless and feeling cooped up," I lie. "And I haven't figured out what to do for Poppy's dinner yet. What do you say we get out of the house for a bit and grab a bite to eat?"

He glances my way for the first time. I swear I can see relief flood through his posture at the lifeline I'm giving him.

"Where do you want to go?"

"How does anywhere but here sound?" I laugh. "Grab a hat and sunglasses. Probably best if you take that BENT shirt off too so we can go incognito."

He nods and a slow, steady smile paints his lips. I haven't seen that all day, and it's all I need to see to know I made the right suggestion. "Okay," he says softly and then turns to Poppy. "We—you, Willow, and I—are going on a date. How does that sound?"

She squeals and runs to his arms. They babble as he carries her down the hall to his bedroom to change. I watch their backs as they go, marveling at what a difference a few months makes.

Night and day and in all the best ways.

And the good mood keeps rolling as we find a wood-fired pizza place and allow Poppy to make her own pizza. To say she was ecstatic is an understatement. Then to a boutique where Rocket spoils her with a new doll that she now has clutched under her arm, right beside her bunny.

We walk a few blocks down, side by side with Poppy on his hip, where the breeze is a welcome relief in this heat. It feels like time slows down and allows us to have this moment. Like it knows how bad we need it.

Laughter is constant, as is Poppy pointing at everything and wanting it. She takes one last bite of a pretzel from the cart we passed when we round a corner and stop when we see a tattoo parlor.

Poppy tugs on Rocket's sleeve and points at the images in the window—the flowers, the dragons, the names inked into skin. She then looks at his arm and points.

"Dadda," she says. "Like you."

"Yes, like me," Rocket says, tugging on her ponytail and holding one arm out so that she can see the similarities.

I glance over to Rocket, curious why he's so quiet, and it's like I can see whatever thought that just jolted into his brain hit him.

His body straightens. His eyes sharpen. That worry he's been carrying seems to shift into something else. Something like resolve.

Fifteen minutes later, we're in a small studio tucked in the back of the shop. Music comes through the overhead speakers, but they turned it down for Poppy. The air smells like antiseptic and there's the constant stop and start of a low buzz from other artists elsewhere in the studio.

Rocket's shirtless, sitting on a black leather chair. I study the various tattoos he does have, each one a story in their own right, but something made him want to add another one.

And this one is different in every conceivable way.

CHAPTER
forty-four

Rocket

THE LEATHER IS COOL AGAINST MY BACK AS I SETTLE INTO THE CHAIR. There's no such thing as getting comfortable when you're about to subject yourself to pain, and yet this is a pain I welcome wholeheartedly.

I've done this a dozen times. Maybe more.

But today feels like it's the first time.

Willow sits cross-legged on a worn leather couch across the room. She's wearing one of my hoodies, sleeves shoved to her elbows, and bare legs tucked under her. She looks like home and heaven and hell all rolled into one.

Poppy's on her lap, head buried under her neck, but eyes locked on me and the tattoo artist almost as if she's fascinated but scared about what happens next.

This probably isn't the brightest thing to show a three-year-old—because over my dead body if she wants a tattoo when she's older—but it feels important for me to do this right now.

It will *show* her what her place is in my life—always.

The needle buzzes to life, and everything—the shop, the sound, the ache in my chest—all fades away.

And suddenly, I'm not here.

I'm back there.

The first time I saw her.

Not Willow.

Her. *Poppy.* Tiny. Silent. Holding a rabbit like it was the only armor she had, and with eyes too big for her face, looking at me like she already knew I was going to disappoint her.

I'd been hungover, still reeking of liquor and regret, staring at her like she was a vicious punishment.

She wasn't a daughter to me that day. She was proof of who I'd been. Of how badly I'd screwed up.

I hadn't seen her as a gift, but rather as a reckoning.

The needle touches my skin, right over my heart, and I suck in a sharp breath as the artist begins.

It burns. Not the needle. Not the pain it brings. More so, it's the meaning behind what the ink is creating.

Because I'm not that man anymore. I've become a better version of myself in this brief time that Poppy has come into my life, and I'm fucking terrified to lose her.

This tattoo isn't a punishment. It's a promise.

I glance at Willow. She's whispering something to Poppy, who's still watching me with eyes wide, and tiny fingers curled around Willow's.

I want to cry. I want to laugh. I want to stay right here forever.

"You were never my mistake, baby girl. You were my beginning," I whisper to myself before gritting my teeth as the needle digs a bit deeper.

As I let it brand me with a representation of the one thing I've spent my whole life trying to believe I could deserve. A family.

Poppy.

Willow.

Us.

And fuck if that thought doesn't start my spiral of thoughts all over again. I finally have something I never thought I wanted, deserved, and . . . *what if I lose it?*

The hearing. The custody battle. The possibility of losing Poppy. The thought of never having had Willow in my life.

I don't want to imagine my life without either ever again.

The artist finishes shading the stem, wipes the skin, and starts lining the petals.

I close my eyes because I'm not just getting a tattoo.

I'm getting marked.

By them.

For them.

Forever.

CHAPTER
forty-five

Willow

The poppy flower over Rocket's heart is both delicate and bold. Soft orange petals. Slender green stem. A flower that grows wild, that comes back year after year, and that looks like it could be blown away with one wrong breath yet still refuses to bend.

It's such a different tattoo from the rest he wears, but this one suits him. The pop of orange brightens all that dark.

He's not just wearing it. He's owning it.

Poppy squirms in my lap, fascinated by this place. She must be able to feel the vibrations of the buzzing or something because it's nap time and she's completely awake. Rocket lifts her up gently, careful of the plastic wrap that's been put on his chest to protect his new tattoo, and points to the spot.

"See, Popstar?" he says. "You're always with me now."

Poppy grins. That sweet smile that owns my heart. She reaches out to trace the outline through the wrap—like she's done to so many of his other tattoos before—almost as if she's sewing herself to him. He guides her finger gently over the plastic and lets her trace.

My heart both swells and explodes.

Because this tattoo wasn't for show. It wasn't to post on social media to brag about. It wasn't to pull up his shirt to show a judge in court.

This one was strictly for him.

This is Rocket Caldwell saying, "she's mine."

It makes me wonder, will he one day say that I'm his too?

The tattoo artist leaves us in the back room while he runs the bill through the register. Rocket stares at Poppy as tears flood his eyes. He catches me noticing, clears his throat, and blinks them away as his cheeks turn red.

"Well, well, well. The big bad rock star gets one tiny flower, and suddenly you're all sentimental," I tease, trying to save him from being embarrassed.

He groans and rolls his eyes, but I can tell he appreciates the levity. "It's not tiny. It's meaningful."

"Oh, of course. Very macho. Nothing says *tough guy* like delicate poppy petals."

"Careful, Adams. You keep running your mouth, I might have to tattoo your name next."

"Better be a prime location."

"How about right across my ass?"

I burst out laughing, and Poppy claps her hands, delighted even though she has no idea what we're laughing at.

And then Rocket steps closer. His smile fades only to be replaced by a quieter expression.

He steps into my space and cups my jaw gently as he meets my gaze.

"Thank you. I needed this today. To step outside of my head. To forget about Monday's hearing. Thank you for knowing what I needed when I didn't."

"That's my job."

"No. Poppy is. I'm you're . . ." His smile returns as he shakes his head like an epiphany just hit him.

My breath hitches. My heart hopes.

"I love you, Willow. I've tried to square it away a million different ways, tried to tell myself it was too fast or too complicated or too fucking risky. But I do. And I don't know what the hell to do with it."

Everything inside me softens and tightens simultaneously.

I stare at him for a long second, vibrating with the weight of his confession. And then I smile. Soft. Steady. Certain. How can I not when I've been waiting to hear those words from this man?

I cup the side of his face and welcome the stubble beneath my thumb. "You don't need to know what to do with it. I'm here and I'm head over heels in love with you too. Have been for some time." I brush my lips against his. "And as to what happens next? We just keep doing what we're doing. Laughing. Talking. Taking care of Poppy. Cheering on each other's successes. Making memories together. Whatever it takes, right?"

I don't need a road map when it comes to Rocket.

I already know where I want to end up.

CHAPTER
forty-six

Rocket

Sandra's sigh is heavy. The kind that sounds like it's dragging the whole damn world behind it. "This is the worst timing for this to come out."

My thumb hovers over the screen of my phone, but the image burns brightly. Me and Willow in the tattoo parlor with my hand on her ass and her lips against mine.

A private moment, twisted, framed, and fucking sold.

It's not just the photo, but rather the headline beneath it that has dread filtering through my stomach. It's clickbait trash designed to shred reputations and smear everything it touches. And what it says about Willow, about her character and her motives behind being with me, makes me see red.

"This is bullshit. Total and utter bullshit. Willow's never dated other dads she's nannied for. Her boyfriend in college was well-off, but she wasn't with him hoping for the money. She didn't get laid off from her teaching job due to inappropriate behavior with a supervisor. This makes it sound like she's some Lolita gold digger who goes from job to job to fuck the husband." I shove up and out of my chair to contain some of my rage. "How do we do damage control? How do we fix this for her—"

"I don't think we can. And honestly, I wouldn't put it past the Whitmores to be behind this. Perfect timing. Public leak the day before the hearing? It's strategic. Calculated. Damning."

I pace my office like a caged animal, one hand tugging through my hair as I fight the urge to break something.

"I told you—"

"I know what you told me. I know you said anyone knowing would mess with her credibility. But . . . Sandra, we were in a private place of business."

"You were, but you know better than anyone that everything is on the table these days. Private or not private. Was the door locked after you went in? Did other customers happen to arrive and wait for an opening after you? Could've been a PI working for the Whitmores. Could've waited for you two to drop your guard."

"Then this is more about discrediting Willow than it is me. Her word. Her character. Her . . . fucking livelihood."

"That would seem so."

"So what do we do? How do we fix this?"

"There is no fixing this once it's in the public like this."

Her words hit and make me feel even more helpless than I already feel. Willow is as pure as pure can be. Until she met me. Until my shadow just fucking tainted her.

"Rocket—"

"Just . . . I need a minute to think." I pace the office, potentially wearing holes in the carpet. *C'mon brain. See past the rage. Try to focus.* I draw in a deep breath. "Do we need to adjust our strategy?" I finally ask.

"No. We stick to the plan," she says but doesn't sound as confident as she wants me to think she is.

Fucking great. Just what I need to hear right now.

"Okay. So stick to the plan, but then what about Willow? Can we release a statement? Can we paint the correct picture?"

There's a pause. Too long.

"We do nothing."

Her words hit like a fucking battering ram. "What do you mean, *we do nothing?*"

"We do whatever it takes to ensure the judge rules in your favor," she says, her voice lacking all emotion. She clears her throat. "Even if that means sacrificing her."

I stop pacing. My synapses misfire. The music I usually hear in my head goes silent, because it feels like something inside me just snapped. "No." I shake my head. I love her. I can't lose her or fuck her over. "We can't do that."

"I understand your immediate refusal. I'm not saying we will, but Rocket if it comes down to Willow or Poppy, Poppy is who we're fighting for."

"I didn't agree to this," I say.

"There are no rules here. Nothing to agree to. If they're going to play dirty, then we might need to as well." She clears her throat. "I suggest you put on some boots and prepare for the mud fight because that's what it just might be."

"Uh-huh," I murmur.

She chatters on a few minutes about what to wear tomorrow and what time to show up. About how she'll contact Willow about what to expect.

And by the time I hang up, I'm still not processing what this has turned into.

"You gotta be fucking kidding me," I mutter and scrub a hand over my face as I stumble to my office chair and sit.

The quiet in the room is deafening. *Fuck.* I grip the arms of the chair, jaw locked and lungs burning.

She didn't ask for this.

Willow didn't ask to be dragged into court battles and custody wars and scandalized headlines. She didn't ask to be part of this family. My band. *This fucking circus.*

But now it's her circus too.

Fuck.

Her words from the tattoo parlor run through my mind.

"I'm here and I'm head over heels in love with you too. Have been for some time. And as to what happens next? We just keep doing what we're doing. Laughing. Talking. Taking care of Poppy. Cheering on each other's successes. Making memories together. Whatever it takes, right?"

She chose me. *Us.*

And now she's the one who's going to be sacrificed because of it.

The panic creeps up my spine like it's ready to devour me. Months ago, the only person I wanted to or knew how to fight for was myself, my band, and now I'm being asked to pick Willow or Poppy when I want to pick both.

How did this happen?

I see something move in my periphery, and I look up. Willow's standing there, and my chest constricts.

Her hair is still wet from the shower. One of Poppy's toys is in her hand like she was mid toy pickup. Her eyes are wide, her mouth is slightly parted, and she's seemingly completely oblivious to what I just heard. To what my lawyer just offered as an option.

To sacrifice her.

To win at all costs.

My stomach pitches. The need to tell her owns me.

I open my mouth to tell her, but then I see the way she looks at me—like I'm her anchor. Her safe place. And the words catch in my throat and die.

It won't come to that.

I won't let it come hell or high water.

"Rocket, I need to show you something," she says and holds up her phone.

"What is it?" I ask but already know.

She holds up her phone. It's the same headline. The same bullshit photo.

"Someone saw us at the tattoo parlor. The story's out."

She doesn't say what else it says. All of the cruel bullshit about her. She neglects to tell me that it trashes her and her reputation and paints her in a horrible light.

She doesn't need to. I already know.

"I'm sorry." Her brow furrows. "I didn't think. I kissed you in public. I just . . . the moment, what your tattoo meant to you. I let it all get to me, and now the moment is ruined."

The moment when I told her I loved her. *She sees her name tarnished, dragged through the mud because of me, and she feels the need to apologize?* Fuck that.

"Please don't apologize. You don't deserve this. I never meant to pull you into this."

And she doesn't know it yet, but I'm not just talking about the picture.

I'm talking about what Sandra said. About what the courts could do. About what circumstances might force us to do.

"This is on me. I've jeopardized—"

"No. You didn't. This is on me."

Tears well in her eyes. "You know I'd do whatever it takes to make sure you get Poppy. The last thing I want to do is risk that."

I reach out, take her hand, and pull her into my lap. Instantly she curls against me like she belongs there.

Because she does.

I bury my face in her shoulder and breathe her in.

"I know you would. But you need to make sure you take care of yourself first."

Because if this gets worse, if they come for her harder than we can protect her, I need to be strong enough to carry us all.

"Promise me, Wills."

She just buries her head into the crook of my neck and holds on instead.

CHAPTER
forty-seven

Willow

THE COURTROOM FEELS COLDER THAN I EXPECTED.

Cold in the amount of people staring at me with impassive looks. Cold in the way every shuffle, breath, and movement echoes too loud in my ears. Cold in this dark wood, dimly lit room with its hard seats that feel anything but welcoming.

I sit stiffly in the witness chair, palms flat against my thighs, spine stiff, and heart pounding so hard I can feel it in my fingers. The gallery is full of reporters and strangers and people with notepads pretending they're here for a headline.

Flashes went off as I entered the courthouse.

Cameras may be banned inside, but that hasn't stopped the damage. My name's already smeared across every tabloid. Each headline twisting the story to outdo the next so theirs is the one that goes viral. "Nanny Scandal." "Sleeping Her Way To a Fortune." "The Rock Star Buys Her Off with Sex."

Their salacious nature is ridiculous, and yet people are talking, are commenting on the posts, and then sharing them to feed this beast.

And to ruin my reputation.

It's been an overwhelming turn of events I never anticipated. Me, being the bad guy in all of this. Me, possibly being the reason Rocket wouldn't get custody of Poppy. I've never had my integrity questioned more than I have in the last twenty-four hours, and it's been disheartening, overwhelming, and terrifying.

Rocket has tried to shield me from it, but it's about as effective as standing in front of a freight train. It's impossible to stop.

But I'm a big girl, and he has way more important things to focus on than protecting me. Like making sure he maintains his cool during these proceedings and proving the Whitmore's claims that he's a hothead fueled by hard partying, recreational drug use, and a hectic lifestyle to be wrong. And while he is a multimillionaire with what I presume is an impressive set of lawyers, they have grief on their side.

And grief is a powerful drug that feeds every other emotion.

My hands tremble, and I brace them on my thighs as the procedural silence in the courtroom continues.

It takes everything I have not to look at Rocket. I know if I do, I might lose what little composure I've scraped together.

And yet, I sneak a glance at the courtroom gallery and am startled to see Gizmo sans Hendrix, who is watching Poppy for us, Vince and Bristol, and Hawkin and Quinlan, all sitting behind Rocket like a phalanx to protect him and show unity.

My chest constricts at the sight. At knowing they're trying to show that Rocket has his own loving and supportive family who'll help him when and if he needs it.

I begged my parents not to come—not wanting to subject them to this circus—and I'm grateful that, despite putting up a fight, they did as I asked.

My eyes shift to Rocket now. He's sitting—stone-faced, beautiful, devastated—beside Sandra. His jaw is set, and his hands fist on the table, like he's holding himself back from getting up and dragging me out of here.

I don't belong here—in this courtroom or in this narrative. And yet I'm here.

Because of Poppy.

Because in taking this job, I made a promise to protect her. To do what's best for her. And this is doing just that.

The judge calls the room back to order. Olivia's parents are seated across the aisle with stoic expressions and stiff postures, and dressed in dark colors.

I take a breath and go through the motions. I swear to tell the truth, but I don't even hear my own voice anymore. Instead, I focus on the court reporter's fingers clicking on her keys.

Sandra moves to the well of the court and stands in its center. "Ms. Adams, can you describe your role in Poppy's life?"

"I'm her nanny."

"And when were you employed and by whom?"

"Child Protective Services contacted me to assist with a traumatized orphan while they located and verified who the father was. I agreed to help, and then when the father was confirmed to be Mr. Caldwell, he asked that I stay on and help him with Poppy's care."

"And that care included what?"

"Everything from daily hygiene, nutrition, and foundational education to facilitating therapy appointments, enrichment activities, and snuggles. You name it."

"And you are on-site, correct?"

"Meaning do I live at the Caldwell residence? Yes. My room is right next to Poppy's for convenience and safety."

"I see," Sandra says as my heart continues to race. I know the questions that will be coming and yet answering them in Sandra's comfortable office is far different from this cold courtroom. "And are you aware if Mr. Caldwell knew of Poppy's existence prior to her arrival?"

"Not to my knowledge, no."

"And how would you describe his adjustment to fatherhood and to Poppy?"

I inhale sharply and look just over the heads of the gallery. "I think he's adjusted well. Understandably, he was shocked initially, as I assume anyone would when thrown into that position as a new parent. He struggled at first. But he's made effort to learn how to communicate with Poppy, he's adjusted things in his house to be safe for a toddler, and when he was on tour with Poppy, he ensured her ears were protected from loud music if she was backstage, and attempted to provide as normal a routine as much as possible. He is patient and funny and . . ." My throat tightens, and my voice breaks. "He's become her most favorite person and vice versa."

Sandra nods. "Thank you. No further questions."

Then the lawyer for the Whitmores stands. Where Sandra came across as welcoming and non-confrontational, this man intimidates me with his slick hair and smug smirk.

"Ms. Adams. Hi." His smile holds no warmth. "Let's revisit your words. Struggled at first. Interesting phrase. Would you define, oh, I don't know, excessive drinking, not coming home until the early hours of the morning multiple times the first few weeks after Poppy arrived, and choosing to be at the studio rather than home as struggling? Was it really struggling or more like absentee fathering while his nanny did all the work?"

My heart races. My eyes dart around the room.

"That was before Poppy."

"Actually, it was in the weeks after Poppy arrived if the gate logs to his community and the metadata on the paparazzi photos taken are correct."

"Like I said, there was an adjustment period. It was a short amount of time, yes. But—"

"But you'll say anything because he pays you too, correct?"

"What?"

The lawyer moves around the well and ticks things off on his fingers as he goes. "Paid nanny services. Room and board. Lavish accommodations. VIP travel access. And as reported publicly . . . certain personal benefits?"

I freeze. The movement in the courtroom stills.

"Objection, Your Honor. Neither Ms. Adams, her compensation package, nor *her* behavior and actions are evidence of Mr. Caldwell's ability to keep custody of his daughter. Please have the comment about personal benefits struck from the records." She pauses and glances toward the Whitmore's attorney. "If Mr. Caldwell is out of the house, it doesn't matter seeing as his employed nanny is at home caring for the child."

"Sustained. The purpose of this hearing is to discuss Mr. Caldwell's custody of his own child. Is there a question about his ability that you wish to ask Ms. Adams?"

"Yes, Your Honor. You say your *employer* struggled with his new role. Can you explain what you mean by *struggle?*"

Heat flushes through my body. I don't want to make this any worse.

"I—uh—I think that is a subjective opinion and my opinions aren't exactly qualified by any means—"

"Your opinions are jaded, are they not? It's hard to remain unbiased when the father of the child you're supposed to protect is also your lover."

The word cracks like a whip in the air. The gallery murmurs. Someone shifts. A throat clears.

"I care about Poppy. That's why—"

"Just like you cared at your last charge where you snuggled up to the father in exchange for admission and a scholarship into your undergraduate program."

"What?" I bark out as the blood drains from my face. "My employer was an alumnus. That's it. Nothing was traded for anything."

"An alumnus that secured you a scholarship to pay for your education. What did you have to do in return for that *help?*"

"Judge, this is out of line," Sandra says.

"I'm simply establishing a precedent here to imply why Ms. Adams's opinions can't be seen as credible," the Whitmore's lawyer says.

"What social media and gossip sites write have no basis in this argument. It's hearsay. For Mr. Sally to ask these questions based on those articles is irresponsible, inflammatory, and shouldn't be allowed."

"Noted and agreed with. I'll allow the answer to this one question to see where you intend to go with this, but you're on a tight rope, here, Mr. Sally. Get to the point," the judge says.

"Of course." Mr. Sally turns back to me. "You were saying, Ms. Adams. About why you're here?"

My body's shaking violently, and I break out in a sweat. I'm flustered, struggling to sound coherent when I answer. I glance to the gallery and see several people shaking their heads, and that only adds to my torment.

"Ms. Adams?" the judge urges.

"I did nothing in return for the letter of recommendation my employer wrote the admissions office." I try to explain away his lies with the truth but fear it hasn't done any good. The judge may get to rule on the outcome, but the hundred or so people in the gallery who are probably posting on their social media channels right now just got more food to feed the fodder.

"No?" Mr. Sally suggests that he knows something no one else does.

I don't know what he's asking, and I can barely hear him over my own heartbeat. "I'm not here to lie for Mr. Caldwell. I'm here to tell the truth. I'm here for Poppy's best interest."

"Of course. Because you've been very . . . well taken care of. Haven't you?"

There's the scraping back of a chair as Rocket stands up. It's the first time I've looked at him. Devastation. Rage. Disbelief. Sandra puts a hand on his arm, whispering fast. No doubt begging him not to take the bait and look like the unhinged, unqualified parent they're trying to paint him out to be.

I look away as quickly as I look at him. One second longer, and I'll crumble.

My chest heaves. I blink too fast. My fingers curl into the fabric of my pants.

"Tell me, Ms. Adams, did Mr. Caldwell ask you to testify here today?"

What's the trick in this question? What is the best way to answer?

I don't know.

I don't want to make this worse.

I swallow over the lump in my throat. "No. I volunteered."

"Of course. It's only normal to want to protect one's lover."

All the breath leaves my lungs and I struggle to reinflate them. I straighten my spine.

"Like I've said several times, but you don't seem to hear. I'm not here for Mr. Caldwell. I'm here for his daughter and what's in her best interest. The little girl who knows more love in his arms than she'll ever find anywhere else."

Mr. Sally's smile is smarmy. "No further questions, Your Honor."

CHAPTER
forty-eight

Rocket

I DON'T REMEMBER GETTING BACK TO THE HOUSE.

One minute I'm sitting in that courtroom watching them gut Willow on the stand, staying after for a debrief with Sandra while Willow rushes home to get out of the limelight and back to Poppy, and the next I'm here, at home, pacing the floor like a fucking caged animal, my palms still damp and my pulse refusing to settle.

Fucking hell. *Her voice.* I hear it in my head on a loop. *"I'm not here for Mr. Caldwell. I'm here for his daughter and what's in her best interest. The little girl who knows more love in his arms than she'll ever find anywhere else."*

Strong. Brave. Shaking. And I just sat there. I didn't stop her. I didn't protect her. I fucking couldn't and felt so goddamn handcuffed.

I scrub my hands down my face and sit on the edge of the bed. But the second I close my eyes, I see her on that stand with her wide eyes and heart on her sleeve, bleeding for everyone to see.

Because of me.

Sandra's words echo louder now than they did the first time. *"Even if that means sacrificing her."*

I should've said no, fought harder against it. I should've stood up in court and defended her from that fucking prick of a lawyer.

But I didn't.

Fuck.

I glance over at the bathroom door. Willow's in there, giving Poppy a bath. I hear the soft sound of water splashing. Poppy giggling. Willow's voice sounds exhausted, spent, and still somehow soothing. She's still taking care of Poppy after what she went through today, and I'm sitting out here like the world's biggest asshole.

It kills me because I know what's coming.

She doesn't.

Not yet.

But I feel it rising like a swell I can't stop. The thought I can't unthink. The truth that no one would dispute. Willow's never going to be safe as long as she's with me.

Not from the bullshit accusations. Not from the stain the ones today will leave. Not from a world that eats women alive simply to spit out headlines.

Because the guy is never at fault. The male is always untouchable. But the woman . . . she's always to blame in their world.

Another round of giggles comes through the door, but they're only Poppy's when usually they're both. That hits me hard because I know, however hard she's playing off the ramifications of what happened today, of social media that is afire with it all, it has truly affected her.

Restless, I stand and move toward the window. I look out at the dark night beyond and question who is out there, watching? Who tricked their way past the guard shack and is out there waiting to catch a random photo that they can spin to further along the fucked-up story?

And when did I stop trusting the world?

Motherfucker.

I shut the blinds, but still stand there, lost in thought. Sure the PR spin is already underway, trying to discredit the photos, deflect the rumors, and repair Willow's public image.

But none of it matters. I know from my own experience. From those of my bandmates. The damage is already done, and Willow's at ground zero.

All because she loves me.

Fucking hell, I love her too, and that's what makes this whole situation ten times worse. Because I know now, deep down, that I'd walk through fire for her. That I'd do anything to protect her.

And after today, I think I might have to.

Just not the way I want.

The bathroom door creaks open, and she steps out. Poppy's wrapped in her bunny towel that has a hood and ears that flop over. Her damp tendrils of hair curl around her face that's red from the warm water.

Willow meets my eyes. They're hesitant. Gun-shy. And the sight of it fucking kills me.

Poppy asks for a snack, and Willow agrees way too quickly. She's trying to escape from having to face me. From having to relive that her presence here fucked her over.

They move to the kitchen, and I follow right behind. She looks over her shoulder at me, and everything inside me hurts. Is her expression one that says she's glad I'm here or one that says she'd rather be left alone?

I follow anyway because that one look did show she's already unraveling. It said the thread is pulled taut, and one more tug might snap it.

Maybe I can at least prevent that.

"Hey," I say.

She looks up at me as she peels and begins cutting a banana for Poppy.

"Tell me it's going to be okay," she whispers, voice thick with emotion.

I muster a smile that I know for a fact doesn't reach my eyes.

"I need to review the documents on this case. There are many, and for that reason, I'd like to reconvene next week at the same time for my decision."

The judge's monotone voice replays in my head. I thought this would all be over today, that we could start repairing the damage immediately, but now, of course, we have to wait a week. A week where it can fester and blow up to epic, untrue proportions.

"Tell me it's going to be okay," she repeats.

I can't.

Because it's not okay.

Not for her. Not anymore.

A quick look at social media has headlines flashing in front of my eyes. Terms like gold digger, slept her way to the top, and lies for money.

All because I kissed her.

All because I love her.

"In time it will be," I finally say.

She nods, but it's a nod that's meant to be brave, not honest. "I got flustered. I feel like I failed you."

"You didn't." And I mean it with everything I have.

"I'm sorry, Rocket," she says, her voice breaking.

"No, please don't cry." My heart sinks. She looks so sad. So vulnerable. "You were perfect."

She reaches for me. Just a hand on my chest. A question if this is okay in the midst of all this chaos.

I let her touch me, but I don't give in to the need to pull her closer.

I don't lift my hand to her waist. Don't bury my face in her hair like I want to. I just . . . stand there.

And her eyes shift. I see it. The flicker of confusion. The fear. *Why aren't you holding me back?*

"Rocket?"

My chest aches. "Let me finish snack and bedtime for Poppy. It's been a long day. You should get some sleep."

She hesitates. The hurt in her eyes fucking owns me. But she nods, presses a goodnight kiss to Poppy's head, and then she walks past me toward her room without looking back.

And I don't stop her.

Because I want to pull her into my arms and never let her go. But in loving her, I know that if I really want to protect her, if I really want Poppy *and Willow* to be okay, then I might have to break my own damn heart.

And hers.

To save them both.

CHAPTER
forty-nine

Willow

Poppy's laughter is a sound I don't deserve. It's like a balm to my soul—something that feels better for now but that I know doesn't fix anything.

She's sitting beside me at the small kiddie table Rocket put in what he's now deemed her new playroom. It's one of the extra bedrooms on his side of the house, situated off the kitchen and before his studio, the game room, and then his bedroom.

Within days of the hearing, it became a kick-ass playroom full of sensory items, stuffed animals, a rocking horse, and every new trendy item I can think of.

He's either willing her to remain in his custody, or he's finding an excuse to be so busy he doesn't have to be alone with me.

Maybe it's a little bit of both.

The matching game that Poppy is playing has her throwing her hands up and cheering each time she turns a card over and makes the match.

Begging this moment and these memories to be enough, but the courtroom's still echoing in my head. That lawyer's voice. The shame burned through me even though his accusations were lies. The way the entire room stared at me, questioning if they were true.

I take my turn and flip over a crown and then a frog. Poppy's eyes light up as she urges me to hurry up and turn the cards back over so she can make her match. And when I do, she hops on the crown card I turned over and then turns another one over to match it.

"Yay, Poppy!" She squeals and claps in excitement.

I cheer too but I also stutter in motion because she just said more words. Two strung together for the first time. And it's almost as if she's so excited, she doesn't even realize the words came out.

And as her therapist advised, I don't make a big deal about it. I let it go and cheer on her accomplishments instead.

I grin as tears burn at the backs of my eyes and hold Poppy's hand up high. "Winner. Winner. Chicken dinner," I shout out loud.

She giggles, and my heart soars.

This fierce, brilliant, big-hearted little girl deserves everything in the world, even if I might've just ruined her shot at staying with the man who loves her most.

The wait until our court date next week is already excruciating. Until the judge's decision is made. And while I appreciate she's taking her time to go through every character statement, every motion, or whatever it's called that's been filed, in the meantime, our lives hang precariously in the balance.

And that's never a good place to be.

It leads to overthinking. To self-doubt. To wondering what I could have done better.

If I hadn't gotten involved with Rocket, if I hadn't followed my heart and my lust, if I hadn't crossed the damn line and let him become my distraction, then none of this would've happened.

My word would have held. My opinions would be valid.

Fuck.

My phone buzzes on the table, so I pick it up, the tears threatening harder now.

"Hey, Mom."

"How's my girl?"

I bite the inside of my cheek. "You mean the disaster barely holding it together?" I laugh.

"I don't like what they're saying about you. What they're implying."

"Neither do I, but there's nothing I can do to stop it."

"Mr. Farley put out a statement. Did you see that?" she says of my old employer, whom Mr. Sally tried to implicate. "He stated that you were nothing but professional in your years working with him and his family. That you were accepted to the university on your exceedingly high marks and that call or no call from him, you would've been accepted into the program."

"That was nice of him, but it doesn't change anything."

"You're right. It doesn't. But maybe his threats to sue various media sites for defamation will lead them to retract their statements and issue an apology."

"The truth only gets a tenth of the coverage the lies do."

"Sweetheart, I wish there was something I could do. Someway I could help."

"I know you do." There's nothing anyone can. Not Rocket. Not his PR team. Not the kind words his bandmates have given to the press. Not my silence.

"Just remember that none of it matters. Not really. The people who love you know who you are."

My eyes sting. "I appreciate the sentiment, but it doesn't exactly feel like that."

There's a pause, then her voice softens even more. "How are things with Rocket? You haven't even mentioned him."

I swallow hard and hate that that one question from my mom has all of my insecurities and worries and heartache that have been building day after day since the hearing bubble up. "Strained, I guess. Distant. It's like we're the same but I feel like he's pulling away."

"Because of what happened in court or . . ."

"Maybe. Maybe not." I'm so sick of thinking about it. Of worrying about it. "He's never been a relationship guy so maybe all this press has spooked him into realizing that's what we actually are even though we haven't actually defined it. Maybe he's afraid of losing Poppy, and since our whole relationship started and has been defined by her, maybe he thinks that means I'd leave too. Or maybe he just realized this is too much . . . I don't know, Mom."

"Why don't you talk to him about it? From what you've said, he seems to be a good listener."

The thought has crossed my mind a million times only to be shoved away by not wanting to add more stress to any of our plates.

"It'll work itself out," I say and beg myself to believe it.

I hear her inhale like she wants to say something but then pauses only briefly. "Do you love him?"

"Yes."

The door creaks behind me. I turn, and Rocket stands in the doorway, Poppy's beloved rabbit in his hand. His eyes flick from me to my phone, then back again.

Exhaustion emanates off him, like the weight of the world is on his shoulders.

"Mom, I'll call you later," I say.

She says something, but I don't hear it. I'm too busy setting my phone down and trying to hear over my pulse pounding in my ears.

Rocket crosses the room in a few strides, and without a word, he pulls me into him. I collapse into the warmth of him and just simply hold on.

We stand like that. No words. Just breathing. Just me holding on.

But his grip says it all. It's too light, like he's afraid of crushing something fragile. Like he's already started letting go.

I bury my face into his chest and hold on tighter, desperate for something to say. "Poppy matched the crowns today."

His lips press against the top of my head, and I can feel it spread into a smile. "She'd make a damn good queen."

I nod against him, the lump in my throat stealing my voice.

Something in his stillness, something in the way his hands don't wander, or the way his eyes don't meet mine, tells me what he won't say.

This is the start of goodbye.

And I don't know how to stop it.

CHAPTER
fifty

Willow

HE COMES TO ME LATER.

In the quiet of the night, in the dark of my room, he walks in, sits beside me in the bed, and brushes his lips against mine.

There's a strange, unsettling to the silence. A resignation in the space. Neither are relayed with words but rather reinforced by the look in his eyes and intensity of his touch.

"Rocket—"

"Shh," he says against my lips and then kisses me so I can't question or protest or wonder.

But I do.

It's all I've thought about since earlier today. It's the only conclusion I can come to. This is most likely over.

Us.

This weird dream I had where I thought this could be more.

And I'm either a glutton for punishment or desperate to prove him otherwise because I kiss him back.

We undress in silence. The unspoken words are punctuated by actions. There is no fervor. No wild hunger. No urgency in our touch.

It is slow and devastatingly tender. As if, in this fleeting moment, we are both carving out a before and after. His body over mine, his hands gentle, his mouth moving over my skin like he's memorizing it for later, when the memory will hurt worse than the loss.

My body feels like it's the only part of me that could tether him here, so I let it. I let him. I need it as much as he does.

I search his face for a hint of what he's feeling, so that I don't feel so alone in this unspoken goodbye—the beginning of the end—and perceive the sorrow in his eyes, the hardened set of his jaw, and the slightest of trembles in his touch.

I hold him as tightly as I can manage, pull him into me as if I might change fate by force, but it's a losing battle. In every breath he takes, I hear the words he doesn't say.

We come in the quiet comfort of each other. Tense muscles and linked hands. Soft kisses and yielding sighs.

And when we finish, he lies beside me on the same pillow so our foreheads meet. His eyes search mine and in them I see sadness and regret.

Long after he falls asleep, I study him. Memorize him. Map every detail to memory.

Tonight might not be our last time, but it's the start of it.

Deep down, I know it.

CHAPTER
fifty-one

Rocket

THE BACKYARD'S QUIET.

But I'm out here because inside the house is even more so.

Out here there are crickets and the occasional car driving past. The hum of the A/C kicking on and off and an occasional plane overhead.

Inside is a smothering silence of disappointment, uncertainty, and yes, my failure.

"No, Sandra, I'm not happy with how it went. The more I sit on it, the more I see the fallout, the angrier I get. Wasn't it your job as my lawyer to protect her?"

"My job is to protect you," she says quietly.

I grit my teeth and fight the urge to punch something. "This is total bullshit. This is character assassination and—"

"You can thank social media for the fuel to its fire. You can thank yourself for getting involved with the one witness from whom we needed credibility. I had to use what I had to work with."

"What you had to work with? What? An upstanding, incredible human being who would sacrifice herself for me and for Poppy?"

"Your relationship created the content. Got people to dig and post and fabricate stuff about her. I did my best to try and protect her as well as let the judge see how slimy the Whitmore's lawyer was. She's a smart cookie, the judge."

"The more you explain, the more pissed I get."

"There was a method to my madness."

"What was that? To fuck over Willow and me all in one hearing?"

"No. To let the judge see how low the Whitmores are willing to go. None of that bullshit he brought in factors into who you are as a man and a father. That's what those dozens and dozens of character witness statements do. Mr. Sally proved he's grasping at straws by chasing social media posts and insinuating facts that have no relevance to you and Poppy."

"So you hung her out to fucking dry?" I state the obvious and scrub a disbelieving hand over my face as my gut churns.

"I told you we had to do what we had to do."

"It doesn't sit well with me."

"It never does until I get the end result that I want. We'll get it this time."

"Great. Fucking awesome. I win and Willow gets fucked."

"Unfortunately, sometimes that's how it works."

There has to be something I can do to set the record straight.

I've been sitting out here for an hour, maybe more, trying to think just what that might be. My glass sits empty, has been for some time, but that doesn't mean its contents don't hum through my blood right now. I feel numb, and I'm not sure if that's because I need to be or because I've already turned everything off—shut it down—to prevent the coming pain.

It's not the hearing that gutted me. It's not the possible consequences of my actions from years ago that I'll need to live with if I lose Poppy, or the massive bender I know I'll go on, if I do. It's how this has affected Willow. *Because of me.*

It's like a nightmare I can't erase. Scene after scene and all because of me. Willow being vilified on social media sites because she's with me. Willow facing the sleazeball Sally's questions and insinuations about her life and how she lives it. It's Willow's picture in post after post, headline after headline about how she's an opportunistic, gold-digging whore who's using sex to get everything she wants out of life—her education, fame, attention . . . who the fuck knows what else because honestly, the accusations are so ridiculous they're not even worth reading.

And now threats from the master's program, where she had planned to continue her graduate degree, is investigating whether she deserves to be in the program or if strings were pulled for her.

Like . . . what the actual fuck.

I brought her into this, and I'll be damned if I'm the reason she never gets out. If her reputation and future is ruined because of me.

The sliding glass door creaks open behind me.

I don't turn. I know it's her.

"Rock? You okay?" she asks, voice cautious, like she already knows the answer and doesn't want to hear it confirmed.

She's asking me if I'm okay when her life is being turned upside down?

I grit my teeth and fight the urge to roll my shoulders. She'll think my irritation is because of her when it's because of me.

I can't do a goddamn thing to right this wrong—and even if I could, isn't the damage already done?

I stare out at the skyline, fighting the urge to reach for her. To fall into her. Instead I do the only thing I know I can't fail at. I breathe in. I breathe out.

And I do what she deserves and is in *her* best interest.

"Willow." Fuck. The words stick in my throat as emotion burns bright around them. "You need to go."

CHAPTER
fifty-two

Willow

MY HEART STOPS.

Not all at once. More like a boa constrictor wrapping around it and starving it from what it needs to beat. To live. *To love.*

He makes the statement so calmly, so nonchalantly, like it's not meant to gut me.

"What?"

He still doesn't look at me. His shoulders are hunched. His jaw is clenched. The ice in his glass makes the perfect move and melts so that it drops to the bottom providing the only sound around us.

"Rocket. I don't understand."

It takes a few seconds for him to turn, but when he does, I see it. Defeat. Distance. The wall built back up.

"You don't have to understand. In fact, it's probably better if you don't. All you need to know is that you deserve better than this. Better than me."

I shake my head before he's even done talking. "Don't I get a say in this?

Nothing has changed between us. Nothing that the outside world has done changes how I feel about you. About us. I don't want better, Rocket. I just want you." *I want to stay. Please don't push me away.*

He chuckles under his breath, and I hate its bitter and broken sound.

"The outside world is trying to destroy you because of your affiliation with me. It shows no mercy. They're trying to destroy you, tear you apart, for something I did, and if you think for one second that this is going to fade away, it's not. It has teeth. It's staying. I brought this fucking shitstorm down on you. The smearing of your reputation. The questioning of your qualifications for your education. Any future job you interview for to work with kids, they're going to look you up and see all of this. Because. Of. Me."

My head shakes like it's physically trying to reject every truth he just spoke. "That's not true."

"Open up any social media site. It's true. It's there, plain as day."

"And me leaving here, you pushing me away, isn't going to change any of it. It's already out there whether I'm with you or all alone. It's something I'll have to deal with regardless. Let it be out there while we stay in this bubble we've created. Just don't . . . don't do this to us, Rocket," I plead.

"The paparazzi chased you on the streets the other day for Christ's sake. Almost ran your car off the road. Your social media accounts have been hacked, and then they posted shit that was vile. How can you stand there and tell me you don't care when your entire fucking life has been destroyed because of me?"

The pain in his voice is raw and real and shatters every hope I had inside that I was misreading his distance. His indifference. The desperation in the last time we made love.

Because we did make love.

There's no other word to describe it and so it makes everything hurt that much more.

"Let me make the decision about how much I can handle. Let me decide what my line to be crossed is." I reach out to touch his shoulder, and he shifts away. That rebuke, I think, is harder than any of the verbal ones.

But he's not wrong about the things that have been said about me. It hurts. My God, has it hurt. But he's also wrong. Those things *are* out in the Ethernet now, never to be removed. But if I stay, if we make this work, they will be proven wrong. *If I run, if I leave, then . . . I'll literally lose everything.*

"I don't care what they say or what they do. They'll be proven wrong if we make this work."

"I care. What kind of man am I if I'm unable to protect you? And if I can't do that, then what the hell am I doing?"

I reach out, but he rises from his seat and physically distances himself from me.

"I don't need you to protect me." I hate that it sounds like I'm begging . . . but isn't that what I am, in fact, doing? "I just need you to talk to me. To let me stay. We can take a break if that's what you need or whatever else, but . . . I can't lose both of you. Not in one fell swoop. I can't . . . Jesus, Rocket."

"I'm better off alone. Can't you see that? Do you think I truly know how to love someone? My own goddamn parents didn't love me—one never even stayed around and the other didn't fucking care—so . . . I just can't do this. I can't give you what you deserve. I can't love you how you deserve because I don't even know what that is. Maybe the Whitmores are right, huh? I'm nowhere good enough for Poppy—even I know that—but maybe she'd be better off without me in her life, just like you will."

"No. Don't talk like that. We haven't worked this hard for you to give up now."

"I'm not giving up, Willow. I'm doing what's best for the both of you. I'm trying not to ruin you because of all that comes with me. I can't let Poppy grow up thinking this is what love is—ruining the person you love and being so selfish, so afraid to let them go, that you just hold on tighter to them at their expense."

The determination in his eyes is something even I don't think I can overcome.

"I hear you. I am trying to understand what you're saying, but you have it all wrong. Staying together, working through adversity is what Poppy needs to see. Using each other's shoulder to lean on when times get tough."

His jaw sets and his shoulders square, but the look he gives me—a mixture of love and pain—will haunt me. I know it. "I want you out of here tonight. I won't let you drown with me."

It would've hurt less if he'd simply shot me in the heart. "What? What about Poppy—"

"She's sleeping."

"But she's already lost—"

"I'm well the fuck aware." His hands fist and his muscles tense.

"What happened to whatever it takes, huh?" I ask.

His eyes close for a beat and then open slowly, before he looks down at his fingers. "I promise I'm trying to do what's best here. For everyone. Please—"

"You can't even stand to look at me," I whisper.

"It hurts too much."

It hurts too much. Four broken words. He genuinely believes he's doing the right thing and nothing will change his mind.

"I love you." The words are barely audible but I can see when they hit him. Three punches one after another, but he doesn't move. Doesn't flinch. He's already pulled away.

And the next time he meets my gaze, his face may be blank, but his eyes are shattered.

"You'll thank me someday."

And then he turns and walks into the house. I track the sound of his footsteps down the hall until I see the light in his studio go on. His safe space. Where he'll let himself feel. Where he'll shut the world out.

I'm tempted to waltz in there and tell him I'm not leaving.

I'm tempted to scream at the top of my lungs so that he sees how much he's just hurt me.

I'm tempted to beg and fight harder for what we have.

But I don't.

I can't change the world around us, and it seems he thinks the world has won.

So instead, I stand here, my hands curled at my sides, tears rolling silently down my cheeks.

He thinks this is protection.

He thinks pushing me away is saving me.

But what he doesn't know, what he'll never understand, is that I didn't fall in love with the man who promised to protect me.

I fell in love with the one who held his daughter like she was his whole world. The one who wasn't afraid to be vulnerable in front of me and cheered on each and every one of my strengths. The man who was confident and cocky to the world, but who was sweet and tender to me.

I chose him.

And I'll keep choosing him.

Even if he won't let me.

Even if it means walking to my room, packing up my stuff, saying good-bye to Poppy, and walking away.

You can't make someone love you. Common sense says that.

But it's even harder to know someone loves you but actively chooses not to fight for you.

I deserve better than that.

CHAPTER
fifty-three

Willow

CHECK MY TEXT MESSAGES AGAIN, EVEN THOUGH I KNOW I'VE ALREADY checked six times today.

For anything from Rocket.

For a response from Poppy through her kid's messaging app. It's not like she knows how to spell, but the emojis came and the silly pictures right behind them that no doubt Hendrix or Quinlan or Bristol are helping her send while they take turns watching her to help Rocket out.

But there is nothing.

I didn't expect one from Rocket—as much as I hoped there would be one—but Poppy has been "sending" me silly pictures. But nope. Nothing new. The last communication in our chat was from me—a short video, shaky and too overtly cheerful, where I told her I missed her and tried to make her laugh with a dancing stuffed bunny I may have bought just for that video.

I've had to leave the kids I've nannied before. It's always brutal, always heartbreaking, and yet it's typically a bittersweet transition. I know they're too old for me, their families are happy with the time I've spent with them, and I've left them in a good place.

This time it's so much harder. So much . . . more everything. My chest hurts constantly, and my thoughts never stop about what I could've done differently. *And I just miss them.*

The problem? I know what I'm missing. I know the hope and the happiness and the feeling of pure contentment that they brought me that is now gone.

Missing her, I scroll up to see her last message. She "sent" a heart and a dinosaur emoji with a picture of her sticking her tongue out.

It's not enough.

None of it is.

My apartment feels empty. Stagnant. Too freaking quiet. There is no babbling toddler. No music being played somewhere in the house, whether it's Rocket humming something he's trying to write over and over or the random piano sessions between Poppy and Rocket. There's not the smell of his cologne or the bark of his laugh.

It's just me. Just an empty fridge because I have no appetite or desire to go to the store.

There's texts though. The endless stream from everyone continually asking if I'm okay.

My mom. Lily. Hendrix. Quinlan. Bristol. Even the guys have checked in, trying to remain neutral but checking in, nonetheless.

Every call or text starts with the same question—"Are you okay?" or "How are you doing?"

And every time, I give the same lie. "I'm fine."

But I'm not fine. I'm so far from being fine that I think I forgot what fine ever felt like.

It's been five days since my testimony, and the judge's ruling can't come fast enough.

In the meantime, Rocket's gone quiet too. He's shut me out so completely that I can't help wondering if maybe he thinks that's how he wins. If maybe he really believes the Whitmores are the better option. That Poppy would be safer in their picture-perfect, retired world.

The thought makes me sick.

Because I know him. I know the way he looks at Poppy like she's his second chance at everything. I know how gently he tells her he loves her when she's asleep.

So how could he possibly believe he's not good enough?

I close my laptop on my course selection site and look around at my apartment, at my home. It doesn't feel like my home anymore.

Because what defines what a home is? It's not where you live. It's where you love. It's where you can fight and make up. Where you can laugh so hard your stomach hurts and sit in silence without talking and it be okay. It's the first person you want to call when you get good news . . . and bad news.

It isn't this apartment that looks like time stood still, that feels like the old me, the before-Rocket me . . .

It was him. And Poppy.

I wipe at my face and open my phone. My fingers hover over Rocket's name before I sigh and scroll down to Vince's instead. It's easier to text him: **Can you just check on him for me? Please? Make sure he's okay?**

It's short and sweet. He'll know what I mean.

I stare out the window after I hit send, lost in thought, and wishing Rocket was sitting there. It's a silly thought, a hopeful and desperate one, but for one second—for one single heartbeat—I swear he is there. I swear that I *feel* him. *Ridiculous.*

And yet, on the off chance he is, I whisper, "I love you," to the darkness beyond, and hope somehow it will get to him.

But when I blink again, it's just headlights and reflections. Just a man with a camera leaning against a streetlamp, already creating a headline to disparage me.

Just me, alone in the quiet, praying Rocket hasn't already decided he's not worthy of the love we have.

CHAPTER
fifty-four

Rocket

THE BEER IN MY HAND IS WARM.

I can't remember the last time I took a sip. I've just been holding it, letting the label peel beneath my thumb while the guys talk around me.

We're in my backyard. It's late afternoon, and the guys showed up without warning. They waltzed in like I'd invited them, loaded my fridge with beer, and brought pizza with my favorite toppings. Vince and Hawkin brought their youngest kids so that Poppy would have someone to play with.

I know what they're doing. It's a circle-the-wagons approach to make sure I'm okay. I appreciate it, know they have my back, but it doesn't help.

The best part? They know I'm in a shit mood and don't expect much from me in return. There's something to be said about old friends.

I glance over to where Poppy's in the grass, giggling as Vince's youngest son shows her how to race matchbox cars down the patio steps.

I sit and watch, absent when I've been anything but that with her this past week. It's almost as if I've been hanging on for dear life instead. Present and trying to pretend I don't feel like I'm bleeding out on the inside.

The wives have been helping as much as they can outside of their own lives. The new nanny interviewing process has been happening—but I don't like anyone . . . because they're not *her*.

So I haven't pulled the trigger on hiring a new one. Just been relying on Quinlan, Bristol, and Hendrix and borrowing their nannies and backup nannies in the interim. Poppy has ramped up the meltdowns, so most nights have ended in sobs that have almost broken me. *I hate that I pushed a person she loves out of her life.* I hate that her tears are because her little heart is broken . . . *again.*

So, it's messy, hard, and confusing but it's what's working. *Sort of.* However it only serves to prove to me how perfectly Willow fits her.

In my house.

In my life.

So that's why the guys are here, showing up unannounced, and circling me like wolves that know I'm wounded. They're not loud. Not aggressive. Just here. Drinking their beers, waiting for the moment I stop pretending I'm fine.

I'm not fine.

Willow isn't here.

My chest hurts constantly. The music has stopped in my head.

And I have to face the judge in twenty-four hours' time.

"I was able to get her to grant it," Sandra says and then sighs in exasperation while relief slowly finds its way through me. *"Now do you want to explain to me why you just demanded I call the judge and ask for another appearance with the court before she gives her final decision?"*

"I'd rather not."

"What do you plan on saying?" she asks.

Like a song that's begging to be written, the things I want to speak in front of the court have run circles in my head, but I haven't found the right words to say them yet.

One last plea before she rules.

"Sandra, I need you to trust me. I'm going to do what's best for Poppy."

She makes a noncommittal sound that says she doesn't exactly trust me or what I'm going to say. "I'm not a fan of surprises, Rocket."

And I'm not a fan of throwing people under the bus to save my own skin.

"Well, I've learned to get used to them."

She snorts. "I'll let you know she doesn't like her time wasted and simply squeezed you in as a courtesy to me. The Whitmores are still in town as they were waiting for her decision before leaving—"

"So they could take Poppy if ruled in their favor," I say absently.

"Yes. I assume. So all the players will be there, but please, don't waste her time or she will hold it against you."

"Noted."

"So we didn't just come here to watch you mope, Caldwell," Hawkin says.

"Shit, man. If you nurse that beer any harder, you're going to need to put a nipple on it," Gizmo adds.

"What we're here to say," Vince chimes in, "is that you're a fucking idiot." He glances over to the kids but they're far enough away that they don't hear his cursing.

I glance up. Don't argue. Don't flinch. I'm exhausted, and my eyes burn from too many sleepless nights and not enough answers.

Gizmo nudges my elbow with his. "You love them. Willow and Poppy. We all see it."

The beer bottle thuds as I set it down harder than I mean to. I can't sit still, so I shove up out of the chair and move around the patio. "Yeah? And look where that got them. Poppy is possibly leaving and Willow is gone."

"Willow's gone because you forced her to go. Not because she wanted to leave," Vince says in his low, even tone. "And look where running from them is getting you."

That one hits. I flinch but keep moving.

"I'm not good for them. You heard what was said in court. You saw what has been said in the papers about her. She's dealing with the ramifications of me."

Hawkin stands and blocks my path. His face is calm, his eyebrows are raised, and there's a hint of a smirk on his lips. "You mean like we have to every day?"

The joke is meant to be funny, to lighten the mood. I laugh. Or try to, at least. It sounds like gravel and hurts to come out. "Exactly," I grate out.

"You're missing the entire fucking point, Rock," Gizmo says.

"Which point would that be?" I ask.

"Willow didn't need saving. She's a grown woman with a stiff spine and a strong resolve. Dating you showed that shit. What she really needed was for you to tell her to stay. To fight for her. To prove to her that by blood or by choice, you choose her."

My throat tightens. "I thought letting her go would protect her. That it would . . ."

"Dude, family isn't something you protect by leaving. It's something you protect by staying. Besides, what's been said has already been said. Can't take that shit back, but you can make going forward better."

The silence that follows is thick enough to drown in. It's only accented by Poppy's squeal and the clapping of her hands. How is it in such a short period, I fell in love with two people and feel like I'm drowning on dry land at the thought of not having them both?

Hawkin leans in, voice low and raw. "You love her? Then go fucking fix it."

That's it.

No frills. No hope. Just the truth like a fucking blade in my heart.

I drop my head into my hands, and for the first time in longer than I can admit, I cry.

Not loud. Not messy. Just broken silence as a tear slides down my cheek that I shove away with the back of my hand like it never happened.

Having made their point—that they're here for me, that they're not going to let me get away with fucking up—the guys quietly pick up their bottles, give me one last look, and leave.

Poppy climbs up onto my lap, too tired to play anymore, as the sky turns orange and the light fades. She curls into my chest, her little fingers finding the poppy tattoo over my heart.

She traces it.

Just like she did the first time.

Just like Willow did the last time.

"I'm going to make this right, Popstar." I press my lips to the top of her head and close my eyes. "I'm going to fight like hell to keep you. And fight like hell to get her back. I don't know if she'll forgive me. I don't know if I deserve her. But that's the thing about love, right? You fight for it anyway."

She looks up at me and smiles like she understands what I'm saying. She presses a kiss to the poppy and just about guts me. Then she asks, "Song, Dadda?"

To find my voice, to use it, even when I don't think it holds much value.

I nod. I smile. I begin to sing her favorite BENT song, the one she always hums and then eventually falls asleep to.

Probably not a good career insight, but what the fuck, right?

Her fingers slow. Her breathing deepens. She snuggles in closer. *She's happy here. With me.* I can't lose her. I can't lose the happiness I found. I can't lose the woman who made my world complete.

My boys were right.

"Dude, family isn't something you protect by leaving. It's something you protect by staying."

"You love her? Then go fucking fix it."

It's time I prepare to fight like hell. I am worth that. And so are my girls.

CHAPTER
fifty-five

Willow

HENDRIX: You need to be at the courthouse. Trust me.

That's all the text says. No emoji. No punctuation. Just nine words that send a current down my spine.

I read it again. *And then I'm moving.*

No makeup. No plan. No idea what the hell I'm walking into, just a thundering heart and a sinking feeling that maybe, this is the moment I've been both praying for . . . or dreading.

The judge has decided. Or Rocket is washing his hands and walking away.

Both are terrifying prospects to me.

The drive is a blur.

The courthouse steps rise in front of me. Each one I climb, I swear my legs get heavier, almost as if I'm not sure I want to see what's waiting inside.

I don't. But I do.

Because it's him.

I slip into the back of the courtroom. It's just as crowded as the last time we were here. When my flustered, unprepared self took the stand and was ambushed with lies. The beginning of our end.

It feels like it was forever ago and yesterday all at the same time.

My eyes find Rocket instantly.

Ooof. Just seeing him. I never expected it to hurt this much.

He's seated at the table up front. His jaw is tight, and in the minute I've been here, he's already adjusted the knot of his tie several times.

The man who commands stadiums is fidgeting like a lost boy. My heart—if there were any pieces that weren't already shattered—is now in shards.

Uncertain whether I'm welcome or not—and definitely not wanting to catch the eye of any reporters or social media influencers who are no doubt in the room—I hover near the back and try to make myself as inconspicuous as possible.

For one wild second, the uncertainty in Rocket's posture has me thinking he's going to give her up. He's going to say the Whitmores are better for Poppy.

Because he thinks that's love.

Because he thinks that's protection.

The judge clears her throat and looks at Rocket. "After having spoken last hearing, you again requested the ear of the court, Mr. Caldwell. I'm not usually one to grant such a request but feel Poppy's well-being is on the line. Therefore I've agreed to grant you that time. In saying that, please know that I offered the same courtesy to the Whitmores in case they wanted to add to anything they said last time. They've opted to stay with the statements they've previously given. So, Mr. Caldwell, what was so pressing that you felt the need to address the court again?"

I suck in my breath as he stands.

"Your Honor," Rocket says, his voice rough and nervous. I grip the edge of the hard wooden bench until my knuckles go white. "I was a screwup in my younger years. There's no point pretending otherwise. Like most growing up, I made bad decisions. I've let people down. I've been too loud in the wrong places and too silent in the right ones. I'm not going to deny that, just as I won't deny the fact that my mistakes have been documented for the world to see and blown out of proportion and into falsehoods because of the public spotlight that my career dictates as necessary."

I sink into the seat beneath me, completely mesmerized and surprised by the commanding presence he has over the courtroom.

"But I'm not the guy they're talking about anymore," he says, glancing briefly to the gallery with a nod to his bandmates who are still sitting strong behind him.

"Learning you have a daughter you never knew about is shocking enough. It would be to anyone, not just a single guy. But coming to terms with it and the fact that I've been robbed of all of her firsts is a completely different type of grief I can't put words to. Believe me, I've tried." He adjusts his tie and gets a nod from Sandra to continue. "Poppy's not my second chance, Your Honor. She's my first real one. The one I didn't see coming. The one I almost screwed up. And that's not because I didn't want her, it's because I didn't know how to be enough for her. But every day since, I've tried. I want to keep trying, and I hope that you'll allow me that chance. I can't account for the reasons Mr. and Mrs. Whitmore were estranged from their daughter. No one will ever truly know both sides of that story, but I know that Olivia thought I'd be a better fit for our daughter than they would, and she knew Poppy better than anyone. Unlike their statements about me, I don't wish to malign their character. I'd rather focus on and emphasize that it's my desire to be the best father I can be, and if that means sacrificing my existing life for her? Then that's what I'll do."

I bite down on the inside of my cheek in an attempt to stop the tears. It's no use—because this is the Rocket I know. Unvarnished. Raw.

No stage. No spotlight.

Just the man I fell in love with, finally standing still. Finally recognizing his worth.

"It's also pertinent for you to know that I believe it's extremely important for Poppy to know her mother's family. The Whitmores deserve to be a part of her life. Having custody of her doesn't mean they get pushed out. That's not who I am. She deserves both sides of her story from the people who know how to tell it best." He pauses. Swallows. And then something in him shifts, and his voice becomes more resolute. "But I want to address that too. I don't want my daughter to grow up in a house where the people raising her think it's acceptable to publicly smear a woman like Willow Adams just to make me look bad. A woman who's done nothing but love that little girl and care for her. Just because I love Willow doesn't make her a liability. She's not collateral damage in this custody case, which is what they made her out to be. Rather, Willow's the reason I became the man standing here today."

My hand flies to my mouth as my body trembles.

"I'll never be perfect, nor do I want to be. I've never needed praise, nor do I want it. I just want to be Poppy's dad. Every damn day that I can be." He pauses, just for a breath, but I see the muscles in his jaw clench, the way his fingers tremble at his sides. "Please know that I'll do whatever it takes to prove that to the court. I'll take mandated parenting classes. I'll submit to random drug tests—even though that's never been my thing—but the Whitmores put it out there, and now it's in your head. So fine. I'll do it."

His voice catches, just for a second, as I wipe yet another tear off my cheek.

"And I'll even put aside the contempt I feel for the Whitmores—for what they've done to the people I love—because I finally understand that kind of love. The kind you have for your daughter. The kind that says you'll do anything and everything to make them whole. I understand it because I have it. Because Poppy isn't just a part of my life. She's everything. And all I want . . . is the chance to prove I can be hers." *Cue more tears.*

No one in this courtroom could possibly understand what that cost him. No one but me.

And I've never loved him more.

"Thank you for your time. For making the time again."

A hush falls over the room when he finishes. Truth has been spoken so loudly, that it leaves no room for rebuttal.

I wipe my cheeks and try to breathe.

"Thank you, Mr. Caldwell," the judge says. "I'm going to be honest and state that I had decided on the matter but feel that I need to re-evaluate my thoughts, the facts, and all contributing factors one more time. While the word for what I'll make is 'decision', it's so much more than that and affects many lives. I don't take that duty or honor lightly. While I said I would have the decision today, I feel it pertinent to take a bit more time. I'll have a decision in the next few days."

Rocket sits back down, but he doesn't turn around.

I can't take my eyes off him. I'm overwhelmed and stunned and . . . more in love with him now than I ever was before.

He didn't just become the man I hoped he could be. He became the man I already loved.

And he did it without me.

I'm unable to move. The past week, the distance, the pain . . . it's all tangled up in my chest. Because loving someone like this doesn't come without cost.

Sometimes, love breaks you.

But sometimes . . . sometimes it shows up in a courtroom, in a suit that doesn't fit, with a voice that trembles and a spine made of steel.

And for the first time in a long time . . .

I let myself believe we might still have something left to hold on to.

CHAPTER
fifty-six

Rocket

THE COURTROOM DOOR CLOSES BEHIND ME, AND I DON'T BREATHE—
can't—until the latch clicks and the hum of the court is replaced by the
quieter hustle and bustle of the side corridor. The business end of the
court and the one Sandra has the bailiff clear to help avoid the media circus
outside.

My hands are still shaking and my heart is still racing, but my feet move.
Step after step, as relief and pride slowly replace the fear.

If this doesn't go my way, I can't say I didn't leave it all on the field.

But it will go my way. I have to believe it will.

Sandra meets me at the end of the hallway. She nods toward the exit
down the opposite way. "The media is waiting outside. It's chaos."

"I figured." I run a hand through my hair. When are they not waiting?
The same *they* that I'm trying to protect Willow from. "I just want to get to
Poppy. Even if I have to wait them out or sneak out another way. She doesn't
need to be subjected to that."

"Agreed and already on it. Working on getting you out through the underground garage." She glances over her shoulder when the door opens and a rush of noise comes in before it shuts. "Poppy's with the girls. Bristol and Hendrix took her out into the side atrium—less traffic. I'll walk you that way."

We round the corner, and I hear her before I see her—that belly giggle she makes without a care in the world, sheltered from the fact that her life is being discussed in a public forum. Hendrix is crouched in front of her, releasing her from a hug.

And just for a second, I let myself feel it.

This is mine. *She is mine.*

What would Willow have said if she saw me today? Would she have been proud? Told me I needed to say more?

I don't know. All I know is I had to fix this, fight for this, before I could fix my fuck-up with her.

But I stood in front of the judge, the court, and pretended like I was talking to Willow. I didn't let my anger speak for me. I didn't throw punches or hide behind my fame. I gave the court the truest version of myself.

For Poppy.

For Willow.

For the life I want back.

"Rocket."

I turn to face the voice at my back . . . and falter.

The Whitmores are standing in the hallway. Up close, it's evident they've aged so much in the few short months. They seem smaller somehow, like the grief has hollowed them out.

I lift my brows and wait for them to make the first move. I'm not sure what that might be though.

Mrs. Whitmore steps forward, clutching her bag to her chest. "You meant what you said?" she asks.

I nod. "I did. Yes."

"I don't understand. Why say that? Why offer anything when we've done nothing but fight you?"

I shift my weight and swallow over the bitterness they've caused. I don't want to, but I have to because Poppy's watching me now. And I need to be the man she deserves her father to be.

"Because I know you're hurting," I say quietly. "And I have no intention of taking Poppy away from you. She deserves to know who her mother was. And I'm going to depend on you to give that to her."

They look at each other, startled. Mr. Whitmore's eyes narrow cautiously.

"You sound like you already know the outcome. What the judge has decided."

I hesitate. "No. I don't." *But deep down, I do.* "She needs us both."

The silence stretches for a second too long, then Mrs. Whitmore nods, slowly. "You're a good father," she whispers. "She's lucky to have you."

I blink hard and struggle for words through the inundation of emotion. "And despite the estrangement between you and Olivia, she felt the same about you."

Mr. Whitmore flinches . . . and then his eyes fill. He nods once, fast, like if he doesn't, he'll lose control.

"We'd like to see her," he says gruffly. "If that's okay."

I nod. "Of course."

We turn, and when Poppy looks up, her eyes light up and she lifts her arms. I scoop her up, tuck her close, and turn just as the Whitmores step into view. For a beat, we all just stand there.

Then Poppy waves her bunny.

Mrs. Whitmore sniffles softly and clutches her chest.

Mr. Whitmore presses a hand over his mouth and nods, like maybe this is the first time in months he's seen the girl and not the ghost of his daughter.

"We'll give you a minute," I murmur as Hendrix moves out of the room.

I kiss the top of Poppy's head and place her down between them.

They kneel on the floor. She smiles before reaching for Mrs. Whitmore's hand.

And just like that, we stop being enemies for the common good of Poppy.

I know it won't always be easy. I know animosity might own them at times. But for Poppy's sake, we'll manage.

I step back, watch the three of them together, and again know that Willow would be proud.

Of how I spoke.

Of how I stayed and fought.

Of how I gave grace, even when I hadn't been shown any.

And that? That might be the first thing I've done right without her beside me.

But God willing, it won't be the last.

CHAPTER
fifty-seven

Willow

I WAIT OUTSIDE THE COURTHOUSE WITH MY HEART IN MY THROAT AND my fingers digging into my leather bag's strap.

People begin filing out—reporters, spectators, the general public—but I keep my head down, not wanting to be noticed, which could feed their malicious fodder.

If there still is such a thing. I can hope that Rocket's comments in there about me will make it out into the world. But the salacious sells better than the boring and so I'm not expecting much.

But he made the effort.

He protected me by defending me.

Now, if he'd just see it'd be better if we were a team together fighting against this . . . and his words today gave me hope that there is.

Another deluge of people exit the courthouse and draw my attention. Their shoes click against the concrete steps, and their conversations are hushed and completely ignorant of the storm inside my chest.

I scan every face that passes, looking for him.

Just one glimpse. One glance. One second of eye contact so I can know he saw me. That maybe, somehow, all the things he said in that courtroom were true and going to fix whatever broke between us.

And then I see him.

Black blazer. Long stride. Head bowed like the weight of the world is still sitting on his shoulders. His face is hidden beneath a baseball cap, the bill tattered at its edges.

My breath catches so hard it hurts.

He's alone, moving fast, and the press hasn't noticed him yet. I take a step off the wall, with my heart pounding and tears clogging my throat, but when he turns . . . my hope crumbles in my chest. *It's not him.*

He's not here. Or maybe he is, and he left through a different door to avoid all of this. But I stay anyway, hoping to see him. Needing to see him.

I walked away without a fight, and therefore I'm no better than him. But he fought today. He took the first step, and I want to meet him halfway.

So I stay just in case. I stay until the courthouse doors close behind the last lingering intern, and the air feels too thick to breathe.

Then I decide to go to him. Because I need to. Because I have to. Because I can't let us go without trying again.

His neighborhood looks the same but different. Like a place I used to belong. I pull up to the gate and roll down the window.

The guard steps out of the booth, adjusting his cap when he sees me. "Evening, Ms. Adams."

"Hi," I say, voice tight. "Is he . . . can I see him?"

His mouth flattens into a frown. "I'm sorry. He's not accepting visitors right now."

Of course he's not.

"Meaning he hasn't changed his accepted visitor's list or he's reconfirmed it?" The first means it's an oversight, and the latter means I'm not welcome at all.

"It hasn't been updated in two weeks." He glances over his shoulder at a car that exits through the opposing gate to the community. "You're not giving up on him, are you?"

"Meaning?"

"Meaning I've noticed you drive by a few times. You just never pull in."

I figure I should be embarrassed that he's noticed but fuck it. There's no shame in loving someone so much it hurts.

"Just making sure he's okay," I whisper, grateful for the sunglasses hiding the tears welling in my eyes.

The guard watches me a moment longer, and then something in his expression softens. "Give it time," he says gently. "Sometimes men have to figure out how to say the big stuff."

I blink fast and chuckle. "One can hope. Thank you."

"Anytime." He winks. "Even if I were to let you in . . . he's not here."

I drive home with an empty feeling.

No verdict yet. No answers. No Rocket. Just this ache that wraps around my ribs and refuses to let go.

By the time I pull into my building's parking lot, the day has turned to twilight with the sky painted pastels I should appreciate. But I don't. *Can't. Because I feel defeated.*

Empty.

I reach for the car door handle, exhausted on every level, and then I see them.

Two figures sitting on the grass. One small. One broad-shouldered and relaxed. They both have ice cream cones in their hands, and a bright pinwheel is pushed in the grass in front of them.

Poppy is the first to spot me.

She jumps to her feet and holds her cone high like a torch before running toward me.

I'm afraid if I blink, they'll vanish, but Rocket stands slowly, his eyes locked on mine like they never stopped looking.

"I brought a bribe," he says and holds out one of the cones as Poppy wraps her free arm around my leg.

"Hello, Popstar. I've missed you so much!"

"Me too," she whispers and then giggles.

"Well, two bribes, technically," Rocket says, gesturing his head at the tiny person still holding my leg.

"A bribe?" I whisper.

"I figured if I showed up with sugar and wind toys, you might not slam the door in my face."

I shake my head, laughing through tears I can't hold back. "You never even knocked."

His smile is small, crooked. Nervous. "I didn't want to assume I had the right. Not after . . . well, after everything."

He steps closer, slowly, carefully. "I fought today. For Poppy. For you. For us. You would've been proud of me."

"I know. I was there. You were incredible," I say.

"You were?"

I nod, words escaping me, and something in him crumples. But it's not weakness. *It's surrender.*

He reaches out for my hand and touches me. All those sparks, those embers, come roaring back to life.

"I love you, Willow," he says, voice breaking. "I love this girl, and I love the life we didn't mean to build but did anyway."

My breath hiccups on a sob.

"I thought letting you go would protect you, but all it did was break me." He leans over and presses a kiss to Poppy's head before looking back at me. "So . . . if there's even a part of you that still wants this, *wants me*, then come back with us. *Come home.*"

Poppy squeezes my leg tighter—no doubt getting her melting ice cream everywhere, but I don't care. This is my happiness. This is my home. This is all I ever wanted.

"Come home, Wiwwow," Poppy says.

Three simple words, but they mean the world to me. They show just how far we've come. I throw my head back and laugh, and then lean over and press a kiss to the top of her head before standing up and brushing one against Rocket's lips.

"Wiwwow, huh?" Rocket says and quirks an eyebrow as he places a hand on my lower back. He looks down at Poppy happily sandwiched between us, looking up and grinning with ice cream all over her face. "I love it."

I smile and pull them both in a little closer.

"Home," I whisper.

CHAPTER
fifty-eight

Rocket

THE COUCH IS TOO SMALL FOR ALL THREE OF US, BUT NO ONE SEEMS TO care.

Willow's legs are draped across mine, and Poppy is curled between us like the perfect little wedge she is. Her hair smells like strawberries, and her frilly pink pajamas are halfway tucked into the throw blanket she insisted on sharing with both of us.

I'm holding her juice box while she tells me, very seriously, about something that happened to her bunny. The words are intermittent, connected by Poppy pointing to things to explain the words she's not saying. From afar it might look disjointed and frenzied, but to me it says she's okay now.

We all are.

In fact, never been fucking better.

Willow smiles over the top of Poppy's head, her fingers brushing my arm in that absentminded way that makes me feel like I've been hers forever.

If this is what normal feels like, I want it for the rest of my life.

Then my cell rings. I hold up my finger when I see it's Sandra, and the room stills.

Willow and I look at it and draw in a collective deep breath before I swipe the call and put her on speaker.

"Sandra. It's Rocket and Willow."

My pulse kicks into overdrive. Poppy pokes my cheek like what's happening, but I can't tear my gaze away from her name on my phone as I wait for her to tell me the judge's decision.

"Hi, Willow. Rocket." Sandra's voice is calm but clipped, giving me no indication of what she's about to say.

"You're killing me here," I say.

Sandra exhales. "The judge filed the ruling this morning. I just got the call from the clerk's office."

My chest caves in on itself. Too many words.

She's stalling.

We lost.

I grip Willow's knee without realizing it.

"You've been granted full custody, Rocket."

The room goes silent . . . like no one knows how to breathe. Poppy stares up at me with wide eyes, clearly sensing the change in energy in the room.

Willow covers her mouth and makes a choked sound that's halfway between a laugh and a sob.

I blink. Swallow. Then blink again.

"I got her? She's mine? Ours? She's . . . *ours?*"

"You got her," Sandra says. "She's yours. It's done, Rocket."

I laugh. Then I break. Tears come hot and fast, and I don't care who sees them. I bury my face in Poppy's hair and wrap my arms around her like I'll never let go.

Willow leans in, kissing the side of my head, her hands cupping the back of my neck.

"You did it," she whispers. "Rocket, you did it."

Behind us, the front door swings open.

Hawkin's voice rings out. "What did we miss? Willow said a big call was coming and to round the troops." He holds out his arms to the whole lot of them. "So I rounded up the troops. Did we win or what?"

The guys tumble in—Gizmo, Vince, Hendrix, Quinlan, Bristol—my brothers, their wives, and their kids too.

"Yes. We won," Willow says. "Rocket has custody."

The room erupts. Gizmo hoots. Vince fist-pumps. Hendrix hugs Willow so hard I have to pull her off her to breathe again.

Bristol lifts Poppy in the air and spins her like she's the center of the whole damn universe, which, for us, she is.

"All right, all right," I say, wiping my face and pretending I haven't cried like a baby. "Time to celebrate."

"Popsicles for the kids. And some drinks for the adults," Willow says.

We pass around drinks, and then someone turns on music. The band is sprawled across my living room like they always belonged here. Willow disappears for a second and returns with a tray of snacks, and I swear I've never loved anyone more in my life than I do watching her pass out tiny bowls of pretzels. *She's looking after my people . . . because they're her people now.* Fuck, I love this woman. Funny how my interpretation of sexy has changed.

Eventually, the conversation turns to how wild it's all been—the trial, the press, the public disparagement.

"By the way," Willow says. "A podcast called Strong Voices wants me to come on for an interview."

"About me?" I ask, narrowing my eyes.

"About advocacy. About this journey I've been on. About fighting for what's right and how easily people believe what's posted online without checking facts. About public perception and private truth."

"You gonna do it?"

She lifts one shoulder. "Maybe. I think it's time people heard my voice and how this all affected me. How keyboard warriors, with their malicious and merciless vitriol printed from behind their screens, can cause genuine pain for others. It's so wrong."

I grin and kiss her cheek. "Look at you. Master's student—"

"Soon-to-be," she corrects.

"Speaker. Influencer. Advocate."

"Careful," she says. "I could start charging appearance fees."

The guys laugh, and I lean back, arm slung across the back of the couch.

"You know," I say, eyes still on Willow, "it's funny how fast the headlines change when you stop giving a shit about them."

Vince raises his beer. "To not giving a shit."

"Cheers," I say. "To finding something better to live for."

Eventually, everyone winds down. Poppy crashes first, curled up on the couch, head in Willow's lap, one hand still clinging to my sleeve like she's afraid I'll vanish. It takes us some finagling to get her into her bed without waking her.

"Thank you," I whisper to the guys and their wives when we return. "For everything."

"Anytime, brother," Hawkin says, and then he and Quinlan lean in for quick hugs.

"You know we've got your back," Gizmo says, kissing Willow's cheek and then punching me playfully in the arm.

"And we're always here. Even when you annoy the fuck out of us," Vince says and laughs, cuffing my shoulder and then pulling in Willow for a hug.

"Same goes here," I say as I hug Hendrix goodbye.

And within seconds, they're gone.

The house settles.

The silence is different now—it's . . . not empty. Just full.

Willow closes the door behind them and turns to me, leaning against it with a slow smile.

I step toward her.

She tilts her head, eyes soft. "You okay?"

"No," I say honestly. "I'm wrecked. I'm elated. I'm every damn thing I didn't know how to want."

I cup her cheek, stroke my thumb over her jaw.

"We're her home now," she says, her voice barely above a whisper.

I nod.

"And you're mine."

Her breath catches. I dip my head, brush my lips across hers, slow and steady.

"Let me show you how I love you," I murmur.

"I'm not saying no to that."

She kisses me again to show she means it. Like we both already know that isn't the end.

It's the beginning.

CHAPTER
fifty-nine

Rocket

I'M SITTING IN THE SAME TATTOO CHAIR I SAT IN WHEN I GOT THE POPPY.

The same buzz of the machine. I feel the same nerves. And I don't give a fuck who's sitting in the other seats wanting to take a picture this time around.

I'm not hiding shit from anyone.

Willow's here, sitting on the same black leather couch with Poppy on her lap, feeding her yogurt bites while talking about the pictures in the magazine she's holding to teach her new words.

I glance down at my chest.

Fresh ink beside the poppy.

Three words, in script—*Whatever it takes.*

It's not a lyric. It's a vow.

A memory. A future promised. A reminder kept.

When it's over, I walk to them—my family—shirt slung over my shoulder and lean down to press a kiss to Willow's lips.

She stares at the ink, at the words that tell her what she means to me—and then smiles up at me.

"You're kind of a softie now," she whispers.

"Yeah," I murmur, kissing her again. "But only for you."

epilogue

Rocket

THE BACKYARD LOOKS LIKE A DAMN PINTEREST BOARD EXPLODED.
Twinkling lights strung from the trees. White tablecloths with black graduation caps in every variation as decor. A photo wall with blown-up pictures of Willow—a nerdy middle schooler in braces and glasses. An undergrad with her nose buried textbooks. A Poppy asleep on her chest with her laptop beside her as she studies.

Hendrix helped organize all of this. The flowers. The food. The old school pictures from Mrs. Adams. Gizmo, no doubt, spiked the punch, which has been moved to a different counter so the little ones don't accidentally dip into it.

This party?

It's hers. Willow's.

Because today she walked across a stage in a cap and gown and was handed a diploma that said she finished what she set her mind to. She checked off one of the last major items on her to-do list. Finished her master's degree.

How fucking insane and incredible is that?

The woman who wants to make the world a better place, just got even better at it—if that's even possible.

God, I'm so in love with her it hurts.

"Rocket." Bristol taps my arm. "You ready?"

I nod.

Poppy's at my side wearing her own tiny graduation gown and cap. We got it custom-made in purple with glitter, which I'm sure we'll be trying to get out of the cushions months from now. She's practically bouncing with excitement.

I kneel beside her. "You remember what to do?"

She nods. "Yes." And then grins before saying, "Love you."

"Love you too," I repeat.

It still hits me in the chest—in the best way—no matter how many times she's said it to me.

"Okay," I whisper. "Go find Hendrix."

She takes off toward the little stage we set up by the pool.

I find Willow near the drink table, laughing with her mom. She's swapped her graduation gown for jeans and a soft white blouse. Her hair is twisted back, and her smile is as alive as her eyes.

"Speech time," I say, sliding an arm around her waist. "You promised."

She groans. "Maybe I lied when I said I'd do that."

"You're the woman who made it through hell and earned her master's with a toddler in her lap. Come on. The people demand it."

She eyes me suspiciously. "You better not have something jump out of a cake or some weird embarrassing thing up your sleeve."

"No idea what you're talking about."

Lie. Big lie.

"You know I hate surprises."

I shrug like I have no idea what she's talking about.

But she lets me lead her anyway.

The partygoers cheer as she climbs onto the stage.

She takes the mic with a nervous smile. "Okay. I was forced into this, so no judging because this type of shit makes me nervous."

A few laughs. A few cheers of encouragement.

She glances around, visibly touched. "I just want to say thank you. To everyone here. For believing in me, for rallying behind me, for being there for Rocket and me during every step of the way."

Her eyes flick to me. Fuck, I'm a lucky man.

"While I'm a firm believer in chasing your dreams. I never imagined I'd be standing here with my master's and as part of a family that feels bigger than anything I ever dreamed. I am so grateful and humbled by your love and support and—"

The mic cuts. She blinks and looks around, but I can see when it dawns on her that this isn't a technical error.

But more like perfectly planned.

The music starts.

A soft acoustic version of the lullaby I used to sing to Poppy starts, and on cue, Poppy walks out from the side of the stage.

The crowd applauds her. Her little hands are shaking, but she says the first line, "You don't need words to know you're mine. My hands can tell you every time . . ."

Willow's hand flies to her mouth.

And that's when I step out behind our daughter—because she is *our* daughter—with a ring in my pocket and my heart in my throat.

Willow doesn't move. She just stares at us, at me, like she can't breathe.

I crouch to kiss Poppy's forehead, then turn back to Willow.

"Willow Adams. You . . . you are something else, you know that?" I chuckle nervously. "You taught me what rhythm feels like when the lights go out. You showed me that there's music in silence. That there's peace in the quiet. That 'safe' isn't just a sign, but rather it can be a promise."

I step closer.

"You taught me that home isn't a place. It's a feeling. And I want to carry that feeling with me for the rest of my life. Every stage. Every night. Every morning after."

Tears stream down her face as her smile widens and her eyes own mine.

"And yes," I add, "I had help with this plan." I gesture to Poppy. "She picked out the ring box. There's a reason it's glittery and in the shape of a star."

Everyone laughs as I pull it from my pocket, drop to one knee, and then open it.

The laughter in the backyard fades to murmurs. People shuffle and lift to their toes to get a better look. The sound of cell phone cameras clicking go off intermittently.

"Willow . . . marry me. That's my plea. I won't promise that I'll always be perfect—because we all know I'm not." Laughter flows through the guests. "And we're always going to be a work in progress, but that's okay because it means we'll never stop trying. But what we have is ours, and I will protect it always. Whatever it takes."

She nods before I even finish the sentence. "Yes," she whispers and then says louder, "*Yes.*"

Our family and friends erupt in a fit of cheers.

I forget about the ring in my hand and pull her into my arms. I kiss her like I've waited years for this moment—because I have.

Poppy's around us, twirling in her sparkly gown because she knows the whole world just shifted.

And maybe it just did.

Poppy came to me scared and shattered—much like I was but in a totally different capacity. We both needed healing, patience, someone to ground us . . .

And Willow did just that. She brought us together. She held us together. She showed me how to fight for us when I wasn't sure I was worth fighting for.

Forever used to seem like such a daunting word.

Until Willow. Until Poppy.

Now, it feels exactly right.

They're my forever. Always will be.

Whatever it takes . . .

Did you enjoy Rocket and Willow (and Poppy) in *Sweet Distraction?*

There are more bandmates in the Backstage Pass series if you want to get lost a little deeper in BENT's world.

You can find Hawkin, Vince, and Gizmo's stories as well as all of my other books by going HERE.

My books always come with a guaranteed happily ever after—*I just might make you work some to get there.*

As always, THANK YOU for reading!
—Kristy

ABOUT
the author

New York Times Bestselling author K. Bromberg writes contemporary romance novels that make you work to get your happily ever after. She likes to write strong heroines and damaged heroes, who we love to hate but can't help but love.

Since publishing her first book on a whim in 2013, Kristy has sold over two million copies of her books across twenty different countries and has landed on the *New York Times, USA Today,* and *Wall Street Journal* Bestsellers lists over thirty times. (*She still wakes up and asks herself how she got so lucky for all this to happen.*)

A mom of three, Kristy finds the only thing harder than finishing the book she's writing is navigating parenthood during the teenage years (send more wine!). She loves dogs, sports, a good book, and is an expert procrastinator. She lives in Southern California with her family.